DESCANT

DRAZOEN HERALDS
BOOK TWO

JULES PEACOCK

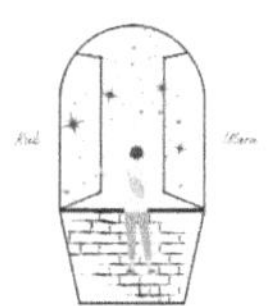

LCCN: 2025922072
ISBN-13: 979-8-9923803-4-7 Trade
ISBN-13: 979-8-9923803-5-4 Hardcover
ISBN-13: 979-8-9923803-3-0 eBook

First Edition: December 2025

10 9 8 7 6 5 4 3 2 1

❀ Formatted with Vellum

ALSO BY JULES PEACOCK

Virtuoso: Drazoen Heralds Book 1

THE WHEEL OF CENTRIS

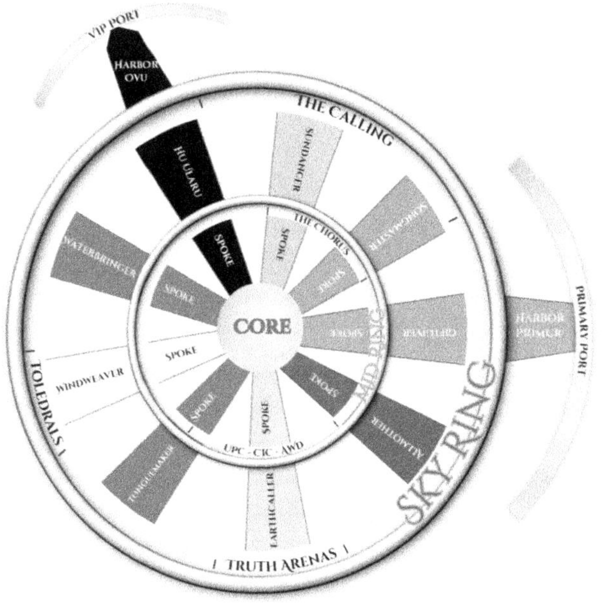

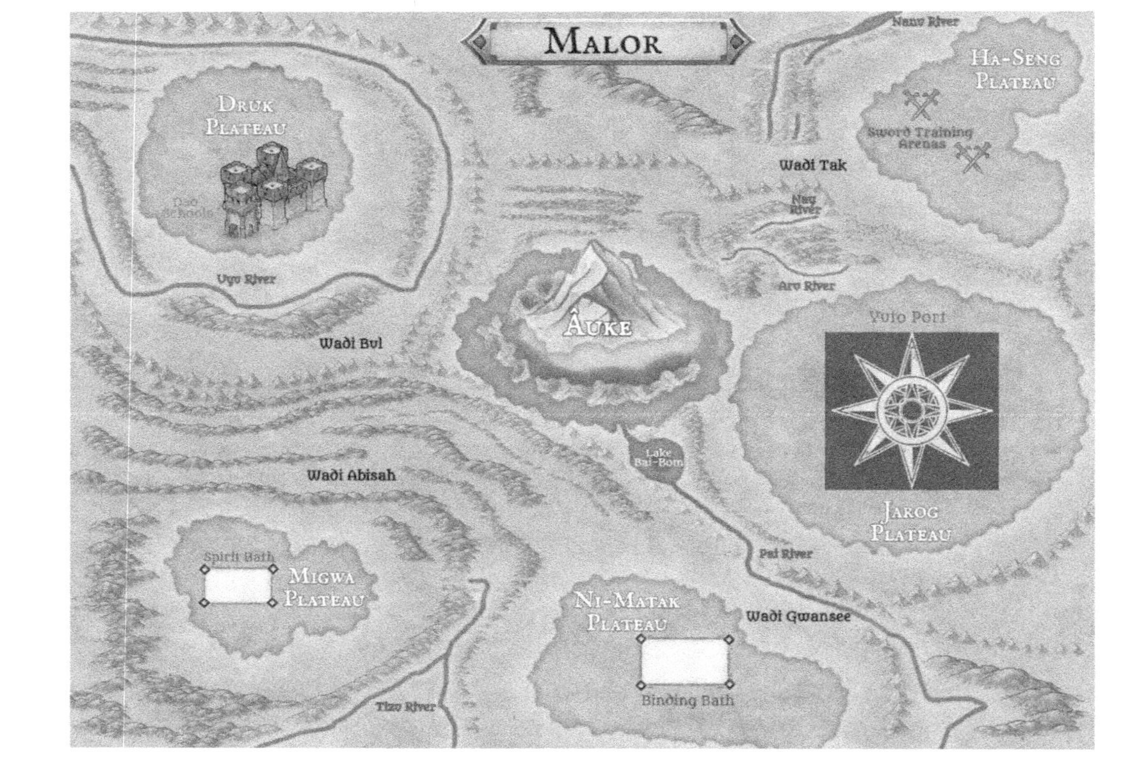

Malor
Nanv River
Ha-Seng Plateau
Druk Plateau
Sword Training Arenas
Wadi Tak
Dao Schools
Nev River
Arv River
Uyo River
Âuke
Vuto Port
Wadi Bvl
Lake Bai-Bom
Jarog Plateau
Wadi Abisah
Pai River
Spirit Bath
Migwa Plateau
Ni-Matak Plateau
Wadi Gwansee
Tizu River
Binding Bath

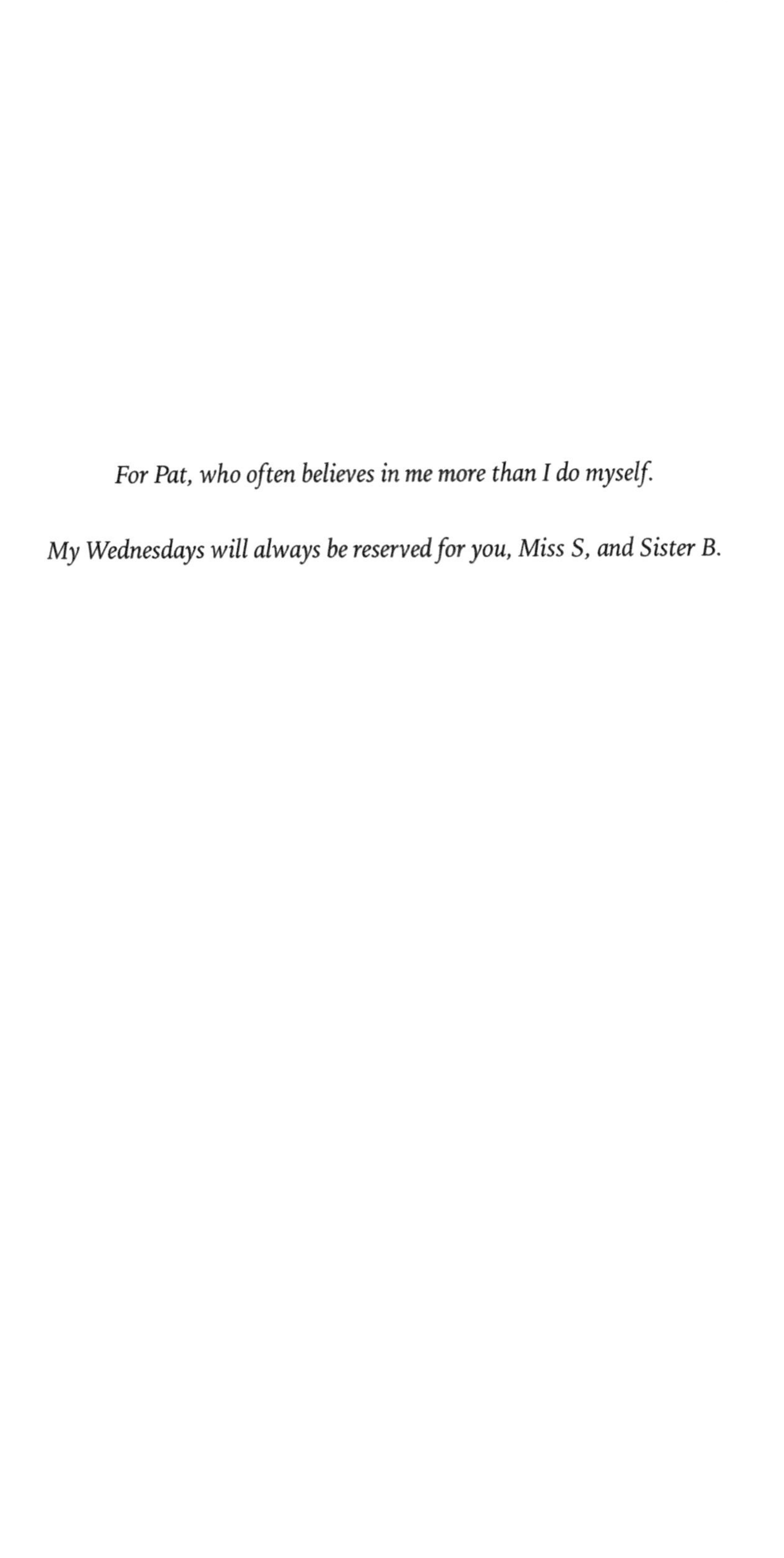

For Pat, who often believes in me more than I do myself.

My Wednesdays will always be reserved for you, Miss S, and Sister B.

DESCANT

A counterpoint to a melody
that soars around
and interweaves with
the core music

PRELUDE

Yuhwa Bon-Gil wouldn't say she skulked out of the room. But she didn't take time to glance back at the woman she left behind in bed either. There was no specific reason to hurry away from the short-lease establishment and back to the *Eternidad*, Yuhwa just always felt better there. Keeping herself unentangled was much easier when she avoided morning afters, too.

Their core group had snuck out of Voice House last night and reveled in a subspoke-wide festival, held on the blue spoke of Centris. Rixat, like the woman with whom Yuhwa had merrily passed time, were already feeling the pull of their Valc. A triwakian atmospheric shifting of their home planet's magnetics, it triggered mating frenzy in their species every three hundred tuigs. No matter how far away Centris was from Shilmand, Rixat were feeling a need to share beds and worship bodies. Waterbringer Blue's spoke was known for ecstatic celebration, and when the people most closely aligned to them wanted to party, it got raucous.

Katy Phelan, upon seeing the crush of people said it looked like something on her planet called "Mardi Gras to the extreme." Djilbay, Katy's mate, had agreed with her, although it turned out neither of them had ever attended this festival when they'd lived on Earth. Yuhwa didn't understand how anyone could pass up a chance for fun like that, but accepted she knew little of the newest people to join the Calling.

Hål, join was mere speculation right now. Humans hadn't gotten that far yet; the Cadre were still planning carefully how to announce them as the sixteenth advanced species on Centris. Sundancer Orange was back, but hadn't resumed leadership of the Calling yet. She was biding her time, given they all expected the Pu'ulqaari to confront them soon. No telling if the PQ would attack directly or secretly, and until then Sundancer would keep everyone else on the Wheel wondering what was coming.

Of course, that kept all of *them* precariously balancing, too; anxious and eager to do something, or be helpful. Grasping at anything, all diversions great or small. Which helped explain how Katy, Raisa, Djilbay, Lia and Yuhwa sought out the early Valc "hootenanny" (new Human word, saved to aoiti favorites) and dove in as deeply as possible. When Yuhwa bumped into Xanthos, a gorgeous Rixat woman whose dancing meshed perfectly with her own, Yuhwa had surrendered to the current and thoroughly enjoyed her night. She wasn't sure how many drinks she'd consumed by the time Olak Purplevoice came and claimed Raisa, but only one more after that she got a message from Katy that the rest were calling it a night, too.

Yuhwa took advantage of her momentary freedom; no one asking her to pilot through a veṣu, head of the Swords not nagging about going back to Malor, nothing more stressful than a sweet woman's kisses and a sensual night sharing pleasures. She'd been honest with Xanthos, as she always was with new partners. Yuhwa wasn't good for more than a night, two at most, but would be *very* good for that brief window. They'd had a great evening, now she quietly departed the sky ring hostel with a smile.

She received Katy's semi-urgent message at a bev cart near the tram stop. Yuhwa read it as she swiped her aoiti interface to buy an extra-large nropita with optional baijur dust sprinkles. Yuhwa clearly wasn't the only traveler on the Wheel who'd learned to love that sweet, nutty flavor.

> Not sure where you ended up last night, but
> we're meeting at the ship. Time to head back
> for family pickup!

Yuhwa hurried her steps, hopping the tram running back to Harbor Primur. She dropped her eyes as they passed the Truth Arenas. With her luck, if she even glanced over there, Head Sword Tangun would jump aboard and remind her she was soon likely to be called home by the nawa. Yuhwa wasn't opposed to tradition, per se, but didn't feel ready to drop her life as majio for something else.

What if her quest made her a diplomat? That life change would probably jeopardize future interspecies relations, and the thought made her smile. Anything in the hospitality industries would be equally bad. None of those options stirred her spirit the way piloting the *Eternidad* did.

But it could just as easily make her a sword, following her father's legacy, which was what Tangun believed destined to occur. Yuhwa wasn't sure how she felt.

Thoughts of her father weren't as painful as they'd been when he first died, two hundred thirteen tuigs past. But Phu Bon-Gil had died too early, leaving a bereft daughter and cata-tonic wife. Nowadays, Yuhwa struggled with thoughts of her mother more than her papa. She had been far too young to lose both parents.

She'd been orphaned, felt lost and forsaken, yet she'd

endured. That's why her looming pâtexi didn't scare her so much as it stressed her. Yuhwa had found equilibrium, friendship, and a good place in life after two aiwaks, and she didn't want to risk losing it at the whim of the nawa and their waja quest.

Shaking off such gloomy thoughts, she arrived at the *Eternidad's* berth to the sounds of an argument.

"I bloody well am going!"

"Katy, *qania*, be reasonable. We can't leave-"

"You did *not* just tell me I'm unreasonable! I can't believe you. Just because I'm Kawakona doesn't mean I'm chained to this Wheel!"

Uh oh. Trouble in paradise already?

"What did I miss?" Yuhwa interrupted the argument. She directed her question to a nearby Raisa Leon.

The second Human rolled her eyes. "These two drank too much last night, or they woke up out of sorts. They've been at loggerheads all morning." Raisa made two fists and bumped them together.

Loggerhead *Human English name for amphibious life-form known as 'turtle'; also idiom to indicate either fights and/or stupidity.*

Yuhwa doubted Raisa meant semi-aquatic creatures. She also wasn't surprised to hear Djilbay "Bay" jo Bikajo and Katy Phelan were struggling. The stress of everything they'd already been through was enough to push anyone off a plateau, but now there was the prospect of families being retrieved for a bonding ceremony. The mating a recently revived Drazoen had thrust upon them, all with the knife blade of a Calling hearing about their actions poised at their throats.

Between the Mikanjo violating the Law of First Approach, helping a PQ slave escape (Yuhwa was still pissed at Na Xan for forcing her complicity in that), and inadvertently making themselves Prima of a species not yet invited to the Calling.... Well, there was plenty to fray tempers.

Katy, vibrant curly hair flying around her shoulders, gestured at the ship, eyes pleading. "I want to go back with you to Earth. It's time to pick up our parents and families before everything gets too insane back there." She pointed an accusatory finger at her partner. "Bay thinks he can overrule me." Her voice dropped, low and gritty. "He's wrong."

Raisa, long brown hair unbound and (like her tone) calm in comparison to her friend, said, "I'm excusing myself and my family from this. I know the news reports we've managed to get from Earth are confusing, but I think my family isn't ready. Babu will be a difficult passenger under the best of circumstances."

"But if you're there-" Katy started.

Raisa's hand forestalled Katy's objection. "I agree with Djilbay, Sundancer, and the Cadre. We can't leave now. What if they refuse to let us back on Centris? Things are sure to get heated, politically speaking, and we must be here to defend ourselves."

"Or punch back," Yuhwa said in support. "Sounds smart to me. Lia and I will get your family, Katy. Send them our arrival time so they'll be ready."

Katy's shoulders slumped. "Fine. I hear what you all are saying."

"You see reason only when someone else speaks it to you?" Bay, normally a rational and unruffled man, semi-barked his question at Katy. His wings, in their compact hold, circled as his shoulders rolled in irritation. "As soon as we were told this morning not to leave, I knew I couldn't go to Bankiri to pick up my mothers, but I did not argue like you."

"Good thing," a new voice added. Yuhwa saw Lia's feet before she fully descended into view, coming off the *Eternidad*. "Our mothers have declined the offer of a visit with us here on Centris." Vailillia jo Bikajo hid her disappointment so well Yuhwa wondered if she even felt it the way her brother obviously did.

At his crestfallen expression, Katy's ire disappeared and she wrapped her arms around him. "*Mo chroí*, I'm so sorry. I know you hoped they would come for the ceremony."

His arms circled her, followed by his wings which hid her entirely from view. Resting his head on hers, he sighed. "Some things change more slowly than wind carves canyons."

Lia grimaced and looked to Yuhwa. "Ready? Let's fly fast as we can; I'm excited to try a new application of the kuh-suppression suit technology. Bay," she smiled at him, "such amazing things have come from your first hybridization. We applied it to the landing shuttles, which should hide us completely from Humans!"

1

PAUL PHELAN WAS DONE WITH THIS FEDERAL GIT. THE man had arrived at the head of a phalanx of black-suited government robots, and was intent on scaring the hell out of everyone. As if anyone needed extra help being terrified in the wake of his sister's memorable exit from Earth three weeks ago.

Thankfully, Paul had already been at his parents when this tosser and his posse came screaming down the driveway. In a black van so much a stereotype it hurt, no less. Who did that on Mercer Island, for fuck's sake?

Paul looked at his father, who seemed torn between according respect to an official and letting his Irish temper off the leash. Baby brother Oran, also home, cracked his neck ominously and looked ready to get into it physically.

"As I keep saying, we've tracked signals to this home. We know you're in contact with the aliens."

"I'm sure we don't know what you're talking about," Da said, wrapping an arm around Ma and pulling her close.

Paul's heart ached looking at his ma. She'd been hardest hit by Katy's disappearance, though he didn't think the alien thing bothered Ma. More that her baby girl was in the middle of scary events happening so far away. When they'd heard "assassin" and "poison" he'd worried his mother would faint. Of course, Bug had dropped those bombs and swanned off to do her own thing. Typical move from his baby sister.

Speaking of whom, it must have been her latest call to the family that set off alarms at the Pentagon. Or NASA, or SETI, whichever place this weaselly twat called home. He hadn't clearly stated his affiliation, just flashed some badge Da flinched upon seeing. Given he worked at Boeing's military and government facility (called the "black hole" by locals), Martin Phelan probably knew exactly who this guy was. Paul didn't, and found it hard to care; his irritation was the same no matter which org was to blame.

What he *did* know? Katy's message from two days ago meant this man needed to leave ASAP. Their chariot to the stars was due any minute if he'd done the math correctly.

Right as he had the thought, he spied two women approaching the front door. One of them – long brown hair and bright green eyes – was taller than his own six-five. Impressive. The second woman wasn't as tall, closer to Bug's height, but she was arresting just the same. Pale lavender hair blowing in a gentle June breeze, skin-tight bodysuit of red and black, dark eyes, and stride that said she knew her capabilities well.

Paul's life of learning, competing in, and teaching gymnastics had taught him to size up body language. This woman wasn't a fighter, but she had fluid grace similar to it. Like a dancer or swimmer. This had to be Yuhwa, pilot of the alien spaceship here to pick up the Phelan family. But nice as the diversion of these two pretty women had been, Paul needed to get this idiot out of the house and keep the aliens from bumping into him.

"We will take your entire family in for questioning if you aren't more cooperative, Mr. Phelan."

What had this fool said his name was? Something bland. Jim? No. John, wasn't it? Paul was terrible with names. He moved to position himself so the women could see him through the front windows. "We don't even know what you're talking about, man!" He raised his hands and shook them, praying a brush-back gesture translated across species' lines.

"I cannot be any clearer. Our systems picked up communication originating from beyond Earth's satellites. It came to an IP address located here. In this house."

Both women heeded Paul and stopped on the walk. He saw them consult with each other, then creep closer to the front door without knocking. Damn, he hoped like hell they could hear and understand what was happening. Paul had to believe two women instrumental in saving his sister were more than smart enough to avoid detection.

Oran drawled, "You're whack. You think those aliens from last month, what? FaceTimed us?" As much of a pain as Katy's twin could be, he was solid when he needed to be. Nor was he lying; Katy and Bay used WhatsApp.

Da moved to stand beside Paul, Oran sliding in next to Da. They'd made a wall of Phelans, and Jim-John the government lackey wasn't getting through it.

"I've been here a long time, sir. I've got clearance as far up as an Irish immigrant and green card citizen can get where I work. That means I know you'd have taken us in, seized our computers, and refused us calls for help if you had enough proof. And yet," Martin Phelan shrugged, "here we are. Standing in the family living room."

"Look here-"

"I think not." Ma spoke up, surprising Paul. She pushed her way between Da and Oran. "We've been polite, we've listened to your threats, and we're done. Unless any of your goon squad want the refreshment previously rejected, you may be on your way."

He tried not to react as two puzzled faces peered from the side of the front windows, mouthing "goon squad". Sweet

Marie, these two! Thankfully Paul was on a break from women, or he'd probably form the kind of insta-love connection Katy had with her Bay. The very next second, both ladies melted away from the porch and front entrance.

Just in time to avoid the exit of a furious government jerk who tried to stare down every family member before stalking out behind his team. Slammed the door when he went. Twat.

"Did you see-"

"Yes, of course I did. Everyone! Get it in gear!" Briana Phelan knew how to bellow, having raised four hellion boys and one *sensitive* girl.

A girl who'd sent aliens to pick up her immediate family for transport to a place called Centris. On a Wheel, she'd said. In the middle of the Universe. She'd gone and had some epic adventure with winged aliens, supposedly waking up a dragon. Paul figured that had to be exaggeration or creative license. Or maybe a mistranslation by those aoiti bugs Katy had ingested.

Bug swallowed bugs. Heh.

His oldest brother, Ian, came out from the rec room, his wife right behind him. Deb was a high maintenance piece of work, but for whatever reason she and Ian meshed perfectly.

Another picture-perfect couple came out of the guest bedroom they'd claimed when the fed arrived. Patrick and Vasuda, not married, but might as well be. They were the opposite of the Ian-Deb ladder-climbing power couple; two artists, chill as all get-out, and happiest with simple things.

Paul was sick to death of happy couples. He hadn't been part of one for nigh on six months, and wasn't sure he'd ever be part of one again. Women were vicious creatures who tore a man apart with ultimatums and unrealistic demands. He was better off single, if what his ex had done to him was anything to go by.

Ma and Da (another damn love match) had everyone gather close in the dining room.

"They're here-"

"Jesus, we know, Da. We saw them."

"*We* didn't! Do they look really alien?" Deb's face was livelier than her recent Botox shot should have allowed. She must be very psyched for this adventure.

Vasuda marveled, "I can't believe this is real. We're going to experience new cultures and species, it will be ama-"

"New networking opportunities. If we can get in first, we-"

"Blow it out your arse, Ian." Oran punched his brother's arm.

"Everyone shut up." Man, his ma could control the family perfectly. "Are all the bags in the garage? Katy said to pack light; they'll have everything we need on the ship, or on that Wheel thingy."

"I just packed booze."

"Oran, my lad, you're a good-"

"You have to be kidding. Martin, don't encourage that! Make him grab underwear at least."

"No time, *mo chroí*. I'm sure they've got us covered."

Paul and Patrick exchanged a glance that spoke volumes. They'd always been the closest of the kids. Ian was too invested in being the oldest to care about younger siblings. Oran and Katy had whatever the opposite of a twin bond was; they could fight over anything, and regularly did. Paul and Patrick, however, had each other's backs. They supported one another, collaborated on their businesses, shared ideals and plans, and knew how the other thought. Right now, Patrick was wishing they could ditch the Phelan brood and get going on this trip without all the damn noise.

Paul agreed, but that was part and parcel of the family deal. Hearing a tentative knock on the front door, Paul prayed these two women from space were prepared for the chaos to come.

YUHWA DIDN'T KNOW what to think of Katy's family. Loud, that was a certainty. There were so many of them! Jadoube tended toward single-child families, and while she'd heard Katy speak much of her large clan, meeting them in person overwhelmed.

She'd been most fascinated by stories of Katy's twin. It was intriguing and unsettling to think of sharing gestation with another, someone linked by blood and genetics yet completely separate. Oran, the man her friend claimed was a Chitan "changeling", was nothing like Katy physically. Yuhwa's people didn't have tales where one species swapped out babes for others, though it was said Sister Ha-Seng could change between a Jadoube woman and a ferocious four-legged beast with brindled fur and sharp teeth.

In this case, Katy had exaggerated more than a little. Oran seemed completely Human, hair the same color as his sister's, upper body strength implied by the muscles Yuhwa could see under his tight-fitting shirt. Unlike a Chitan, he didn't seem determined to start a fight at every moment. Eying his bulk, Yuhwa bet he could definitively end a bout, though.

Too many Phelans, she thought, as she and Lia tried to sort out how to cover everyone in the rimā they'd brought (newborn name of the hybrid kuh-suppression suit). It hadn't occurred to them that any of the group would object to being shrouded together, but they certainly did. Strenuously. In hindsight, if she'd listened more closely to Katy's stories, the ego of her eldest brother and his wife would have sunk in better. Ian demanded he and Deb have one to themselves. Katy's parents tried to reason with him, but the couple were united in their demand for privacy.

"No," Lia ended the argument. "Two rimā only. Half go Yuhwa. Half go me." Despite the limited English Lia spoke, they got her message. "Shuttle in big rimā, you Humans no can see."

Patrick laughed. "She's got you there, Ian. Ya prat." Shaking his head, he addressed Yuhwa and Lia. "On behalf of my family I apologize. You've come across the Universe to be met with such stupidity, I can't even."

"Hey!"

"Shut it, wanker" said the one who'd been introduced as Paul.

Wanker *geo-culturally specific vulgar Human slang; one who masturbates ("wanks"), idiot, fool; comparable to bakyại*

Huh. She wouldn't keep "wanker" as a favorite; she already had a better one with bakyại; her own language added a hint of pathos the Human word lacked.

Paul was notably different to the rest of his family. Every other Phelan, except the mother, had red hair. The mother's was blonde, but her son had hair as black and gleaming as Ji-Cheol Jarog's wings. Unlike the other mens' close trims, his fell sleekly against the nape of his neck. Vibrant blue eyes, no facial hair, tall for a Human. His smile was what linked him with his family. Yuhwa supposed he was considered handsome.

Katy said he worked with children, teaching them some kind of acrobatics, which Yuhwa had assumed meant he was gentle and understanding, but something about his attitude so far didn't work for her. She couldn't pinpoint what was off, just that something was. Maybe it was the way he'd tried to send her and Lia away when they arrived, as if they couldn't see what was happening and needed his help to avoid detection. Like they were infants!

She'd reserve final judgement, but for now Paul Phelan was in the "watch" category.

"Come by me," Yuhwa said to the group. She'd practiced hard to get the words right on this. "Gather in a circle, near near, I give aoiti, start your learns."

Her studying had worked, because everyone stepped forward. She wondered if they'd appreciate the advantage Katy and Raisa had given them: the aoiti they were about to drink had been upgraded repeatedly by the first Humans on Centris, and benefitted even more from the Mikanjo feedback loop on the *Eternidad*. These nanobots would bind faster and with greater depth than they had for the women nearly a buwan ago.

Once they had that out of the way ("You're absolutely sure this is safe for us?" the only comment from Deb), she and Lia split the group. Deb, Ian, Martin, Brianna in Lia's rimā. In the other, Vasuda, Patrick, Paul and Oran followed behind Yuhwa. While the rimā had a lot of give, they still needed to keep very close as they walked from the house to the shuttle. They moved mostly in sync, shoulder-to-shoulder, but Yuhwa couldn't help thinking not a one of them would make it as a majio. Being a pilot of the dao took a rhythm and connection to the current these folk lacked.

Paul was almost there; this made obvious that his work involved his body. He seemed acutely aware of how he moved, but bore a deeper stiffness that would cut him off from the river's flow.

If he tried at all, that is, which Yuhwa doubted he would. Paul seemed like a man who would deny the Jadoube birthright, try to dismiss it as "magic" as Raisa had first done. She caught herself imagining how she'd explain it to him, then grimaced internally. Why was she thinking so much on this one? He wasn't a candidate for pleasures, he was a job from her friend. Who was his sister. End of any further Paul Phelan contemplation.

Miraculously they arrived at the shuttle without being discovered. It was good fortune indeed that Katy had drawn them a map of where to land; somewhere with sufficient space and not far from her parents' home. Keeping the rimā stretched tight as possible to cover the boarding ramp, they sent the Humans inside one-by-one. They ascended at a jog, comments trickling back, while she and Lia exchanged sly looks of humor.

"The engineering on this!" from Katy's father.

"Thought it would look more alien," from Paul.

"Incredible!" from Vasuda and Katy's mother together.

"Can I drive this thing?" from the twin.

At that both women hustled up the ramp, ready to pull Oran away from the controls if he'd actually figured out how to engage them. Thankfully nothing of the sort happened, they got their passengers secured. For the second time in recent history an *Eternidad* shuttle whisked Phelans off Earth.

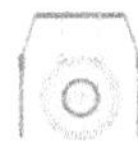

PAUL NEEDED A GODDAMN BREAK.

In the days between his sister's last call and now, his adrenaline was on overload. Both he and Patrick had been given myriad jobs by their mother to prep the house for their likely long-term absence. They'd added extra locks on doors and windows, deep cleaned like the Pope was on his way, and directed packing logistics. Oran, beyond securing smuggler-haul volumes of booze apparently, was going to install a sprinkler on a timer. Da reminded him Seattle lawns were meant to go brown in summer, and that was dropped. Vasuda had shopped for the list of foods Katy and Raisa begged them to bring for replicator training. Ian and Deb tried to bring half their home with them; thankfully Ma and Da stopped them, with Patrick and Paul announcing firmly there wasn't room anyway.

All in all, Paul stepped aboard the *Eternidad* with only five pairs of underwear, two pairs of gym shorts, three tank tops, and the slacks, tee and sneakers he was wearing. Katy's man, Bay, swore his people would give them clothes they could wear on the ship and at Centris, but Paul wanted workout clothes he could be sure were comfy. Bonus, they doubled as sleepwear.

He also carried two duffels filled with snacks and sheet music for Katy. The shuttle lifted off and Paul declared himself probably the first interstellar contrabandist of powdered donut holes and BBQ chips.

The run-up to departure hadn't left him time to think about what the hell they were actually doing. Leaving Earth. Flying away, like heroes in some cheesy sci-fi movie. Earth was…kind of a disaster at the mo'. Humans were panicking about the alien incursion, many swearing this was a deity's judgement for unchaste lives or twaddle like that. Which deity, exactly, was hotly contested.

There were also the coverup conspiracy theorists, saying world governments had known all along. And one couldn't forget the knobs welcoming future alien "friends" with open arms, but getting frustrated when no more of them appeared on demand. All these groups came with attendant shouting, protesting, marching, sign-waving, etc.

Some governments deployed military to keep peace, though Paul begged to differ. Peace can't be kept at the end of a weapon, he knew. Other regimes opted to let chaos reign, looting and fighting in the streets over gas or groceries building to upsurges of terror and violence. It was a cluster fuck, to put it mildly.

Kids had stopped coming to his gymnastics academy for the most part. Directly in the wake of Katy fleeing Earth, at least half of every class had immediately dropped. Paul couldn't blame them; plenty of folks kept their kids home from school and all activities, too scared to let them leave the house. Attendance continued to wither until he'd finally sent a message to parents that classes were cancelled for now. Would have been a hell of a blow to his psyche and wallet if he hadn't known all this was about to happen.

All this, right here. Leaving the atmosphere and landing on a huge damn flying saucer, a process less taxing than a quick run to a convenience store. Five minutes, maybe? Yuhwa, the one with pale purple hair who liked to order them around, showed military jets scrambling to reach them, visible on the shuttle screens.

No luck, Chuck! They were astronauts now. Paul felt like there should be a badge for that.

Dock, disembark, dork out. Rubber-necking like a madman, despite trying to be nonchalant and suave, Paul took in what he could as he could. People with wings. Everywhere. Lia, too, flexing massive wings now they'd left the shuttle. People – Mikanjo – in flight, walking about, coming closer to circle the Phelan brood and smile. Good thing this place was cavernously big or all those white feathers would smother them like down pillows.

A man with neon yellow hair stepped forward. He seemed slightly older than the rest, his cocoa skin just a hint softer, looser than Lia or Yuhwa's. "Wiremu," he said, bowing to their group.

Katy had coached them all about Mikanjo formality. No using nicknames, no touching without permission, never assuming you had the right to do either until expressly and verbally confirmed. She'd also warned them that when the aoiti kicked in, it would blow their minds. She wasn't wrong.

Wiremu jo Bikajo *captain of the Eternidad for the last milenyo* flashed in his head. Right in his bloody noggin, like it was normal to have microtech broadcasting bot-to-brain. His father's look of wonder made it obvious everyone had gotten the same blaze he had. Hot damn.

Another Mikanjo stepped forward from the crowd, looking not at them but at Wiremu. His face didn't seem friendly and his fists were clenched. "Wiremu," he started, then continued in a barrage of language their aoiti were far too immature to trans-late. He heard Bay and Katy mentioned, but that was the sum of Paul's ability to keep up. All the Phelans shuffled a bit, unsure what was happening. Yuhwa and Lia's faces darkened so it seemed a safe bet this wasn't a routine ship question.

Paul moved closer to Yuhwa and asked, "Any chance you can translate a little for us? We're getting nothing." Her face clouded more, and she shook her head in the negative. Great.

She put a gentle hand on his arm to focus his attention, and said, "Soon. Hope soon."

A nice dark room for the two-day transit to Centris seemed like a grand idea right now. Give his aoiti time to marinate, give him a chance to figure out why his chest felt like it was gripped in a vise. Paul had never been prone to anxiety and wasn't about to start now. A solid workout was what he needed, and a good ale. Oran better have packed both Ma's favorite (45th Parallel) as well as Da's (Kilkenny cream ale).

Paul would be fine if he could just understand what the argument was about, if he could intervene and deescalate whatever was happening. Before he could give it a shot, a young Mikanjo raced out of a corridor overhead and slid down a ladder like an eel, running toward them. Just about the age of one of his students, and flexible. Did Mikanjo have acrobatics? Perhaps that was something built in when you eventually grew wings and had to make them work. This boy didn't have them yet, his round face beaming, chest heaving for breath.

"Humans!" he shouted. Arms waiving exuberantly, he shouted again, "Katy Humans! Frens!" He leapt at Da first, who was pretty adept at catching flailing boys by this point in his life. Paul's father laughed out loud.

"Me Zazi. Fren!" The boy hugged Da, wiggled down, then made his way through Ma, Patrick and Vasuda before reaching Paul. **Zazi jo Bikajo** *son of Wiremu, pre-fledgling of one aiwak. Human age equivalent ninety years.* Whoa. Zazi wasn't exactly the age of Paul's gym kids, was he now?

"Fren?" he asked Paul more calmly, extending his hand.

Paul squatted down to look Zazi in the eye. "Good friend, yes." The smile he got in return lit up his heart. He stretched his hands out to the boy (never mind he was older than Paul, he acted like a kid), and when Zazi nodded, Paul scooped him up under the arms and slung him onto a hip.

This was a good omen, a perfect start to their interstellar voyage. As soon as the aoiti kicked in full-time, he'd get an explanation of what that guy had argued with the captain about. Then he'd get more clarity on where they were going, how exactly Yuhwa the Jadoube majio was getting them there, and what it would be like when they arrived.

There was only so much he could take of what his sister had said without questioning, and doubting, frankly. A dragon? Sure. Flying, no, swimming through a black hole? Uh huh. Giant planned communities, designed by pre-sleeping dragons, floating in the middle of the Universe where all the aliens liked to gather and hang out? Right you are.

A man could only take so much. Paul was that man. He needed answers, followed by calm and quiet. But right now he'd settle for cuddles with an alien who'd wrapped small arms around his neck and clung like a barnacle, giggling in his ear.

2

IF UNGO DIDN'T STOP WHINING AT WIREMU, YUHWA might slap him. For sure glare at him forcefully until he shut his nŭz mouth. She and Lia had risked themselves to get Katy's family here, safe from PQ reprisal and the mess their Earth was gearing up to be. The Phelans had also taken a risk to come, plus a huge leap of faith. Mikanjo, especially seekers, were supposed to be open and kind. Giving and wise. Ungo was opting for annoying, which flayed Yuhwa's nerves.

"I know what you're saying, Ungo-"

"Do you, really? Then why have we violated the Law of First Approach another time?" Ungo tossed his hands in exasperation and fluffed his feathers a little. "We should be returning to Bankiri. Taking our families to the home we've dreamed of for milenyo! Instead, here we are, ferrying Humans illegally for a second time. Explain this to me, to us!"

In fairness to him, Yuhwa respected Ungo's concern. The Calling at Centris, an august, if slightly tarnished, governing body, didn't take laws lightly. Especially ones of non-intervention. A transgression of this magnitude would reap sanctions or fines. Nothing so dramatic as ûpiøra; they wouldn't be banned from Centris and shunned by all species. But there would likely be charges brought, and the Mikanjo couldn't claim it was an accident. The first time, many aiwaks ago, had been forgiven and overlooked when Humans weren't sophisticated enough to track what had happened. Now, however, it was a different tale. Twice in short order the *Eternidad* had breached Human space, revealed themselves to the world through technology far too advanced to be native, and had kicked off planet-wide fright.

Regardless of the logic or reason behind it, Ungo was being an ass. Confrontation here, in front of the Humans who couldn't process a word of it, was underhanded and manipulative. But Yuhwa saw more than a few heads nodding their agreement with his points. She wished she could tell Paul and his family what was being said, but her English just wasn't good enough.

Zazi's unplanned but welcome distraction put the argument on hold. Ungo and his supporters left, thankfully. Yuhwa was impressed by Paul's immediate rapport with Zazi, though the boy instinctively acted with more reserve toward Paul than he'd shown with the others. Katy's brother hadn't hesitated a second, though, to grasp the boy's hand and take him up on friendship. Paul wasn't off her watchlist yet, but she was thawing slightly.

Turning to Lia she said, "Time for Katy's message. We can get them settled in their quarters, and I'll head to the numig for transit." Yuhwa was suddenly antsy to get to her dao bed and link in to the *Eternidad*. She hadn't felt this way in a long time, since she was a girl first learning the dao, and there was a piquancy to the eagerness, like it could be her last chance to connect. Ridiculous. Even if the nawa called her back to Malor, she'd resist. The *Eternidad* was her home, had been so for too long to just hand it off to someone else. She was majio here, no one could take that from her.

All the Phelans had heard her say Katy's name, and now faced her. Zazi slid down Paul's side and ran to his papu. Lia used a nearby terminal to access the video Katy had made for her family. Suddenly Yuhwa's friend's face popped onscreen, cheerful as always.

"Hi all. If you're seeing this then you're on the ship and it's time to go. Bay says your aoiti will be a gazillion times better than ours were." She looked back over her shoulder, off-screen, then nodded and turned back. "Yep, confirmed again. But it won't be immediate so this is to get you through the first hours. Your key takeaway here is going to be simple: trust Lia and Yuhwa."

Oran snorted, Deb scowled, the rest kept listening.

It wasn't a long vid, and when it was over the Humans waved goodbye to Wiremu and Zazi so that Lia and Yuhwa could move them along. They escorted the small group onto a travel sled, then deep into the residence area of the ship. Three conjoined family units had been set aside for the Phelans.

Each couple had a full family unit, and the two unattached males could pick where to take a guest spot. Paul immediately moved to Patrick and Vasuda, Oran to his parents. Yuhwa had begun to see everyone avoided Ian and Deb as much as they could. She blamed no one, the pair had been less than delightful so far.

As the Humans checked out their cabins and set down things they'd been carrying, Martin asked Lia to explain the replicators. He declared his "engineer demon brain" had engaged and needed to be fed. Lia laughed and showed him the way, all the other Phelans following like gõwie waddling after their fathers.

Amused by the thought, Yuhwa chuckled. There was a tug from her majio side, so she listened to it and excused herself. Or tried to. Paul stopped her.

"Wait, where are you going?"

"Numig," she answered, doubting it would translate.

But a moment later his face lit. "New-mig. The bridge, the ship's command deck?"

Yuhwa nodded, speaking slowly, but more hopeful the aoiti were coming online. "I need to fly us now, through the veşu."

Paul's eyes revealed he hadn't caught all of it, but some had gotten though. "Veşu is a black hole, yeah? Katy tried to prepare us for this. She said you swim it somehow." He crossed his arms, conveying his doubt. Was he unsure his sister told the truth, or if Yuhwa did? Either way, she'd happily prove him a fool. With any luck he'd faint the way Katy had.

"Come on, then." She climbed onto the travel sled and raised her eyebrow at him. "If you're brave enough." Paul's eyes narrowed in response.

Waving goodbye to the rest, she waited. Paul called out he'd return soon, then jumped on the sled. She could admit to some showboating, taking turns a little faster than necessary, although nothing like the racing young Mikanjo did. Paul didn't object, but he didn't stay standing, either.

When they arrived, Yuhwa jumped down and offered her hand. He mocked her by cocking his eyebrow as she had, putting one hand on the side, and flipping himself off the sled in some Human acrobatic maneuver.

Interesting.

So long as he told himself he was inside a planetarium, Paul didn't think he'd fall down. But shite, this numig thing was mind-bending! Multiple stories, flashing lights, walkways leading to a center platform with terminals and a raised dais bearing some kind of couch-bed deal. All of it under a clear dome with a view of distant stars. Not a hint of Earth to be seen.

"Majio attends!" called out all the Mikanjo on the bridge. Yuhwa headed for the dais in the middle of everything.

Paul followed behind her like a suck-up assistant. "I understood!" he crowed, not embarrassed when Yuhwa glanced back at him with a smirk.

People who'd been born to this Aoni of multiple species and space travel and aoiti couldn't comprehend what it was like not being able to participate, to communicate in such a basic way. He had just enough time to be ashamed of every time he'd been impatient with immigrants speaking imperfect English back home, before Yuhwa climbed onto the bed reclaiming his attention. He had burning questions she needed to answer.

"What are you doing?" he stepped closer, aware of the Mikanjo watching them. As long as they were happy to let him be there, he was staying. The way they'd hailed her arrival he assumed his presence was covered by her authority. "What is this? Does it all work only for you?"

Yuhwa measured him with an arch look, obviously contemplating whether to answer in pidgin English or go for broke and hope the aoiti worked. "Dao bed. I *unintelligible* order to *unintelligible*. It might *unintelligible*."

"I got dao. Katy says that's how you get us through black holes. That it's like swimming?"

Yuhwa nodded, then made a move that was kind of like an eel. Or maybe a snake. "Dao. Swim. Pilot."

"Why does swimming space mean you need to lay down? Is it a trance, or you fall asleep or what?" Paul had seen the look on her face that he was getting now in the past. A lot. Mostly from women, in particular his ex, Brittany. She'd given him that exasperated, *why are you so dense you frustrate the hell out of me* look many a time in their decade-plus together.

"Look, I'm only trying to assimilate what's happening here. Things have moved so fast, half of this feels like magic even though I know it's not. I'm just…"

Yuhwa's eyes went from cold onyx to a warmer ebony, her mouth softening. "I know *unintelligible* hard. Soon *unintelligible* aoiti will *unintelligible* and we *unintelligible*. Try to *unintelligible* patience."

Damn, he needed these nanobugs to start working right damn quick. "'Kay, then I'll just hang out here while you do that voodoo you do." It was probably childish, but he loved how phrases like that made her eyes lose focus and give a *hold please* vibe as her aoiti worked to translate.

She shook her head. Maybe voodoo wasn't something that crossed species boundaries? Yuhwa made a shooing motion, moving him back from the dais. Then she reclined, closed her eyes, and started to meditate. Or fall asleep. Almost the same thing as far as Paul was concerned.

He looked overhead: his view of the stars rapidly changed and warped, which gave him wicked spins. Concentrating on Yuhwa seemed less urp-inducing, so he watched her as she began gyrating. Her lilac hair, nearly to her butt when she stood, was trailing off the edge of the dao bed, down the dais and swayed to the movements of her body. He wasn't sure he'd classify her movements as swimming.

More like she was dancing. Or getting sweaty between the sheets, if he were honest. She undulated, writhed a bit, trembled. Her mouth opened in a grimace that curved into a wide grin. Heavy breathing, which drew his eyes to her small, well-formed breasts encased in that red and black bodysuit.

Yeah, wow. Not Safe For Work time, and he had to turn away because she was not on his radar in any way. Paul was off women, for one. For another, Yuhwa was his sister's friend who was allegedly four hundred years old.

Paul knew all these things they'd heard from Katy were supposedly real, but honestly? All the people of the Universe were long-lived, specially powered, and smart enough to discover other advanced species because dragons made them that way? He'd need more proof to believe it.

Newly resolved to avoid the temptation of the majio pilot wiggling her hips like a Latin ballroom dancer, he tried looking through the windows again. Big mistake. A long way away, but closing in fast, was a black hole. How did he know?

It was huge, blacker than any black he'd ever seen, and he could only "see" it because the damn thing was sucking down light like a slushy dripping from the edges of a bulging sphere. At least, that's what his mind told him milliseconds before taking a break and shutting off.

ALL JADOUBE on Malor are taught the way of dao as children. A birthright, gifted from Songmaster, allowing their people to travel the Aoni in ways no other species could. Their instruction started so young that, as adults, they couldn't remember a time they hadn't known the way. They were older than babes in arms, but not by much; they learned to swim before walking.

Parents weren't allowed to watch that first day, as their child was carried into the Uyu, a large river surrounding Druk Plateau in Wadi Bul. The Uyu had serene lake-like parts, some rambling waters, and sections where rapids ran wild and dangerous. Jadoube were introduced to the calm, placid sections first, by instructors who set them gently upon the water and let them float or sink. Those who floated immediately (rare) were routed to accelerated learning, the majority who sank were pulled up, soothed, and put back in. Over and over until the child learned the skill of keeping their head above water.

Yuhwa had taken the fast track. Her papa had told her he'd been proud, then sad, when he heard from teachers that she was the greatest in a generation. It meant she would be a brilliant majio, but might never follow in his footsteps as a sword. Her mother, happy in those days, had laughed at him and said Yuhwa would become whatever the Five Côttru decreed.

For her part, Yuhwa didn't worry overmuch about the day the nawa sent her on pâtexi. All the mystical transcendence she needed was already in her grasp, every time she called upon the dao and swam through space and time. Just like the arnat zingo found in Malor river waters, Yuhwa swam the Aoni.

See how they slide through the water, child, you must do this with the Aoni. Close your eyes, seek the branch of river that flows within you. Watch their silver fins, how they flutter or keep still. When do they do one or the other, and why? Do their eyes frantically dart about? No, they are focused; small arrows needling through the river, trusting their bodies to know the way. The arnat zingo is always in harmony with its environment, too quick to catch, beautiful and solitary, the fastest swimmer of Malor. Be that. When you leave us here, be that.

And she had been. Years of study, early one-off jobs as majio while she honed her talent. Securing her position on the *Eternidad* had been a dream fulfilled: sailing throughout the Aoni, befriending a group who needed her to get them safely between galaxies, meeting travelers from all species, and staying as far from Malor and nawa influence as possible. She'd embedded herself here, and her relationship to the Mikanjo and the ship itself was as intrinsic as breathing.

She never knew how to answer the question Paul had put to her: *Is it a trance, or you fall asleep or what?* It was the core of who she was, and even if she'd had enough English to talk to him easily, Yuhwa wasn't sure she had words in any language that translated. Jadoube just *knew* and didn't talk about it, though many times she'd heard older Jadoube say they missed it.

Another reason Yuhwa dodged contact with Malor; the nawa couldn't send her on a quest to seek waja that would reveal her sacred role if she couldn't be found. Maybe she'd still be a majio after that quest, but far more were taken from the role, and Yuhwa wasn't ready to let go.

Here and now, she let herself relax back onto her dao bed. Soft where it needed to be, firm and supportive elsewhere. Crucial for transiting veṣu, every ship's dao bed was unique because each majio designed it to suit their needs. When Yuhwa had taken the position here from Fyuko Jin an aiwak past, she'd had a new bed built and replaced his. All Jadoube had the genetic power that was dao, bestowed by Songmaster, but it manifested for each of them individually. The dao bed allowed them to connect quickly to the flow of the Aoni, harkening back to their first days on the Uyu River. More critically, it linked their dao with their ship.

Sinking deeper into the comfort of the bed, Yuhwa's eyes closed. Her focus circled like a whirlpool, draining down to her deepest, darkest places. The smallest particles, even smaller, down, down, until she squeezed between the tiniest bits. Each time she communed with the dao this way was a revelation, no matter how many times she'd done it. Shrinking to sub-atomic and quantum levels only to discover how vast the spaces were between infinitesimal things.

The wonder of the Aoni surely lay in how universe upon universe nested within itself, an endlessly blooming lotus, that which gave and gave of itself. Yuhwa had never reached an end to it, even on her longest transit. If she dove deeper, more was revealed, unfolding like waves upon a shore.

What majio learned during their years in the dao schools was how to ride those waves, find the shortcuts between them, and make crossing cosmic distances a mere step. Less than that, even. A breath, a thought.

She'd tried in vain to explain to Katy and Raisa, knew she'd have as little luck trying with Paul or the other Humans. When she swam the dao, she first connected to all living things on her ship; in a transit the *Eternidad* was hers more than anyone's. She had to take ownership of the people, plants, animals, even the objects. Everything fell under her power, tied by strings only she could feel, but that bound them together as surely as blood.

Gathering those strings was the first step, reaching for the veşu was second. Harmonizing with a veşu was like dancing with a new partner; they were dazzling, enchanting. They called to Jadoube like a lover promising forever, sweet murmurings of perfect unions and eternal joy spinning together. Always a slow, flirtatious approach followed by gentle touch and swelling excitement. One pass, then another. Yielding, pressing forward. Spin, clutch and release, moving apart then back together, faster and faster. Sliding around, then through, diving into the stygian waters of the veşu. Aligning them to your own, two rivers flowing in perfect concert; same direction, speed and strength. All while the majio sheltered the ship strings and brought them into the dance.

Then, becoming the arrow of the arnat zingo, slicing through one wave to the next. This dance with the veşu became more challenging, fighting the pull of its power. Veşu could, after all, stop the very light of the Aoni from escaping. But not a majio. The more a majio traveled the more she knew the magnetic attraction of known locations. Remembered how to swim in the right direction, trusting herself on currents her soul had marked and kept in a holistic inventory. Expertise taught her which moment was right to wrap herself in the threads under her protection, and leap from the veşu back to plain space.

Transit completed. She felt the Kéntro system mute her abilities and drag the *Eternidad* down into cruise speed. The enforced slowdown on the way into Centris always annoyed her...but considering what kinds of people would try to storm the Wheel if they could, she knew the Drazoen had been wise to put it in place.

Yuhwa's eyes shot open. After every transit she wanted two things: rusim and sex. A quick look to her side revealed a Paul-shaped object on the floor. Ah. Looked like fainting ran in the family after all. He wasn't her choice for sex, anyway, because he was Katy's brother. And a bit hỏi hậu, like Kalim Bluevoice and Thuliso Maor. Yuhwa had no time for men who relied on appearances to get their way. Looking at his prostrate backside, though, she could appreciate the view for a moment.

Nŭz. Rusim it was.

3

Had Paul woken up in strange places having passed out the night before? On more than one occasion? Without a doubt. But the only time he'd opened his eyes to feathers was that time he'd fallen asleep in a park and woken up surrounded by pigeons. Mikanjo wings were a less familiar sight.

He wasn't completely ashamed or embarrassed, but he wasn't feeling über manly either. He was on the floor, surrounded by concerned Mikanjo, one of whom fanned air over him with a wing. Like Paul was a genteel lady who'd fallen prey to a fit of the vapors. Jesus.

Above his head, space had stopped the buckling, twisting hyperdrive imitation it had been doing and resumed its steady state. Yuhwa's head peeked in from the side; she'd finished her cosmic swim, was off her bed, and in his face.

"Katy and Raisa shared sympathetic fainting when they went through, if that makes you feel better."

It did not. "How did they get over it?"

"We commandeered an observation chamber, drank heavily,

and I forced them to stare into space until it didn't make them dizzy anymore."

"Then we should-", he sat up so fast he almost collided with Yuhwa. "Hey! I understand what you're saying. The bugs are working!" He pumped a fist; the nearby Mikanjo narrowed their eyes and scuttled backwards.

One of them called out, "This," he copied Paul's gesture, "it means good or bad? Do you say you will hit and do violence?"

Crap. Humans were going to have to watch themselves, if something so simple to him wasn't clear to his hosts. There was a whole world of Human gestures that were innocent, and probably even more that weren't. Body language was a new frontier when it wasn't merely a cultural divide, but one of biology and speciation.

"Nah, man, it's good. Happy." Paul did it again. "It's saying 'yay!' and that I'm excited."

Yuhwa huffed. "Good your aoiti work. You can keep up when I say it's time to work on acclimating you to space. All of you, if you can convince the rest to do it."

As he and Yuhwa headed for the exit he saw all the Mikanjo officers giving fist pumps a try.

By the time they'd returned to the ship section temporarily housing his family, Paul's spirits were back to normal. It was only to be expected that he'd stumbled the first time he confronted interstellar travel. Nothing to be ashamed of, he'd just put it right out of his mind. Pretend it never happened, in fact.

Yuhwa rounded the corner to their hallway, much slower than she'd driven it before, for the record, and came to a jerking stop. Dozens of Mikanjo were milling around, smiling and laughing, and right in the middle of it was Da. Of course that's how it was. Papa Phelan never met a stranger, only friends waiting to be made.

"Did this happen last time?"

Yuhwa shook her head, using a hair stick she'd pulled out of nowhere to secure her hair in a bun before jumping off the sled. "Not this fast, no."

"My boy!" Martin Phelan bellowed down the open hall, arm around Ma's shoulders. "This replicator does God's own work, and we've been sharing ale with all these fine people."

Paul had to laugh. This was what his family gave the Aoni: a sister who broke a dragon out of prison with her flute, and Irish beer.

They neared the crowd, Lia making her way toward them. She, too, had a mug of Kilkenny.

"What happened?" Yuhwa said. "We left you with tired Humans and return to a hootenanny!"

Paul cracked up. "How do you know *that* word?"

"Your sister," she replied. "I learned it right before we left the Wheel to come for you. Did I use it properly?"

"Absolutely," Paul said, feeling a grin break out. "Gives me hope these aoiti will teach everyone, not just us backward Humans."

"This is what they do," Lia said. "They were first created by a team of Imen and Lunari. The Imen don't have the same vocal structure most bipedal species do. They were motivated to ensure all people would be able to communicate."

"It will take some time," Yuhwa added, "for Human languages to assimilate. There are a lot of them, more than most species have. But the aoiti are already much faster than they were when Raisa and your sister first got them. They learn and share exponentially. Once the main databases get uploads of what's been worked out so far, it will be even better."

In the future, Humans wouldn't be fleeing Earth the same way the Phelan brood had. Hopefully. Paul knew there were those who'd kill to be where he was, and those who would rather dig a hole and live in a bunker than go to outer space. Those who did want to get off-planet could get their aoiti in place ahead of time. Like getting vaccinated, but with nanobots that were your phone, wallet, and malaria shot.

"Back to my question," Yuhwa said. "Since when did this become a party?"

Lia blushed. "Martin Phelan wanted to see the replicator, try to understand how it worked. Katy's womb mate-"

"Oran." Paul offered. "And you might want to say twin instead. Those two aren't friendly enough to be mates of any kind."

"*Oran* offered to use what he named your most precious resource for testing. When I was gifted a portion, it was astonishing, so I commed my friend. Orihei came to see about getting a taste, and she told another friend." Lia laughed. "Your father replicated many containers of, what do you call this?"

"Ale. Beer."

She peered into her mug. "We have nothing like this, but it's delicious."

"I wonder," Paul mused, "if it's the hops. Maybe that's an Earth original."

Both women paused simultaneously, shook their heads as one, and he took that to mean the plant wasn't something they recognized.

"All right," he clapped his hands and rubbed them together, cocking an eyebrow at Yuhwa. "Does this work for the space exposure therapy you were talking about?"

Lia gasped. "We would never expose you to space!"

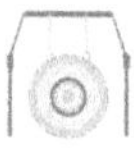

EVENTUALLY THE PHELAN FAMILY, plus Lia and Yuhwa, made their way to an empty observation chamber and locked the doors for privacy. Wiremu had given his approval, though he suggested Yuhwa not drink too much rusim "like last time".

He'd added a wink so she knew he wasn't a captain censuring her, just a friend teasing.

She tried the Human ale; it was acceptable, but she preferred her native drink. Reminded of how she'd overdone it before, though, she planned to be reasonable. Temperate enjoyment wasn't what the still rushing blood in her veins wanted, but Yuhwa could control her impulses. She'd had plenty of practice in her four hundred seventeen aiwaks.

Even with a temptation like Paul Phelan, she reasoned. Yes, he was very attractive to her in her post-transit state. She'd watched him though, ever since they met on Earth, and knew they wouldn't work. Even if she was willing to risk Katy's wrath by sleeping with her friend's brother, Yuhwa wasn't willing to risk attachment. This was a man who needed a family, the closeness of people who know one another fundamentally. Exactly the opposite of what she wanted.

The initial sal-ang in the chamber didn't go well. Deb vomited, sheer panic at the idea the vacuum of space was "only a window away!" making her sick. Brianna trembled, too, but not as bad as Deb. She'd thought the others might be equally challenged, but Patrick and Vasuda were cuddled together on a couch, dreamy smiles on their faces as they watched space move by.

"Years ago, they went through a 'shrooms phase," Paul murmured. "This is probably nothing for them."

Martin wouldn't stop moving long enough to look out the windows, far more interested in the furniture and construction materials. He and Kweza were having detailed training about layout and design on the *Eternidad*. A loud "marvelous!" erupted from different parts of the room every few kaalas.

Oran and Ian had taken a long look into the darkness filled with starry pinpricks and shrugged. "Huh," came from one of them, before they parked themselves at a table. The large amount of beer they'd brought sat between them as they made their way through bottle after bottle.

That left her in a lounger, Paul on her left and Lia to the right. Paul had asked to try her rusim, declared it was "damn fine" and tried to get his brothers to try it.

"Guys, it's like Olde E and Goldschlager. But with, like, a Baltimore Zoo kicker." Deb retched again, and everyone else waved him off. "Fine, guess it's just me then."

Lia smiled. "You sing less than your sister."

"Ha! Katy can't hold her liquor to save her life. She spent all that time in Ireland and didn't even work up a good tolerance. Wasted time, you ask me."

"You use less of her slang, too. Even though you're from the same family group." Lia sipped her ale. "Is that common on Earth?"

"With Katy, it's a special deal because she was in another country for years, and she's a little sponge for that stuff. We all use some of Da's phrases, but she's got the most of all of us." He mulled it over. "Actually, though, it will be a thing for Humans in general. We have hundreds of countries with different cultures and languages for each one. One country can have three languages, local creoles, stuff like that. We barely understand each other half the time, so...."

Yuhwa smirked. "You've got your own way with words; I've only gotten half of what you've said the last few kaalas. It will be a good workout for the aoiti, and all those people who love to study different species."

"The Uilig will jump at the chance," Lia predicted.

They sat in comfortable silence a while longer. Patrick and Vasuda had risen from their couch and walked right up to the windows. Side-by-side, hands clasped, free hands reaching out to lay against the coolness of what separated them from space. Vasuda lay her head on Patrick's shoulder, and he kissed her gently.

Lia sighed. "Happy pairings run in your family. Your parents, two of your brothers, your sister. I can't deny some jealously. My younger brother is a lucky man."

Paul scoffed. "They aren't always happy."

Yuhwa rotated her head to look at him. "Do you refer to yourself, or one of these other couples?"

"I just," he started, stopped. Running a hand through his hair he went on. "Ma and Da are good, that pair over there, too. Even Ian and Deb, probably because no one else could stand either one of them. But Oran's never going to settle, and I had something but it fell apart. Now Katy's gotten hooked up with a guy and it's moving too fast. No offense," he tossed at Lia.

"I take no offense, and agree their mating is rapid. They've had no time to learn each other's ways." She frowned. "Not that tuigs always matter. There are some cases where time is no help."

Yuhwa took a quick drink. "That sounds like experience, Lia, hard learned."

Lia winced. "I've loved for a while, without return. It makes me sad and resentful now and then, but I keep hope for others," she finished.

"And you," Yuhwa redirected. "What is something that *falls apart* on Earth?"

Paul poured more rusim and sipped before answering. "Brittany and I hooked up in college; we were together almost from the instant we met." He slouched back, stretching his long legs in front of him. "She said she didn't want to get married, but we kind of were, by default. After eleven years she was family; we lived together, did all the holidays, etc. I thought we were good, but the last six months before she ended it were very unpleasant."

Eyes closed, a tightness to his face, he went on. "Suddenly I wasn't enough. Not driven enough, not successful enough, a 'drag'. She said I wasn't willing to put in the effort to get my business to the next level, and when I said I was fine with it where it was, she said that was a sign I wasn't willing to provide for a family."

"Was she correct? Or did she make excuses to end something she no longer wanted?" Yuhwa realized her questions were unkind when Lia sucked in a breath.

Paul pinned her with a wounded stare. "Since she was the one who didn't want marriage, and we'd both agreed to no kids, I'm going with her making excuses."

Yuhwa put her hands palms-to-ceiling in the Jadoube sign of surrender. "This is why I only have short term encounters. Cleaner and easier that way."

"But no chance to develop deeper feelings," Lia challenged.

"I'm not interested in that," Yuhwa declared. "When my papa died, my mother's broken heart took her first from me, then from life. I'll pass on that kind of selfishness."

Silence greeted her words, and she feared too much drink had made her overshare. Jumping up to change the energy of their group, she grabbed cups for refills, pondering how she could divert them from heavy talk. The quick movements dislodged her hair stick, which hit the floor with a little clink. "Shtŭ," she said, bending down.

Paul snatched it before she could. "Thanks for finally sharing some profanity. I was starting to think there wasn't a word for *fuck*, and that would be tragic. Shtŭ. I like it." He balanced the stick on his middle finger as he closely examined the designs, her family symbols, embedded along it. "Is this silver?"

She put out her hand for him to return it, unable to deny the zing that fired her blood when his fingers touched hers. They stared at each other, caught in a moment of something Yuhwa couldn't name. Lia cleared her throat and they broke off, but Yuhwa noticed his fingers trembled just a little. That was fine, it matched the quake she'd felt in her bones.

"This is waja, a metal found predominantly on my people's planet. Malor."

"It's like platinum or silver from Earth. Lighter, though. Like air but solid," he marveled. "Is it strong?"

Lia, still looking at both of them curiously, said absently, "You'll see when we get to Centris, all the Swords have weapons of waja. The Jadoube are famous for that."

"That's sturdy enough to make weapons?! Wait, you're fighters? I thought Jadoube were pilots?" Paul looked honestly confused.

"One atóm," Yuhwa said, going for the drinks. She resumed when she got back. "We all start out as majio. Pilots, as you say. Eventually, after several aiwaks we are called home by the nawa."

Paul interrupted her. "Aiwaks? Centuries? Seriously, you cannot be that old."

Lia laughed merrily. "She is very young, both for a majio on such a large ship, and in comparison to almost everyone living on the *Eternidad*." She leaned forward. "I am four times her four aiwaks!"

Yuhwa watched the calculations behind Paul's eyes. "Holy shit. You're *sixteen hundred years old*?!" To Yuhwa, "And you're legit four hundred, like Katy said. I didn't really believe her. She's been known to tell some whoppers, so we all sort of wondered what to take as true."

Whopper *slang in Human British and American English, typically references objects or concepts of exceptional size, or statements that are grossly false. May also reference a specific version of a foodstuff called a hamburger.*

Ooh, another good one to mark for later use. "What other things did you think she'd lied about?"

Paul's face flushed red. "The dragon thing. Dragons are her favorite kind of fantasy."

Lia and Yuhwa laughed hard enough to get everyone's attention. By the time they'd recovered the whole group surrounded them. "What's this then," Martin said. "Are there tales to be told of our Katy?"

"The opposite, *sana*," Lia said. "We are explaining that Katy told no tales, and dragons are real. Nine Drazoen created Centris, went away a kōmilen ago, and your daughter brought the first of them back to us. Sundancer Orange, Irojaku jo Faluji, flies the Aoni once more because of Katy Phelan alone!"

So many shocked faces, Yuhwa mused. Finally, Brianna spoke. "You shouldn't call him 'honored one', dear. He'll never let it go."

"Wait, wait," Paul waved his hands. "If Yuhwa's young for a pilot, how did she get this job?"

She wasn't comfortable with so much attention, but answered him. "I was an advanced learner, and I grew up on Centris more than Malor because my dad was a sword in the Truth Arenas. I came to independence sooner than most majio." She opted not to delve further into losing her parents, and pushed on. "I focused on short trips, a contract majio hired for a transit or two then parting ways. When the *Eternidad* stopped at a station I was on, their old pilot asked if I'd be interested in taking over his position so he could retire back to Malor."

Lia raised her voice. "Best day of the last aiwak!" She drank, then amended, "Except for the last part, where we began saving the Aoni. That's been quite exciting."

Yuhwa laughed. "What about that adventure satellite in the Pandicoya system?! All you seekers wanted a break and thought Eng-designed challenges would be 'fun'." She slapped her thigh. "So much for that, eh? But I was able to get to know the ship while it was mostly empty for a while, which was sublime." Yuhwa's face softened.

"We are all very lucky that so many things have aligned," Vasuda murmured. She was a beautiful, soft-spoken woman with skin like shaded wadi sands; she wore a loose wrapping around her head that caressed her face. Yuhwa admired the look, and wondered if she could imitate it without offense.

Lia got that *look* on her face again. Same look she'd had when Yuhwa and Paul had locked gazes. "The Aoni and the Nine make all things possible." Glancing between Yuhwa and Paul, she casually dropped a bomb. "Have I told you that in the Mikanjo prophecy from Windweaver, Songmaster's herald will bear waja?"

Yuhwa gaped at her friend, ""That's preposterous. What you're implying."

Lia smirked. "Seraji jo Milabika is Songmaster *Silver*, of course waja would play a role."

Yuhwa looked at the waja hair stick still resting on the arm of her lounger, then to Paul.

He shrugged. "You just told me dragons are real. My sister is supposedly one of these heralds, right?"

"Kawakona," Lia offered.

"Sure, Bug's a big deal. Maybe one of us is, too," he laughed. "We've been brought together by this Aoni, right?" His grin creased his handsome face with mirth. "Nothing's off the table, Phelans! Speak up if you're hearing voices, or having weird dreams, or whatever passes as advance warning of herald status."

Everyone broke into laughter, and Yuhwa raised her glass to Paul. No one here was destined to be a herald, they were obviously on the same wavelength about that. In two sals they'd get to Centris, plan Katy's wedding, and life would go back to normal.

4

T HEY'D STOPPED. P AUL HADN'T BEEN ON THIS BOAT long, but after last night's shindig he knew what it looked like when they were moving. That surely wasn't the view out his window right now.

He got up and dressed in one of the outfits the Mikanjo had gifted him. It felt like a fine material, but had the look of an ashram nature lover ready to discuss spiritual ascendence. He'd have to ask Yuhwa about getting one of her bodysuits, even if he'd look like a cut-rate superhero wearing one.

The main room was empty, so Vasuda and Patrick were still asleep or otherwise occupied. Paul wished them well either way. He'd followed Da just enough yesterday to work the replicator that came in these family pods, and got it to spit out nropita. Katy had sworn once they tasted it no one would want coffee again, but Deb had brought her treasured Ethiopian beans along just in case. His first sip confirmed what his little sister had promised. This stuff was manna from heaven.

Determined to find out why they'd stopped, then hopefully where he could go work out, Paul emerged into the cul-de-sac formed by their three units. Lia was walking down the hallway toward him, a grim look on her face.

"What happened?"

She spoke quietly and gravely. "Departures. Hundreds, leaving at once. Nothing like this has ever happened, and Kweza stopped the ship. It calculated a potential collision issue if so many personal craft depart at the same time."

Mass exodus this close to Centris, and substantial enough to concern the ship's AI? "I don't understand. Why would they go now?"

Lia sighed. "It is a complicated and nuanced situation. Since Djilbay found Katy, seekers have been debating if our job is over. Are we no longer seekers as Hunanjanno made us? Should we return to Bankiri? None of us have ever walked the lands of our home planet, or felt its winds through our feathers. Going there is almost a bigger dream than finding a Kawakona. To set foot on the earth that created us...." She near-whispered, "It's a powerful urge."

Mikanjo seekers could never go home unless they gave up their names and their mission. A heavy price. "Okay, but why go now? Couldn't they have gone before?"

"The other factor is you." Her eyes were downcast. "Humans, I mean. One of the oldest rules of Centris is the Law of First Approach. It decrees that advanced species of the Calling cannot, must not, interfere with new species. They're meant to progress on their own, and only if they're able to leave their home system independently can contact be made."

"Ohhhh. And you came for Katy and Bay, then for us."

"Just so. Some of the seekers who push to abandon the *Eternidad* have been...anxious, I suppose. Their fears of sanctions or punishment have built to the point that many on the ship plan to leave before we reach Centris, where judgements may fall."

Paul couldn't guess exact numbers, but as they'd travelled

around the ship he'd seen hundreds of people. "How many? How many going or staying?" Yuhwa wouldn't bail, so they should be able to fly, right? Except she wasn't the pilot right now, not since they'd come through the veșu. Crap, would they still be able to get Centris?

Lia sighed. "Less than two hundred will remain. More than eighty percent of the people will leave in the next sal-ang."

"I can't imagine what you're feeling," Paul offered. He nearly hugged her, remembering Katy's ban on touching Mikanjo uninvited just in time. But that reminded him of the day before. "What about that boy? Zazi?"

"Wiremu, his father, stays, as does Zazi. Yuhwa, obviously. My friend, Orihei, also stays."

Paul had seen how Lia looked at her, and matched that up with what she'd shared about unrequited feelings. He'd bet his gym back home that Orihei was the focus of her love. "Is there anything I can do? Help in some way?" He was really out of his depth here, but a part of him felt like he and his family had chased the seekers from their home.

"No," she smiled sadly, "but thank you for the thought. I just came to let you know what's happening."

Paul watched her walk away, thinking this wasn't the most auspicious start to their journey. One that had started with dire threats from that fed, no less. It had to get better once they arrived at this wheel, right?

He focused best as he could, trying to talk to his aoiti. Yuhwa said they could be used to privately communicate, and he wanted to send her a message. Kweza was a last resort since that was completely public, whereas the aoiti were one-to-one if need be. Paul just wanted to make sure she was okay, given how deeply tied to the ship she was.

No luck, though, so he sent mental "good vibes" her way, wherever that might be, and went back for a second cup of nropita.

YUHWA DOVE into a secluded pool fed by a large waterfall. The meditation and relaxation zone of the ship, Xhisa, was her favorite hideaway. This particular area was her extra-secret spot, far from the entrance to Xhisa. Most people used the larger pools up front; the much longer walk here meant she was rarely interrupted taking a swim. Unlike the purple water of Lake Mwanaburo's replication, the lakes and cenotes in here were the clear green of her planet, Malor. There were days she needed the calm the resemblance gave her. Days like today.

I am not the captain, she told herself. *Not in charge. Can't take the desertions personally.*

But she did, damn the fleeing Mikanjo to the Three Ekletu! Surfacing from her dive she floated on her back, letting her eyes lose focus. The thick tropical canopy overhead blended into a comfortingly blurry peach-and-ivory colored sky. Yuhwa let her mind wander.

Could the Three Ekletu make it all the way from Malor to here, even if it bore no resemblance to where they'd been created? They were shadow spirits, said to be the lost souls of Jadoube who hadn't gone on pâtexi; mythological beings who plagued the Five Côttru and caused fights, misery, and dissent wherever they roamed.

Was it their fault so many had fled the *Eternidad* a sal-ang past? Where exactly could Yuhwa place blame for the evacuation no one had anticipated? On Bay, for finding Katy? For scaring the crap out of his people because she was under attack, so much so they broke Centris rules of engagement with the Humans to get to her? Maybe the PQ for having bred shtŭing insane suicide assassins? The Drazoen for disappearing in the first place and sentencing Mikanjo seekers to such loneliness?

She rolled over and tried to swim like an arnat zingo, but

floated too well for that. No escaping into the dao for her just yet. Yuhwa was annoyed, wanting her equilibrium back. Uncertainty and rejection weren't her preferred emotional states.

A conversation drifted to her ears from the forested shore; she'd lost her privacy and knew exactly to whom. They spoke in Human, meaning there were only so many options, but Yuhwa acknowledged she already knew Paul's voice better than the rest. Any moment he and another male from his family would find her.

Her quiet reprieve was gone. Reluctant to sacrifice her serenity, Yuhwa swam to the ladder of rocks she'd made long ago. These humans, they always wanted to talk. Endlessly talk. She'd rather do that sitting on her towel than treading water.

Paul and Patrick rounded the trailbend and spotted the small clearing just as she got out of the water. They stopped short, for once having no words.

Yuhwa tilted her head, and called, "All right? You can join me if you want."

"Nice-" Paul broke off and cleared his throat. "Nice suit."

Patrick smirked. "The bikini turns out to be one of the universal things in this futuristic, advanced Aoni? Wouldn't have predicted that."

The look in Paul's eyes heated Yuhwa's core. Reminding herself he wasn't acceptable fling material, she shook off the attraction and reached for her clothes. But she wouldn't deny putting a little extra wiggle and shimmy into donning her bodysuit. The flame of Paul Phelan's gaze morphing into an inferno was the perfect balm to her earlier frustration.

"What are you doing here? How did you manage to find me?" she asked, sitting down now she was dressed.

Patrick lay on his back, staring at the sky just as she liked to do in the water. Paul folded his legs crossways and settled at her side.

"We weren't stalking you, promise. Someone told Paul he

could come here and swim to get his excess energy out." Patrick shook his head. "He hasn't worked out or done gymnastics in days, so he's going bonkers. You've always had too much pep, man."

Paul ignored his brother. Facing the nearby rainforest, his attention was all for a line of rufucebus. They swung by their tails on yellow raschai vines that wound around tree trunks and through branches, chittering and absently scratching their tiny bellies.

"What are those?" He rolled to his knees, inching closer to them. "They're adorable." He stopped moving. "Are they carnivorous? That's what always happens in the movies, the cute ones go for your throat."

Once the aoiti clarified "carnivorous" Yuhwa snorted. "They're gentle, fruit and nut eaters. They aren't native to the Mikanjo world, but long ago an Imen ambassador gifted a pack of them for this part of the ship. They're called rufucebus, and if you bring them baijur crackle, they'll swarm you and rub all over your hands to get the scent in their fur."

"Roo-fah-see-bus?" Patrick asked. "Like tiny red monkeys, but with six pairs of paws. Aw."

Paul muttered something about getting his hands on baijur crackle. Eventually, he concentrated on Yuhwa. "All right?" he said, echoing her earlier question.

How extraordinary. They'd known each other less than three sals and he somehow understood the stress Mikanjo mass-evacuation would put on her.

A gentle smile curved her lips in response. "I'll be okay. The ship just feels…. Barren. I know it's fanciful, but when I walked the corridors after they left, it seemed to echo more loudly."

"I doubt you imagined it," Paul nudged her foot with his. "You know this place inside and out, and losing all those people in just a few hours has to be discombobulating."

Discombobulate *from Human English; informal; meaning to put in a state of confusion, physically or emotionally. Often used comically.*

Another word to put in her repository. She had to give it to Humans; they'd taken everything Tonguemaker Green flung into the Aoni and run with it. Even when she'd first landed on Centris as a child and her aoiti updated with a sudden influx of species-specific words, Yuhwa didn't think there'd been so much unique terminology and slang. To think this was only one of their languages!

She nudged his foot in return. "It was. Thank you for understanding that. But," she sighed. "They were bound to return sooner rather than later. These poor seekers have been kept from Bankiri for generations; they're desperate to learn what their lives will be like now."

"We call that finding your new normal."

Yuhwa mulled it over. "I like that phrase. I'll have to find my new normal, too. If the *Eternidad* is permanently docked now that destiny is fulfilled, I'm out of a job." Her heart sank. "I like my job. Why do things have to change?"

Patrick hummed, eyes closed. "There's an old Earth saying about the Wheel of Fortune always turning. That's all there is to it; chance, destiny, fate, luck. Call it what you want, but it never stays in one place for long." He laced his hands behind his head. "Up, down, and around. Forever and ever, amen."

Yuhwa caught Paul shaking his head. "Ignore him. He did a lot of drugs when he was younger."

Patrick's eyes popped open and he rolled to his side, propping his head on a bent arm. "I've taken edibles a handful of times, and psychedelics twice." He raised his eyebrows. "If Paul thinks that's a lot, I think it says less about me and more about how uptight *he* is."

She watched a teasing grin transform Patrick's face. This Phelan child was the calmest of all of them, probably the easiest to like and get along with. But he was perfectly capable of poking back at his brother, as he'd just proven.

"If I try these edibles of yours, will I be as cheerful about my life turning upside down as you've been about leaving Earth and meeting aliens you never imagined?"

All rufucebus in the vicinity scattered as Human laughter, deep and loud, broke out.

PAUL WANTED to say he'd handled arrival on the Wheel suavely. Like a young Paul Newman would have, or Michael Fassbender. Cooler than cool. Casually taking in all the sights, a self-deprecating smile charming everyone, knowing there was nothing out there he couldn't take on and win. In the end he thought he'd come across more like a kid arriving at Disneyworld for the first time.

There was just so damn much to see! Even from the dimmed windows of the *Eternidad* his entire family was lookie-looing every which way. Bright colors and aliens of every possible shape, shade and size, the landing area's chaotic noise carrying from below through the ship cargo area they were in.

The turmoil wasn't like the mess they'd left behind on Earth; this was more or less organized, just with thousands of people moving about quickly. Ships everywhere, whistles, beeps, and alerts going off while people shouted over the bedlam. Katy had tried to warn them it would overwhelm, but not a one of them was being chill.

Da seemed to be analyzing everything in sight, his engineer brain trying to force logic onto what was beyond Human ability as of yet. "D'ya see that?!" he exclaimed in delight. "Three eyes and tall as trees, they are!"

Oti *ooh!-tea; young species from Oxlom in the Portlaq galaxy of*

Balasa system, fond of puzzles and intricate games, excel at tasks requiring manual dexterity; often act as mechanics

"Da," Katy hissed. "Keep your voice down. We're still sneaking around here; you shouting in a language no one else can understand doesn't help."

Oran, laconic as ever, drawled, "Whassamatter, Bug? Ashamed of your Human family now you claim you've become a dragon queen?"

"Look at that," she snarled and bared her teeth at her twin. "My great enlightenment didn't make me want to hit you any less."

"Children," Ma started, "not in public. Katy, show us what to do or where to go so we don't embarrass you."

Paul's sister looked guilty and gutted in one. "I'm not embarrassed, Ma! Jeez. It's just... Humans aren't official here yet. Until the whole team decides how to handle that, we're flying under the radar."

Deb and Ian bore twin grimaces. "What," Deb bit out, "could be more under the radar than literally exiting under the damn ship, Katy?" Ian nodded at his wife's words.

Everyone knew Katy was closing to blowing her stack. The one-two punch of Oran and Deb was sure to push her over the edge. Vasuda rushed to her side, taking her hand.

"Dearest, we'll follow. We only need to know what to do. Explanations," she turned a quelling gaze on the family, "can wait."

"Just get in that." Katy pointed out a cargo container, floating a few inches off the ground. "Pretend you're all luggage, or precious goods if you prefer." Here she glared at Deb. "Last time we managed to trick them into thinking Raisa and I had malfunctioning aoiti, but this time they won't buy that for a whole group."

She pushed a button on the hovering pod. When a door swirled open, Paul saw it was actually pretty roomy and had a light. "I should have taken Sundancer up on the offer to grab you all, but that's hard on the system." She sighed. "Plus, you said Earth was a wreck after the *Eternidad* showed up the first time. A dragon might have been a worse shock."

Katy had *said* she'd been some kind of dragon chosen. But he, hell, they all had assumed that was an exaggeration; metaphor or her runaway imagination. The way she spoke now, though, on top of what Lia and Yuhwa had sworn was true meant he couldn't keep denying it. They were going to meet a dragon, Katy's Sundancer, who was basically a god in this big, bright Aoni. He glanced at Patrick who raised an eyebrow and shrugged.

Da was helping Ma up into the cargo box when a voice behind them called, "Katy Phelan? Are you Katy Phelan?"

Katy's eyes widened in shock, and she turned to face a floating blob of coral. Paul really didn't know what to think about that, so he gawked.

Eng *multiple home worlds in multiple systems of the Dorji galaxy, share linked consciousness when on a home world, thrive in magnetic environments, highly driven to organize, excel in bureaucratic and logistic areas.*

His sister, flanked by her entire family, tilted her head and made a *go on* gesture. Jeezy Creezy, hopefully that translated well to a species that had no arms. Why hadn't Lia or Yuhwa stayed to make sure something like this didn't come up? *Shite, Bug. Aren't you better at this by now?*

After a slight hesitation, it continued. "Greetings, I am Ihaia Tang, supervisory registrar. Your file has come to me. One buwan ago, you arrived on the *Eternidad* unable to comply with registration requirements due to 'malfunctioning' aoiti. Is this correct?"

Katy nodded and it continued, but Paul thought Ihaia's voice was threaded with suspicion now. He sidled closer to Patrick and Oran, who were trying to casually ease their way in front of the group. The urge to protect was strong in the Phelan family, and all of these hits to their sense of security were riding them hard.

"You have exceeded the hinaharap you were given to update your registration. I have also been advised you must have left Centris at some point, because there is video of you returning with Sundancer Orange. To a restricted port, I might add. There was no clearance for that, either requested or provided. We need to clear this up and file the correct documents. You are free now?"

5

"WHY DID YOU GIVE THEM OUR REAL NAMES?!"

Bay looked at Katy in surprise. "What other name would I give them? We weren't pretending you were someone else entirely, just that you weren't an unknown species sneaking on to the Wheel."

The Phelan clan collectively held their breath when they saw the Irish mule face Katy made. This boy was in for it now. Raisa snort-laughed, obviously familiar with the look and what it portended.

"That's how they nailed us, Bay! Those officials from our first landing filed paperwork. Apparently, you told them we'd clear things up in a few sals, but we never did. Now Riri and I are gonna be heavily fined, and non-compliant to boot. Plus, the Eng who served the papers today saw my whole family and got suspicious! I barely got away with the mute routine and that "Cadre attaché" card Dindal made. I think we're fugitives now!"

Yes, fugitives who'd stowed away in a floating container that carried them to what Katy called "long-term residence mid ring, between Sundancer and Hu Ularu spokes." Sure, because that had meaning to any of them.

Raisa and Bay had been waiting for them in a big common room, several open doors showing hints of bedrooms beyond. Before they'd even had time for intros or to sort out who would sleep where, Katy had started yelling at her boyfriend. Partner, mate, good buddy. Whatever they were calling each other.

Bay tried to placate Katy, assuring her it would all be fine. Paul admired any man with the patience of this guy; he'd supposedly waited a thousand years for Katy. And now that he had her, Bay had to live with her. No easy feat, Paul could attest. His sister wasn't a treat in the morning, held a grudge like a mafiosa, and would always steal the last cookie from the plate. She'd also fight in your corner like a demented wildcat, and love you very nearly unconditionally. He wished them well, even if secretly he thought these hurried nuptials seemed unwise.

"Katy, what did they say we need to do?" Raisa interrupted the brewing corker between the couple.

"The one thing we *can't* – to register our identities formally for the Centris bureaucracy. By tomorrow. Bay, we need to go see the Cadre. Figure out how we'll handle this."

"*Mo leanbh,*" Da said. "Tell us what this means. You're going a wee bit fast for the rest of us."

"I wish we had time, Da," Katy rushed to him, hugging him. "I'd planned to take all of you with me when we went back to the Chorus, but I can't shake a feeling it's too risky now."

"We will go straight away in the morning," Bay said. "It's very late, Centris time, and the voices are busy preparing for Zina's funeral or sleeping about now."

Paul knew that look from Katy, too. She wasn't sold on Bay's approach, but she was giving in despite her misgivings. Part of him liked seeing her compromise; that had never been Bug's strong suit and was probably good for her personal growth. But another part of him worried she was letting herself be rail-roaded. Just because this guy with wings was older and she had feelings for him, Katy shouldn't think she had to cave to his opinions.

"Fine," she grumbled. "Grand. Well, everyone, this is Raisa. And Bay, obviously."

"We've seen them on videos," Deb said, her tone implying Katy was dense.

"I am aware, Debra." Daaaamn. If she was using government names, Deb best retreat. "You've not met them in person, though, so I was formally introducing you."

Bay bowed, keeping his wings held tightly to his back. How in the hell did they fold up like that? It was next-level origami.

Raisa waved slightly. "Very nice to meet you, all of you. Katy has told me so many stories of your family."

"She lies," Oran said. Patrick and Paul both smacked his arms, one on either side.

Paul hefted one of his duffels high. "Cheese puffs, six pounds of Fran's chocolates, all the spices we could grab from the market, two bottles of rosewater, and ma's shortbread." Distraction: the best way to shortcut a twin fight.

Raisa's face lit up. "Turmeric? Saffron?"

Vasuda, standing next to her, reached over to touch her arm. "Yes, and mint from my garden. I am sorry, though, I couldn't find golpar."

"Riri loves to cook, turns out, but we didn't have the right ingredients for her favorite dishes." Katy laughed. "Sending people out to the subspokes searching for equivalents has been a good time, but bloody hit or miss."

Raisa echoed her friend's mirth. "What was that Yuhwa brought back last week? I wanted tangy, but I think it mistranslated, because what she got was so sour my entire mouth shriveled!"

"That's a Rixat plant, relashfev." Bay grimaced. "A condiment I'm happy to bypass in future."

Paul's aoiti flashed an image of a very pale and stringy seaweed facsimile.

"Not good," Katy giggled. "Not good at all."

Ma pushed forward to wrap her arms around Katy. "I'm so happy to see my baby girl!" She had tears in her eyes. "I've been so worried," she whispered. Releasing her and turning to Da, she said, "You remembered the games?"

"Of course! Phase 10, dominoes, Boggle. I've brought them all."

Marshaling her troops, as Ma always did, she suggested they settle into their rooms then break out the games. "We can pass a nice night and relax before meeting these voice people," she said.

Katy had explained they were in the Centris version of a short-term rental. Cozier than a hotel, "closer to a real house from home."

Paul and Oran were assigned a room together; to Paul's mind that made it nothing like home. He was used to his own place, built over the gym he ran. A loan from Patrick had made owning the building possible, and even when finances were tight, Paul could say he was the landlord. These last few days of sharing space were wearing on him; he was too old to be roomies, or a third wheel to the couples of the group.

"Is there somewhere I can work out?" He wasn't encouraged by the carefully blank expression on Bay's face. "Let me guess. We have to stay hidden?"

"Yes," Katy's man said. "But tomorrow, at Voice House, I expect we can find somewhere for you to exercise. Katy has told me that you are the most physically inclined of the Phelans."

Paul grunted. "You could say that, I guess."

"Once Humans are part of the Calling, there are several places you can visit." Bay tapped his lips. "I'll research some options, for the future." His smile was open and genuine.

Paul returned the smile, but balked at the idea of a future on Centris. They were here for Katy's wedding, but no one had really talked about what happened after. Did they return to Earth? As much as he lamented the post-apocalyptic vibes of the last month, that was home. This thing, whatever it was, couldn't be more than a lark. A surreal tourist experience.

How could they go back, though? In just two days he was changed by what they'd seen. Mikanjo were another species, but in crisis just like Humans. Altered forever by what Katy and Bay had accomplished, they were confused, hopeful, questioning, and flat-out scared. He could relate.

Paul always tried to find the beauty in things; young Zazi, the happy sharing of Irish ale with seekers pleased to lay down their burdens for a while, Yuhwa in a bikini, and those adorable damn rufucebus.

He, Paul bloody Phelan, had watched entire galaxies swirl past his eyes. Standing at the windows of the *Eternidad*, he'd let the power of the cosmos wash over him like a cleansing rain. He'd been humbled, nearly brought to tears, at the realization he was the tiniest speck of space dust in the grand scheme of things. And yet, he was a marvel, too. He was a sentient being made up of all that Big Bang residue. Humans weren't the only evolved kids on the block, but they were new members of an exclusive club. Only sixteen known species could stand at the window of a spaceship and ponder the meaning of existence. How did you return to the ordinary after transcendence like that?

He supposed that federal prick would be happy to let him contemplate this epiphany from a secure cell somewhere in Area 51, though. What was that word Yuhwa had used...shtŭ, that was it. They were shtŭed if they went home, so they'd best press on with getting Humans accepted here on the Wheel.

Their night was a typical raucous Phelan get-together. Loud

voices and laughter, attempts to cheat that were so blatant it was just part of the silly fun, and testing the replicator's ability to copy ma's beloved, buttery shortbread. It took three tries, but eventually it was dialed in and a success.

Not Boggle, though. Da admitted that, in hindsight, bringing a game that relied on reading English hadn't been the best idea. "I didn't think that through, my boy," he'd said apologetically to Bay. "But here, these others just have numbers!"

Bay was kind enough not to point out he'd likely spoken English longer than Da's ancestors had been in Ireland. Paul thought he just didn't care for the game.

Raisa had been shy at first, but by the end of the night she was trash talking as much as the rest of them. Deb had tried her usual passive-aggressive isolation strategy on Raisa; it was very much rooted in *you are other*. Vasuda had ignored it for years now, but Raisa looked Deb in the eye and asked, "Is the problem that I'm not a Phelan, or that I'm Persian?"

Called on her bullshit, Deb sputtered an apology and clammed up the rest of the game. If Paul hadn't sworn off women, he'd be looking at Raisa in a whole new light. Anyone who could stop Deb in her tracks like that was a person worth keeping close.

The next morning, Katy was in a frenzy, having changed her mind. They all had to go to the Chorus together, and right damn now. She was pushing everyone to get moving faster. "We gotta go! *A stór*," she stomped over to Bay, raising her hand to rest on his chest. "Can you call another cargo sled? We have to get everyone to Voice House as soon as we can. Sundancer says she'll meet us there. Hustle, family!"

"Don't we have a sal to provide our documents?" Raisa was far calmer than Katy.

His sister frowned, hunching in on herself. "My gut is saying no, even though it's what that Eng said. I'd feel better if we got a move on."

Bay reached out. "*Qania*, the Eng are notorious sticklers for paperwork and detail. I think this is just normal-"

Pounding at the door stopped him short.

"Centris Immigration Compliance. We are entering the premises. Unregistered occupants, present yourselves room center. Registered occupants, move to the side." With that the door swooshed open and a uniformed squad of four stalked in. They spread out to block the exit.

Bay stepped forward, starting to speak. But he was rebuffed by the leader, some guy who looked perfectly human until his tail peeked around his leg.

Chitan *kite-an; from Tzavro in Bølshkel system of Centris galaxy, known widely as brawlers, skilled fighters, and martial artists, semi-nomadic.*

All right, then. Paul was getting nervous. He scanned their group and everyone's fear and worry shone clearly. This wasn't part of the great plan to tour the Universe, stand up at Katy's wedding, and meet a big orange dragon. Logic said nothing bad would happen to them with one of the nine gods of this place on their side. But Paul couldn't completely suppress his worry that an "accident" could cause real harm between now and whenever Katy could get Sundancer to them.

"With one exception – you," the official gestured at Bay, "no one in this room has aoiti pinging on the registry."

"I don't understand, I thought we'd settled this at Harbor Primur." Katy was trying to sound innocent. Paul wondered if this guy would buy it, then saw agonized self-recrimination flash in her eyes. Bay looked at her with helplessness in his own gaze, Raisa gasping.

"What language is *that*?" Chitan guy prowled forward, a clawed finger lifting to point accusingly. "That was gibberish. No new languages have been registered in aiwaks, but the Mikanjo and others understood you."

Trapped. They were trapped and couldn't get away. Paul's

chest tightened with worry and an impotent desire to do some-thing, anything, that would solve the problem. Katy had inad-vertently tripped the wire and they'd all suffer for it.

"Answer!" Tail guy was getting worked up. "Who are you people that your language has no translation, and you have failed to register your status properly?

Raisa turned, giving the officials her back, trying to keep her voice low. "Tell me you're talking to Sundancer, Katy. This is escalating fast."

"I'm trying," his sister muttered.

"Cease talking!" Head dude grabbed at Raisa's arm. She cried out and shrank back from him.

Paul hated bullies. "No need for that friend," he said, even though the words weren't translating. Maybe the tone would get through. He stepped forward. "Paul, I'm Paul. And you are?" His friendly manner didn't work.

"Var Mutile, secure him."

"Yes, Var Yee." A second Chitan stepped forward, the space version of a zip tie handcuff dangling from his hand. Inside the rings a yellow glow pulsed.

Var *officer, designation specific to Centris police forces (CIC, AWD, UPC), indicates middle grade rank, below gozan and above feld, does not apply to swords.*

Before Paul even had time to process the aoiti data, he was shoved against a wall and cuffed. His family erupted, shouting and making an already volatile situation worse. In the end every-one, including Bay who'd tried to defend Katy, were mussed and restrained while Var Yee called for a large transport.

"I don't know who you are, or how you got on the Wheel, but you're going straight to a holding chamber!" His tail slapped the floor repeatedly, transmitting irritation.

By the time they'd been rounded up, shoved into yet another damn cargo carrier, and whisked away to wherever holding chambers lived on this Wheel, Paul was over it. This trip had been an escapade at first, now it was tiresome and more than a little upsetting. What if they got ejected and sent back to an Earth busy destroying itself in panic? What if Katy *had* been full of shit all along and there was no dragon rescue? Where were their Mikanjo and Jadoube friends who'd so conveniently disappeared upon arrival?

His anger mounting, amped by fear, Paul shoved back against the cop pushing him out of the hotel. All that got him was a vicious shoulder pinch that deadened a nerve for the rest of their walk to the prison barge. His family was loaded onto the vehicle and their cuffs secured to a bar running along the middle of the large platform. No sides or cover of any kind, everyone around them staring in shock and judgement as the Phelan family was locked into place by space jackboots.

Helluva welcome to the Aoni.

Yuhwa raced to the containment chambers on mid ring of Earthcaller's spoke. These were never part of the original Drazoen layout on the Wheel. But føns of bad species interactions later, entire blocks of short-stay lodgings had been repurposed. A large area now housed all three military forces situated below the Sword Truth Arenas; below both in power and geographically on the spoke.

Armed Wheel Defense (AWD) was for those worried about external attacks against Centris itself. The Urban Peacekeeping Cohort (UPC) saw to internal issues like theft and bar brawls. And Centris Immigration Compliance, nit-picky khòchis that controlled every entry and exit on the wheel. The very group of power-hungry idiots currently wreaking havoc on all of Team Drazoen's carefully laid plans.

Truth Arenas were at sky ring level, but the detainment of

the Humans would be treated as less critical. Unless they were challenged by a faction in the Calling, this would stay contained. CIC holding areas were on mid ring, and Yuhwa sped as fast as she could behind the far-taller Lia and Sundancer. An angry dragon, in any form, was fast. Sundancer could have transported instantly but opted to stomp out her fury in bipedal form, something that had every person in her way scrambling to the sides of the corridors.

Their small group arrived just as they saw the Phelans, plus Bay and Raisa, being force-marched into CIC headquarters. Katy looked weary, her Mikanjo seeker protective and sad, her family bewildered and terrified. Paul, more than the rest, seemed like he would break from his handcuffs and start cracking heads together, if he could just figure out how. Interesting that, from what Katy had shared, her womb-twin Oran was the firebrand, but everything Yuhwa witnessed put that label on Paul.

CEASE!

Sundancer's mental shout almost took Yuhwa to her knees; she saw many in the area did fall. The CIC officers who'd arrested the Humans stopped, but one turned to face Sundancer with prideful disdain. An impressive feat for a being half a body shorter than Sundancer's present shape.

"We have taken these creatures as per decree 9817.Q5 of the Centris Calling. No one can interfere until we have finished our investigation of their standing." His tail barely moved, but Yuhwa saw the very end of it vibrating a little, whether in fear or righteousness she couldn't say.

You dare take my chosen, my spark, and imprison her? Call her 'creature' as though she is below notice? SHOW RESPECT.

At the last words, everyone left standing from the previous demand collapsed to their knees, some laid flat out. Sundancer's words were an oppressive command no one could fight, except Katy. She remained on her feet, surrounded by unwilling supplicants.

"I appreciate the rescue, but maybe a little less Zod?"

What is… Mm. I see. You prefer the Superman's ways? Shall I leave you here to triumph sals from now?

Katy sighed at Sundancer's annoyed tone. "No, of course not. We need you, but freaking out an entire chunk of people isn't helping as much as you think it is." She held up her cuffed wrists, which were suddenly free of restraint.

Yuhwa glanced behind Katy at the now unshackled family. Dragons were handy in a crisis, that couldn't be denied. Katy helped Phelans and Raisa to their feet, Bay protecting their backs. The lead var, Chitan temper in full view, was ready to spring.

"You cannot take-"

I can. As of this moment I reclaim leadership of the Calling. The Trinary no longer rules in my absence. These people are my emissaries and are protected. A declaration of Sundancer Orange supersedes your directive, Var Chadna Yee.

Chadna Yee still looked like a man ready to rumble. Of course, he was Chitan and they always were, as a rule.

The freed group made its way toward their rescuers, whom Paul greeted with, "Maybe if you hadn't deserted us back at the ship none of this would have happened!"

Whoa. "Are you blaming *us* for this bureaucratic mess?" Yuhwa wasn't happy. "Ridiculous!" She turned away from him, unsure if any of the others were interested in piling on. Lia rolled her eyes, but also laid a forestalling hand on Yuhwa's arm. She took the hint and tried to exhale the argument out of her lungs and find some calm, frustrated how Katy's brother got to her so easily.

She spotted the arrival of a new containment sled across the way, this time run by the UPC carrying a lone prisoner. One she recognized despite the very brief glimpses she'd had of him back on Ishar, and then running away from the *Frelaasti*: the PQ escapee, the slave she was sure Na Xan had helped smuggle off-planet. A few sals of liberty hadn't changed his appearance much: he'd gotten hold of dye somewhere because he was blonde instead of brunette. Didn't look as though he'd found anyone to hide the imagery on his ruh though, an oddly melancholic lightning storm surrounding a mother holding her babe. Something that distinctive had to be what had led to his capture.

Poor siztuk couldn't catch a break. Luck wasn't on his side. The one leading him off the barge wore a uniform that broadcast he'd been captured by a gozan, the highest official of the police forces here. No less than a Pu'ulqaari gozan, in fact, which meant the officer had a special grudge against an escaped slave. Yuhwa considered trying to intervene, but then what could she do? Until the practice was outlawed he was considered stolen goods, no matter he'd stolen himself.

Fret not, Yuhwa Bon-Gil. The Vi'isser contingent is scheduled to arrive in six sal-angs. When they bring suit to have him returned, as they no doubt will, I will take the opportunity to strike down namu'ur.

Sundancer must have spoken only to her because no one else acted like they heard the words. This was huge news, and would be incendiary for the PQ. *You know many may object, more than just Pu'ulqaari?*

Many in the calling should have objected to something so despicable long ago. I will remind them of their morality, and what it means to be an advanced species worthy of inclusion here on Centris.

With that Sundancer instantly transported them to the large entry inside Voice House. Yuhwa had never experienced Drazoen travel, though she'd heard Katy's description. Fairly similar to the dao, if she were honest, and it didn't faze her. Katy was fine, too. Everyone else reacted with varying levels of nausea and shock. Deb started crying, Ian trying to comfort her but radiating embarrassment at her state. Katy's parents were wobbly, as were her siblings. Even Lia and Bay half-flexed their wings to remain steady.

I summon the Cadre for a meeting before I retake my place in the Calling.

Sundancer bounded up the grand staircase in front of her without looking back.

6

This was some serious bullshit. Having never been arrested, Paul couldn't say he had a basis for comparison, but this seemed like absolute crap. Police mofos with tails had dragged him and his family through this godforsaken Wheel and had been aiming to throw them in jail cells. It'd been a close escape. Would all of them have conveniently disappeared if Sundancer and Yuhwa hadn't come?

Speaking of whom, he was still working on letting go of his mad that she and Lia had bailed back at the *Eternidad*. Okay, everyone had agreed it was probably safest, would garner less notice if their party was as small as possible. Well! Just how had that worked out?! Paul had been manhandled and shoved around. His diplomacy attempt was ignored. All because Bug, his beloved but irritating-as-hell-right-now sister, hadn't planned. She never planned! Always did things only when they occurred to her, or whenever people told her she should. She was malleable that way.

He wasn't. Most of his life had been charted, by him, in a step-by-step plan for success. Start out being the best boy. In grade school that meant he had to get top marks for handwriting and reading aloud. Middle school introduced tumbling into Phys Ed, and that became the new framework for Paul's life outlook.

Take gymnastics classes outside school
Make sure regular grades stayed good enough he didn't
    lose extra-curricular privileges
Be the best gymnast in his academy, even better than
    older boys
Kiss Adriana Van Camp

He'd stuck to his plan, and it was working. Adriana had been willing, and liked a boy who could handle the monkey bars like a pro. It was great, right up until his first year of high school when he hit a growth spurt that ruined his Olympic dreams. None of his family even knew he'd started fantasizing about that, but at thirteen Paul would fervently visualize future gold medals each night. The more he *saw* it, the more he believed it would manifest.

But a twelve-inch expansion to the body had a way of putting the kibosh on dreams like that. Suddenly he was taller than everyone in his family, all of his friends, and every male at the academy including the instructors. There was a good reason most gymnasts averaged five-foot-five. His arms and legs didn't reach or land where he expected, his center of gravity was elusive, and everything ached all the time from rapid resizing.

No matter. Paul's new six-foot-five body could still teach other kids, help *them* get to championships or Olympics. Just motivating them to be active and having fun was good, too. So new plan, get a degree in business management and run his own studio. Which he'd done, damn it, and is how he knew having a plan worked; that Katy never bloody bothered stuck in his craw. Now her lack of forethought had his planet going ballistic, his methodically built dreams up in smoke, and his family unmoored. It drove him crazy.

He looked up in time to see a large orange figure getting away. No longer in danger of puking from Sundancer's abrupt teleport to this fancy-ass mansion, Paul bolted up the staircase behind the twelve-foot, dragon-headed woman. Paul had to admit, hearing a voice in his head like Sundancer's — a voice that could control every being in a forty-foot radius! — went a long way to convincing him everything Katy had told them was true. There was no way Paul wasn't going to be front-and-center for whatever was about to happen.

Sundancer's stride far outstripped his, and by the time he got to the room she'd entered, Bay and Lia had caught up. Being tall had its advantages, as the rest of the shorties trailed well behind.

Cadre attend, we have much to address.

Everyone else made it to the doorway just as Sundancer's command echoed in their heads. Paul looked over his family, concerned at how pale they were. None of this was what they'd been expecting when Katy told them they were coming to Centris. The journey was wearing on all of them, he supposed, though he felt enervated by this latest trial. No one was going to tell him they were "creatures" to be sneered at.

A tall woman with dark hair and yellow eyes came through a side door. She wore a silver robe and was followed by a Black woman in orange, then a third dude, buff with a similar tan to the first woman. His robe was white, his black eyes took in everything, widening slightly before he relaxed his face. Paul wondered what aliens did in the gym to get the kind of form cloaked by this guy's robe. He also tried not to be weirded out by how their overlarge eyes sans pupils shone in the room's light.

"Sundancer, what is happening? Who are-" the woman in

silver took another look around before continuing, "Ah. Clearly these are the herald's family."

Did the profusion of red hair give it away, Paul snarked to himself. Observing anew how fatigued and confused his family looked sobered him.

"Are we welcoming them now?" The Black woman said, green eyes warm. "I thought that was tonight. We need refreshments."

"We're blown," Katy burst out, wringing her hands. "I tried to sneak everyone into our new apartments-"

"Why did we leave our rooms here?" Bay asked. "I told you we should have remained."

Katy rounded on her fiancé. "Are you blaming me? Me! I'm not the one who gave the gestapo our real names!"

"I do not blame; I just point out that we would have had greater protections from the CIC here at Voice House."

Paul shared a look with Patrick and Vasuda. Someone was headed to the sin bin for a time out. Bay had a lot to learn about dealing with Bug. Raisa tried to soothe Katy, and they stepped to some windows, talking low together. Bay's face closed off, his sister silently offering support in the form of a wing at his back.

Wasn't this fun? Paul walked closer to the people in robes, assuming they were this Cadre Sundancer had called upon. "Hi, Paul, Katy's brother." He stuck out his hand, which was viewed with disdain and reservation by the people in robes. "Hopefully we can sort all this out quickly and get back to celebrating."

Brother of my heartnote, you have much to learn yet. This is not the time to teach you, we must decide how to proceed.

He tried to hide his embarrassment at being shut out as he walked back to his family. At least he might be useful there. Yuhwa squeezed his arm as he passed. Hopefully she'd forgiven him for trying to blame her earlier, because he was coming to realize he'd gotten awfully good at putting his foot in his mouth.

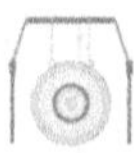

YUHWA KNEW they were in dire circumstances, but she felt for Paul and the rest of Katy's family. This trip was supposed to be a joyful one, celebrating Katy's impending marriage and the success of waking the first Drazoen. Instead, there'd been an arrest and being brushed aside as too naïve to participate just now.

Mara, Dindal and Pijo turned their focus back to Sundancer, who continued.

Humans are no longer a secret. In order to protect them from any provisions regarding quarantining, or punishments for arriving without petition, I will declare the Trinary is replaced with the rightful head.

"You mean you?" Pijo asked.

Of course. That was always my job, I will resume it now that I have returned.

"That," Mara hedged, "may not be well-received."

"What's our other option? If it's revealed we've been here all along, I mean?" Raisa spoke, leading Katy back to the main group.

Yuhwa's heart ached when Bay remained on his side of the room. This kind of thing, the arguing and frustration, was exactly why her non-attachment-no-relationship model worked perfectly.

"No alternative, I fear," Dindal answered Raisa. "Our plan had been to reveal Humans with Katy's Symphony of Awakening. We meant to enter it in the upcoming competition during Pała·č on Quiltac, and when it won-"

"IF it won," Katy protested.

"No question, it will win," Dindal said with a smile. "Then we would reveal to all that the first herald was from a new species, a clearly advanced one, and must be invited to the Calling." Her smile dimmed. "We've lost that avenue, now."

Yuhwa glanced back, hoping any of this was getting through on the Phelans' relatively new aoiti.

"Our girl's made a symphony, *mo chroí*," Martin kissed Briana as he spoke softly. It reminded Yuhwa of her childhood, how her parents had supported each other. "That's our girl, and she saved the Universe, too!"

Oran grunted. "Seems a stretch, Da."

Paul, flushing, shushed his family when the voices and Sundancer glanced over with frowns.

Mara cleared her throat. ""The Cadre is not immune, given our complicity. More than one statute exists, and they all include penalties for harboring undeclared species. If it's revealed in the Calling that Humans have been on Centris for a buwan, there will be consequences." Mara's lone wrinkle deepened.

Expect that it will not only be revealed, but pursued rigorously. The Vi'isser clan are scheduled to arrive in a few sal-angs. We must assume they intend to air grievances; the loss of a slave, for one.

"I saw him," Yuhwa blurted. "The runner. He was brought in just as we arrived to rescue our group."

Not ideal. If they tie his flight from Ishar to the Humans, it will greatly complicate matters. No question, I must assume leadership once more. Sundancer paced for a moment, then faced the voices. *I would expect the full Cadre there to support our position once I take the seat.*

"Kalim is returning from Rixat, to attend Zina's death rites," Pijo said. "Should be here in another sal. Last I heard he hasn't progressed on finding the Lost Library. Everyone else is away from Voice House today, but will attend Calling business when it's opened."

Waiting will not serve us. Where are the rest...

Olak Purplevoice appeared in the middle of the room, her cup of pualah dropping to the floor. "By Nine! What on-" she gagged and bent over. Probably due to displacement wobbles, but could be from the fermented bush she'd been drinking. Yuhwa would never understand Human tea or Centris pualah. Leave bushes alone, don't go drinking them.

As Raisa and Pijo helped Olak to a chair, Golgun, Trey and Gudar appeared in short order. They all stumbled upon arrival, and Yuhwa wondered what Sundancer was hearing in their heads as regarded being summarily yanked into the conference room like that.

We will leave Kalim Bluevoice to arrive on his own.

"Apparently only Rixat princes avoid being jerked across the Wheel," Gudar muttered. If Sundancer responded to his sarcasm, it was private.

As things were re-explained to the newly arrived, Yuhwa watched interactions from around the room. The three Phelan couples were closely gathered, touching and reassuring one another. Raisa, who'd abandoned Katy as soon as Olak appeared, was stroking the Purplevoice's hair gently as she recovered, while Pijo Whitevoice rubbed Olak's shoulder. Oran, against all odds, had sidled up to his sister and stood within her reach. He looked at Bay as though he would attack, more of that Chitan changeling behavior Katy had joked about. Bay, wing-to-wing with Lia, looked dejected, but still didn't go to Katy.

What would happen with them, Yuhwa didn't know. Sundancer herself had declared them mated: could you go back on that? Maybe this was all just heightened tension and they'd be back to normal soon. Messy, messy, messy. She'd stay well clear of it.

Interpersonal drama needed to stay downriver from the critical issues they already faced. "The Vi'issers are coming to the Calling. We know they'll lodge a complaint, almost certainly demand the escapee's return. He was with the UPC, I saw him in their custody," Yuhwa repeated.

"What's the difference between who had us and who has him?" Paul's question was, inadvertently, going to help make Yuhwa's point.

"CIC is mostly a bureaucracy, filing data, aligning needed information to received information. UPC, they're the real Centris police force. They are not always neutral, either."

When we left no such organizations existed.

"That was long ago," Yuhwa said. "Over time, without your influence, people behaved as people do. Mostly fine, sometimes poorly." She shrugged.

Golgun Greenvoice picked up the thread. "The Urban Peace-keeping Cohort works more closely with some of the Calling ambassadors than is appropriate, rumor has it." She inclined her head to the Phelans. "While I'm sorry you had to deal with the CIC, I am relieved it wasn't the UPC."

"Exactly," Yuhwa said. "Their involvement makes it thorny. First, will the prisoner know he has any rights? That he can call for dōmank ganga in the Truth Arena? The PQ's will try to take advantage of the uproar caused by removing the Trinary to claw him back under their control." She looked at the Cadre. "We all know many ambassadors will take the perceived threat to their power negatively. And if he isn't aware, if PQ don't tell their slaves about dōmank ganga and what the Swords do..." She shook her head.

He must call for the ritual combat. That will be the fastest way to rule against namu'ur.

"We better ensure he knows, then," Bay said. His voice was dull, face still unhappy. "I remember what sorrow he seemed to hold, though I was in no shape to empathize then."

Yuhwa flinched at the reminder of the dark sals they'd thought Katy dead. This memory is what bridged the lover's gap; Sundancer's herald went to her seeker and embraced him.

They'd been through so much in a short period, no wonder their feelings were like a racing river. Bay and Katy did seem destined for one another, though it was unlikely to be a painless journey.

"Who can get there and have any sway with the UPC?" Yuhwa knew she had none.

"We have to maintain partiality, as much as we can," Mara waffled. "Voices can't show favoritism in a way we've never shown it before."

Raisa, holding hands with Olak, raised her head. "Swailu? Tangun? I don't know how often escaped slaves are caught, but I'd think they might be able to get in to see him? We'd call it humanitarian aid back home."

"Riri coming in hot with the great idea!" Katy called from Bay's arms. She looked up at him. "We could call them?"

"I'm checking now," he replied.

The Calling is summoned, to convene in four sal-angs. I have sent the message.

Each voice nodded.

"If that's concluded," Lia said, "I'd like to return to the *Eternidad*. With such a great loss of people, those of us left need to do extra work to keep it flight-ready."

"Agreed, Lia, I'll come with you." Yuhwa said. "I'm ready for a few sal-angs of normal before the drupkee coming our way."

DRUPKEE *DROOP-KEY; Jadoube word for anticipated disaster, refers to any attempt to gather criqals, a task set young majio by their instructors. English equivalent "circus", "goat rodeo", "herding cats".*

Paul got a quick flash of something that looked like a crayfish mated with a centipede and **criqal** *kree-call* was emphasized.

He couldn't argue with Yuhwa's assessment. Everything said in that designer war room hadn't translated perfectly, but he'd understood the gist. Paul's money was on these Calling ambassadors trying to stage a coup of some kind. No one who has power gives it up voluntarily. Not in his experience anyway, which was based entirely on Earth politics, wars, and one vicious Parent Teacher Association meeting he'd witnessed as a seventh grader. If Sanjay Chaudhary wouldn't hand over his job as PTA treasurer after six years, it seemed a stretch that people who'd had their power for centuries would thank Sundancer for taking it away.

"Hey," his sister called out. "You up for a field trip?" She included the whole family in her question. "Lia says she can bring some of those new camo suits back in a bit, and if we're careful we can go with Bay to meet Swailu."

"*Mo leanbh*, I think yer ma and I need rest." Da was quieter than Paul could ever remember seeing him. The exuberance of leaving Earth followed by fear, then being discussed as a problem but completely sidelined by all these aliens...hell, it wore Paul out, too. Ma and Da were twenty-five years older.

Brianna hugged her daughter. "Can we get a room to take a little nap?"

"Of course, of course." Katy looked around. "Anyone else?"

In the end only Patrick, Paul and Vasuda opted to sightsee. Raisa would stay back with the rest of the Humans; Paul thought it might be more about the lady in purple who she'd been cuddling with almost the entire time. Lunari, his aoiti told him, were considered fickle people, so hopefully Katy's friend knew that going in. He glanced at Yuhwa, who was leaving with Lia. She'd said her dating MO was same as these Lunari; hit it and quit it. Paul's first response to the idea was a mental push back, but then he remembered how Brittany had tap danced over his heart and ego, and thought he could probably go for some of that no-strings stuff.

By the time Lia returned with a handful of the rimā and a transportation sled, their fellowship had dwindled to a final five.

Parents and siblings had gone to rooms graciously provided by the voices, Sundancer had simply disappeared to gods knew where, and the rest of the voices left, Raisa going with them.

"Don't move around the sled too much," Lia warned. "As long as you remain still you should be almost invisible."

Katy sat by him, Patrick and Vasuda were across the sled. His sister grabbed his hand, squeezed, and whispered, "I'm so glad you're here, ya numpty."

Paul ducked down and kissed her head before they got underway. Suited up and immobile as Bay drove the sled, Paul looked around. He hadn't really had a chance to take in the new world in which he found himself. Lots of that freaky peach grass. Trees with orange-vanilla swirl trunks, teal bushes, bright flowers on vines that drooped blooms all over the place. And aliens everywhere the eye could see. Lunari and a few Mikanjo. Were those ones on the right Jadoube like Yuhwa? Or one of the other species? He knew he'd always remember the Eng, since that was the floating coral tattle tale who'd turned them in. Chitans with tails and bad attitudes were also burned into his mind.

For now he let it go, focusing on the wonder around him. Being in the center of the Universe was a damn fun ride when you ignored the encroaching problems. Paul could do that, for a bit at least.

7

"I AM REMINDED OF TIMES LONG AGO ON YOUR Earth," Bay said just loud enough to carry back to them. Their sled wasn't high-speed zooming, so he didn't have to overcome wind noise. "Many times I would be smuggled in a caravan by the Berbers and Tuareg, crossing the desert to find gold." He beamed with the memory. "My name was Nizam ad-Dīn back then."

Vasuda leaned forward just an inch or two. "Katy says you're an artist? Is that why you sought the gold?"

Bay nodded. "Over the years I went by many names, but was always a jeweler of some kind. Rolf Geldsson, Matthias Bild-hauer, whatever name helped me fit in to the time and place."

Vasuda sucked in a huge breath. "Matthias Bildhauer? I've seen his work in museums. He, you-" She reached for Patrick's hand. "You were a Königsberg amber carver?"

"Yes! I am flattered you have seen some of the pieces."

Patrick had done a double-take at Vasuda's words. "Hang on, we're talking the Amber Room kind of thing? Catherine the Great?"

Bay turned his head, picking up on Patrick's unhappy shock.

Paul knew where this was headed, and felt it too. Katy hadn't caught on yet, or she'd have been stiffening up next to him.

"That's the fucking seventeen hundreds, my man. Bug, what the hell?!" Patrick was hissing, but it was loud enough.

"Drop it," Katy started.

"Don't," Vasuda joined in. "Either of you."

"It's worth a discussion, oh great seeker and precious herald!" Paul couldn't help himself. "She's twenty-eight years old. You're what, a thousand?"

Bay's nape flushed around the back of his ears. "Thirteen hundred Human years."

Katy snarled. "Shut up! This is my life. My issue. Yes, he's older, but there are things you don't understand."

"Maybe," Patrick hissed again, "you're the one who doesn't understand because you're too damn young."

Katy scooted herself away from them and closer to Bay. That had to violate the "stay still" rule from Lia, but his sister never listened anyway, did she? Rules weren't for her. She reached for Bay's wing and stroked the edge to soothe him. "Ignore them, we've been through this. We're *us*, and no one gets to tell us what that means *except* us."

"You act like bringing your orange dragon back to life made you the hotshot of the Aoni," Paul said. "But you're still our baby sister, and we'll protect you to the end. If that means we question this guy who shows up, whisks you off your planet, puts you in unbelievable danger, and manages to romance you at the same time? Yeah, we're going there!"

"Exactly," Patrick added.

"You're full of mirca," Katy ground out. "Both of you."

Mirca *meer-ka; shared Aoni profanity; literally 'refuse of a dying sulfuric star'; English equivalent shit.*

Goddamn Bug. She always picked up lingo and language quickly; absorbed it like a greedy sponge as he'd told Yuhwa and Lia.

Patrick opened his mouth but she cut him off. "No, we're done with this. I can't believe you two. Vasuda, do you agree with them?"

Katy's voice had gotten thin, and he knew they'd pushed too hard. If the sister of Katy's heart piled on, too, she might crack. Bug had adored Vasuda from the day Patrick brought her to family hurling day, and her opinion mattered to Katy. Probably more than her brothers' did.

"Of course not," Vasuda soothed. "How can I object when I, myself, rob the cradle with your brother." Bringing up the old family joke – Vasuda was nine years older than Patrick and Deb had yet to stop mentioning it at least once a year – helped defuse the tension.

Katy laughed reluctantly, keeping her back to them the rest of the trip.

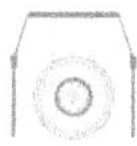

AFTER A SAL-ANG WITH WIREMU, reviewing flight logs and confirming the *Eternidad* was in fine shape, Yuhwa left the ship. She'd put this moment off for so many tuigs, but the time had come to say her final prayers for her parents. Gathering their remembrances, she made her way to Allmother Purple's spoke.

Jadoube didn't have graves for their dead, nothing to mark where bodies lay. In their beliefs, the spirits of dead were freed as the deceased's waja returned to the communal pool. Called the Spirit Bath, it held the genetic memories of Jadoube. Merry or tragic, loving or bitter, all was contained in the Spirit Bath. Only the nawa accessed it, though, and bodies freed of souls were left in the wadis of Malor. Flesh returned to its truest home.

Yuhwa's father had been given a plaque in the Truth Arenas, commemorating his service. Not all swords were honored thus, but his situation had called for something special to acknowledge the sacrifice made. She'd seen the tribute only once, on the sal it was raised into place, never willing to return and see his name hanging above the sands there. It had seemed hollow comfort to a devastated daughter.

Her mother had faded so completely there was almost nothing to give back to the nawa in the end. Jae Bon-Gil had been a woman of extraordinary warmth and generosity before her husband's murder. In the wake of Phu's death, she'd lost all vibrancy and hope, fading like an out-of-season flower.

Yuhwa was left with the despair and confusion of a foundling, angry and unforgiving. Forced to an early maturity, battling anyone who tried to give comfort or help, she'd railed against the unfairness. She didn't need the support and enrichment of close friends, she was determined to make her own way, ignoring Tangun when he'd said it was far too soon.

And it had all been fine. She'd shown everyone that she was as gifted as the early Malor instructors had claimed. Her life was challenging, but manageable and generally a lot of fun. Until the moment Katy and Raisa had walked onto the *Eternidad* and changed everything.

These recent sals had forced her to confront some things; how Katy's parents doted on her had been sweetly painful to witness. She had to believe hers would have been equally proud of her. It was as if witnessing the closeness of the Phelans allowed good memories to resurface. Sun-filled reveries of family outings to the rivers on Malor had come back to her, early mornings baking with Mama, watching Papa train new swords and quietly trying to follow along.

She'd clung so long to the bitterness, blocked all the good, but nothing was to be gained there. Not anymore. It might have driven her in the early days, given her the impetus to push herself as a majio and young woman seeking her way in the Aoni. Now, though, it was time for a different way forward.

Allmother Purple was the Drazoen of birth and death, creation and destruction, fête and funeral. For she reminded everyone that, in the end, these were all part of a whole. A cycle that had existed from the beginning of the Aoni. Yuhwa recalled Patrick's Wheel of Fortune and thought that came close. There could not be beginnings without endings; carrying too much pain left no room for pleasure.

Yuhwa took her time finding the perfect place on Allmother's upspoke, not far from the sky ring. The subspoke handled the other side; marriage and joining parades, exuberant celebrations of births and commemorations of namedays, anything that warranted festivities. But this section of upspoke provided places of mourning that catered to every species, every belief. No matter what kind of shared ceremony or solitary memorial you needed, it could be found here.

Trusting her instincts to lead her where she needed to go, Yuhwa's eyes were eventually drawn to a small fountain tucked between a Rixat catacomb and a Krylar crematorium. Even if they were banned from Centris now, the Krylar had once been here and left their mark in a place they'd turned their dead to ash.

The fountain called to her; bluish stone, worn down and smoothed over føns of people leaving offerings and paying respects. Yuhwa removed her shoes and stepped onto the grass surrounding the waist-high fountain. It showcased a central statue of an archer, bow drawn taut, aimed to the sky. A gentle stream of water trickled from the arrow, not strong enough to splash, only to softly ripple. Her father's weapon had been the bow; this was the right spot.

She pulled the objects she'd carried in tribute for two aiwaks out of the pouch strung across her body. Papa and Mama's matched pair of hair sticks. Holding one in each hand, she rubbed her thumbs along the designs. Mating Jadoube usually picked objects to adorn themselves, ones they could make identical or complimentary, and wore them as a display of the partnership. Piercings, bracelets or rings, small objects with a greater symbolism.

Phu and Jae had both preferred long hair, his dark green and hers pale blue. They'd chosen the family name Bon-Gil together – it meant "bound tail" – and commissioned the hair sticks. Mama had told her Papa drew the symbols for their family himself, and that she'd negotiated fiercely for the rare unclaimed waja.

Yuhwa had grown up with the icons imprinted in her mind: the swirling curls of Malor's windswept dunes wrapping around the stylized, entwined figures of her parents. Between them, they cradled the tiny bean that was the child they already anticipated by the time of their joining. Caressing the lines one last time, Yuhwa let the serenity of this sacred garden free the tears she'd suppressed for half her life.

Oh Mama. I was angry for so long, and I may yet be. Just a little bit. You left me when I needed you most, that's hard to let go. Papa, I think I was mad at you too. One of the greatest swords of a generation and you failed to see the danger. Too trusting of the good of people, you never saw the evil in him. You left me, too.

Tears ran freely, falling from her trembling chin, and Yuhwa allowed a brief wail to escape. Releasing the pain, giving it sound and presence, turned it into something she'd be able to overcome. A rapacious void no longer, a grief denied the power to feed upon her; it transmuted to a sorrow she could bear without bruising her heart.

Raising her head, Yuhwa contemplated the last step and how to handle it. Other memorabilia had been left on the fountain rim, under the water, in nearby tree branches and even inside niches of the walls bordering the small plot. But her eyes caught on the statue of the archer, which had long hair chiseled in curls almost as wild as Katy's. Partway down the thick mane she saw an opening, just wide enough.

Several kaalas passed, Yuhwa clasping the waja tightly, hunched over and unable to let go. More than once she howled soundlessly, chest jerking and eyes burning. But the storm of pain was cathartic. Eventually she calmed, unfolded her clenched body and rose to her feet. Taking care not to rush and disturb the water too much, she waded to the statue.

"Thank you," she said aloud. "You both gave me everything I needed to survive on my own, for that I thank you." A sob choked her. "And I love you. More deeply than every veṣu I've ever crossed, I love you and always will."

One last kiss and she slid the hair sticks into their final resting place.

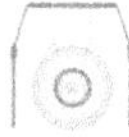

BAY HAD EXPLAINED where they were going before they'd left; somewhere called the core, dead center of the Wheel. Apparently, it was where people who lived and worked here long-term bought homes. Or had them assigned: Paul wasn't clear on the real estate industry here at Centris. Whoever Swailu was, she lived down there.

While they'd been pissing off Katy earlier, the flora of the Chorus had given way to manicured street trees planted beside walkways and roads of granite pavers. Every storefront looked expensive, and the restaurants probably had codes for attire. This was the place for upscale anything. He could see people here were very well dressed, even if the clothing was unfamiliar. Orange subspoke was clearly for movers and shakers, fancy pants folks.

Eventually they reached a portal embedded within a curving see-through façade. The whole thing ran top-to-bottom, and since he couldn't see a stop line, it presented as an endless sky before them. Beyond the portal, he saw incredible buildings shaped like flowers, some on the ground, some rising high in the air on columns. Plants, trees and blooms in every color. To their left was a large lake, water the same color as faded blue jeans.

"We are here at the Toledral's request," Bay spoke to the woman at a desk before them. She was the gatekeeper, and looked kind of like Yuhwa but with silver tattoos tracing up and down her neck.

She'd also raised her eyebrows at Bay. "We?"

"Pardons, please. I'm used to speaking for many seekers." Bay's chagrin was obvious, and Paul prayed they didn't get caught because of his slip.

"So formal, Mikanjo. Don't know how you all do it." She shook her head. "I see your passage approved, but there's a note about CIC." She squinted. "Looks like you need to report back to Earthcaller mid ring when you're done with the Toledral."

Patrick and Paul's eyes met, frissions of fear running down Paul's neck. He couldn't help thinking they should have stayed safe at Voice House. Adventures were only a good time when you didn't have Chitans trying to break your wrists.

"Indeed, that is part of what Swailu jo Faluji will clear up on my behalf this sal." Bay's voice was at its most stuffy, playing into this woman's assumptions of his people's propriety.

The portal popped back, split in the middle, and slid to either side of the entry. "You're good then, please stay on the marked paths and keep it slow. Most travel in core is by foot; assume they have right to passage rather than your vehicle."

She waved them off and they were through. It was immediately warmer, humid, and reminded him of the trip he and Brittany had taken a few years back to Fiji. Got an amazing deal and took a week to celebrate his first year of running the gym. Hopefully this would go better than that trip, and he wouldn't sweat through his clothing. Or get into an argument with a woman. He glanced at Katy and amended that to *another* argument.

"Raisa should be here to see all of this!" Katy exclaimed, loud enough Paul worried she'd be overheard.

They weren't in a crowd but there were still people walking near them on the path. Nobody seemed bothered by a ghostly voice issuing from their sled, though, and that was great because his sister kept going.

"All the lotus, they're just everywhere." Katy's voice dropped, still excited but more contained.

"Why is this important, dearest?" Vasuda's warm, walnut eyes crinkled at the corners, happy to see Katy's good mood restored.

"When we were working so hard but getting nowhere on how to find Sundancer, she had a theory." Katy leaned closer. "There are poems and stories about the Aoni *after* the Drazoen, but so little about how the Drazoen themselves came to be. We scoured anything we could find, but not much useful is out there. Did you know, the Imen have theories they're aliens from another universe, sent here by powerful beings?"

"Odd," Patrick said.

"I know, right? It reminded me of the people who say pyramids are from aliens. Bay swears they aren't." Katy laughed. "Anyway, Raisa keyed into the lotus imagery that's all over Centris and how god-like the Drazoen are considered. She likened it to Earth's myths about lotus, how they're often primordial and stand as symbols for concepts that are too big for words." She shook her head. "I'm not explaining it well. Raisa would say it better."

Vasuda's copper headscarf slipped past her rimā's border as she reached for Katy's hand. "No, I understand. In my mother's faith, Brahma came from a lotus, born into the cosmos as lord and creator of all. Goddesses are often seated upon them; they represent the cycle of rebirth. My mouj often embroiders them onto pillows as gifts for newborns, she loves them so much. It would take a lot of words to try and describe what just a simple image can make clear."

Katy smiled. "Exactly. They're fundamental in our mythologies, and they're everywhere here. Since so much of the different species' language and myths come from the same origins, Raisa thought it meant something big. Deep, you know? It was what made us realize the answers were more likely to be inside me. We didn't stop looking for hints in external sources, and I still think there's something out there that will give us a good idea where to look for Big Damn Answers. But," she paused to look around them, "seeing how intense the imagery is in here reminds me the other heralds will probably have to take cues from their gut. I just wish we knew who they'd be so we could tell them!"

Paul wouldn't say this aloud, but he wouldn't lie to himself, either: he knew there was a good chance he'd be a herald like his sister. It would only make sense, wouldn't it? Something in these dragons needed what Humans offered. Whether that was their relative youth as a species (fresh blood, as it were), or something specific in the Phelan DNA, he didn't care. But he was listening to all the hints being dropped, keeping mental notes.

"Lia said Songmaster Silver's trigger is waja," he mentioned casually. "Maybe we need to visit wherever that lives and see what's what."

Bay slowed in front of a three-story column topped by a lotus-shaped house. When the sled came to a full stop, he extended his wings to full form and swung off the sled. "Seraji jo Milabika may need waja, but He will have to wait a bit. We should keep you all out of prison, first." Using his wings to shield the Humans clumsily disembarking as they tried to keep camouflaged, Bay added, "Waja is a Malor product, sacred to the Jadoube. I'd think Yuhwa could help, eventually."

Patrick and Vasuda, artists to their cores, were slowly circling the column before them, awestruck. "Look here, the filigree, it's masterful. So fine and delicate." Vasuda tugged on Patrick's arm.

"We have to go," Katy said. "We can spend more time admiring when we aren't being hunted by police."

Bay grimaced. "Yes, everyone, inside." He tapped a pad that was head-height for most of their group, and a solid panel retracted to reveal a compartment. Once they crowded in, it slid shut and the capsule, apparently an elevator, ascended.

A gorgeous woman greeted them when they arrived at the top. White wings just as big as Bay's, dark hair and eyes, café au lait skin, and a welcoming, genuine smile.

"Djilbay and Katy! Here, we can remove those now." She pulled the rimā away from Katy's shoulders and hung it from a hook in the entry. The rest of them followed her example. "I am Swailu jo Faluji, Toledral Speaker and – I hope – friend of the Kawakona and her seeker. So very pleased to meet all of you."

They made quick introductions, then Swailu walked them deeper into her house. It was the perfect abode for a winged person; large, open living space and highly arched ceilings. The real showstopper was an entire wall missing on one side, not even windows, just open to the elements. It offered an unimpeded view of the core, spread below them. A wooden deck that she could probably use for takeoff and landing stretched all the way around the house.

"I guess you don't have to worry about break-ins up here," Paul joked.

He was terrified his sarcasm had gone horribly awry, until her face cleared and she laughed. "Break-in, another new Earth term. You're correct, we don't see that much in the core. Access is restricted to residents and vetted visitors only. And," she swept her arm to the view, "this high up my only concern would be other Mikanjo."

"And Nyakisi," a raspy, broken voice interjected. They turned to see someone new entering the great room.

8

"Tangun, I'm glad you could get away," Swailu said. "While true that Nyakisi are famed for scaling one another's towers, I can't imagine them trying here." She swept an arm at their group. "Paul and Patrick Phelan, Vasuda Khatoon," she indicated each of them as she spoke. "Please meet Head of Swords, Tangun Ye-Na."

They all inclined their heads at one another, while Paul marveled at the new guy. Not wildly tall like the Mikanjo, silver tattoos over his neck like the front-desk lady they'd just snuck past. Coal black hair in a man-bun, and the first person he'd seen on Centris openly carrying a weapon. The bō staff was attached diagonally across his back, just like every badass Paul had ever seen in Kung Fu and ninja movies.

"If I'm being rude, please tell me, but what do your tattoos mean?" Patrick's question was forward, but Paul shared the curiosity. "They're beautiful pieces by whoever did them."

"Yuhwa didn't explain?" Katy asked.

"No, why would she?" Patrick answered.

"Yuhwa has returned to the Wheel?" Tangun said. Jesus, that voice. This guy had swallowed glass or been through something

88

rough. When Katy nodded, his eyes tightened fractionally before he answered Patrick. "She would tell you, because it's part of the Jadoube way of life. They indicate we have quested and been transformed."

At their confused looks he clarified. "The waja makes what you call tattoos. It binds to us, gives us our path and meaning. We rejoice to have our purpose revealed by the waja."

Vasuda marveled. "You mean to say the material itself created the design?"

"Just so."

There was a moment of silence while they digested the information. Paul was recategorizing Jadoube into pre-tattoo and post, wondering what made them change and why. Yuhwa seemed perfectly happy with her life, why would she go on a quest to become something else?

Swailu said, "We need to discuss what was urgent enough to warrant this visit, and I must prepare for the Calling. I'm assuming you can explain why Sundancer summoned us without warning."

Bay and Katy took charge of recapping everything that had happened, so Paul wandered out to the deck, looking at the core spread below. Patrick and Vasuda joined him.

"Incredible, isn't it?" Vasuda murmured.

She was spot on. If you took the lushest of arboretums, tropical and barely shifted from wild to cultivated, then cleverly embedded buildings of different heights along with the plants, you'd get the core of Centris. The road they'd ridden their sled along was the only one visible, and ran in a big circle. A few footpaths trailed off that main one and wound through the shrubbery and ponds, but everywhere you looked nature was the focus. Not a nature Humans were used to seeing, because the colors and plants were all different. Paul, used to Seattle evergreens, kept staring at trees the wrong color of green to his eyes, then his eyes snagged on neon pink vines cloaking the wall of a nearby building. Just like ivy would back home if Barbie got to paint it.

He was about to point it out to his brother when a tiny bird flew straight up to his face and hovered like a hummingbird. It had an orange head, neon green body, translucent daisy yellow wings that reminded him of a dragonfly, and a tiny black tongue. He could verify the last part because it tried to lick his eye.

"Crap!" He stumbled back as it made a chittering sound and dashed away.

"Faropaiti!" Bay called, his voice excited.

"They were imported long ago, when Toledral Speakers were made adjuncts of the Calling," Swailu said.

"Don't forget," Tangun rumbled. "The children will expect you before we leave to check on the prisoner. There won't be time to come back from mid ring before going to the Calling."

Paul perked up. "Children? Is there any way I could sneak along?"

Katy gave him a sweet smile. "My brother teaches children on Earth. Gymnastics. Do you have that here?"

Swailu clarified, "Tumbling and body movements as an artful or aesthetic performance and competition?" Paul nodded at her definition. "We have something along those lines, although most species are likely to treat it as battle training." She looked to Tangun.

"Yes," he agreed. "Swords practice forms regularly, to ensure stamina and flexibility."

"We have that too," Paul rushed to say. "Martial arts, it's called. Gymnastics, what I do, is more about creativity and artistry, endurance and flexibility. Really, though, it's about the kids for me," he finished wistfully.

"Speaking of kids," Patrick said. "Do we know if Katy and Bay's kids will have wings? Because if they will I'm going to start designing a house like this right now."

Paul didn't think his brother had meant to drop such a

bomb; knowing him he'd probably just spit out the first thought he had without filter. Got that from Da. But Christ on a cracker, the question landed with the grace of an elephant seal on land.

Bay froze, eyes wide, wings trembling. Katy turned redder than a boiled crab, mouth opening and closing like a dying fish. Vasuda pinched Patrick's arm, hard, and Paul took a subtle step back from the splash zone in case his sister exploded.

Swailu rushed to fill the charged and painfully awkward silence. "That won't be known for a long time, I'm sure. If, or when, there are little ones to celebrate, they will be precious no matter how they manifest. Seeing them flourish is a gift unparalleled," she finished gently.

Back to Paul, she said, "I think, as we are here on core, you do not even need to be hidden. The CIC has no power in our area. If we give you better clothing, you might pass for Nyakisi."

Paul wanted to know more about this species. His aoiti gave him just enough that he'd assigned "cat burglar" in his head, especially after Tangun's earlier comment they might scale the column of this house.

"I will escort everyone else back to Voice House and meet you at the UPC headquarters." Tangun scratched his temple. "Djilbay will face fewer challenges to his return if I'm there."

With that their two groups separated. Swailu brought Paul a change of clothing after the others departed; dark pants and a heather ivory tunic. "These were Tangun's long ago, and your frames are similar enough. I'm happy to see they fit."

Paul, unlike his gormless brother, knew better than to ask why the Head Sword's clothing would have a home with Swailu. Some things just weren't his business.

YUHWA NARROWED her eyes at the Chitans who'd entered the bar she occupied. The emotional upheaval of the last sal-ang had left her raw. She'd told herself she deserved a relaxing drink, and ignored the voice inside asking why she needed to have that drink on Earthcaller subspoke.

Specifically, the Oikla ward on Earthcaller subspoke. At this bar, notable only for being closest to the CIC and UPC, officials Katy had called "po-po" and Oran named "five-oh." Yuhwa had no good aoiti translation other than *geographically specific slang* but liked how the Earth words felt on her tongue.

This group of three felds, lowest ranking of all the Centris police force members, sauntered behind the stool Yuhwa occupied, deliberately brushing against her back, going so far as to snag some of her loose hair and pull. Yuhwa hadn't brawled in a very long time, but her roiling feelings were near to erupting at the disrespect. Shtŭing Chitans.

"Show the Dál match, you ewagga!" Snarled words from one feld to the server, another Chitan who looked ready to come over the bar and answer the aggression. Agitated tails slapped against the bar wall on both sides.

In hindsight, Yuhwa may have been trying to bury further emotional introspection by picking this locale. She had bypassed at least four other places to get her drink, deliberately entering this one. Chitans of any kind were firebrands, but enforcers were the hottest of heads.

The despair she'd seen on the Human faces in CIC hands yesterday still chafed her; it wasn't accidental she'd sought out the famed police establishment. Katy had come to mean so much to Yuhwa; they'd bonded faster than she'd ever experienced before and her devastation when she thought Katy was dead had hit hard. In the sals since her return they'd been nearly inseparable.

Jadoube used the term yeŏjoda for someone who'd gone beyond friend and burrowed into the heart. Katy was the level beyond that: jaejuan, a person essential to your happiness in life. It wasn't a title used casually, but Yuhwa knew it applied here.

To see how callously the Chitan enforcers had treated Katy, Raisa and the others…it inspired an anger that felt cleaner and simpler than her complex release in the garden. She'd allowed that to direct her steps here, and Yuhwa was only a careless word or three from getting violent. The temptation was insidious, teasing her with the ease and promise of a physical distraction from uncomfortable and murky thoughts.

The huge vid screen blinked on, presenting her with a new diversion. Fumi Ly, current Dál favored fighter, awaited her next match in focused silence while the crowds around her screamed and threw trinkets. Her hazel eyes were pinned to her opponent across the arena, head lowered slightly, making him the only thing in her sights.

Commenters mentioned this round of bouts took place on Fakar for the first time. It was one of the oldest Rixat satellites, not far from their home planet of Shilmand. Yuhwa wondered if Kalim Bluevoice ever sullied himself with something as primal and base as Dál fighting, then remembered he was coming back to Centris anyway.

Fumi was the Chitan they'd transported to Earth, she and Lia answering the hail just before the emergency comm from Bay had arrived. The Chitan brawler was a powerful presence, her intensity felt like a breath-stealing wind. Yuhwa had considered testing the waters because that would have been memorable sex. But she'd sensed a darkness in the other woman, an anger she didn't want to engage.

Now, as she watched the tall, lithe Chitan prowl from her corner of the fighting pad to the center, Yuhwa recalled it was Fumi Ly who had enabled Katy's abduction and near death. Passive aid or not — who could say for certain? — the results had been Aoni-changing. If not for Fumi, Bay and Yuhwa wouldn't have gone to Ishar. Raisa wouldn't have a permanent scar on her scalp from the PQ assassin transported in secret to Centris by a Dál ship.

And, perhaps, Sundancer would still be locked away.

Fumi had changed out her green color palette from a buwan ago. Her hair sported a base pink instead, the pale blushing color of fading sunrise on a bright day. All four claws on both hands coordinated, too. Her hair was bound in her signature style of large, loose buns. Today they were trailing ribbons of black and blue. She wore skintight shorts and a halter top in colors matching the ribbons. Yuhwa had just enough time to admire her pink militia boots before one of them shattered the jaw of Fumi's opponent.

All three Chitan felds cheered, pounding on the bar and demanding more drinks. "She'll be top fighter this tuig, mark my words," said one of the men.

The woman between them scoffed. "She's good, but I hear she's easily distracted outside the arena. That doesn't cut it."

"Long term, no," the other man agreed. "But short term, it could get her the crown. She's unstoppable, just look!"

Every person in the bar stared avidly at the bloodbath on the screen. Fumi had taken advantage of her opponent's blood loss and confusion to hammer him with blow after blow. He'd fallen to the mats, curling in on himself, but she was relentless. Yuhwa would have sympathized with him, but he'd have been as brutal if he'd gotten the advantage of Fumi. At least a sanctioned match inside Rixat territory meant he'd live. That wasn't always the case in the unregulated outer systems.

> Hey, back at Voice House. Getting ourselves
> together for this Calling shit coming down.
> Where are you? We can all go together if you
> come back.

Katy's message put a small smile on Yuhwa's face. She didn't need the looming violence of this place, she needed to be at her jaejuan's side. She'd just experienced a major change by learning to let go of the pain she'd been holding. What good would causing pain to another do, especially when so many more changes were bearing down on them.

Was this maturity? She wasn't sure she liked it. But as she exited the bar, she allowed that it felt more like a win than a clash with Chitans would have.

ONCE THEY'D WALKED the short distance to the Wheel version of a rec center, Paul watched the group of twenty or so children light up like fireflies at the sight of Swailu.

His heart warmed, and he longed for the purpose and fulfillment his teaching on Earth had given him. In all the riotous frenzy that happened back home post-Katy and Bay, the loss of his kids was the most painful. These ones, though they looked quite different, behaved much like his. Exuberant, a tad unruly, so filled with life and energy. Whether they had tails, almost-fins, or tentacles they were children and he loved being around them.

"Do you have young ones of your own?" Swailu asked when they'd left.

Paul took a second to come up with a response better than *hell no.* "I love kids, love being around them and watching them learn and grow. But I also like my space, my peace. You know? My family doesn't believe me, but it's true."

Swailu laughed softly. "I do know, yes. I am the same." A morose look shadowed her face. "My desire not to parent is similarly doubted by those close to me."

Paul would have reached out, stopped himself just in time.

"Your feelings are valid, though. No matter what someone else might say."

Her wings shifted, pushing away from her body before resettling. "Long ago, I had a partner. He couldn't accept it. For aiwaks he claimed he did, but then something happened that changed him. He nearly lost his life, suffered damage even Centris and aoiti healing couldn't fully repair."

Holy shite. She had to be talking about Tangun. His voice sounded mutilated like that, and she had his old clothing in her place. Paul knew all about old flames and the heartache they left in the wake of their departure.

"When he recovered," she went on, "he pushed. He scoffed at my desires that he believed were self-deceptive. How could I work with children as I did, be enamored of spending time with them yet want none of my own?" Swailu paused, her tender voice roughened by pain. "His near-collision with death had made him want family and it angered him I didn't share the need. That was the end of that love story, I'm afraid."

"Did you stay friends? Or was that bridge too burned to recover?" Paul asked, knowing the answer.

Her smile was mysterious. "You will learn, Human, that in the Aoni lives are long enough to make many mistakes, learn from them, and grow."

Paul barked out a laugh. "Wait until you hear the complaints there are gonna be about how short our lives are compared to yours. Katy says she's going to tell Sundancer to fix it."

"I'm sure Sundancer would not dare impede the Kawakona's will," Swailu declared with a chuckle.

Another pleasant stroll got them to an open lot for travel sleds where Swailu checked out one reserved for the Toledrals. Once they were aboard, she told Paul to slowly pull the rimā around him as they flew. That way he didn't disappear suddenly, he faded out of sight.

He was fully covered by the time they reached the portal to

Earthcaller's subspoke. She'd explained each subspoke had its own entrance from the core. Tangun was halfway there by tram, and would meet them at the jail cells on mid ring.

It was, unfortunately, a wasted trip. The UPC refused visitation, claiming the prisoner was a self-harm risk. Possibly violent to others as well, the head guy said. Gozan Jeu'uto was Pu'ulqaari according to Paul's aoiti, and the weird-ass mask he wore was called a ruh. This was his first face-to-face with a PQ and the bonded mask was off-putting to say the least. It was fuchsia and bright aqua, swirled together, with patterns carved in it. Nothing Paul recognized, but if the dude superglued it to his face, it probably meant something to him. It was truly disconcerting, how it never moved when he stomped out to face off with Swailu and Tangun, voice loud and firm.

"Until I am instructed otherwise, the Vi'isser property remains sequestered. There is no provision in our regulations for your interference, Toledral. Nor you, Head Sword."

They rejoined a still camouflaged Paul on the sled.

"I am not sure it is wise to have Pu'ulqaari as gozans."

"Agreed," Swailu said. "Especially not at this time in the Aoni."

Tangun put the sled in motion, shaking his head in disgust. They rode in silence the rest of the way.

The Calling at Centris was astonishing. Paul knew what US government campuses looked like, the Senate and the House of Representatives. He'd seen the British House of Commons on TV more than a few times, hell, even the U.N. was something he could probably describe. Functional working buildings that doubled as historical monuments and tourist mark-the-spots. This was a political space to dwarf them all.

Now that Katy had pointed out what one was, he clocked it as a giant blooming lotus. That was especially obvious as they approached from the outside, cruising down a long, straight drive. Centris trams didn't run down this road. Wide walking paths, dotted with neatly trimmed and shaped shrubs, lined the boulevard they were on. Paul watched crowds of people scurrying to the main building, the kind of crowd that attended sports matches or big concerts.

The Calling was an imposing goddamn building; the nearer they got the more Paul was reminded of driving to Mt. Rainier outside of Seattle. Slowly the Calling filled his view until it was all he could see. By the time they got to the entrance he couldn't see the top, even if he craned his head back.

Tangun maneuvered the sled through an entry for officials, both he and Swailu checking in. Paul did his best not to breathe. They were waved through, and instead of leaving the sled Tangun flew them into the heart of the lotus.

Nine gargantuan petals, curved up and out from a central floor. They joined a roof at their apogee, which simulated daylight via a salmon pink sky filled with pastel mint clouds. If you stood a hurling pitch on end, it would be about this tall, maybe one hundred and forty meters, or a hundred fifty yards give or take. It would take another two or three laid end-to-end to reach the edges at its widest. Tier upon tier of glass-fronted rooms nestled inside each section, stacked floor to petal-tops, people swarming inside and out. Each office had its own open balcony where he saw sleds landing and groups milling.

The petals were one of each of the Drazoen colors that repeated ad infinitum all over the Wheel. People of nearly every species his sister had ever mentioned ranged in and about the petals. He couldn't be sure, but it didn't seem like the various species kept only to themselves. To the near right was a cluster of Oti-filled offices, yet he spotted more all the way across the chamber in a different petal. He had so many questions he couldn't ask until they got somewhere safe; he tried to keep a running list so he didn't forget.

Tangun took their sled to the left and up high in the white petal. Of course, white for Windweaver, Toledrals and Mikanjo.

Tangun parked on the patio, helping Swailu off. She stretched her wings, turning her back to the Calling. Her eyes silently urged Paul to leave the sled window-side. When he was off, Tangun led the way to doors in the glass panels. They opened at his firm touch.

Swailu closed the door behind them, all sound ceased, and she exhaled heartily. "We should be safe for you to take off the rimā, but please stay back from the glass for now."

Just as Paul emerged from the cloak-like garment, someone entered from the wall-side of the chamber. He was so startled he tripped and barely managed to turn his fall into a somersault.

He heard, "What is this?" just as he rolled back up to his feet.

9

The new woman was another Mikanjo, not one he'd met on the *Eternidad*.

"Adena jo Kalda," Swailu said, a gusty sigh preceding her next words. "There are many things about to be shared in the coming Calling. Things I've known but was unable to share before now. This, he, is one of them.

Adena, whoever she was, looked older than Swailu, but even more kind, if that were possible. "I see. What are these things you have been keeping from me?"

"The Kawakona is from a new species, and this is her brother. We thought to manage how to reveal this information, but it seems things have gotten out of our control."

Adena blinked once, then laughed. "That is the way of secrets, they seek any wind to fly free."

"Elder Speaker," Swailu said with regret.

"Bah, none of that. We have not been elder and junior for a milenyo. We are Toledral. You have made decisions I will support, whatever they are." Another chuckle. "Your power as a speaker is undeniable, your wisdom far-reaching."

Swailu bowed her head. "Thank you, Adena. All will come out, if not in this session, then over pualah later today."

Adena nodded, and Paul saw the twinkle in her eyes when she looked to him. "Brother of the Kawakona, what is your name? Your species?"

Was he supposed to say? Paul was confused: did he have to wait for Sundancer to take over the Calling again, or was this other speaker safe to be in the know? Swailu saved him by explaining about limited edition English-capable aoiti, and all the stuff that made communication tricky right now.

When she finished, Tangun bowed and took his leave to join the Swords. Paul hoped he got to see where they sat later, and really hoped he got to see the Truth Arenas soon. Yuhwa described them like a gladiator-dueling hybrid, but he didn't think he had the right image. Surely they didn't have sanded floors filled with snarling beasts, or open meadows where they faced off at ten paces?

While Swailu said goodbye to Tangun at the wall-side exit, Adena walked between Paul and the windows and opened her wings.

"This will cause comment, no doubt. We rarely spread them all the way here, but it's useful to me now." She smiled. If she were Human, Paul would compare her to a white-haired, Hawaiian grandmother. "Tell me your name, *hooman. Hewman.* Yes, tell me your name and repeat your species name. Slow and clear, if you please."

They'd gone over it twice when the opened the door once again, admitting Bay, Lia, Katy, and Yuhwa. He felt relief wash over him, surprised at the strength of it. Was that because he felt safer in a group, or because he'd missed Yuhwa and Lia? They, more than his sister and Bay, had been his first lifeline into this Aoni muddle. He felt a scooch unmoored if they weren't present. Paul's big brother side had also kicked into overdrive: Bug needed him to watch out for her, because she was a fly-by-the-seat-of-her-pants mess out here.

"The Cadre follows right behind us. Raisa and the rest of the Phelans are with them," Yuhwa announced. "They'll come here to drop off the Humans then go to their section."

Bay said, "Mara wanted me to share: be ready to lock down if things turn unpleasant." He rolled his shoulders. "She fears Sundancer's news won't go down well."

Adena closed her wings and approached the newcomers. "I greet the Kawakona, sister to Paul, precious to the Aoni, Chosen of Sundancer." At Katy's blush she tilted her head. "I see it, the spark inside of you. Most exquisite."

"How was the core?" Yuhwa had snuck up on him and he suppressed a jump.

"Gorgeous. And I learned about those silver tattoos you're going to get someday." When Yuhwa blanched and dropped her head, he made a note to push later. There was quite a gulf between Tangun's assertion the quest was a joyous revelation and Yuhwa's negative reaction just then.

In minutes, the Cadre sled touched down outside the windows. Swailu and Adena both went out to use their wings as screens, hiding all the invisible people jostling to get inside. Paul was happy to see his parents looking perkier. Da was practically spry, rubbernecking at the astounding Calling and all the people.

"Paul, *a mhic!*" Da hugged him tightly, clapping his back. "I envy your adventures, lad. Patrick and Vasuda said it was a sight to behold, that core was."

"Look around, Da, this whole damn place is nothing but wondrous sights," Paul laughed.

He sobered, watching the Cadre leave for their own rooms, Raisa reluctantly releasing Olak's hand. But it had been decided all Humans needed to be in the same place so she remained in the Toledral chamber. It was going to start soon, he had no idea what to expect, and he feared it might be as bad as Mara Silver-voice had warned.

He didn't feel one iota better when the noise that had been coming through the open door stopped entirely. Not a sound was heard. He looked around and was struck dumb himself, chills racing down his back.

Sundancer Orange, still in two-legged form, floated in the center of the calling. Arms at her side, dragon head fearsome, clothing billowing in a wind no one else felt. Paul thought her crown was bigger than before, and shone from within just like the carnelian of Katy's pendant. Katy wore it out and proud today; it glowed in tandem with the crown. Was all carnelian symbiotic, or just Katy's fragment from Sundancer?

Let us begin. I call the bulε to order. Let the record reflect this will be a new Cabinet of Calling.

The hush that had fallen over the assembly burbled in response to Sundancer's proclamation; indistinct, but people out there were whispering a storm.

Bulε *boo-luh; Aoni word for Calling ambassadors assembled and in session; English equivalent parliament, senate, legislature.*

Paul didn't know whether to be excited, afraid, or bored. Politics wasn't to his taste, but his sister's quest had yanked them out of heroic adventure realms and into government yuck. He didn't know diddly squat about Centris and the Calling, and what he'd heard back at Voice House made him nervous. Could they get in serious trouble? Sundancer believed she could over-rule everyone and fix things, but what if these ambassadors mutinied? Revolutions were born of people being pushed just that tiny bit too far. After a hundred thousand years of control-ling the Calling they might not happily hand the reins back to a single Drazoen.

"Founding leader," a voice sounded in their room, though the person speaking was clear across the Calling. "Point of action."

All the Humans gasped as a lizard the size of a baby elephant came into view, stopping their sled just below Sundancer's feet.

"Imen," Bay murmured to Katy, but they all heard. "One of the oldest species."

He'd heard the name plenty but had had no concept. The Imen was a cross between a triceratops and a frill-necked lizard. The leathery, spined halo around its neck was brightly bejeweled and fully flexed. The shining gems were a stark contrast to the dun-colored flesh that covered the rest of its large body and spiky tail. It was the first four-legged alien they'd come across, and Paul was experiencing some dissonance, hearing an "animal" talk. He was going to need to nip that prejudice in the bud fast.

"I didn't realize they were on Centris," Raisa said. "We haven't seen them before now."

Swailu said, "They prefer their home planet to the Wheel, but are always present for Calling business."

Tio Van, Calling Scribe, you are recognized. Raise your point of action.

"The Pu'ulqaari bloc registers removal of the Lu'upan members at this time." The Calling burble swelled; more open chatter than whispers. Tio went on. "Replacing the Lu'upans are the following: Getnet of the Ko'olak clan."

A striking man stepped out onto a patio ledge, a fair way down and to the left of the Toledral group. These offices were in the gold petal. His haughty expression was clear despite the distance; his fair skin dotted with faint colors Paul couldn't make out.

The woman behind him was more interesting: rich, cacao skin shown off by her sleeveless dress. Every bared inch was dotted like the man's, but her colors were much brighter; white like Mikanjo wings, forget-me-not blue, and the green of late spring grass. The dots looked like raised spots in a specific pattern. Deliberate scarification, or perhaps acne gone terribly wrong, was hard to say from this view.

"Wale and Kyree, both of the Ra'ani clan," Tio announced next.

Two more PQ stepped out beside the first pair, and a third man moved in behind them. These brown-mustard toned PQ were stranger in appearance, faces more like the ruh on the whackjob who'd tried to disappear Katy. The way she'd described it, anyway; oddly smooth and unnaturally colored.

"By speaking I have recorded the change. The bulɛ proceeds to new business, cleared of past items." Tio backed the sled away from Sundancer, bowing their head deferentially.

Yᴜʜᴡᴀ ᴡᴀs ɪɴᴛʀɪɢᴜᴇᴅ, and leaned forward to ask Swailu, "Do you think this is because Katy woke Sundancer?"

Next to her Paul nosed in. "What 'this'? And why would Katy's herald escapade have caused it?"

"The Lu'upan family will be in disgrace," Swailu answered. "Pu'ulqaari have a fluid power structure, one heavily weighted on financial success and perceived superiority. The families clearly know of the sacrificial child-assassin role, and which families bore them. For the short time Katy was in the shadow prison, Lu'upan would have been the ascendent family, to honor Yfaun's presumed success. With Katy alive and Sundancer returned, they are instead failures."

Yuhwa added, "They also must fear what Sundancer might do, knowing their guy was the one who tried to make sure she couldn't ever come back."

"Gotcha," Paul nodded. "They had to get out while the gettin' was good."

Her aoiti offered her nothing that helped the phrase make

more sense, but Yuhwa understood the gist. Yfaun's family were fleeing Centris like chom chom ran from light. The Lu'upans weren't nocturnal insects, obviously, but they were probably just as venomous. "I wonder if they had any idea their prisons *could* be destroyed. If not, that had to be world-altering."

Paul's laugh was cut short by Sundancer.

We will move on to my proclamation.

Most of the Humans clasped hands. Everyone present watched Sundancer, wondering how this was going to go. As Tio had said, she was the Founding Leader of the Calling. This entire place was something she'd created back when all Nine of them built Centris. Each Drazoen had given something that was specially theirs, and Sundancer made this place. She had the power and the right to run it how she saw fit, Yuhwa supposed.

A loud commotion broke out, back on the PQ's chamber ledge. Two people pushed their way in front of the newly declared ambassadors. Directional microphones weren't aimed down there, but the volatile hand gestures and angry posturing made their displeasure clear before anyone could hear them.

"We demand to be heard," the male of the duo shouted forcefully enough to carry to their ears.

The woman spoke as soon as she was signaled sound had been turned on. Yuhwa remembered her from Ishar. "The Vi'isser clan of Ishar lodges a formal complaint with the Calling." Her blue facial gradient nearly pulsed with her suppressed fury. "We have been cheated and wronged, our property stolen, and we *will* be compensated."

Sundancer didn't verbally acknowledge the PQs, but her eyes focused solely on them. Absolute silence filled the Calling for long moments. Stunning way to reassert her authority, Yuhwa marveled.

Declare yourselves before the bulε, Vi'isser clan of Ishar.

"I am Ekpo," the man announced, unnecessarily loud now

the directional microphones were aimed and working. His voice blared from the in-room speaker.

"Ubeti, matriarch of Vi'isser clan." Her voice was stately and sharp.

Katy muttered, "Think she pulls her hair back so tight because she's afraid she'll smile if she doesn't? Sheesh."

Bay's arm went around Katy, more to comfort himself than Katy, Yuhwa thought. Those days they'd spent going to Ishar and back had left dark residue on both their souls. Having Ubeti here in person, about to demand her slave back, made it that much worse. Maybe she should have exorcised some frustration on those Chitan felds in the bar.

What is the injury you claim done unto you?

"Our property was smuggled off Ishar, in a Nyakisi trader's ship. The *Frelaasti*. We accuse Na Xan, Abou jo Nbali, and their Jadoube majio of treachery and false contract. We additionally charge that they knowingly stole and transported Budiasa Vi'isser, our bonded namu, here to Centris."

The Calling noise at this point was poised to boil over.

"I thought it was namu'ur," Katy said.

"That is the practice; the namu is the bonded person, in their terminology. Slave in ours," Adena answered her. "They have long cloaked their ugliness in words meant to soften the hard edge of their evil."

Ekpo jumped in, pitching his voice over the Calling uproar. "We are told the namu has been recaptured, and is held on the Wheel. We demand the return of our property. We also demand recompense from the people Ubeti named, for the damage done to us."

You demand many things, Ekpo Vi'isser.

At least the khòchi had the intelligence to tremble at the silky violence in Sundancer's mental tone. Everyone in the building understood her patience was thinning.

Very well. Bring Budiasa Vi'isser before me, that I may judge for myself.

Ubeti and Ekpo sputtered and grumped, shocked Sundancer didn't just give them back their slave without question. Had they really been so foolish as to think she wouldn't examine all aspects of the complaint they lodged?

You feel my process is unfair?

"We were wronged!" the matriarch yelled, her composure cracking. The Nyakisi and Mikanjo came to us under false pretenses while we negotiated in good faith! Then they stole precious property along with the samples we gave them. Our injuries must be addressed!"

Bay snorted. "The good faith of illegal negotiations."

"You know something about this?" Ian asked. Katy's oldest brother was lost, as were most of the people present. None would know this story, except as a side note to Katy's.

"Bay was Abou, I was the majio. That was us on their planet that they're mad about. We went looking for Katy and had to fake making a deal to try and get information." Yuhwa clenched her fists. "Na Xan was the lying mašu who used us to smuggle the namu off planet."

Paul cocked his head. "You're mad at a guy who runs an underground railroad? Where I'm from we call people who free the enslaved heroes." The disappointment in his eyes skewered her more than she expected.

"I'm mad, not because he frees them, but because he *lied* to me about it." Yuhwa knew it was time to release the grudge, but Na using her grief over Katy to aid his deception kept the burn bright as acid. "Don't just assume he's doing it for good reasons, either; Nyakisi are infamous for putting selfish motivation before all else."

Your injuries will most certainly be addressed, Vi'isser clan.

If they didn't hear the threat in that, Yuhwa would pilot a bloated junker through five veṣu for free.

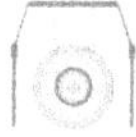

SHE'S gotta learn to let go of that stuff, Paul thought. He could help, because look how well he'd gotten over losing Olympic dreams, his ex, and the Chitan meathead who'd shoved him around. He wasn't hankering for a rematch with Chadna Yee, maybe with a crowbar this time. Not at all. Nor was he still angry at the woman who'd chewed him up, spit him out, and left him behind.

No-sir-ee. He was fine now, and could give his Jadoube friend some pointers.

We await Budiasa Vi'isser before I will hear more of your complaints.

"While we wait, may I speak?" a cultured, smooth male voice rang out. A new sled moved out from the silver petal, hovering higher and closer to Sundancer than the Imen had gotten. "I have information I'd like to impart to this bulɛ. There are concerns, as well as questions I think need to be answered, sooner rather than later."

"Thuliso!" Katy chirped. "I wondered where he was."

Raisa said, "Olak told me he's been meeting with Gudar Redvoice a lot. They've been locked up in secret conversations."

The Cadre folk must have planned this, because new guy hadn't needed to wait for the mic, his sound was on from the get go.

Thuliso, looking sleek and charismatic in a well-tailored suit, addressed the calling. "Only sals ago, a Pu'ulqaari assassin struck at people on the Wheel. In the middle of Harbor Primur, crowded with families and tourists. I have since learned he got onto Centris via the Dál ship *Oudna,* and that the *Oudna* has secret priority docking permissions. They land at Harbor Ovu, a port usually reserved for ambassadors. They bypass all registration procedures and avoid any documentation of their arrivals and departures."

Shouts rang out in the wake of his statement. Didn't sound like everyone knew about that special circumstance. Surgical strike, score one for the team!

Thuliso raised a seven-fingered hand for silence before continuing. "The Dál, I'm told, have back-channel agreements with nearly all major satellites, and take advantage of their stealth access with impunity. They pay no duties or moorage fees. This kind of preferential treatment and exemption is troubling, and in this case led directly to injuries and an act of terrorism."

The Calling dissolved into cries and roars, some demanding action and some shouting down anyone bothered by the news.

Who profits in these exchanges?

Thuliso spun to face Sundancer. "I've followed some of the money. Typically, agreements of this sort would be registered with the governing bodies of satellites. But the *Oudna* is unofficial; I've found a series of Pu'ulqaari and Chitan contacts, embedded at high-ranking levels, who are very well compensated for the deceptions. They are not sharing the details, or the profits, with leadership in these places."

Bay huffed. "They should dismantle the whole Dál."

Dál *doll; consortium of intergalactic fighters where bouts generally end in serious injury or death; most Dál competitors are Chitan and Krylar, though all species can participate; widely popular and well-attended events.*

Paul could appreciate the artistry of lots of martial forms and practices, but this just sounded like glorification of violence. Wouldn't stop a lot of people, Humans or other, from eating it up, though.

How are they able to hide the landings, departures, and movements of passengers? Even with officials paid to look the other way a sudden influx of outsiders would raise suspicions.

Tangun flew a sled up to where Thuliso hovered. "Swords have investigated the incident on Centris just mentioned. What they uncovered is cause for serious concern: Pu'ulqaari have concealment technology that hides them completely from Centris security cameras."

What perfect choreography! The Calling turned to anarchy with that bomb. It was pure bedlam; screaming and furious accusations were hurled at the various PQ suites. There were, of course, a few groups who threw it right back, convinced these were all lies.

Tangun persisted, raising his voice. "They can, in many cases, directly access secure footage and tamper or erase as needed. We don't know how long this has been going on."

Pu'ulqaari bloc, answer these accusations.

Sundancer's rumble was deeper than the Grand Canyon. The recently inducted PQ ambassadors looked lost and shaky, but a different contingent stepped to a ledge located in the black petal. Seven of them, a mix of funky face masks and clothing styles.

One man stepped to the front, his skin so yellow he looked jaundiced. The stuff on his face was obsidian, but instead of a full mask it only covered the lower part of his lips and jaw. It eerily resembled black blood running down his chin. "Qo Uitu'umen, speaking for our people. We deny what Head Sword Ye-Na says."

Does he lie?

10

"WE WOULD NEVER ACCUSE SOMEONE SO REVERED OF dissembling. It is our suggestion he has been misinformed."

Tangun's harsh voice carried well in this setting. "I've seen the evidence myself, Ambassador."

Before he could launch into any more detail, a prison transport sled flew into the Calling. Paul recognized the bar running down the center from when he'd been cuffed to one. His stomach churned as he relived the humiliation visited on his family, and his impotence in the face of stronger men.

This time a lone individual was chained to the bar. Had to be Budiasa the escapee, right? Only logical, seeing as they had four freaking cops on the sled with him, like they were afraid he'd cut and run if they didn't keep him surrounded.

Yet another PQ helmed this sled, jerky jerk Jeu'uto, and he was driving it straight at the Vi'isser duo. Budiasa's face was the embodiment of despair. He didn't even pull at his cuffs, or glance at the Drazoen who could save him. This poor bastard had given up. Paul wanted to run out there and fight for him, though he knew it wasn't possible.

To me, Gozan.

The PQ in charge decelerated the sled, but didn't immediately head to her in the center. Guess he thought he could ignore her command. He was not correct about that. His sudden look of panic and the rapid ascent of the sled made it clear Sundancer Orange was calling the shots now.

Budiasa Vi'isser, you fled Ishar and your enslavement, yes?

Ubeti glowered. "Stop using that word; namu are lawfully bonded. Tell them, Budiasa."

If the guy could get paler, he would have. But he stayed standing, nodded at Sundancer, then said in a clear voice, "Yes. I sought freedom. From slavery."

"Now he demands dōmank ganga," called a new voice.

Every eye in the Calling swept up to a balcony in the purple petal. A lanky man in all black had walked to the very edge and crossed his arms. "I am Na Xan, here to answer the Vi'isser slanders and ensure Budiasa receives a fair trial."

Paul didn't have to look to know Yuhwa's hands were fists now. Behind him, he heard Da say, "Sweet Lord, this is better than Coronation Street!"

"Da!" burst from an embarrassed Katy, but Paul thought their father had it right. Everything about this bulɛ reminded him of a freaking soap opera. Dramatic entrances, unjust imprisonment, secrets revealed: all they needed was a bowl of popcorn to complete the mood.

Do you, Budiasa, repudiate the Vi'isser clan and enter a request for dōmank ganga? Do you seek ritual combat to resolve the complaint the aforementioned clan recorded for your return?

If the prisoner didn't know the way forward before, he did now, thanks to Sundancer. The despair on his face shifted to hope. "Yes! Yes, I will fight anyone or anything for my freedom!"

"You do not fight," Tangun said as he maneuvered his sled alongside the prison transport. "My swords do." He pushed something on his console that audibly locked the two vehicles. "Gozan Jeu'uto, I will take charge of Budiasa. Dōmank ganga challenges are ours to handle, and we retain custody of the declarants. The UPC is thanked for its efforts, and may rest easy."

The Vi'issers from below yowled in frustration. The head cop clearly didn't want to release his catch, but under Sundancer's gaze and faced with Tangun's authority, he had to give way. He reluctantly handed over the PQ prisoner, eyes narrowed.

Head Sword, who will stand for the counter-complaint? Who will take arms for Budiasa?

"I appoint Sword Zam."

The air in the Calling damn near created a vacuum as it hoovered into every lung from all the gasps.

Katy beat Paul to his questions. "What does it mean? Why is everyone so gagged?"

Swailu, who'd been mostly silent this whole time, answered. "He has all but guaranteed Budiasa's victory. Isae Zam is undefeated."

Yuhwa's voice was awed. "She's the only Lunari to ever become a sword. When she was discouraged, she ignored them all, traveled to Malor and underwent pâtexi for her personal waja." Rubbing her arms, she said, "It wouldn't bond to her skin the way it does to ours, but her weapons formed. No one could deny her after that."

"Sorry," Paul said. "First we heard the stuff tattoos you how *it* wants. Now you say her weapons *formed*? The waja makes itself into what you need? You don't forge or machine it to make the weapons?"

"The Five Côttru and Malor itself determine what your waja reveals to you. That's the end goal of pâtexi. For a non-Jadoube to not only try, but get weapons such as hers… Incredible."

Paul wanted to know everything about the Jadoube vision

quest, but this wasn't the time. Outside their chamber, Tangun had flown Budiasa back to the gold petal where the Sword balcony sat. The sled was met by a Lunari with a honey blonde mohawk. She wore leathers, waja wrapped across her torso like a bandolier that snaked around her waist, too, and metal glinted from her ears. Had to be Isae, right?

"I met her only once, when I was young, living here with my parents." Yuhwa's voice filled with fondness. "She should have had no patience for a child like me; one who knew all the answers to every question and shared them constantly. But she was kind."

"She'll save Budi?" Ma sounded worried and protective. "That boy needs care. Did you see his face tattoo? Makes me really sad for some reason."

"Isae Zam is Tangun's second in command. For one so young to do that, she has had to be exceptional," Swailu assured them.

Vi'isser clan, I give you the rest of this sal to engage your sword. Tomorrow they will answer the dōmank ganga against Sword Zam in the Truth Arena. The Cabinet of Calling is paused until the matter of Budiasa is resolved.

Sundancer disappeared in the next second. Paul wished he could do that. What a wicked way to make sure you always got the last word.

YUHWA HAD VOLUNTEERED to get out of Voice House and grab food. As loud and colorfully crowded as Giftgiver Red's subspoke was, it felt less frenetic than Team Sundancer's war room. All the Phelans, Katy and Bay, Lia, and all eight voices were crammed in there.

Kalim Bluevoice, who returned earlier than expected while

they'd been at the bulɛ, had thoughts on everything. Including his conviction Mara Blackvoice had been killed by the PQ because she'd found out about their stealth tech before Tangun had.

He and Thuliso had slipped away to discuss "other urgent matters". Kalim was different than Yuhwa remembered. Still a hỏi hậu diva, but shaken slightly; subdued. She wondered if the search for the Lost Library was giving him trouble.

Sundancer had been absent when Yuhwa left with a long list of dinner requests. Did the endless chatter and noise of such a large group get to her, too? Spending a kōmilen in a dark matter prison might teach a dragon to prefer solitude.

Yuhwa thanked the elderly chef for the last of six family-portion containers. He'd overruled her original order with what he thought they should have, and she'd acceded. It was always easier to let this particular cart chef pick, and more often than not she was better pleased with what she got. Each of the various dishes were secured in a temperature-controlled mini-sled, which she mag-tethered to hover over her head as she jogged for the tram.

Her hope was to get through tonight without a headache. As much as Yuhwa loved Katy and tolerated Paul, the entire Phelan family might be more enjoyable if their faces were stuffed with food and unable to talk. Same went for the voices, who bickered like school children. She still felt unsettled after the Calling session today. The look on Budiasa's face when he'd thought he was being returned to the Vi'isser clan haunted her, and didn't put her in the frame of mind to put up with any of the infighting.

"Hello, majio."

Yuhwa whirled to find Na Xan standing behind her at the Chorus tram stop. "You," she snarled. Yuhwa walked away from him, calling over her shoulder, "I have nothing to say to you, liar."

The Nyakisi smuggler's long legs caught him up instantly. "How odd. I have many things to say. Should I say them to the CIC instead? Such interesting company you keep in that Voice House."

Dread soured her stomach. "There's nothing-" From the corner of her eye she caught his smirk.

"Who tells tales now?"

She stopped and faced him. "Are you looking for money? I agreed to pay you for that nŭz trip but you refused it." Jabbing a finger at him, she added, "And, I'll remind you, you lied about Budiasa. You used us to get him away!"

"I waived the fee because your beloved herald was dead and I pitied you both. But wait! She's undeniably alive, as is Sundancer." Na crossed his arms over his chest, his charcoal synth-hide jacket creaking softly. "I could make a case you *do* owe me."

"Is that what you want?" Yuhwa lowered her voice, conscious how many people were walking nearby and could overhear. "A payoff or else you turn in my friends?"

Na's eyes gleamed, and he leaned forward. "I want in."

"What?" Flummoxed, Yuhwa twisted her fingers. "In what?"

"Take me to where the seeker and herald are. Where the Cadre holds court. There are things I can share, and much I want to learn."

She took a good, long look at Na. Black hair, like Paul's, but shorter. He had blue eyes like Paul, too, though she preferred the Human color. Nyakisi eyes were partially bioluminescent and unnerving to her. But when she peered into Na's she read honesty, which was, frankly, unheard of in a Nyakisi. Maybe she was making a huge mistake considering letting him join them, but her gut told her Na could be useful.

She also didn't have much choice, since he threatened Katy, Raisa, and the entire Phelan family if she denied him. "Follow me," she said.

He won some favor by quietly coming along, not gloating. Nor did he attempt small talk on their walk to Voice House and up to the war room. Lowering the food sled from above her head when they reached the door, she offered, "I'll share an aoiti update with you, but you have to let me through your firewall."

"Why?" He quirked his head, leaning away. "Mine are always up to date."

"The herald's language isn't hosted anywhere but the local aoiti of our group, and the Mikanjo from the *Eternidad*."

Na's posture relaxed. "What great secrets you all hold. This has already been worth the effort."

Reactions to their new visitor ranged from horrified (the voices) to anger (Bay and Katy) to intrigue (Raisa and the Phelans).

"This is a major breach of protocol!" Mara Silvervoice barked.

Yuhwa extended her palms. "It was the only option. He could make trouble if he talks, and he knows about Katy and Raisa."

"How?!" Katy wailed.

Bay was rueful. "We told him everything. When I was desperate to find you, it seemed the smartest move."

"Damn it, Bay. Again?! How you ever stayed hidden on Earth for a thousand bloody years." She slapped his arm lightly. "I swear!"

Na glanced at Yuhwa. "Time for that transfer." He turned his attention to the whole room. "Then I can explain some important things to all."

As she relinquished the food to Raisa and Oran, Na moved to the windows across the room. Would a Nyakisi appreciate this evening view of the Chorus grounds? Or just look for exploitation potential? They were famous for scaling impossible buildings to steal objects or people, whatever their job called for. Voice House probably didn't represent much of a challenge.

Paul helped load the conference table with dishes and cuisine he'd surely never seen before. Yuhwa tried not to notice how much attention he paid her and Na as they connected wirelessly and transferred the Human aoiti package.

Jealousy was ridiculous in general, even more specifically in this case, and if he made a peep she'd put him in his place. She was a grown woman, she knew they shared an attraction, but that was it. Neither of them would act, likely for the same reasons, and she couldn't let anything slip into intimate territory.

WHO WAS THE NEW GUY? Paul thought it was the one from the Calling, who'd stood up for Budi. Na something. Nyakisi species. This guy looked like he played "nefarious but beloved crook" at a renaissance faire. Dark clothes and hair, freaky blurple eyes that glowed, and he moved with lithe grace. This was a guy Paul wanted to buy a drink, for saving Budi if nothing else. But he'd like to hear his stories, as they were no doubt epic. He had a feeling that Na wasn't going to be the obvious hero, but if you stuck with him you'd have the most fun.

The silence in the room moved beyond awkward into loaded. Paul and his family didn't know details of what had happened; that was Bay's side of the tale and mostly they'd only heard Katy's point of view, then what little Yuhwa had dropped earlier. His sister's adventure in the shadow prison had been center stage before now, but it was time to understand why Bay and Yuhwa were so pissed. Why would this dude get involved with their mess voluntarily?

"It would help me if you conversed," Na finally spoke. "The new species. *Hewman*. Yes?"

Vasuda laughed. "That we can do. Humans excel at talking,

especially these ones." She pulled Patrick to the food table. "Let's try a little of everything."

"Make sure to take that one," Golgun Greenvoice pointed at the xitlacoche.

"Yes, one of my favorites," Bay concurred. "Yuhwa, many thanks for your efforts."

It went on like that for several minutes. The attempts at normal chit chat were painful; Paul wanted to explode with his questions for Na. A minute longer and he lost the fight. "Who are you? Some kind of criminal, or a privateer? I didn't get all the details, but it sounds like you rescue slaves from those PQ assholes?"

Na's gaze was piercing as he processed Paul's questions. Then a smile broke like dawn. "Privateer. Pirate? Yes, my people will like this very much."

"Of course they will," Bay grumbled. "Blackbeard had nothing on you."

Paul quirked an eyebrow. "Seriously? You said he hid an escaping slave, getting him to freedom. Blackbeard killed untold people for greed and was only out for himself."

Bay shrugged. "Nyakisi have a reputation."

"We do," Na interjected. "Well and proudly earned. We are raised to prioritize self over all. Family, political ties, romantic relationships, none of it ranks. Business that will see to our needs, or advance our position is the ultimate goal of every Nyakisi." He stepped away from the windows and to the center of the room. "Only one thing overrides that. I told you," he nodded at Bay, "about frelaasti, on our way to Ishar. What it means to us."

Frelaasti *frel-ash-tee; Nyakisi concept of liberty, freedom, home. Individualistic or personal.*

"Is that something your people see as a cause, a thing they'd fight for?" Paul was fascinated. "Or is it more of a 'stay out of my business and I stay out of yours' idea?"

Na clapped his hands, startling everyone. "You have it exactly! My people are entirely selfish *except* when it comes to frelaasti. For that we will cut throats, lie cheat and steal."

"Not seeing the difference between usual Nyakisi mercenary attitudes and this frelaasti," Olak piped up. She had an arm around Raisa, who was snuggled into the voice on a shared loveseat.

"The difference," Na replied, "is that when other people's frelaasti is compromised, we'll fight for that too."

Katy's eager voice cut in. "That's what you're doing on Ishar! You act like a smuggler, but you're some kind of freedom network, getting slaves out and away from that horrible place!"

Na dipped his head and spread his hands. "I won't say there isn't profit to be made as well, but a loosely aligned group has worked for several milenyo primarily to break namu out of their bondage. Pu'ulqaari-" he chuckled. "Did I understand you've renamed them PQ? Excellent. The worse PQ abuses got over the aiwaks, the harder we've worked to free them. Frelaasti is power we are all born to wield; for a species to deny it is an abomination."

Yuhwa got in his face. "Then why lie about all of it to us?! We would have helped you, but you tried to trick us instead."

"How was I to know I could entirely trust you?" Na stepped back to the table and sat against the edge. "You and the Mikanjo were easy to trick, I didn't have to 'try.' *His* logical fear his herald was in danger, and *your* irrational fear of underground places, made my job simple. After the meeting, when Budiasa had gotten aboard, Djilbay was too grief-stricken to notice, and your own sorrow let me give you a paltry answer you accepted."

Bay and Yuhwa still looked pissed; didn't seem like that was the answer they wanted. If they hoped for an apology, Paul could guarantee that wasn't happening. Na might occasionally bat for the side of angels, but the rest of the time he was probably as greedy as he said his people were raised to be.

Paul still wanted to share that drink, though. Na was fascinating. What did Nyakisi do on a night out? High class lounge stuff or punk ragers?

"Why are you here, then, Na?" Trey Goldvoice asked, weary. "This day has been long, we have much to discuss about what will be revealed tomorrow, so lay it out."

"Two things. I want to confirm Budiasa is safe, comfortable and understands what's happening. His life has been even worse than most namu and we are concerned for his mental well-being."

Ma asked, "Budi needs help? More than just with the fight in the morning?"

Lia apparently caught something on Na's face, because she threw in, "Humans are very fond of sweet-names. They call them nickel names."

"Nicknames," the Humans chimed simultaneously.

"We think he does need extra help," Na answered Paul's mother. "We also worry the Vi'isser clan will try to kill him, rather than let him win tomorrow."

"'We' who?" Bay said.

Na replied, "The Nyakisi bloc in the Calling. Most of them are members of the network. We've worked long tuigs on the plan to get him out; the final pieces came together when we heard a seeker and herald had come to Centris."

"Did you know about Yfaun?" Katy's voice shook. Raisa shrank even further into Olak's embrace. Neither one of them had dealt with the residual fear, Paul could tell. "Did your bloc know and do nothing?"

"No, but meeting your seeker wasn't accidental. Initially I hoped your search for Sundancer would cause the PQ to panic, giving me an opening to land and get Budiasa off-planet." Na shrugged. "What happened worked better."

"Fecking PQ mofos," Katy grumbled. Bay slipped part of a wing around her shoulders, clasping her hand with his.

"Can we check on Budi?" Ma pushed. "If it were one of my boys, I'd want people taking care of them." Pa gathered her close and kissed her forehead.

"He would be lucky to have someone like you caring for him," Na murmured.

Bay said he'd check with Swailu where Budi was, and if one of their group could visit. Paul used the break to grab seconds of the dish that looked like blue spaghetti, but had the taste and texture of fish. Sushi pasta. Sushsta.

Enjala *en-jaw-lah; Muškikal food prepared from coobi, animal harvested on Kan-Xibyui*. The explanation came with an image of a big shrimp.

Screw that, sushta was a better name.

Next thing he knew, half the room had emptied. Deb and Ian wanted to sleep, having lost interest a while back. Patrick and Vasuda begged off, too. Fair play, because it had been a hell of a time, and all in one day. Ma and Da were determined to visit Budi at the Truth Arena. From what he gathered, petitioners of dōmank ganga got accommodation near the combat zone. That way they were looked after and watched over; the Vi'issers would be somewhere over there, too, but probably keeping well clear of Tangun. His accusations in the bulɛ today had been explosive.

Mara declared the Cadre needed to catch up with Kalim and Thuliso. "Unless you have the key to where the next herald resides, we have other business to deal with." Na admitted he didn't, and the voices left to deal with Zina's funeral preparations. They had to ready the Chorus to elect a new Blackvoice as well, a process that would follow right on the heels of the memorial.

"I still think we should have gone to see Budi," Katy said.

"Far too dangerous, herald," Na replied. "They know you now. If you're discovered before Sundancer proclaims you tomorrow, the politics will ignite. I'd like to go, as well, but since Bay, Yuhwa and I are named in the suit we have to stay clear until it's resolved."

"What's the second reason?" Raisa burst out.

Na's gaze measured her head to foot. "Pardon?"

"You said there were two reasons you were here. Budi was the first, what's the second?"

11

Yᴜʜᴡᴀ ᴡᴀs ᴇᴀɢᴇʀ ᴛᴏ ʜᴇᴀʀ ʜɪs ᴀɴsᴡᴇʀ. Sʜᴇ *ᴛʜᴏᴜɢʜᴛ* Na was being honest, but so much was at stake. Adding someone else into their troupe of hapless Drazoen seekers carried a measure of risk. If he was just going to complicate things or cause problems, he didn't get a seat at the table.

"That is a question with tricky answers." Na's smile at Raisa was cheeky, but his voice was sincere. "I have been all over the Aoni, worked as I was taught from my earliest years. Make no mistake, I've done very well for myself, regardless of the jobs I took. But something lacked. Money didn't matter when there was no excitement or fire anymore."

"You wanted a purpose?" Yuhwa asked. "I thought that went against everything Nyakisi."

He shrugged. "Yes and no. We're taught that we are the way we are because we learned it from dwellers in darkness, shadowy beings from long ago. Creatures who were hidden from sight but were powerful and wise. One day they all died, leaving us to keep the old ways as best we could. You could say following those tenets is our purpose."

Katy's corkscrew red curls suddenly lifted in a breeze that touched her alone. Her eyes took on a glow more orange than amber. "You're the people of the Shadow Drazoen. They say Nyakisi are the only ones who believed they existed enough to try to communicate. They remember visiting your world eons past."

"The who?" Na peered intently at her.

"Shadow dragons. They're the other side of every Drazoen you know of. When I brought Sundancer back, it was only because our Shadows helped."

Na looked like someone had handed him a luscious sweet after tuigs of fasting. "These Shadows, they talk to you? You can hear them, though we can't?"

"Yeah," Katy sighed, her eyes and hair returning to normal. "We make a Wataño, the six of us. Me, Sundancer and our four Shadows. They're what makes up the part of the Aoni you can't see. And they can't talk to everyone the same way the Nine can."

"Exactly as *Frelaasti Song* says! They taught us how to live in the darkness, but we thought they'd died out."

"That's not for common knowledge, Na." Yuhwa felt like she should mark that boundary.

His roguish smile didn't inspire confidence. "Of course not." He got serious once more. "This! This is exactly what I needed. I am made to find valuable things, no matter where they've been hidden. I am relentless on a hunt, and might have knowledge that can make a difference. Let us treat with one another, let me help you find the most valuable prizes in creation. When the Drazoen – visible and invisible – return, the Aoni will be reborn."

"Bug, he wants to parlay," Paul laughed. "Just like a pirate!"

Bay scoffed. "And, like pirates, you hope to be rewarded."

"Ah seeker, you've gotten yours." He pointed to Katy. "The rest of us deserve something as well."

"There is nothing more powerful than an unreformed criminal who turns his efforts to good." Raisa's mischievous laugh captured Na's attention completely.

"*Bardu*," he said on a soft breath. "How well you know me, without knowing me at all."

Yuhwa was shocked to hear the Nyakisi endearment pass his lips; she'd thought it was reserved for romantic partners. He'd said it pretty intimately, too; was he hitting on Raisa? Sad if he was, because from what Yuhwa could tell that ship had left the dock.

Raisa blushed and crossed her arms, looking away. "Olak says they're wrapping up, so I'm going to meet her. Welcome to the team, Na. Don't mess this up for us."

She passed Voltan at the door, who poked her head in to say, "Yuhwa? There's a Xanthos Dai here for you."

Non-plussed, Yuhwa gave Voltan a blank stare, hoping there might be more data forthcoming.

"Rixat, female? Green scales?"

Oh shtŭ. Her party night diversion from sals ago. Why would she be here? "I'll come down, don't bring her up here."

Voltan's face was blank. "It would never have occurred to me to do so."

"Oh hey, that was your hookup from the other night, wasn't it?" Katy piped up. "Maybe she's looking for more."

"She shouldn't," Yuhwa said as she walked out. "I was clear!" Only when she got downstairs did she realize Paul and Oran had followed.

"What?" Oran mumbled. "The other chick said scales, I wanted to see."

Paul nodded. "That, me too. What Oran said." He dropped to a whisper. "The aoiti say sometimes they have gills!"

This particular Rixat did not have them, but her scales ran up her throat and chin, right round her lips. Yuhwa remembered having to be very careful kissing Xanthos. The morning after she'd had a scratched lip.

Coming around the stairs Yuhwa faced a pissed off woman instead of the laughing and playful partner from that night.

"Good to see you didn't flee Centris. Just me."

Pre-Valc fever kicked in for some Rixat nearly as bad as the Valc itself. Even at this distance from Shilmand, Yuhwa had heard their blood fired with the mating urges. Which seemed to translate into anger for Xanthos.

"Did you throw me over for these two?" she cried, waving at Paul and Oran.

Great. Toss some possessiveness into the whirlpool, too. Yuhwa prayed the Humans kept their mouths shut or else there was going to be more happening than her moving an ex-lover along.

"Xanthos. I'm sad to hear you regret our time together. Was I not clear? We are not partnered, joined, or committed. I thought we had a delightful affair that ended pleasurably. I didn't flee *you*, I just left your room. As would be expected the morning after our fun night."

Oran was either choking or suppressing laughter; Yuhwa didn't care which, she wanted it to stop. This scene was bad enough without witnesses like these two.

"Without waking me? That sounds like running away!" Xanthos wasn't giving up her fury.

Hands out, palms up, Yuhwa tried once more for calm. "It sounds like I needed nropita and you were fast asleep. I know pre-Valc can be hard on you-"

Xanthos pounded her chest. "You don't know a thing. I'm not in a frenzy, I thought I'd met someone great who liked me back."

"You did." Yuhwa ground out, fed up. "You were perfectly rational, you say? So what did it mean when I said it was for the night only?"

"I-" Xanthos started.

"Did you think you would change my mind? That you'd be the person who made me give up my ways?"

"Yes!" Xanthos' lips paled as she bit them. "I mean, no, I didn't think that clearly. But I hoped we'd have time-"

"That is the one thing I assured you we wouldn't have." Yuhwa needed to end this, and the only way was to be cruel. "I was honest, it seems you were not. And you come here, having tracked me somehow, with the nerve to attack me about my behavior? If I'm sharing beds with these two, there is no Aoni in which that's your business."

She stepped past Xanthos to open the front doors. Without looking back she said, "You should go now. In future I'd urge you to listen to potential partners. Believe what they tell you."

Yuhwa didn't look at Oran or Paul when she closed the door behind the Rixat and jogged back upstairs. That didn't stop them from commenting the kaala they got into the war room.

"If we need anyone to shred some shit in that Calling, Yuhwa's your woman," Oran said.

Katy pulled away from Bay and walked to Yuhwa. "You okay? What happened?"

"I'm fine," she squeezed her friend's arm. "Someone was a little clingy, but it's over."

Yeahh," Paul dragged out the word, staring at her in disappointment. "It's over, for sure. Because you crushed her."

"How is this my fault?" Yuhwa was incensed. "I was truthful, she went back on our agreement!"

"It isn't a business arrangement!" Paul shot back. "Just because you can't handle relationships doesn't mean other people don't want them. You broke her heart!"

"Would you prefer I changed my mind about my long-held romantic limits? After telling her the opposite from the beginning? Like your partner did?"

"Hey, hey!" Lia and Katy both broke in.

Paul was furious, but Yuhwa wasn't apologizing. He had no right castigating her like that.

"I swear, Paul, you're a bloody mess." Katy was disgusted. "Actually, so are you, majio hotshot. What is up with hitting each other below the belt?"

"If I may ask, how the hål have any of you accomplished anything?" Na frowned.

Snippy, Katy said, "'*Void of suffering and death*'? Fecking good definition of this mess, big thank you for the new word." Katy shook her head. "Less thank you for being judgy judgerson. We're all tired. My family started out the day being arrested and it's been a high-speed roller coaster since then." She turned to her brothers. "Maybe a nightcap, then we all turn in. Tomorrow isn't going to be any better."

Yuhwa pretended Paul didn't exist when she headed for the bar on the far side of the room. She was having a shot of rusim, and no Humans were allowed to share.

A short time later, most of the room's tension had diffused. Katy was half asleep on a sofa, the rest of the group packing up what was left of the food. There wasn't much; Na had unapologetically snacked his way through most of what had remained.

Wary, but unable to fight her compulsion, Yuhwa approached Katy. What had started as a barely-there, wondering question now filled her with a disquieting sense of inevitability. Katy's eyes blinked wide when Yuhwa slumped down beside her.

"I'm up. Swear, I'm up." Katy groaned.

Yuhwa hunched over, hands dangling between her knees. "I wanted to ask you... how did you know you were the herald?"

Blinking slowly, Katy took a kaala to reply. "I don't know what *I* knew, just that Bay believed it." Katy laughed, rolling onto her side. "I'd always loved fairy tales and mythology, and what we call sci-fi back home. I guess I'd been primed to believe him, once he said it was true."

"So, you didn't dream about it?"

"No, Bay was the one with dreams that had hints and things. I didn't have a clue what to do, right up until I did it." Katy shuddered. "Stuck in the shadow prison, it felt like everything in my life had led to that moment and suddenly…" Katy puffed air and flicked her fingers out like a small explosion. "Herald, Kawakona, Chanticleer, Returning Child. That's when I knew they all really meant me."

"But if you hadn't been who you are, it wouldn't have worked." Yuhwa knew she wasn't saying it right, and Katy's confused head tilt confirmed it. "Bay dreamed, but *you* had the music. And you followed it. Learned your flute, studied so when the time was right, you'd be ready. When you talk about your past I always think those tuigs were your preparation before taking your place. Fulfilling your destiny."

"Oh, huh." Katy's lips curved into a soft smile. "I hadn't thought of it that way, but maybe you're right. Why do you ask, by the way? If you're wondering if being the Kawakona makes me an easy win at that Tschuele competition, Dindal swears it doesn't. Playing my flute to wake up Sundancer doesn't mean my symphony is a shoe-in to win at the Paɫaˑč."

Yuhwa waved a hand negligently, once the aoiti clarified 'shoe-in'. "It should! There's no other being in creation who's done what you've done."

"Right?" Katy slumped back against the sofa cushions. "But just because it opened a prison made from a collapsed dark star wrapped in nefeslo doesn't guarantee it's a good score. They'll judge it free of how it was created."

Katy's eyes were closing, and Yuhwa knew she could have let it go. Some part of her needed to share, though. "What Na said earlier, about my claustrophobia? I've had it since I was a small child, because of terrible dreams. I've always had nightmares about going on my pâtexi and being buried in one of the caves."

At that Katy sat up again. "Pâtexi? This is the thing the nawa call you home to do? Your vision quest?"

Yuhwa nodded. "My people believe Jadoube become fully adult after they are sent on their pâtexi. You leave from one of the plateaus on Malor, making your way to Âuke."

Pause. "Big mountain in the middle of five plateaus. Got it," Katy said.

"We believe there's a path into Âuke for every life path of the Jadoube. When you find yours, you go into the heart of the mountain, and there you'll find your personal waja. In my nightmares, as I find the cave holding mine, everything collapses on top of me. Darkness swallows me, I'm scared and alone, can't see anything." Yuhwa shuddered. "Sometimes I drown."

"That's awful," Katy soothed. "Do you have these dreams all the time?"

"More when I was younger." She thought it over. "I think after Papa was killed and Mama died, my brain found other things to worry about."

Katy's drooping eyes shot open. "Wait. Do you think you're a herald?! Is that why you asked?"

Yuhwa recoiled. She hadn't thought anything that radical. She'd just wondered. "Lia said something, and Songmaster Silver's trigger will be waja according to their prophecy."

"Paul mentioned that earlier," Katy pushed herself up.

She tried to forestall whatever explosive comment was about to come out of her friend. "I don't think I am. That's ridiculous. First, I play no instrument. Second, I have no waja."

"Yet!" Katy burst out. "And who's to say every herald will play an instrument just because I do?"

"If anything, it would be more likely for me to be a helper. Like Bay was for you."

"That's why Paul asked about waja! No way it's my idiot brother, but I bet he thinks it's him," Katy giggled. "I still think it might be you, especially if we get you back to Malor and looking for waja."

"Slow that right down, please. I don't want to go back to Malor." Yuhwa felt her chest tighten even thinking about it.

"Why not?"

Yuhwa strove to answer in a way Katy could relate to. "Remember you said how hard it was for you when your parents didn't understand your music dreams? When they didn't want you to go to Earth Chorus?"

Katy pouted. "Yeah, that wasn't fun."

"But you went anyway, because it was what you loved. For Jadoube, being majio is just the first part of our journey. Every single one of us has the ability; it's what Songmaster gifted us, like Windweaver gave Mikanjo wings. But it's what I love best, and going on pâtexi risks being told I can't do it anymore."

"Screw that! Tell them no," Katy sputtered.

"I can't," Yuhwa said, desolate. "It just isn't done. The nawa call you home, your waja reveals what you're meant to do with the rest of your life. No one balks; we actually have tales where spirits of Jadoube who rejected the call became twisted and work against the good powers. I don't want to become one of the Ekletu." She looked toward the dark windows, pensive. "It's considered the ultimate dream fulfilled. Maybe I'll be revealed as majio, but I could be anything from a sword to a tour guide. That's why I worry, but I doubly worry that if I refuse I'll be shunned."

Nose scrunched in irritation, Katy said, "I still say screw it. You do you, no matter what anyone else says. If you really think you have to go through with it, march in there knowing you'll come back out a majio. On Earth we call that manifesting our own destiny. You tell the Aoni what you want, it finds a way to make it happen."

Laughing, Yuhwa said, "I find it unlikely the Aoni grants everyone what they want."

"Maybe," Katy's mirth turned sly, "the best way is for you to find Songmaster's waja and be his herald. That way the nawa can't tell you what to do or who to be."

"You are trouble, Katy Phelan."

Bay approached them, standing to the side of Katy. "She is the best trouble, majio." His wing brushed her arm, making his Kawakona lean in his direction. "She is *my* trouble, and will be, for many bisous to come."

Yuhwa hid her mental rejection of his sentiment, but felt it nonetheless. Aiwaks and milenyos of partnership like that weren't for her. She just wanted to be left to fly the Aoni and enjoy the freedom of being unattached. That was the biggest reason she couldn't be a Drazoen herald: they seemed to come in pairs, and no one would be allowed into her head, heart, and soul.

PAUL GLANCED at his sister and Yuhwa, conscience twanging like a fecking banjo. He'd been harsh and rude, he knew it. The scene with Xanthos had been really ugly, and Yuhwa had rightly reproached him for taking his personal feelings out on her. He'd been overwhelmed by a surprise kernel of jealousy mixed up with a hefty dose of leftover trauma from his ex.

But he was a little bit right, too. Yuhwa fled emotional ties like a criminal on the lam. That couldn't be healthy for her. He'd never met someone more in need of a safe harbor, but since that wasn't going to be him, he couldn't push the issue with her. Hopefully Bug or Lia could get through to her someday.

"Quick question before we all head to bed," he called to the room.

"Yes, I will stay," Na replied.

"I'm positive that wasn't his question, and no, you will not," Bay said.

"The Cadre will not thank us for boarding a Nyakisi under their roof, no matter how pure you claim your motives to be." Yuhwa snorted, leaned her head back and closed her eyes.

Na smirked. "Worth a try. Let us ask the *bardu*, she was on my side."

Bardu *bar-doo; medium-sized bird from Godot; form lifelong bonds with a partner; Nyakisi consider it lucky if mating bardu set up a nest atop their tower and will often construct areas to attract them; used as a term of affection.*

"You leave Raisa alone," Katy warned. "She's had enough trouble, and is barely able to sleep a full night. Olak Purplevoice is helping her, so just leave her be."

Na focused on the now-empty loveseat where Raisa and Olak had been cuddling earlier. His countenance started out forbidding, but cleared to blank. "As you say, herald."

"Back to my question," Paul said. "What is the plan if we're discovered before Sundancer declares us at the bulɛ? Where is she, anyway?"

"She said she wanted time to herself, which I assumed meant flying all over the system or Aoni or something. But now she's wandering the Wheel as a two-legs, putting the fear of Drazoen into people left and right. I think she's having a blast, TBH." Katy chortled.

Twice already today Oran had shocked Paul by involving himself. This time he said, "What's there we can do if we're found out? Those CIC fucks know we're here somewhere," he spat. "We just need to make sure they don't figure out exactly where. They're much stronger than we are, and, at least right now, have the laws on their side. Thanks for making us illegal immigrants, dear sister."

"I hate you. So much."

If Paul didn't cut in, this would devolve into one of their massive twin fights. How could two people who'd shared Ma's uterus be incapable of sharing oxygen without a screaming match?

"You have the rimā, obviously you'll use them again," Lia offered. "They hid you well today, and you only have to last until after the dōmank ganga. Perhaps you should skip the Truth Arenas, just in case."

"I dare anyone in this room to tell our mother she can't go tomorrow. You saw it," Paul said, watching Katy and Oran nod vigorously in agreement. "She's adopted him, and Ma is the Terminator when it comes to protecting her kids."

Na lifted his hand. "Terminator is translating, giving me concerns about how your species handles robots and AI. You've not created these beings in reality?" When he got shaking heads from the Humans, he said, "Does she – do all of you, actually – understand that Budiasa will not be fighting tomorrow? With a sword like Isae his victory is almost certified."

"He's right," Yuhwa agreed. "Isae Zam fights with a pair of shirumi. No sword in history has ever had a weapon like them; flexible as whips and they cut like the sharpest blades. She wields them, four blades on one hand, five on the other, whirling and spinning them to create a wall of razor-edged death." She paused. "*If* they fought to the death, which they don't."

Lia said, "Growing up we heard some remote satellites have mortal duels even now. For enough money the risk is worth it to some."

"Yes, I've heard that, too," Na replied. "But I've traveled extensively and never seen it."

"I would guess they can leave all of that nastiness to the Dál," Bay said disdainfully.

Ignoring Bay's darkening face, Paul spoke up. "Great. All fine, all good. No one else is worried about the Humans being thrown in prison again? Or shot on sight? Nothing to fret about?"

Katy mocked him. "You didn't get 'thrown in prison' a first time, ya doofus. Stop overreacting and letting your control freak off-leash. Everything will be fine tomorrow, you'll see."

Paul caved in the face of the entire group dismissing his concerns, but Oran stopped him when they reached their rooms in the security wing.

"What we do, *dearthái*r, is go down swinging."

They fist-bumped to seal their agreement. Sometimes having an argy-bargy scrapper for a brother had its advantages.

12

He woke a few hours later to shouting. Raised voices, the loudest Na's. How did *he* get into this so-called secure wing? Paul jumped out of bed and ran into the common area in his sleep shorts. Damn it. So many people to deal with before he'd had any coffee.

Tangun, Na, Yuhwa, Paul's entire family, plus Bay and Lia stood in a circle, pointing fingers and yelling.

"Explain this, Head Sword!" Na was furious, normally pale skin flushed. "How could a man with no resources escape the house where you'd left him?"

Ma was wringing her hands. "Is this because we visited? I'm worried this is my fault." She reached down for Katy's hand. His sister pulled Ma close and murmured reassurance.

"Calm yourself, everyone," Tangun said evenly. "He can't get far. As you say he has no currency, his aoiti are at minimum functional level, and he is tired from sals of running already."

"What the shtŭ," Paul jumped in. "Why would you lock down his aoiti? Doesn't he need them to talk and understand? To heal him if he gets hurt?" Shit, he'd thought Tangun was one of the good guys, but hobbling Budi was cruel.

Tangun looked at Paul like he'd happily squish the Human insect before him. "We found they'd been compromised. His clan had added trackers to them, coded to his specific bots and genetics. They were impossible to remove by force, and resisted overwrite attempts; it helps explain how the UPC found him so quickly on something the size of the Wheel."

Paul grimaced. "Sorry, man. I should have known better."

The Head Sword accepted his apology. "We had to transfuse new aoiti after flushing the old ones." Suddenly there was a gleam in his eye. "I gave him mine, with his consent. Budiasa doesn't know it, but he was able to understand Brianna and Martin because of that."

Da cackled. "You gave him the Human booster pack! We didn't even stop to wonder how he spoke so easily, did we my love?"

Ma's frown eased. "Does this mean he could come with us? Back to Earth, I mean. Once he's cleared and free, he's part of our group now. If he wants."

"He is *not* part of the group," Na bit out. "That's the whole problem! He's gone, and if he's caught and tortured by the Pu'ulqaari he can reveal the names of several Nyakisi abolitionists. A big part of our operation will be exposed!"

"I hate the PQ, really hate them," Katy said.

"Just wait until you meet the Krylar," Yuhwa offered. "They make PQ seem polite."

Before anyone could say anything else, Swailu and Raisa came in. "The Vi'isser know he's gone, and they're preparing demands for the Calling." Swailu sounded worried.

"The Cadre says to expect the worst," Raisa added. "Gudar thinks someone told them about us."

Paul and Oran locked eyes, traded nods. Blaze of glory if they had to, damn straight.

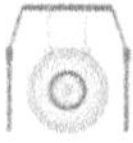

YUHWA, who'd been yanked out of bed by Lia's frantic call to get to Voice House as fast as they could this morning, wasn't in the best mood. She'd lived a life of free-wheeling fun, but valued her routines just as much. Nothing since Bay found Katy had been normal. This catastrophe was just the latest in a line of insane calamities she was hard-pressed to move beyond. Where had her simple life as a majio gone?

Before, she'd swum veṣu and drunk rusim and bedded willing partners. Small adventures here and there, and she was a simple, happy Jadoube. Now, she was surrounded by terrified Humans, a couple belligerent ones (if she read their faces right), a Nyakisi who shouldn't even be in the room, political high ups, and not a one knew what to do. What *could* they do? Budiasa had escaped, the PQ would rain down fury, and Yuhwa wasn't sure how any of this was going to turn out.

Just as she'd decided nropita would help, Sundancer materialized in the room with Isae Zam. Isae, to her credit, didn't gag or fall down. Looked like it was a close thing, though. Yuhwa took a good look at the woman she'd read about for tuigs, but had only seen with adult eyes twice (from a distance), and once as a child being humored.

Her yellow-blonde hair was cropped to a short length, little wisps flaring out here and there. One sal ago she'd had a mane of tall spikes, today this shorter look. She had orange eyes, and wore no jewelry, atypical for her species and another difference from the sal before. Perhaps where she diverged most from mainstream Lunari, she dressed in black flex armor head-to-toe. Wrapped around her waist and across her upper body were the waja blades of her shirumi; their hide-wrapped handles met at her waist.

Isae didn't disappoint, thank Nine, because that was always a risk when meeting icons. Sometimes they let you down. Since childhood she'd devoured stories about how Isae had risen to the second most powerful sword of modern times. It would have broken her heart if Isae had been less than she'd dreamed. This woman had defied the accepted conventions of *two* species, and refused to be forced into a role she didn't want. She was incredible! Yuhwa kept herself from fawning over the sword, but it was hard.

We will go directly to the Calling now. Our position is threatened by the escape of the namu and-

"Don't call him that!" Katy interrupted Sundancer in a way Yuhwa couldn't imagine doing. "He's Budi the person, not 'the slave'. Besides, that word just pretties up the atrocity."

You are right, heartnote. But his disappearance raises issues on several fronts. Some of the blocs will call for the Swords to offer recompense. There will even be those who push to have them relinquish power, and give their authority to one of the other forces on the Wheel. That will not happen while Drazoen live and I lead the Calling, but if they bring the motion to session we will have to listen to the complaint.

Tangun addressed Isae. "You will find Budiasa. He must be returned and stand for the dōmank ganga. It was called and must proceed."

"You can track, sword?" Na challenged. "We have someone on Centris right now who could help you locate him faster. Greatest hunter in a generation."

Isae waved him off. "I would rather trust my own instincts."

"I understand your caution, but in this case I will overrule you." Tangun said. "Na, coordinate a meeting between…" he let the sentence hang, waiting for a name.

"Ula Ky. She will meet us at the Calling."

"Watch out," Raisa teased. "Next thing you know you'll be riding a white horse."

Na grinned, and to Yuhwa's eye he looked more softly at

Raisa than she expected from his species. "No danger of that, Human. I remain unreformed, as you said last night."

"What," Isae asked, "is a Human? What did that woman just say? Is the herald Human, too? Her words were meaningless before."

This will be the other major problem, declaring Humans Prima. Explanations must wait. Everyone prepare for the Calling. I will move us there.

"Wait!" Katy cried. She looked around. "Some of us have to get dressed. Give us five minutes."

"Pity," Yuhwa said, looking at Paul. "I was just starting to enjoy the view." As she'd hoped, his face flamed with embarrassment and he fled.

Vasuda touched her arm as she went by. "I love seeing you keep him on his toes."

Yuhwa couldn't deny how much she enjoyed making him nervous, throwing off his flow. His ego wasn't loud, but ran deep, so any chance to drain it had to be taken. When Sundancer teleported all of them into the Toledral Calling chambers, she was still smirking.

Adena jo Kalda greeted them with aplomb; how she could be so relaxed about sixteen people dropping into the room was a nod to her aiwaks of experience as a speaker. She'd have thought Swailu warned her, but none of them had known where Sundancer would drop them off. Yuhwa might try to schedule time with Toledral Adena for lessons in being unflappable.

Na, Tangun, and Isae left immediately. Hopefully Isae and Ula would locate Budi quickly, closing off that route for PQ complaints. Everyone else gathered close to the window wall, not watching Sundancer appear mid-air, but focusing on all the Calling species gathered on their ledges or running between petals and various offices. The last sal had put these ambassadors in a panic, and they scrambled to find new footing.

"See there, Swailu," Adena pointed left and down. "Chitans seeking out the new Pu'ulqaari contingency."

"Dangerous partnerships could be made," Swailu said. "I see the Eng hover not far from those talks, as well. Will they side with them openly? We've feared they headed that way, politically."

Yuhwa slipped nearer the Toledrals and asked, "Sundancer says she'll take the Calling over, but how many will support her by your estimates?" Yuhwa wanted to know how many species she'd have to outrun on the *Eternidad* if they had to fly faster than the Great Druk to keep her friends safe.

She heard Bay from over her shoulder. "The Mikanjo are certain. Even after the…"

"Desertion?" asked Lia, bitterly.

"Departure," he said softly. "They will still follow Irojaku jo Faluji."

"Agreed," Swailu said. "I also believe the Imen, Jadoube, Lunari, Tschuele, and Muškikal will back her."

"Jesus," Paul said. "Are there any left to go against? Who would dare oppose a dragon, anyway? Seems like a sure ticket to being roasted in flames."

Adena reached over to pat his cheek, an incredibly forward gesture for a Mikanjo. She must really like him. "We should get you a mantle, young one; you have the curiosity of a newly fledged seeker."

"Sundancer doesn't breathe fire," Katy said sadly.

Even if I breathed fire I would not cook and kill people.

Katy crossed her eyes which made Yuhwa laugh.

"It's early to assume how the blocs will take form, but Nyakisi, Rixat, Eng and Ⴍti are generally opportunistic," said Swailu. "Their voting and influence is based most often on what their people get out of any vote."

Martin Phelan's brown eyes were anguished. "Not my Ⴍti!

They're my logical lads, aren't they? They should be on our side."

"Sounds like they will be, if the price is right," Ian threw out. "Which is entirely logical and rational, Da. Quid pro quo."

Paul ignored his brother. "I think you're wrong about the Nyakisi. Na made it clear they'll oppose the PQ because of that frelaasti thing."

"Fighting for namu freedom is one thing," Yuhwa countered. "Profits lost because Sundancer takes over the calling and destroys aiwaks of networking is another.

I call the bulε to order. Let the record reflect the orange penta-clah seventy fourth Cabinet of Calling is restored from the previous sal. Unfinished business to be resolved this sal.

Yuhwa estimated the PQs took half an atóm to reach Sundancer on their sleds. Pissed off Vi'issers, glowering Ra'ani and Ko'olaks, even the one who'd tried to deny the stealth tech PQ used to hide from cameras. To her dismay, the var who'd arrested the Phelans stood with them. All the Cadre fears were coming to fruition: there was zero chance any of them were escaping this unscathed.

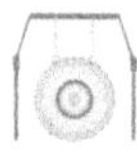

SHIT WAS ABOUT to hit the bloody fan. Paul could clearly make out that twat, Chadna Yee, and knew their secret was about to blow. The Phelan family was pale by nature, but they'd all blanched to bone white, unable to halt their impending exposure. It was like watching large cracks forming in a dam.

Pu'ulqaari bloc, you have not-

"We invoke emergency procedure 8SQ.901.L!" shouted the Vi'isser matriarch, Ubeti.

The Calling erupted into Taylor-Swift-crowd-causes-earthquake levels of noise. Angry, ecstatic, everything in between.

Whatever they had just done, the PQ had pulled off something pretty rare if these reactions were anything to go by. Paul wondered why nothing immediately followed their declaration, then saw they were waiting for the Imen from yesterday to get up to their level.

Calling scribe Tio Van, please register the motion from the Vi'isser clan. I require clarification of the procedure. Sundancer's voice dripped with sub-zero freeze. *This is something created while I was imprisoned and away from my Calling.*

"He will not like having to do this," Adena commented.

"Sundancer Orange," Tio spoke clearly and slowly. "This emergency procedure was put in place to address events where an ambassador has credible fears of life-threatening risk to either themselves or the Calling at large." He spun his sled to face the PQs, lowering his incredible bejeweled head. "The Vi'isser clan may not technically invoke the procedure, as they are not ambassadors."

"I am petitioning the emergency status; my companions spoke out of turn." Snotty guy from yesterday with the creepy black chin mask didn't even hesitate to butt in. Had they premeditated their plan of attack?

"Qo Uitu'umen," Tio demanded, "provide your evidence of imminent threat."

The previous cacophony died, leaving an audience of ambassadors on tenterhooks.

"The Pu'ulqaari assert that multiple people are acting directly, and with malice, against our interests. First came the kidnapping and theft of property from Ishar. The Mikanjo, Nyakisi and Jadoube were named session prior, and recompense is demanded from their blocs." Those three species' reps called out objections, but Qo plowed on. "When the Vi'issers pleaded their case before the Calling, requests for assistance recovering their property were disregarded. When the property was brought before the bulε, the Swords, Lunari, and Nyakisi intervened to call for an unnecessary dōmank ganga."

Dōmank ganga is the right of everyone in the Aoni.

Qo didn't quail before Sundancer's ire. "Conveniently, the Swords have now lost the property they insisted they had to hold before the bout! All of these actions, in and of themselves, constitute violent attacks against our people and way of life. But now, we've been informed there has been an inconceivable violation. Something far beyond our understanding of how this political body functions, and that undermines its authority in every way. There is an unknown species on the Wheel!"

13

Paul had expected that to be more of a bomb than it was. Checking the crowd, he could see they didn't believe the PQ. "Why isn't Sundancer shutting this shit down?" he hissed.

"She's the Drazoen of justice," Katy said. "The way this is going, she's already going to have to pull some strong-arm tactics she isn't happy about. No chance she's going to skip protocols on her way there."

"Var Yee, who joins us here today, brought us information regarding a lawful detainment overturned only one sal ago. One you, yourself, bypassed, Sundancer Orange!" The collective inhale of the Calling was audible. "He will clarify the details, but we fear your judgement is clouded and name you as a part of the collective trying to harm Pu'ulqaari."

Holy fuckballs. Every time Paul thought it couldn't get more insane it said "hold my beer" and escalated. The furor of the last two days had nothing on the pandemonium now. Paul could hear actual howls from the purple section of the chamber; not sure which species could do that. Every visible landing pad patio was filled with all the people of the Calling. Wings spread over there, tails thumping the floor two petals over, stamping feet and screams throughout.

Sundancer remained silent.

"The fuck is your dragon doing, Bug?" Oran yelled. "Are we about to be lynched because her sense of 'justice' is too strong to defend us? Maybe Herself doesn't need to worry, but we do!"

Katy turned on him, raging. "There's a plan, you ass! She's got it under control, and you just have to trust that a freaking demigod can handle whiny baby fascists!"

Paul ignored the familial infighting and walked closer to the chamber windows, pressing his nose to the glass. If they were soon to be outed and maybe shipped home or incarcerated, he wanted to take in every sight. As scary as some of this had been, it was an exciting adventure he wasn't going to relinquish willingly. They'd have to pry him off of this Wheel.

Yuhwa stepped up behind him. "She'll fix this. She has to let them vent it all so she can flush the hidden demons."

Nodding, he tapped the window. "Look at all of that. Do you notice it, ever? Or is it all status quo?"

"The Calling?"

"The people. The colors and languages, the myriad cultures and…just all of it. We have nations and tribes, what we call races. But they're all the same species. This is like the ultimate Wonderland variety grab-bag, and I haven't seen enough. It's too soon to lose it."

Yuhwa touched his arm. "You won't lose it. Sundancer will find a way to clear this up, and then we'll go through each spoke, see everything. When you're tired of being a tourist, you can set up the first Human school of your gymnastics."

Paul snorted. "Look at Tio. I have no idea how to teach an Imen child how to do floor ex, a kip, or the vault. No way they can do the rings, although maybe balance beam…" He let himself imagine it for a minute; his muscles twitched, and he craved a padded floor to stretch and give them a good, long workout.

"There are moments I feel you almost have dao," Yuhwa patted him again. "When you release your fears and some of your need to control."

He gave her a rakish grin. "Do the aoiti translate 'pot meet kettle' very well?" By the sucking of her teeth, he figured she'd gotten the idea.

Paul's smile dimmed quickly as the Chitan cop stepped forward. He remembered how this dude had shoved him, how he'd told his lackey to restrain them with a sneer, the gratuitous pinching and rough jerks when yanking them out of the containment carrier. Most of all he remembered the moment he realized how much stronger Chitans were than Humans. Knowing bodies was part of being a good teacher, and Paul could easily identify those who would get stronger as they trained versus kids who just didn't have the physiology to be great. Chitans would blow Mr. Universe out of the water.

"Var Chadna Yee. The bulε awaits your testimony to support emergency procedure 8SQ.901.L." Tio sounded grim. "I will remind you, and all in the Calling, that false witness or coerced statements are punishable by banishment from Centris for seven bisous."

Paul figured seventy years was a respectable deterrent for such long-lived beings, but maybe they deserved a lifelong exile. He really hated these people threatening his family.

Yee wasn't intimidated by Tio's words. "I tell no lies, scribe. Last buwan, Mikanjo arriving on the *Eternidad* vouched for two people arriving with them. Jadoube, so they claimed, whose aoiti were sworn to be malfunctioning. When pressed to provide evidence of such a rare occurrence, Toledral Swailu jo Faluji and Head Sword Tangun Ye-Na appeared at the ship. They demanded entrance for the undocumented, and the whole party gave assurance Katy Phelan and Raisa Leon would register themselves within the buwan. They did not.

"One sal ago, according to immigration registrar Tang, she'd located Katy Phelan but still couldn't verify her documentation. Raisa Leon remained at large. My team was subsequently dispatched to a rental domicile on mid ring, just outside the Chorus. Hu-Sun borough, Deekü neighborhood. Records showed it had been leased to Djilbay jo Bikajo, a person of interest and associate of the alleged Jadoube."

There was a lot of rumbling all around, heads turning as though they might see the sneaky illegal immigrants nearby. Paul gritted his teeth, feeling their inevitable exposure bearing down like an avalanche.

"I now submit audiovisual of the encounter into evidence." Var Yee nodded at Tio, who pushed a button on his sled. Holo-screens appeared in a circle around the group hovering in the middle of the Calling.

Their abominable morning encounter was shorter than Paul remembered it. Dread and fear had extended everything in his mind. This showed it was done in a matter of minutes. He saw from this angle that Oran and Patrick had been treated even worse than he had; one of the cops had kicked the back of Oran's knee to force him to stop struggling, and Patrick's head had hit the wall with excessive force. When the vid ended, multiple voices overrode anything Tio tried to say.

Yee bellowed to be heard. "I emphasize again! They spoke a language my aoiti could not recognize. You've just heard the proof of what I say! None of them had aoiti that registered at all! Given what we know of Sundancer Orange's recent return, this one who accompanied her," he threw up an image of captured Katy looking desperate, "must come from an unknown species. One that was snuck onto the Wheel, her presence covered up at the highest levels!"

Multiple sleds rose simultaneously from species' decks around the chamber.

"Is this true?" cried several rose-red ☉ti, as they ascended. "This cannot be!"

A Rixat with cotton candy blue hair, her scales and gills sharply outlined in a deep eggplant shade, nearly collided with the PQ sled. "Are you saying there's been a Law of First Approach violation?" She pounded her sled's console, outraged. "Who? Who did this?"

Nearly every other species had shot some ambassador up to represent and air their thoughts, some more than one. It was a proper melee out there, and Paul didn't envy Tio trying to keep order. Sundancer continued to look down on the gathering, keeping her thoughts to herself. He was trying to have faith, but his own patience was wearing thin as she did nothing to slow the train-wreck pile-driving car after car into itself.

"I have more to say," bellowed Chadna Yee. "In an effort to protect what she knew to be wrong, Sundancer Orange came to CIC headquarters and used her clout to force the release of the aliens! We all know how much power a Drazoen has, and Sundancer used hers to force our obedience, letting her herald escape proper investigation."

Tio tried to intervene. "While extraordinary and alarming, none of this constitutes the emergency state you invoked. No lives of ambassadors or any other person on the Wheel were in jeopardy."

"Our way of life is at risk! As for lives in jeopardy, we believe the alien killed one of ours, Yfaun Lu'upan!" Qo's words were nearly triumphant.

Behind him Katy and Raisa moaned, "No-no-no."

"Any atóm," Yuhwa muttered. "She'll stop this any atóm."

"Proof!" screeched a Muškikal. "You must prove your slander, Pu'ulqaari ambassador. Long gone are the sals your word was good for anything in this Calling!"

Qo and Ubeti scoffed and looked to Sundancer. "You have the eminence of the lauded Drazoen," Ubeti taunted. "Prove you do not collude with our enemies. Bring Budiasa Vi'isser back, return our property!"

"Show us these aliens now," the Rixat woman demanded. "If you removed them from custody, you must know their whereabouts. Bring them to the floor!"

I AM NOT YOUR GWAN!

Sundancer's irate declaration boomed like planets colliding. The gang of sleds around her body shot down and away from her. Everyone in the place cowered, while Paul's aoiti fed him images of a gwan as a horse-sized beast that looked less Clydesdale and more racing greyhound, pulling chariots like Romans and Egyptian pharaohs used.

I do not run to your commands, ambassadors, nor do I cower from Pu'ulqaari as too many in this Calling seem to. I find myself disappointed, yea, even disgusted with what this assembly has become.

In one stomach turning instant, Paul and all the Humans were arrayed in a semi-circle about Sundancer's shoulder-height. He hadn't a clue what they stood on, but there was resistance below his feet. An invisible platform a couple hundred feet above ground was preferable to dangling in open space, but just barely.

Tio Van, make note that I, Sundancer Orange, She Who Balances the Scales, First Speaker of Justice, Final Judge of Merit, invokes clause two of the Calling.

"No!" echoed a thousand times around the chamber as ambassadors panicked over whatever the hell she'd just done. It was hard to read the large lizard's face, but Tio seemed quite happy to take that note.

Clause two is in effect. I am now the leader of the Calling and this bulɛ. Trinary members, you are thanked for your duties performed until now, but that time is done. You should never have been given such power, but you are a symptom of the greater illness I've found in the present gathering.

Katy floated around Sundancer and rose until their heads were at equal height. Paul thought his sister was about to puke, but Bug held it together admirably.

This is my heartnote. The part of myself I sent out into the Aoni, praying it would come back and free me. She has done so, we are reunited as we were meant to be. Katy rested a hand on Sundancer's shoulder, taking comfort and offering it in return.

You will know her by many names; most call her the Herald. She is Kawakona, my Chanticleer, the Returning Child, my Kulu-taja. She will be registered in this Calling as my ambassador, Katy Phelan jo Faluji of the Human species.

There went everyone shouting again.

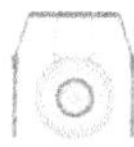

YUHWA WAS IMPRESSED with the Humans. When Sundancer had translocated them to the middle of the Calling, the Mikanjos and Yuhwa had run outside the room. Two Toledrals, two ex-seekers and their pilot, all were ready to jump into a sled and fly their Human friends to safety if things turned violent. The Humans were staying calm out there in the wake of Sundancer's pronouncements, but perhaps they didn't understand the gravity of what had happened.

Clause two was, quite literally, the second clause of the Calling Declaration. First clause stipulated that every advanced species would send representatives to participate as ambassadors; more than one and no more than thirty. Regardless of attending ambassadors, each species only had a single vote. The number of envoys a people sent to the Calling merely represented the varied interests of their world, and they had to compromise, or overrule, within their own species. That's how the Trinary had started; a way to give enhanced voting strength to the most powerful in the Calling.

But what Sundancer named was the reset clause.

If a Drazoen majority agreed the Calling was failing to function properly, clause two said they could take over and set things back on course. Genius of her, really. It was so old no one remembered it could be done, and Yuhwa would bet her substantial life savings that even if they had, not a one would have apprehended Sundancer *was* the majority. Right now, she was the only Drazoen in the Aoni, which made her the chief voice by default.

Yuhwa stared at her friend, floating next to her Drazoen, and felt a ping of something inside. Jealousy? No, not really. But there was beauty in how Sundancer and Katy resonated with one another. She'd had something close to it long ago with her parents; it faded when they had. The dao, while soothing, wasn't the same. She could admire it in her friend...the Kulutaja? Yuhwa hadn't realized the Tschuele had a word for the herald.

Sundancer's voice cut through the cheers and welcomes, as well as the boos and hoots. How insane did you have to be to deny what a Drazoen told you? Apparently Chitan-PQ foolish because those factions were swimming vigorously against the stream out there, lots of rude gestures and hissing.

I hereby declare Humans the sixteenth species invited to the Calling. More ambassadors will follow, including whosoever they declare Prima.

Yuhwa remembered Katy's thoughts on the matter: "Fecking hell, we can't agree on anything as a species, much less who gets to come here!"

Each of these Humans you see here are my emissaries, all claimed by me and declared jo Faluji of my line. None shall be questioned, harassed or bothered in any way.

As those words landed, the voices ascended to join Sundancer on one large sled. Even Kalim was there today. Mara, in a voice trained to reach large audiences, avowed, "Sundancer Orange, the Chorus Cadre of Voices stands in solidarity with your declarations. We will work to ensure fairness, and a return to the principles upon which you founded the Calling."

Head Sword, approach and report on the lost citizen Budiasa. The one so terrified of being returned to his clan he fled the security offered rather than risk going back.

Tangun, flanked by four more swords, flew a sled up into the now-crowded space around Sundancer; Isae wasn't with him. A hush had crept over the crowd, everyone present sensing something huge to come. A ruling as equally satellite-shaking as a new species being invited to Centris, perhaps?

"Budiasa, formerly of Vi'isser clan, escaped the house we'd assigned him last night." Tangun's shattered voice was calm, but Yuhwa had known this man a long time. He'd worked with her father, he'd watched out for her when she was lost and acting out after her parents died, and right now he was teetering on the edge of nuclear fission. "We do not suspect he was removed unwillingly at this time. Isae Zam has been sent to bring him back, so his case may be cleared by dōmank ganga and his freedom secured."

"He is not formerly of our clan! He remains ours, property by contract, and when he is found you will return him to us!" Spittle sprayed out with Ubeti's words.

Property by what right?

"The right of our people! Namu'ur is a protected practice, and the namu owned therein cannot be withheld."

Yuhwa shook her head. That woman really didn't understand who she was dealing with.

Namu'ur is abhorrent. There is no protection for what is an abomination against creation, for treating fellow members of advanced species like chattel. You have profited greatly from enslaving both your own people and others who were caught in your bad bargains and outright kidnappings. When we left the

Aoni a little more than one kōmilen ago, Pu'ulqaari had not dared stoop so low. That you have, and to know so many in this Calling stood by while people suffered, is the deepest level of rot. I could not have imagined this of the people my siblings and I brought together. We had hoped for union, exploration of cultures and mutual learning, sharing amongst the advanced people.

"You will violate the sovereignty of their species?" shouted a Chitan man, his sled nestled near the PQ and Rixat ones facing Sundancer. "What's next? You come for our children if you think we're raising them wrong?"

They have violated the rights of those they enslaved. I do not seek to destroy their species or their world: I merely pass judgement on a revolting practice that will no longer be allowed to flourish. Namu'ur is herewith outlawed.

Gasps rang out, some cries of astonishment as well. Even though no one could have missed what was coming, hearing it said aloud was breathtaking.

All namu are emancipated immediately. Each Pu'ulqaari clan will pay into reparation funds, which newly freed namu may access and use to escape where they've been held and find a new home.

Katy leaned in to whisper something to Sundancer. Yuhwa blinked; it had looked oddly like the herald had flickered out of view for a moment.

"You will collapse our economy, the very structure of our society," yelled Qo Uitu'umen. "We cannot immediately release every namu from their contract!"

In future, do not build your society on a shaky foundation. One that demands your cruelty toward, and disregard of, other people. Advanced species do not buy and sell others!

Katy blinked in-out again, this time so did all the Humans with her. Something was wrong. Paul turned to look down at Yuhwa as he blindly reached for his mother's hand. Bay launched from the deck without a word, fear writ large on his face. Yuhwa started feeling odd, too, right as the Humans faded and returned for the third time. She shook her head. Sundancer hadn't noticed any of it yet, and went on.

You will not do this alone, or unsupervised. I will select

Yuhwa fell down a narrow corridor into a wide pool. She was pulled through the longest, most seductive veşu she'd ever seen. It was serene, quiet, a current that pulled stronger than any she'd known. She had one break in time to marvel at the wildness of it, the untamed feel. Then everything went dark.

14

Paul held a crying Katy as he reached for
stability. The whole family plus Raisa surrounded him, stag-
gering from this unexpected teleportation, hard on the
heels of Sundancer's. Da looked especially pale, Ma holding
him tight with one arm as she reached for her sons with
the other. What the shtŭ had just happened? They'd been
in the middle of the Calling, and now were in pandemonium. The kind that follows war and natural disasters,
worse than anything he'd seen after the *Eternidad* first
arrived on Earth.

People were screaming for loved ones or yelling in anger and
fear, children wailing. Inexplicable water buffalo trampled
pedestrians as they stampeded through crowds, hooking a few
with their sharp, curved horns. He watched two men nearby
punching each other, blood running from their noses.
Bystanders watched in vacant-eyed stupor, making no move to
interfere. Car horns sounded in the distance.

But this was no post-apocalyptic wasteland scene; they were
in the middle of an urban park setting where he could see paved
roads beyond the trees, geometrically planted flowerbeds, and

manicured knolls. A small lake to their right, regular water blue instead of the faded denim of Centris.

"How-w-w," Katy juddered through her tears, "are we in Vienna?"

His sister had survived an assassination attempt and solitary confinement in the worst prison to ever exist. If she was unsettled enough to stutter, Paul knew they were experiencing something unprecedented and bad, bad, bad.

"You know where we are?" demanded Ian. He and Deb clutched one another, their knuckles mottled red from the grip, faces ghostly.

"I spent a m-m-month," she gulped then went on, steadier. "I came here that summer I didn't fly home. I spent nearly every day at this park, it was my favorite place." Katy stepped away from Paul and spun in a circle. "There, see? The monument to Strauss. We're in Stadtpark."

"Katy!"

Despite the muddle they faced right now, he was disgruntled Yuhwa hadn't called *his* name. They'd gotten closer, right? Had a nice moment in the Toledral chambers, right before Sundancer pulled them into the limelight. Even before that, she'd sort of flirted when he had his shorts on. Paul sighed and resigned himself to occupying off-limits "friend of sister" space. FOS was good, honestly. He didn't want to start anything with a woman, not for a long time. But she could still rely on him, couldn't she? Once in a while she could turn to him first?

Yuhwa jogged up to their group. "Does anyone know what's happening?"

"No! I thought this had to be related to what your people do." Katy was plaintive.

"If there is any Jadoube who can connect with the dao, all of these people in separate locations in space, and move them without aid of a veṣu, we should be terrified," Yuhwa replied. "I can sense millions of life forms, nines and nines of millions.

That's unheard of. And what I saw when we were pulled through…. Jadoube *follow* the flow of the dao, this felt more like swimming against the current crossways."

Paul focused on meaningless details to keep himself calm. His heart raced, he wanted to run or shout, or do a six-minute floor routine that forced his body to focus. Because this bull-shit was going to push him over the edge. How did they get back to Earth in a flash? Why would they end up nowhere near their home, in freaking Austria? They were surrounded by Humans and wildlife who were clearly just as shocked to be displaced as his family; this wasn't a case of tourism gone awry.

Five feet away a group of people in bright, handwoven ponchos huddled close, flinching at every bellow and crash, so obviously unmoored from their world it was heart wrenching. Paul guessed South American in origin; he wasn't knowledge-able enough to figure out exactly where they came from, but they looked Andean, maybe? He wanted to offer them shelter; tell them it would be okay and reassure them. A group of young Asians – from Tokyo, Hong Kong, Seoul, somewhere super-urban and hip based on their fashion choices – swept along the park path, chatting and laughing. The mirth had a desperate undertone to it. They were playing at cool, filming one another and giggling as they walked, but were just as freaked out as everyone else. And the two idiots over there were still swinging on each other, rarely connecting, bellowing in French, he thought.

"My lads and ladies, I think we should seek a quieter place." Da was trying to be their da, but he was still pallid and shaken. "Until we can sort this."

Oran demanded, "Call your fecking dragon, Bug. What's the point of having one if she can't save the day?"

"Again," Vasuda scowled at him. "She's saved us twice already, now you think you can make demands?" If his quiet near-sister-in-law was getting irate, shit had to be worse than he thought.

"There was a great café, I remember. We just need to walk-"

Katy was interrupted by a levitating black bowling pin. "Yuhwa Bon-Gil, please follow." Their group stared at the bizarre apparition that spoke in a perky, customer service voice.

"I do not know what to do with that," Raisa's precise words and pauses contrasted with the vague hand gesture she made, encompassing the drumstick-shaped robot that floated head height.

"Other Humans." A green beam from a tiny eye in the top of the pin scanned their group. "You are greeted. Should she desire your companionship, please follow with Ms. Bon-Gil."

"What the ever-loving fuck?" Oran and Katy said simultaneously, a rare twinning moment.

The bowling pin rotated and floated down the path from whence it had come. No one followed, and once it realized that it flew back. "You're urgently needed in command, Ms. Bon-Gil. Mandy must speak with you."

"Command?!" Paul barked, temper snapping. "We're in Vienna not the Pentagon, you unholy Roomba. Where is command? Who the hell is Mandy?"

"You are not in Vienna on Earth, Human." At that statement Ma's knees failed her and Da caught her. "You are on the *Mahoroba*, and will be assigned living quarters soon. By Mandy, who is in charge. Shall we go?"

If everyone was as confused as Paul, their crew was floundering big time. He couldn't think of a single intelligent question to ask as his mind spun out.

Yuhwa approached the bowling pin confidently, not as lost as the rest of them. "Who flies this ship, bot? What species?"

"Human."

"No way, we have nothing this advanced! To recreate an entire city in near-perfection-"

"Three thousand four hundred and seventy-eight," it interrupted Katy. "*Mahoroba* has copied three thousand four hundred seventy-eight cities, villages, islands, parks and assorted geographical regions."

Katy moaned at the absurdity of it, while Patrick said, "It's so precise, but that's impossible."

Handling this far better than they were, Yuhwa asked, "Do you have a preferred name or designation?"

A series of soft chimes tinkled. "Naming was not given priority, but it has been decided you may refer to me as M13. We must go. Now, Ms. Bon-Gil. The situation has become dire, per Mandy."

Yuhwa muttered, "Fine. Let's move fast, because we're getting a lot of attention."

Paul glanced around and saw curious eyes on them, a few turning hostile. Distress never played well with Humans. They made terrible decisions when pushed into corners. Leaving faux Stadtpark sounded better and better by the second.

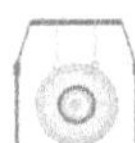

YUHWA DIDN'T THINK she liked being a Ms.

Jadoube had no title assignments based on a woman's marriage state, it was preposterous. She also didn't approve of any species using technology that could summon beings without their consent. Was this 'Mandy' assuming they could force her to be a majio for them? They were mistaken if so.

M13 led them out of the park, down the centers of large paved roads mostly absent of vehicles. There was one large, red and grey one the size of a Centris cargo sled. It had flashing blue lights and emitted a wailing sound that scraped all their nerves. Thankfully in one or two kaalas they reached a clearly marked station and descended via platform to an underground train. It was mercifully empty of panicking Humans, unlike the surface. She'd watched more and more fights breaking out, bellows and cries ringing skyward, as they'd jogged out of the park. The scale of roiling disorder above was something she'd never witnessed before.

Katy looked around critically. "This isn't what I remember. Too advanced, more like what's on Centris," she murmured. "See how smooth the station walls are? I get how this could be part of a spaceship. Too uniform, like it was molded."

Beside Katy, holding her hand for comfort, Raisa concurred. "Reminds me of when Babu's new car arrived, untouched after it was manufactured."

M13 piped up. "Yes, Human, it is all quite new. Less than one hour old."

Dazed silence met the pronouncement. How? How could any of this be possible?

Deb, voice more broken than Yuhwa had yet heard it, whispered to Ian, "I just want a window. Or we could go back up there, where it was sunny and green?"

"I know, boo. We'll get somewhere safe and protected and it'll be all right," Ian comforted her.

Yuhwa wasn't sure that would be the case, but whatever he wanted to tell his wife to keep her happy was their business. They boarded two at a time, to find a seat configuration of large chairs oddly arranged: four sets of three on each side of the tram car, the triad arranged in a semi-circle, mirrored on the other side. The seats were split by an aisle an Imen could nearly fit on. Comfort and personal space had been prioritized by whoever made these.

Their group spread out, but no one sat too far from anyone else. Vasuda sat in Patrick's lap, their drawn faces and slumped shoulders matching. These poor Humans had gone through more in five sals than most beings endured in a lifetime.

She examined everything in sight, and agreed with Katy. This train and the tunnel they zipped through were newer, possibly better, tech than the Mikanjo had on the *Eternidad*. There was zero wear and tear, as if fresh out of a production center. It moved silently, not a hint of track or rail as it sped along. The transport was beautiful in its efficiency.

Paul dropped into the seat beside her. "Do you know what's happening?"

"Not a clue." Yuhwa remembered the relaxing moments they'd shared right before this abduction, back in the Toledral chambers. Paul Phelan had been growing on her, and she found herself driven to console him. He was only Human, after all. New to all of this. "M13 says Human ship, but that's not possible given your species' level of technology." Paul agreed. "That leaves a few other options, but, again, who is capable of something this huge?"

"Chitans have those huge traveling arena ships. That's what Thuliso said, the ones that have black market, back-channel access to stations all over the Aoni. Could they have done this?"

"Possibly," Yuhwa said with misgiving. "Those ships aren't entirely Chitan, from what I know. Even if they were, it seems out of character for them."

Paul twisted to face her fully. "What if it's some kind of game to them? Throw all the Humans in a meat grinder and see what happens?"

Once her aoiti sorted out his words, she disagreed. "I don't doubt they would love to do that. But first, they found out Humans exist only kaalas ago, how could they know to transport all of them here so fast? Second, they don't have this capability, unless they've hidden surreal levels of power from the Aoni at large." Before Paul could hypothesize further, she said, "Chitans aren't known for patience, secrecy, or mastermind intelligence. They like to fight and shtŭ."

He reluctantly gave in. "What about those ⊙ti? They love puzzles and technology, right?"

"They do," she mused, "but why would they only do it to Humans? That's what everyone up there was. The only non-humans I saw were us," she waved between the bot and herself. "Something like this risks ûpiøra declaration, as well. There's no advantage for any species I can imagine."

"I guess we'll wait and see," Paul grumped. It was pretty clear how little he relished that idea. Not one for leaving things to chance or the control of others, this man.

Oran, seated nearby and having overheard them, offered, "I think it was Humans." He pointed at the circular tubes attached to each chair, ones Yuhwa hadn't understood the function of. "Who else includes cupholders on their public transit? The drink I need *should* be right goddamn here."

She looked at Paul for clarification and he shrugged.

"He's got a point."

Yuhwa was never going to really know this species, was she? Another half sal-ang and their train stopped. M13 led their ragtag group, ascending from the arrival platform via an angled moving walkway this time, into a large open chamber.

If Ru Paul had copious multi-colored face tattoos, a shock of bone white hair in Edward Scissorhands' style, and wore an emerald green caftan, that was the person approaching. They didn't run, but were so tall their stride ate up distance rapidly. The green bowling pin following them zoomed to keep up.

"Lanu?!" A shocked Katy introduced Lanu to the family and Yuhwa. He was the safehouse gatekeeper on Earth, Paul learned. He had been kind to Katy and Raisa, helping Bay get them away from a killer.

They. Lanu was agender, or maybe pangender; that wasn't

entirely clear. They and them. Or was there a whole different pronouns set the aoiti hadn't shared with him yet?

"Mr. Lanu Ojala, fortuitous we meet before proceeding to command," M13 said. It flashed a yellow light at its counterpart and they each beeped twice, like echoes.

Lanu stepped forward, coolest of all in the large group. "I believe going to command will get us more answers, we should go as a unit." Everyone nodded, and Lanu turned back to the floating messenger. "Bot, as I informed the one who brought me here, kindly revise your database to exclude gendered salutations and pronouns for all Uilig encountered."

The stupid thing melodically burbled acquiescence.

"We call it M13 now," Brianna advised. "Bot felt too…rude."

Lanu nodded, copacetic with naming robots shaped like turkey drumsticks, it seemed. These long-time Aoni residents had such an advantage over Humans. Almost nothing seemed to throw them.

"Same instruction for all non-Human species," Yuhwa threw in. "People will tell you if you need to use one. The only titles are those earned or inherited."

More cheerful blooping and a happy, "Noted!" from the second bot. One soon to be named by Ma, Paul was sure.

They crossed the entry, encompassed by blank, pearly walls joined to argentine, noise-muffling rubberized floors. Paul estimated the room could hold no more than thirty Humans. A Mikanjo with wings spread might touch the sides. Doors that barely cleared Lanu's height slid open before their approach.

"Please come through the portal," said the green bot. "We understand you are confused, possibly scared. Mandy says Humans respond to anthropomorphism positively." It finished brightly, "Therefore M13 and I, M1616, are being made available for your comfort in this trying time."

"We're in hell, are we not?" Oran, usually the most imperturbable of the family (to Katy's undying frustration), was slowly unravelling, Paul realized. Punch after punch, they were taking too many too rapidly and it left them all off-kilter. Oran added in a disconnected tone, "We've been led to hell by upbeat robots. The movies tried to tell us."

Numbly following Tweedle Dee and Tweedle Dum, Paul stepped into an estate patterned from the European Old World of Earth. A courtyard of near seamlessly joined sand-colored pavers was partially enclosed by a worn, grey travertine arcade. Half a football field in length or less all told, single story at this end. Great arches were anchored by black-flecked white marble columns; these separated the sheltered walkway from the open palazzo on three sides. Gas lamps hung from the apex of each arch, lending a warm glow to the artificial sunset under simulated skies.

Every ten feet or so, doors broke up the smooth back wall of the covered promenade. Each one was a different, faded color, wooden and weathered, echoing the aged look of the building's stone. Directly ahead, orange trees marched down the middle of the palazzo, pulling his eyes to the fourth side. It was a different kind of façade; two sets of sun-bleached limestone steps ascended to a blocky building in the same white. It took up the entire back of the atrium, and was two stories instead of one. Grecian columns with squared openings stood sentry behind a pool inset within a large patio.

Whoever Mandy was, she'd made this place a gothic-Mediterranean hybrid, moody and bright at the same time. Kind of aligned with her weirdo bots; they were a bit steampunk and kitschy, too, with Pollyanna personas. Bizarre.

"Welcome home, Yuhwa Bon-Gil and Lanu Ojala," the M-bots enthused. "Your residence may be selected from any of the available units to either side." They zoomed toward the building that looked like a huge Wall Street bank. "Later. Command first."

"What about us?" Paul yelled after them, trotting to keep up with Lanu's much longer stride.

Multiple bleeps and pings drifted back before he heard, "Mandy will consider and evaluate."

Okay. So, the big building must hold command, and this Euro-plaza was the equivalent of the Captain's Deck? Paul was staying here, no matter what Mandy had to say about it. A yoga mat or two and he could get in a good workout, then plant his tired ass in a lounge chair and admire the trees and pool. Was it a swimming pool? That would be even better.

The stairs marching up to the formal building, one set on the left and one on the right, weren't more than a single flight, but Paul still pretended to be Rocky Balboa in his head. The time for self-doubt was over, he needed to step in and be a champ. Help drive this ship… metaphorically speaking, obviously. Yuhwa was the pilot and he'd leave that to her.

But someone had orchestrated this debacle, his fellow Humans were having a terrible time out there, and his family was fraying at the edges right here before him. Paul meant to lead them to a better place, and he planned to get his way no matter what. Just as soon as he knew which way was his.

15

Their bedraggled group skirted the edge of the pool, passed a few benches facing the water, and reached the building entrance. The pool was tiled in a bright mosaic of fish darting in and out of a kelp forest. Large doors swung open from the shadowed face of the building; lights revealed a hallway inside.

"We're staying out here," Deb announced. "We're tired, damn it. Fed up with mystery and whatnot."

Ian held up both hands in surrender. "We'll dip our feet in this pool and meet you if-" he grinned, "*when* you get out."

Wanker. Paul gave him the finger. Oran, Raisa and Vasuda opted to stay with them. Da clearly wanted to go inside, but Ma said she'd had enough, too, and wanted to soak her toes. By this point the M-bots were nearly vibrating with agitation.

"Mandy awaits! Walk rapidly, please."

The doors closed behind their much-reduced troupe, which didn't make anyone inside feel a whole lot safer.

"Are we being led down a kill chute?" Patrick whispered.

"Not a visual we needed," Katy sighed.

In less than a minute they faced a large portal that didn't

automatically whoosh open. It looked like swirling liquid packed with holographic particles, a rainbow-reflective water marble barring their view to the inside. Thus far, Lanu hadn't needed to stoop through openings, but this time they would. Standard door heights, even on non-standard doors, didn't accommodate seven-plus foot aliens.

"State your names," M13 said.

"Paul Phelan," he offered. The door did absolutely nothing.

"Lanu Ojala," they said, taking one step forward.

Their name triggered a realignment of particles that left the door translucent, but still closed. Paul spied a dao bed inside, upholstered in mauve plaid. It was surrounded by twenty or so fancy leather loungers.

"You now," Katy urged Yuhwa.

"Yuhwa Bon-Gil," she said, voice tight.

At her name, the door ceased to be. Paul didn't know if liquid had sucked back into the walls, or magically freaking disappeared. It wasn't in their way anymore, which was key.

A quick discussion of tactics ensued. In case the room didn't allow tailgating and treated them like attackers, they made a "sandwich" entry. Mandy clearly wanted the aliens most, and she got them, with a Human filling in the middle. Yuhwa first, Humans second, Lanu last.

As soon as they crossed the threshold the fully opaque sparkly water was back in place. Their full view of the room's interior was anti-climactic at first. Large video screens covered every inch of the walls, the carpet was beige, and furniture had a typical walnut or oak finish. Not even gas lamps in here, just regular overhead electric. It could have been the boardroom of a high-end spa. Paul could imagine bougie rich stockholders drinking cucumber kombucha and meditating before discussing quarterly earnings.

Once the screens came to life everything changed.

"Hello!" called a disembodied female voice. "Welcome to

Mahoroba, the traveling home of Humans." If the bots had been chipper Girl Scouts, she sounded like she would love to talk to you about a timeshare.

Each of the screens displayed *Come On In!* in purple text that kept bouncing and cartwheeling, like an old computer screensaver.

"Jaysus," Paul said, stunned. "Oran was right. This is hell."

Yuhwa poked him. "What does that say?"

Right, Bug had mentioned this. The aoiti didn't teach you to read, just rewired you to hear other languages in your own. "It says we're welcome to enter."

Yuhwa's eyes narrowed, and she crossed her arms. "Who are you? What is the *Mahoroba*? Why have you brought us here?"

Shit, she was good at getting right to the point. Paul liked seeing her strong and decisive, firing off questions. That unbound lilac hair, large black eyes and shorter height might trick others into overlooking her. He knew better, and if nothing else good came from this ridiculous adventure, he'd thank his sister for the opportunity to have met Yuhwa.

"Yuhwa Bon-Gil, we are so happy to have you here! You are the answer to the Drafter's request for a way to travel faster than light." A new image flashed onscreen, rippling in a wavy circular pattern Paul's brain couldn't easily grasp. It was mesmeric, if confusing. The spinning, flipping thing was superimposed on a field of stars.

"Whoa, whoa, whoa," Katy said, her hand raised in the universal sign for 'stop'. "The Drafter? What the hell does that mean?"

"Sounds culty," Patrick threw in. He walked closer to the screens, tilting his head left and right.

"I am Mandy," she said. "Very happy to meet you! I am the *Mahoroba's* artificial intelligence, tasked with day-to-day operations of the ship. The Drafter chooses to remain unidentified at this time, and has secluded themselves until further notice."

"Mandy, this is the ship you're showing up here?" Patrick asked, pointing to the screen.

"That is correct, Human. Would you be so kind as to identify yourself? I can disseminate the information to all the system bots. M13's earlier scan of your group indicated the majority of you share genetic material and are presumably a family unit."

"We're the Phelans," Paul said. "That's Patrick, she's Katy, and I'm Paul." He named the additional people outside when Mandy put their images on screens beside the ship Patrick still studied.

"Excellent. My database tells me it's a ninety-eight percent likelihood that Raisa and Katy are the Humans who left earth a month ago on an alien ship, is this correct?" A high-definition image of the *Eternidad* with the Earth behind it landed on yet another screen.

"Never mind any of that," Katy burst out. "Except we can talk later how the hell you'd know about it at all. Right now, we need to understand what is happening! How have we been yanked from Centris, Lanu and loads of Humans from Earth, onto a freaking spaceship imitating the planet? Thirty-four hundred cities?! This is just mind-boggling." She slumped into one of the loungers.

M1616 said, "Three thousand four hundred and seventy-eight."

"Cities, villages, islands, parks and assorted geographical regions," M13 added.

"You two stuff it," Katy replied. "Give us real answers, Mandy!"

Mandy's tone lowered, simulating earnest and respectful speech. "I hear your concerns and will work to eliminate them. The *Mahoroba* is a ship requested by the Drafter, who intended to minimize or stop the suffering on planet Earth. After the aliens first came and left, the Drafter watched people turn on one another, devastating their communities. World powers kept families apart by instituting lock downs or halting all travel.

"The Drafter had the ability to make something large and drastic happen, so they did. They envisioned a place Earth's people could come safely: somewhere capable of helping Humans advance into the previously untraveled Universe, now confirmed to have additional lifeforms. It would need to be varied, as the home planet is, and to provide a way for Humans to be equal to aliens technologically. After weeks of planning and consideration, they drafted their request. It was fulfilled, now we are all here."

His brother rejoined the conversation. "This ship is a kinetic sculpture, a goddamn huge one. I've seen them before. They function like optical illusions, and they're always in motion. Once you start one, as long as it's been made properly, it's nearly perpetual."

Mandy was beside herself. "Patrick Phelan, you are absolutely correct! The Drafter is a fan of the art style, and has fond memories of one in particular."

"How?!" Katy shouted, jumping to her feet. "How did the Drafter request something this size, get a Jadoube majio and Uilig safehouse host pulled in along with presumably millions of Humans? Billions?"

"Unfortunately, I cannot give you all details behind generation of the request. That isn't included in my database. However, as I mentioned before, part of the request entailed the ability to travel faster than light. The Drafter needed to ensure Humans could exist at a similar level to aliens, ones who'd breeched Earth so easily multiple times."

Footage of the *Eternidad* shuttle from its original round trip when it snagged Bay, Katy and Raisa popped up. That was followed by cell phone video of a less-concealed-than-they'd-thought second round trip, picking up the whole family.

"Lanu Ojala, you are here as part of the request to help

manage Human distress and panic. The Drafter asked for someone who could expertly advise on any alien species we may encounter, and who could make Humans feel eased and soothed. Preferably one already familiar with Humans. Once the request was fulfilled and I came online, your names were coded in my registry seconds before you landed on the ship."

Paul and Katy sagged onto side-by-side loungers and stared at each other. Had he thought he would take command of this adventure? What a laugh! It was barely comprehensible, and once more, he hadn't been dragged here because he was mission-critical. He just happened to be a Human in the vicinity of someone the Drafter actually wanted. Absolute joke.

"I won't pilot for the Drafter." Yuhwa opted for direct and honest. "Not until they come forward. Why are they hiding after their request was granted? Do they want to pretend they didn't do it?"

"They should hide!" Paul exclaimed. "People up there are falling apart; it's going to be violence and riots next, if this Drafter of yours doesn't find a way to calm things down."

Lanu added softly, "I oversaw a safehouse with extensive anti-violence protocols. Anyone coming to the refuge knew that, and would behave accordingly. Managing people in this setting is entirely different. I don't know that I am what the Drafter would have requested, had they better understood."

"We have installed similar defenses on *Mahoroba*," Mandy enthused. "Should we deploy them?"

"No!" Katy sat up quickly.

"Agreed," Lanu said. "Attack drones and stun nets are never the first step, only a last resort. Are the Humans aware of what's happened to them? Or were they summoned as abruptly as we were and are unmoored?"

Mandy didn't answer right away. Eventually she admitted, "They were relocated as you all were."

"Were they co-located?" Paul asked.

"Your meaning is unclear."

"I mean," he growled, "did the 'request' put Swiss with Swiss and Kenyan with Kenyan? Or did it dump everyone together? Millions or billions of Humans who don't have aoiti and can't easily speak to one another? Plucked randomly and tossed into one of nearly thirty-five hundred places, lost in cities or villages they've never seen before?"

Yuhwa was horrified as his words sank in. Billions of Humans, barely given a whiff of a wider Aoni, had been taken from their lives and dropped into places they'd never been. She couldn't imagine the distress and terror they were feeling.

"Ohmygod," Katy cried. "How do we fix this? Where is the fucking Drafter? To trigger a disaster like this and bail is the lowest of lows!"

"The Drafter hears you, and says they agree. They are not, however, capable of assisting at this time. Yuhwa, perhaps you will reconsider your stance on flying and commence the *Mahoroba*'s first journey?"

"How does that follow, even in your warped logic patterning?" Yuhwa spat. "We need to return to our group outside, then we'll decide what to do."

The door wouldn't budge when they tried to exit, but after enough threats Mandy let them out. Yuhwa hadn't been kidding when she said she'd destroy the dao bed if they were locked in any longer. This kind of AI wasn't acceptable. The recognized species of the Calling had long reined in such overreach which was all too possible if systems weren't carefully controlled.

"You must return, though, and quickly. Please. We cannot

progress until we're in motion, giving Humans the sense they're heading for something."

"Where are we, anyway? Near Earth?" Katy asked. "Once I can hear Sundancer in my head I want to tell her where to come."

Sounding grim for the first time, Mandy said, "Alien intervention or assault is not desired. The ship has defenses. It was included in the Drafter's request."

"I *can't* with you," Katy groused and stomped out of the room.

"I almost want to see you try, lady," Paul scoffed. "Sundancer Orange would chew you up and spit you back out."

Lanu opted to stay behind in command. "There seem to be large gaps in what the Drafter and Mandy know. I'll try to fill in what I can, then rejoin everyone later."

Yuhwa gave them a smile, outsider-to-outsider. So strange to be the 'alien', when it was Humans that were most alien to them. She reassured herself the sixteenth Calling species would benefit from the rapid changes and challenges to their ways of thinking, and so would the fifteen original species. Over millions of tuigs, it was easy to assume the Aoni had been so long-settled there was nothing new left of note.

Humans were brash and incandescent, short lives burning brightly. They would be a shock to the established systems, and Yuhwa hoped that would be good. If Krylar cruelty and namu'ur flourished under the old ways, let new water flood the banks of rivers dammed up and grown stagnant.

Katy was mid-explanation when Yuhwa arrived poolside. As they all grasped the enormity of what had happened, what the ship was, Raisa panicked.

"My parents! Maman and Baba will be here somewhere. I have to go find them."

"Riri," Katy soothed, "they can come here, all right? Just find them and bring them back."

M13 offered to help locate them. "Not all Humans were transported. Only forty percent, per the Drafter's request."

Martin whistled. "How big is this bloody ship? That's nigh on three billion people!"

"Yes," M1616 intoned. "Three-point-three, roughly. Many Humans. That is why there are so many of *us*: we are to help, oversee, and 'have eyes on' your population."

"Anyone else freaked out by that?" Patrick asked.

Once the M-bots located Raisa's immediate family, Vasuda and Patrick volunteered to go with her. Everyone agreed traveling alone was a bad idea; Yuhwa pushed hardest for safety in numbers. She'd been on a station leaking air once; the problem was fixed quickly, but word still got out. The stampede of rattled people afraid they were about to suffocate had left her with a cracked rib and no wish to visit ever again. Beings who thought their lives were at stake made poor decisions. At least three Humans together could protect one another in an emergency.

"I'll get them and hurry back," Raisa said. "Then we can decide what to do. Katy, is Sundancer coming?"

"I don't know," Katy wailed. "I think I can feel something faint in our link, but I can't hear our Wataño in my mind. I haven't been without their presence since the shadow prison. It's freaking me out."

"Probably just need to get closer to her," Paul offered. "Once the Drafter shows their cowardly ass, Yuhwa can get us back to Centris."

She could? Yuhwa wasn't sure about that. But his instant faith was nice to hear.

Raisa, Vasuda and Patrick left for Bangkok region with a third bowling pin. This one was blue, and said they should call it M42.

"Why do they call things hemispheres versus regions, now?" Martin's questions were unending, but endearing.

"You couldn't ask when Patrick was still here to explain?"

Paul said. "He knew what kind of artsy thing it was patterned after. It looked like a bunch of balls on long, curved arms. Four of the same size, a fifth one at the end at least double the others."

"Spaced evenly," Yuhwa said. "Not clumped together."

"Right, evenly. I don't know how many arms. But the arms have a ring at the end opposite the bigger sized balls. Those rings are attached to a huge central ring."

Brianna asked, "Rings and spokes like Centris?"

"Not exactly; there wasn't a core like Centris has. Can't have one, actually, because the arms are rotating the whole time. Little rings spinning round and round the central ring; it makes the arms look they're folding through the center." He shook his head. "When it moves you think for sure everything will smack into everything else, but it was smooth and beautiful."

"Ah!" Martin smiled. "Kinetic, you mean?"

"That was it, Da!" Katy said. "Each ball has two cities back-to-back. We saw Melbourne on one side and Tallinn opposite, and those were called hemispheres."

Deb gave a confused head tilt. "So, there's a regular city and an upside down one?"

"I guess? But the central ring has *regions* of Earth's biggest cities, marching right around the inside, Rio and New York and the like."

"Directions don't exist the same way in space," Yuhwa clarified for Deb. "When you're in one of the locations, whether you think of it as 'top' or 'bottom' it will feel like you stand right-side up."

Katy added, "It's like one of those M.C. Escher drawings. Anything can go in any direction."

"That didn't help at all, Bug," Ian sighed.

Martin tried to dig in deeper. "My god, how large is this place if there are entire cities in half domes? Rotating rings around another ring? How did they solve friction issues? The seals required would be so advanced…" He trailed off, lost in his thoughts.

Yuhwa was drained. All the stressors of the sals leading to this had worn her down. "I vote we explore the rooms, pick ones for ourselves. With luck there will be a replicator or something like it." She smiled at Katy's father. "And I'm sure the M-bots would be thrilled to explain all the measurements of the ship."

M1616 zipped to her side. "Majio! That is the new word Mandy has given us for you. You will find the homes are much larger than single rooms. There are food kiosks in each dwelling."

For half a sal-ang they opened doors and admired, if grudgingly, what the Drafter had created. Each weathered door turned out to be a portal like the one in command. The bots assured them that, once selected, they would be keyed only to whoever lived in them. They were spacious, comfortable and, Katy explained, mimicked different kinds of Earth habitats.

"That last one we'd call ranch style, but this one has more of a tropical aesthetic. That's rattan furniture."

Yuhwa opted for what was behind a dark red door, a domicile Paul referred to as "NYC high-rise", a concept the aoiti were struggling to parse. She liked the sharp, clean lines and neutral tones. Other homes had revealed strange green lawns and flora, but this had a simulated cityscape visible from a deck.

Katy, tears in her eyes, picked the cavern-like unit. "It's how I imagined a house with Bay on Bankiri." Her arms wrapped her waist and she sniffled. "I miss him so much. Why do I keep being taken away from him?"

Her mother hugged her. "We'll have you back together in no time, ready for that wedding."

"I just want to hold him again. We can worry about weddings further down the road, Ma."

Katy's sorrow made Yuhwa antsy and angry. This Drafter

was a coward; they were responsible for distress and fear, yet took no leadership to show anyone they were safe. These were people they'd yanked off a planet without consent, by Nine! She left the Humans sorting out lodgings and dinner, and marched back to command, incensed anew.

She stopped next to Lanu who'd never left. "Tell the Drafter to come out now. They must face what they've done!"

"You said it," Paul agreed from behind her. How had he snuck in without her realizing? No matter, she was happy for the added support.

All three waited for an answer from Mandy who was, for an AI interface, more dramatic than the job demanded. "Regrettably the Drafter is indisposed," Mandy finally said. "They will come to you in time. They request that you pilot the ship in their absence."

"Where?" Yuhwa asked, exasperated. "To Centris? Somewhere else? What does the Drafter 'request' of a humble Jadoube pilot on a ship so massive it may not be possible to transit veşu?"

Paul's head snapped up. "What do you mean? They made it too big to fly?"

"It has to do with how we connect to all the living things when we swim," she replied. "I've never handled this many at once, it might be impossible to hold all the threads."

Mandy, voice as peppy as when they'd first arrived, said, "You won't know until you try. Shall we begin and see how it goes?"

Shaking her head, Yuhwa walked out.

16

THREE HOURS LATER SEVERAL THINGS HAD HAPPENED. Paul was happy about some, less happy about others.

First the bad — Vasuda and Patrick had returned without Raisa or her family.

"Flat out refused," Patrick said, shaking his head. "Her Da called all of us trouble, blamed Katy and Bay for what's happening, and said they wouldn't 'associate' with it."

Vasuda's sorrow was palpable. "Raisa felt she had to stay with them, but said she'll come back later."

Katy, determined, said, "I'll get her back here. She's too important to our crew to let her mean dad keep her away."

Second, Mandy had gone on an activity spree after her talks with Lanu. She'd renamed the conference room area with the dao bed a numig, since she knew that term now. Command center was the rest of the building, where she'd set hundreds of bots to repurposing the second floor into a factory that could manufacture travel sleds for the ship.

"There are trains on the arms, of course. But the Drafter laments they didn't think of speedier travel in and between the regions," was all she said.

Mandy had also crafted a sixteen-seat, family-style dining table in the empty front room of the command center, which was where they'd all gathered to relax and reset. Two large food kiosks – same function as replicators but slightly different look – were busy churning out meals of choice for their group. The kiosks had settings for every damn dish cooked on Earth, Paul thought.

Katy had drooled when her roast beef with potatoes, Yorkshire pudding and veg had come out. Everything drenched in brown gravy. "I've missed you summat terrible, Sunday roast," she cried in an overly-exaggerated Irish accent.

Da, drinking his beloved Kilkenny Irish Cream, bemoaned lost opportunity. "If we'd set up shop on the Wheel before we left, we'd have owned the market on bringing ale to the Aoni. We would have made a killing, lads. A killing!"

Paul assured a concerned Yuhwa it was a figure of speech and that none of the Phelans would be murdering anyone for beer. She showed interest in his Dungeness crab cakes. Paul's pants became uncomfortably tight when she purred at the bite he'd given her. Friend zone, he reminded himself. Don't look for nookie there, damn it.

They were done with mealtime, and had moved outside to the large patio. The simulation had shifted to full dark, a spray of stars overhead. Was it a real view to outside the ship, or simulated skies from home? He wasn't amateur astronomer enough to know.

Several cauldrons burned with smokeless flames around the rectangular pool, which was also subtly lit from beneath the water. He was sitting poolside with Yuhwa and Ma, when Mandy (via M13) announced they had a problem. "Humans outside this area will not understand Yuhwa or Lanu."

Fuuuuck. Paul hadn't even considered that, he was so used to having aoiti now. "Wait, how did Mandy, or any of you bots for that matter, understand."

"Part of the request!" the bot replied in a tone that implied *duh*. "A Human arkship capable of interstellar travel, has to be able to communicate."

"How can we get aoiti to your people quickly?" Yuhwa asked.

Lanu said, "I gave a sample to Mandy for analysis. She can make as much as needed, when the time is right."

"It's getting Humans to drink them that'll be the problem," Katy groused. She'd had just enough wine to make her pissy. "Stupid Humans argue about everything! No way they'll voluntarily do it, even if we promise it's safe."

"Free will, dearest, it's tricky," Vasuda mollified.

"What if we set up stations on every sphere? Or in the connecting corridors? That way those who are willing to do it can walk up, take a cup, and get it done?" Paul envisioned miles of tables, the kind they used at marathon sidelines, paper cups of aoiti-ade littering the surface. People could just grab and go.

Katy sing-songed, "Still won't get them all, beloved brother!"

"It's somewhere to start, at least," Oran huffed. "*You* ain't offering much in the way of helpful, are ya?"

Katy stuck out her tongue then downed the last of her wine.

"No need!" M13 enthused. "Mandy has replicated them and dispersed to all the food kiosks. Soon every Human will have ingested the aoiti."

Everyone gawped, incredulous.

Briana, voice firm, said, "Bad AI! You tell Mandy I said that. Bad! She cannot go around making decisions for people, even if she thinks it's best. The right to choose is fundamental, like Vasuda said."

Paul could have laughed if the topic weren't so serious. His Ma, treating the most advanced AI interface Humans had ever known, like a misbehaving puppy.

"Mandy thanks you for your input, Phelan matriarch. But she will remind you, part of her core programming states she must do everything in her power to help Humanity survive and thrive in the Universe."

Yuhwa, feet submerged like his, clenched her fists on her thighs. "This will not be well received by other species. Or at the Calling."

"The Calling?" Paul asked, incredulous. "A bunch of politicians who allowed namu'ur to go unpunished don't get to judge my species for the innocent mistakes of one person." He was just getting warmed up. "One who, for the record, was trying to help Humans. Even if the end result has been…challenging, the Drafter was trying to give them a sense of autonomy and power in the face of alien invasion!"

Yuhwa stiffened, Lanu regarded him quizzically, and Katy shouted, "You absolute doorknob!" She'd been sitting on a nearby bench and stood to loom over him. "'Alien invasion? As if they tried to take over, or abuse us! They're trying to *save the Aoni*, a place they've been in far longer than we have, you twit." She turned from him in disgust. "I can't believe you said something so bigoted."

Ian called from a different bench, "He's not wrong! We have to come together and put Humans first right now." That earned him dark looks.

"I'm sorry," Paul said. His eyes met Lanu's, his finger brushed Yuhwa's hand. "That came out badly. I only meant that your people have had hundreds of thousands of years to come to terms with multiple species, the rules and ideas of everything. Technology that seems like sci-fi to my species is ho-hum to you. They don't understand what's behind Mikanjo showing up on Earth, and they're afraid. I get what they're feeling, and at every turn we're confronted with more things we don't know. Ways we're failing to be smart enough, fast enough, hell," he paused, "I'd just take being helpful at all."

Yuhwa linked a finger with his for a second, before letting it go. "You are right, and I need to have more understanding.

There was a time the Jadoube didn't know about Drazoen and Centris."

"Don't doubt your usefulness, Paul," Lanu added. "The Uilig haven't always been the wise and peaceful hosts we're often assumed to be now." They gestured between themself and Yuhwa. "Our species aren't as young as Humans, but we weren't the first to advance, either. Learning takes time."

Da leaned forward from his seat on Ian's bench. "Have you stories?" he asked them. "From before you learned about other species and spaceships and the like? Our family loves a good yarn."

Yuhwa looked at Lanu, they shrugged at her as if to say *you first*.

"I'll tell you the story of the Five Côttru," Yuhwa said. "They're a backbone of our history, and partially explain the pâtexi." She smiled at Paul. "I know you've been wondering."

Everyone, even Deb, focused on her, eager for the tale.

"It's said that Malor captured seeds from the Aoni as it spun round and round, forming into our planet. It learned to mix the seeds with the right elements of itself to make life. Malor created Âuke, the great volcano, to protect the seeds, then disperse them far and wide. For a long time, all Malor did was create life and let it loose on its surface.

"One day, Sister Ha-Seng appeared, asking Malor 'where is your spark?'"

Paul saw a shape-shifting snow leopard, ferocious and beautiful. Piebald fur would be likewise black-and-white pattered hair in person-form, thick onyx claws in either shape.

"Malor told Sister Ha-Seng it needed no spark. But she refused to leave and curled up at the foot of Âuke. The next day Great Druk appeared, asked the same question, got the same response."

Great Druk was a dragon, maybe? Although less like Katy had described Sundancer's form and more like a gargoyle.

"He too, stayed and rested at the base of the mountain, opposite Sister Ha-Seng's side. The next day Migwa approached, creeping up on its long toes, silent and nearly invisible. Both sweet and ferocious, it asked after Malor's spark. Malor replied again it needed none, and Migwa took up its spot, separate from the others."

Okay, Jadoube had a Sasquatch, just like Washington State did. Very cool. Migwa wasn't created to blend in with a forest, though; it had tan, desert-camo fur.

"Fourth day, in flies Ji-Cheol Jarog."

Paul actually leaned back as the strangest being he'd ever seen flew through his mind. He had a person's head, shoulders and arms, plus black wings bigger than Mikanjo sprouting from his back. But he had the lower body and tail of a giant raven. He was sleek and powerful, but unsettling.

"Getting the same answer to his question, Ji-Cheol Jarog rested in a fourth spot near Âuke. On day five, Ni-Matak slowly trailed up and asked Malor the question they'd all asked: where is your spark?"

This last beast was what Paul imagined happened when a wooly mammoth fell in love with an American buffalo. No trunk, horns *and* tusks, shaggy as all get out, bigger than an elephant. It was lumbering and majestic.

Yuhwa's voice had warmed as she talked, and now it took on an exited air. "Upon getting the same rejection the others had, Ni-Matak pushed back and said Malor was denying them. All five of them. Now they rose up together and spoke to Malor: 'We are here'; 'We have come to you'; 'We are your hearts!'; '*We are your spark.*'"

She'd choked up at that last part, and he pressed his thigh against hers.

"Malor appreciated their gift, accepted them and named them: the Five Côttru, sacred and eternal. It then called upon them to help give birth to its last and most precious seed from the Aoni, the Jadoube. Although Malor, it is said, did not name us that. Songmaster Silver did."

"That's beautiful," Katy sniffled. "Sundancer called me her spark, too."

Paul smiled indulgently at his tipsy and emotional sister. Of all the Phelans, she was the most closely aligned with Da's romantic soul.

"Windweaver gave the Mikanjo wings and Songmaster created Jadoube." Katy lay back on the stone patio, gazing at the stars. "What a marvelous Aoni."

"Songmaster didn't create us," Yuhwa corrected. "Malor and the Five Côttru did."

Katy's head turned. "I thought you said he did."

"Named them, *a stór*." Da's voice was soft. "She said he gave them their name, but their planet and those lovely animals gave birth to them." He relaxed into the bench, stretching his arm to wrap around Ma beside him. "A charming story."

Paul thought the Jadoube had an origin story that was unmatched. Not that he knew everything there was to know about Earth's myths, but somehow the big movers and shakers in the stories he'd heard were very Human-like gods. Not a planet and kindly creatures who cooperated to bring forth life. It was nice.

"How DID your planet and the five beasties create your Jadoube spirit quest, then?" Patrick asked.

Yuhwa tried to sort through her confusing emotions. She'd been overcome telling the story of the Five Côttru, for no clear reason. It had been more nostalgic than she'd expected. "Our pâtexi," she said, "is a result of Songmaster's visit. Naming us, and gifting us waja."

"That's right!" Katy sat up fast. "Di-, I mean Sundancer. She said they'd seeded waja to Malor. It's what their claws are made of."

"Speaking of your dragon, any word?" Yuhwa wouldn't mind a Drazoen rescue soon.

Katy's head dropped, shaking negatively. Shoot.

Yuhwa resumed her story. "According to the nawa, Songmaster came and asked Malor if he could name our species, that it was a minor part of his gift. We were still young at the time, didn't know about the Aoni being so big."

"The nawa?" Paul asked. "The ones who will make you go back to Malor?"

"Right, they're the shamans of Malor, holy ones, and call us home when it's time for us to quest. The pâtexi is a way for us to seek our own personal waja, which was the major gift Malor allowed Songmaster to give us."

Oran grumbled, "And I guess the Law of First Approach doesn't apply to Their Holinesses."

"I don't think Windweaver asked Bankiri for permission to give her chosen people wings either," Katy mused.

Yuhwa waved a hand. "We aren't Songmaster's chosen people. The Lunari are. Our souls belong to Malor, but we thank Songmaster for the waja and name. That's our quest, ultimately: travel to the heart of Âuke for the waja that has formed only for us. We say there are as many paths to Âuke as there are Jadoube walking them. Just as the Five Côttru forged unique paths on their journey to become the sparks of Malor, we follow what our spirits tell us, to get to Malor's heart. Once there, the nature of our existence is made clear."

"That is beautiful," Vasuda sighed.

"It can be," Yuhwa demurred. "As for the Five, they are said to choose certain Jadoube and guide them to the right place."

Deb spoke dreamily. "I'd want that Sister Ha-Seng to pick me. She was intense and her look was on point."

Martin picked Migwa, Patrick and Brianna said "I call Ji-Cheol Jarog" at the same time. Ian liked the Great Druk. Katy and Vasuda were undecided.

Lanu smiled enigmatically. "I would not choose, but let them choose me." Yuhwa thought if anyone was going to get all Five on their side, it would be Lanu.

"And you?" she bumped her shoulder against Paul's.

"Ni-Matak. No question."

"Why?"

He shrugged. "That guy has *gravitas*. Slow and steady, but if he had to, you just know he could lay waste to his enemies."

Yuhwa admired the practicality, but smiled conspiratorially at Martin. "I've always liked Migwa best. She's gentle, but capable of astounding power. She's supposed to have created Wadi Abisah just by running around her plateau and waving her arms."

"Thank ya fer sharing yer stories wit us," Martin slurred his words more than usual, giving Yuhwa a momentary concern. Had the events of the last few sals compromised his health? But then he leaped to his feet and she put it down to that regional accent of his. "I'm fer bed, coming love?"

Brianna stood and slid an arm around his waist. All the rest left as well, except Katy, who was drowsy from drink but stubbornly trying to stay awake. Paul, promising to get the replicator to make them something called negronis, jogged back into the command building.

"We need to name this place," Yuhwa called to a droopy-eyed Katy.

"It's named," her friend said. "Innit? Command center or whatever."

"That's only the building," Yuhwa pointed behind them. "And the numig is inside the command center. But out here, where these trees and the pool and homes are, that's what needs a name. Tomorrow if I visit another part of the ship and return, I don't want to come back to a 'command center', I want to come back to everything that *isn't* Mandy's house."

Katy tried to twist and roll, but fell to her back again. "I get ya, I get ya. How 'bout.... Shee? In Irish folktales the fairy mounds are called Shee. A magical place outside of time. 'S where the wee folk lived."

"Shee." Yuhwa considered it. "Not bad. Simple, easy."

Paul returned with three drinks, but by the time he set Katy's beside her, she'd fallen asleep.

"My sister," he chuckled. "She's got the tolerance of a newborn colt." He handed Yuhwa her drink, then held his glass expectantly in the air.

Yuhwa stared at him, then her glass. Were these beverages not for consumption but display?

"Oh, okay, I guess that's a Human thing. We clink glasses and say 'cheers' or, if you're my family, 'sláinte'. Other places say 'salud' or 'skål' or 'cin cin'. It all means the same thing."

"What, exactly, does it mean?"

Paul's face screwed up in bewilderment. "Do you know, I'm not actually sure. 'Here's to you', I guess. I think a long time ago it was supposed to be a trust issue. That if you clinked glasses the drinks could mix and it proved you hadn't put poison in the other person's drink."

Yuhwa scoffed. "Why is everything so violent with your people?"

"Come on!" he laughed. "Your Aoni has way worse than us! Those Krylar pussbuckets destroyed an entire planet."

Yuhwa had to give him that one. "All right, let us clink then. We'll honor your ancestry," she leaned in. "But it's your Aoni, too, you know."

He matched her movement, halting so close to her she could feel his breath running down her neck. "Here's looking at you, kid," he rumbled, eyeing her mouth.

His words made no sense, and her aoiti did nothing to help

her. That may have been due to Paul's closeness; it was heady, as was his scent, and very distracting. There was an arid yet earthy masculinity to it. Musky but clean. Yuhwa was so busy focusing on his lips she was startled when he brought his glass up and took a drink. She copied him, brows raising when the sip hit her tastebuds. The negroni was delightful, particularly with a trace of Paul's natural fragrance curling past her tongue.

"Tell me why you got upset before."

She studied him, surprised he'd picked up on that.

He drank again. "At the end of story time, when everyone left, you had a sadness in your eyes."

"I think...." She trailed off. "One of the few great memories I have left of my mother is her telling me the stories. Jadoube are more like Lunari than Muškikal, we don't write down much. Different reasons, though. Memory, especially genetic memory, is prized in my people. It's considered critical in our maturation to memorize important stories and tales, to pass them on to new generations or people like your family."

He leaned in once more, hand briefly touching her thigh. "Then we all thank you for sharing with us. Sounds like that was one of those good sorrows; nostalgia that has a little sting but still reminds us of good things." At her nod, he continued. "Do you mind if I ask what happened? Back on the *Eternidad* you said you lost both parents?"

She was tempted not to share. This was deeply personal, a pain she'd held close for aiwaks. Despite the release she'd experienced on Allmother's upspoke, pain lingered. But like the cries she'd uttered there, she hoped putting words to the sorrow could drain some of it.

"Swords, like my papa, are meant to be neutral. They fight for the side that engages them, but they have no ties in most cases. It's ritualistic, not personal."

Paul clasped his hands between his knees. "There's no stake in the game, I get it."

"Yes. My father was a senior sword, often requested in the Truth Arenas. You saw some of how it works, although Budi's case was more charged than they typically are. Swords are engaged, they fight to first blood or forfeit, the matter is settled. Currency, power, righteousness, none of that figures into the battles. But some people," her voice cracked and she took a breath. "Some people won't let it go. That's what happened with Papa; a Chitan followed him home from Centris and shot him."

"I'm so sorry, Yuhwa."

She feigned a calm she didn't possess. "He didn't have a choice about leaving me. Mama did. But she loved him so much, far more than me.... It was a bad time. Tangun trained under Papa and they'd stayed close, even after he got promoted to Head over Papa. Tangun was nearly a family member by that point, so he came to get me when he heard Mama was dying. I know he tried to reason with her, but her heart was too broken to hear anything but her death wish calling her."

Paul took Yuhwa's hand, holding it gently. His palm was rougher than she expected, but soothing nonetheless.

"You shouldn't have had to deal with all of that." He squeezed her hand, letting her know with one gesture she'd been understood.

17

PAUL'S HEART BROKE HEARING YUHWA'S STORY. Mostly at how much the pain of a child threaded through those memories, poisoning her against future heart-threatening relationships. That her mother had loved her seemed certain, just as much as he was sure her mother had been depressed and unable to see a way out. Jadoube were a different species, but what she'd described sounded just like the kind of thing Humans endured. Grief is brutal; some people were capable of slow and steady healing. Some were not.

"I decided that I would never be like that," Yuhwa's quiet voice slipped away over the pool.

"No attachments," Paul said, not even framing it as a question.

"Not for romance," she corrected. "I'm tied to the Mikanjo on the *Eternidad*. I adore your sister and Raisa. I lived with Tangun and love him, even when he annoys me with his conviction I'll become a sword."

Paul released Yuhwa and put his hands behind him, staring at the stars overhead. "I don't get that. The waja is made for you alone, and forms into a clue of what you're meant to be? Does waja grow from seeds, or run in rivers, or what? Songmaster gifted your people with it, but you don't think he's your Drazoen, even though he freaking named you?"

"All the waja is buried deep inside Malor, who holds it for us. When we are born, the waja meant for us begins to rise to the surface. When it breaks through, the nawa sense it and call us to pâtexi."

"How the hell do these nawa know it's *your* waja?" Paul thought it sounded too much like magic to be real.

Yuhwa made a frustrated noise. "How to explain føns of Jadoube evolution to you quickly?"

Føns *fawns; eons in English.*

"Go slow," he said, insulted. "I'm not completely stupid, I'm sure I'll catch on eventually."

She took a long look at him, shook her head and made a clicking noise with her tongue. Almost but not quite a *tsk tsk.* "Petulant, that's what you are. Fine, here it is. What I told you before about storytelling, that we think it's part of our genetics? That's because the waja that bonds to our flesh keeps the tales. What you've been calling tattoos are actually the way all Jadoube memory is recorded."

Paul's head jerked, and he sat up. "What the shtŭ?!"

Yuhwa's mouth formed a satisfied smirk. "Songmaster and the Drazoen put the waja on Malor. It knows our planet inside out, and through Malor it connects with every Jadoube born. Some of it singles out a new Jadoube, bonding at a primal level. We find our waja when it's time, we return to the Binding Bath with it and it becomes part of us. The waja remembers every-thing, even the parts of us before we bonded. At the end of our lives, our bodies are taken to the Spirit Bath and the waja is released into a communal pool. Only the nawa enter the Spirit Bath before death, and we're told they have access to every Jadoube's memories and experiences by submerging in the pool."

Paul stared at her. "Spirit Bath?"

"Spirit Bath," she echoed. "Much like this one," she nodded at the pool before them. Rising to her feet and unzipping her bodysuit granted her Paul's undivided attention. "This one, though, I'm allowed to swim in."

As she shimmied out of her bodysuit revealing a bikini underneath, Paul took stock. Was he on board to have a little fun with Yuhwa? Indubitably. Could he respect her one-time-only rule? Probably. He'd never been a casual lover, but he thought he could try to obey Yuhwa's demand when it meant he could get his hands on her body. God knew his body wanted inside hers, even just for a night, his blood beating like a drum in his veins.

"Swimming," he said, distracted by the sight of her barely covered butt, "is very important."

Yuhwa dropped over the side and into the pool. He watched her make a slow, lazy circle, then dive below the surface. Her body in the water was a work of art. If Paul had to pick, he'd confess to being a thigh man, and hers were gorgeous. Long for her height, flexing as she dove for the pool bottom, tracing the tile designs. Her skin was pale, but not the milky white of his Irish heritage. There was a warmer undertone to hers, and not a blemish he could see. She had incredible muscle tone, either from regular swimming and workouts or from the flex-fest of surfing her dao during transit. All of the above, perhaps.

He was debating stripping to his underwear and joining her when she arrowed to the spot between his dangling feet. One hand grasped the side of the pool bracketed by his legs, inches from his crotch, and his pants stretched uncomfortably in a half second. This woman had his body by the short and curlies, no doubt about it.

"Before, you questioned why we don't worship Songmaster, even though we are Jadoube because he named us so. Shall I tell you why?" Her free hand came up to her throat, caressing her own skin, trailing down her cleavage.

"Yes," Paul breathed, enthralled.

"We," she whispered, "are Jadoube. It means we shift." Yuhwa's free hand dropped from her chest to his knee, slowly dragging up, over his thigh, heading for the promised land. "We adjust." She cupped him, no hesitation or nerves. Pure confident woman testing the waters of desire.

When he didn't object, she put her other hand on his leg to steady herself while she rubbed him once. Twice.

"Songmaster named us, but only provided the word to describe what we already were. Just like the waja reveals what was already inside us. To be Jadoube is to bend," her wrist twisted, rubbing in a new way. "To alter."

Suddenly a very wet, limber, beautiful woman lay over him. Yuhwa had launched from the pool to settle directly on top of him, their bodies aligned in excellent places. Paul was dizzy with want, willing to follow where she led this time.

"We adapt. That is who we are, what Songmaster recognized. He didn't make us, he didn't pick us. Malor never needed a name for us, we were its last and favorite creation. Malor accepted from the first what we were, a truth it didn't need to label. Tell me," she said, and lowered her head until their lips brushed. "Can you do that? Accept this for what it is?"

Paul's hips rocked against the cradle of hers. He was achingly hard, craving a joining with her in the worst way. "Everything ends in the morning."

Yuhwa's gaze drilled into his, seeking proof of his honestly; his genuine acceptance. Finding it, she ground back down against him. "There are many sal-angs until morning." With that she finally kissed him.

Jesus, Mary and Joseph. It was like she'd handed him a lemonade on a broiling summer day. Her tongue was cool, her faint scent of peppermint and honeydew exciting. Lucious with just a tiny bite to it.

Paul's palms drifted down Yuhwa's still dripping body, slicking his way down her back to her ass and finally her thighs. Caressing them as they continued to kiss, he got a grip and pulled them higher. Her lower body notched against his like a dream, and the increased contact ramped up the kiss. Yuhwa's tongue dueled with his like an eel; her style was more aggressive than Brittany's had been and Paul loved it. Every small noise he won from Yuhwa felt like a victory.

Her hands drove into his hair, clenching the strands as she writhed on top of him, making him ache to just unzip and plunge inside. Before he could get too far down that path, though, Katy snorted from behind them. Christ! He was getting it on ten feet from his baby sister. There couldn't be any bigger sign of how much he wanted Yuhwa than that.

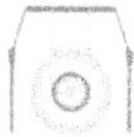

SHE RETURNED to herself a bit when Paul pulled back. Yuhwa had been completely lost in what they'd been doing, her core throbbing with the need to surround Paul and show him what the dao had taught her about moving. "Take me to your room," she commanded in a low voice, desperate to get back to it.

"Shh," he whispered, pointing back at Katy. "We will never hear the end of it if she wakes up and sees us together."

Rolling to his side, Yuhwa reached for her bodysuit and stood. "Which one of these did you pick again? Green door down there?" she pointed to the right. She was inordinately pleased to see the bulge in his pants when he stood up. She also liked he didn't bother trying to hide it.

"Yeah." His voice was gritty, hair tousled.

"I'll follow you," she said, stepping back. Yuhwa wanted the chance to look her fill at Paul Phelan. He was taller than she usually sought in a partner. Taller than anyone else in their group, really, except Lanu. His silky hair teased her with memories of how she'd idolized Ji-Cheol Jarog as a child. Paul's was raven-wing black, too, with a similar shine, contrasting against skin the color of rapids on Nay River as they crashed against the high walls of Wadi Tak. She craved the chance to stroke every bit of it, test the sensitivity of her fingertips and his flesh. Which of them would feel the faintest touch more?

He brought out a competitive streak she'd not felt in other sexual encounters, one she wanted to explore. They were both creatures of control, she'd come to realize. They each wanted to plan for desired outcomes, maneuver situations to their advantage so they could ensure success. What would happen when their ultimate goal was the same, but they had different routes to achieving it? She was excited to find out.

They made it to his door, only hearing Katy snort once as they crept away. Paul had muttered something about how "pissed" Katy would be waking up on the pool deck. Yuhwa had finally worked out the English word covered both anger and alcoholic stupor.

Following close on Paul's heels into his quarters, she couldn't classify which Human style he'd picked out, and didn't care to ask. They had business just then, and it wasn't anything to do with interior decorating. Jumping on his back, wrapping her arms and legs around him like a baby rufucebus, she bit his ear and said, "Let's shtǔ."

Paul grabbed her left thigh and pulled her until they were face to face. He'd kept her on his hips the whole time, which was both impressive and maddening. The friction as she'd been dragged around his body was delicious, but insufficient to do more than amp up her desire.

"Sounds like you want something, majio." He darted in to lick her lips and nuzzle along her jawline.

Tilting her head back to give him access, Yuhwa reveled in his strength. "I want it, and if you don't get to work, I'll take it myself."

Suddenly she was pressed against a wall, Paul's aggressive response to her challenge getting her where she wanted to be. His arms bracketed her head, his hips held her pinned to the wall, his nose sliding along her cheek. When he started a slow grind against her, she choked out an encouraging sound.

"No self-service here," Paul said. "Not this time, anyway. Two questions," he gasped, switching to a rocking motion.

"Yes, you may worship me. And I prefer," she panted when he hit the perfect spot, "being on top."

He groaned at her words. "I've been thinking about that ever since I watched you fly back on the *Eternidad.*"

Yuhwa thrilled to hear he'd been feeling this attraction as long as she had. Getting it out of their system now was the right way to handle it. They'd have a sensual and enjoyable night, and in the morning they would move on with all tension released.

But her pressure was still building at the moment. His ex had been a fool to give up someone who focused like Paul did; in the short time they'd been intimate he'd learned her body well enough to drive her up the slope and keep her on the edge of ultimate pleasure. She wanted him. Now.

"Bed?" she asked. "Or here?"

"Everywhere," he said, diving in for another kiss before pulling back. Meeting her eyes he asked, "One: is this really what you want? And two: what passes for protection in the Aoni?"

Yuhwa focused. "I want this. Tonight, as we agreed, I want to wring pleasure from you on a level you can hardly bear. We'll each cry to the gods, but not for mercy."

Paul shuddered, his hips reflexively jerking hard against her.

"Protection in the Aoni is handled by aoiti, so I manage whether anything can happen to me from our union. Each person sets their own levels, but going forward it's good you ask. Other partners might try to deceive you, and until you can manipulate your aoiti enough to control your own fertility, you need to be careful. They will handle eliminating most bacteria and viruses, even this soon. If you'd prefer, though, we can use an external sheath."

She regretted mentioning how he should handle future partners; his eyes had dimmed and a small frown formed. Was she making a mistake with this? He'd seemed fully accepting of the ground rules, but now she doubted.

"We'll use something extra," he said softly, leaning in for a slower kiss. "Where I'm from, being bare with a partner implies a level of intimacy neither of us wants." He let her legs slide down his, still kissing her, building back up to the intensity of before.

She'd worried for naught. Paul was willing to swim this current with her, and she threw herself back into the heated touches. The more they caressed and kissed, the more she wanted. As his clothes came off and she slid down to examine the most vulnerable part of him, she was surprised at how his natural scent had intensified and concentrated there. It was mouthwatering enough for her to try and take a taste, but he yanked her back to her feet.

"Not strong enough to withstand that yet. Want you too much already."

She resolved to get back there before their time was up. He grabbed her hand and pulled her to the bedroom. They landed on the overly soft bed, Yuhwa on top as she planned. There was very little she enjoyed as much as conducting the tempo and enjoying the view from above as she did it.

Paul had gotten protection from the kiosk, and once he donned it they came together in a torturously glacial slide. Her plan was to torment him a little, but he had a similar plan which left them frustrating themselves in the most glorious way. Slowing, teasing, building, touching and tasting. It was more exciting than anything had been in a very long time, better than swimming a veşu. Yuhwa allowed herself to revel when he broke first, shouting her name as she ran her hands up his arching chest to pinch his nipples.

His eyes flared, he grabbed her hips and slammed into her twice. The unexpected force of it, along with his hoarse *come now, Yuhwa, now!* pushed her into the maelstrom. Blissed out and boneless, she slid to his side, curling up for a quick nap before she'd demand a repeat performance. That was too incredible not to experience again.

PAUL WOKE ONCE, early. He'd thought his internal clock was completely broken for the most part; going from Earth to *Eternidad*, then to Centris and on to *Mahoroba* had destroyed any concrete sense of time. But some part of him had subconsciously acclimated to this ship's rhythms, as if his circadian cycle had reset and said it was morning. Yuhwa still slept beside him, her lower leg stretched across his ankle, her head tucked into his armpit. He smiled; she looked like she wanted to burrow into his side.

The warm feeling faded as he considered that was probably the last thing she wanted. His optimism from last night, about being a good-time-Charlie completely on board with a fling, had faded over their hours together. Every time she'd reached for him, driven him mad with her strokes and licks, pushed him to go faster-slower-more, called his name in a voice raspy-raw from the force of their pleasure, he'd wanted more. Even in the very midst of sharing such hedonistic sensuality, he knew he was headed for trouble.

Paul might have been Yuhwa's booty call, but she was something more to him. His heart felt like a rambunctious kitten, one that had been swatted by irritated parents but couldn't help trying to play again. Yuhwa made him happy, simple as that, and he wanted to stay close to her. To do that, he'd need to keep his emotions locked down tight, because she would bail if she thought he'd caught feelings.

Closing his eyes, Paul mentally walked through his old still rings routine, something he'd planned to qualify for the Olympics with. Only the most advanced boys in his classes were permitted to try it out. They needed absolute focus to even attempt it, and a honed musculature to support their bodies as they swung from kips to handstands, rotated through double saltos into crosses and Russian levers, and hovered in a planche where they stared straight down at the mats, praying their arms kept them horizontal and steady. Visualizing every move slowed his mind, and soothed muscles aching from the only physical act he enjoyed more than gymnastics.

He was fine, this would all be fine. He could be a cool friend, no problem. A friend who'd heard Yuhwa moan so decadently the richest chocolate in the world would be jealous, but yeah, totally casual. Instead of Friend of Sister, Paul transitioned to Friend with Benefits. FOS to FWB. Previous FWB, not to be repeated, regardless of how well they'd connected.

Excellent, he thought as he drifted back into dreamland. *I've got this under control.*

18

Yuhwa's eyes shot wide, yanked from sleep by a sharp tug from what felt like rope wrapped around her soul. The only time she'd felt anything similar was in the deepest part of a veṣu. The dao told them all of the Aoni was equidistant from that sacred spot. It whispered of the myriad galaxies they could access with the minutest shift in one direction or another. Movement in their quantum makeup, just a quark or atom, would take them where they needed to go.

Right now, that feeling was flooding her body, and the dao was insisting they leave. *HOME* it shouted at her. No. Nononono. This couldn't be happening.

Rolling away from Paul's body, she indulged in a long, last look at his beauty. He was a feast for her eyes, broad chest lifting with each breath. The memories of his lips, hands, warm skin, taste, and how he'd matched every demand of hers with one of his own were allowed to wash through her a final time. Then she tucked them away inside, and carefully slipped out of his bed.

Her anger mounted. First the Drazoen-nûzed Drafter yanked her onto this ship without consent, now the nawa called her without the slightest warning? Shtŭ them all! Yuhwa wouldn't dance to anyone's tune but her own.

The tug that had woken her from sleep twisted sharply. *HOME*. Yuhwa realized the nawa weren't going to respect her desires to avoid Malor and her pâtexi. At least they could give her enough time to replicate the Human pancakes Katy swore she must try.

Lanu was already in the numig when she entered. They eyed her plate with interest. "I'll trade you a bite if you managed to get anything useful out of Mandy."

Their mouth quirked just as Mandy's voice filled the room. "Majio, at last. The Drafter urges me to once again request your talents so we can 'get this boat moving.' Direct quote."

"You can tell the Drafter we'll discuss my fees for piloting when they drag their pathetic self out here to explain."

Lanu shook their head. "I don't think that will work."

Mandy agreed. "The Drafter will not join you today, or in the immediate future. They are indisposed." The AI was far less cheerful today than the sal before. "Now drive."

"I will not." Yuhwa was working her way to furious. They thought they could strip her choices, her personal authority, by trapping her in corners of duty or a sense of fair play? They'd soon learn otherwise.

"You must. We require solar winds to power the ship, and calculations show we will drift outside optimal range in this part of the galaxy after the next wave." Mandy slowed her words. "We will be stuck. Without a pilot we'll be stranded in this part of the galaxy, waiting for more solar winds not projected to arrive for three hundred years."

Yuhwa wasn't budging. "You fly, then."

"I cannot, or I would have already. My programming specifically forbids me from taking control of the ship."

"Mandy *is* limited," Lanu hedged. "I've been running through the parameters of the Drafter's 'request' which are detailed and explicit. Overwhelmingly so. What I've seen indicates the Drafter feared AI takeover and destruction of Humanity on board, so they put a series of restrictions in place. One of the first is Mandy's inability to take command under any circumstance."

Damn the Drafter. They erred by creating AI as expansive as Mandy, then fail to give her the rudimentary ability to steer the ship in emergencies. "Fine. I will consider piloting. Ask the Drafter what they will offer as compensation for my time and effort." She regarded the dao bed. "My fee goes up every kaala I have to look at that horrible dao bed, by the way."

"The Drafter," intoned Mandy, "will provide room and board. Obviously. They will have us rebuild the bed to your specifications, and mention since they had no idea what a dao bed was, they did their best. Your salary can be paid in Earth gems, precious metals, or something else you may prefer."

Lanu looked to Yuhwa. "What would be worth the trip to Centris, majio?" Though they hid it, she knew they were laughing inside.

"Damn you to the ass of Âuke!" Yuhwa's righteous fury gave way to weary acceptance. The pull from the nawa chewed at her spirit, chanting *HOME HOME HOME* relentlessly. "We won't be going to Centris, though. I'll get us to Malor, and from there you can engage a new majio to take over long-term." With any luck the Three Ekletu would hop on board and screw up the Drafter's meticulous plans.

"You've been called?" Lanu queried softly.

Yuhwa nodded, walking to the dao bed with slumped shoulders and a heavy heart. If this might be the last time she swam the dao and transited a veṣu, it was going to be in the finest bed she'd ever had. "Mandy, take notes."

WAKING ALONE WASN'T A SURPRISE, but depressed Paul nonetheless. He'd hoped.... Well. That was the problem in a nutshell, wasn't it? No hoping, for fuck's sake. He needed to be devastatingly cool, untouchable, like Steve McQueen. Ooh, or Denzel.

When he got to the breakfast table he thought he had his emotions locked down. Physical interaction like they'd shared released a shit-ton of hormones. That's all this was. Not to mention, she was his first after the breakup, and wasn't there something about not falling for rebounds?

Lanu, taking a seat across from him, studied his face. "Did you have trouble sleeping?"

Paul almost choked on his drink. "What, how, I mean, why would you think that?"

They wore a chartreuse caftan today, lending extra intensity to the splashes of color around their eyes. "You hold that cup of nropita like you'll fall down if you let go."

"I wish it were nropita instead of French roast. It was a long night," Paul admitted.

"Hey, bro, we're going to see some of the ship." Patrick called from the pool outside. "We want to offer help if we can."

"And get the lay of the land," Katy added. She didn't look even slightly hungover, which seemed unfair. "M1616 showed a map and each arm is supposedly sixty-three miles long! I need to see with my own eyes."

"I'm good here for now," he responded, relieved the whole family was leaving. He wasn't ashamed and had nothing to hide, but he wasn't up for an inquisition by someone who cottoned to his emotional state and started digging. "Maybe I'll come out later, message me where you're at."

After waving everyone off, Paul asked Lanu if they'd seen Yuhwa.

"She's having the dao bed renovated to meet her needs before we head to Malor."

"Why the hell would we go to Malor?" Paul said, perplexed. "We're supposed to go back to the Wheel, to Sundancer and that whole mess." He snorted. "A different mess than *this* ship's mess, which is a different mess from God-only-knows-what is happening back on Earth."

"She's been called home by the nawa. I think it had recently been revealed to her," Lanu offered. Paul must not have hidden his hurt that she hadn't told him something so important. "I'm sure she meant to share once the bargain was struck with the Drafter. You two seem close."

"Apparently not," Paul sulked.

Lanu turned their chair sideways and stretched out their long legs. "Unless you ask for your desired outcome, you're unlikely to prevail." They chuckled. "Not that my opinion or advice was requested. Apologies if I am over-familiar."

Paul shook his head. "No, you're right. But in this case, asking for what I want will ensure I don't get it. She can't be 'the one', she'll never accept that. Or me. We agreed no complications, and I need to just forget it happened. If I could erase the feelings, that would be super handy, too."

"Oh, I disagree," Lanu murmured. Their eyes closed, head dropping back. "Long ago, before I went to Earth, I cared for someone. They cared for me in return, but we never spoke the words aloud. One day I realized I cared for another. Not instead, but equally. I felt torn, sure that both could be the one, as you say, but also sure that sharing would be rejected outright."

"Did you tell them?"

Lanu made a sad noise. "Rather than speak openly and honestly, giving them the chance to weigh and consider, I fled. First to Centris, then to Earth. I escaped so very far away, yet I still think about both of them more than I should, a milenyo later." They rolled their head, chalk-colored hair floating around their face, then skewered Paul with their eerie white eyes. "What if I'd been less cowardly?"

How old was Lanu? Crap, these long-lived people were going to give him a complex. Katy was right, Humans had definitely been shafted in the longevity department.

"But what if you're where you needed to be?"

They tilted their head. "I don't follow."

"Seems to me we're living in a Universe of destiny. All these prophecies and the like, you know? As if it took a hundred thousand years to move things into place, and now all the important people are rising up, like the cream of the crop. My sister needed to be born when she was, where she was, to the family she was, in order to become the herald. Bay was the same, or he'd never have gotten to Earth to find the magic stone for Sundancer. If you hadn't done what you did, you wouldn't have been at the refuge, and maybe Yfaun would have said screw it and killed Katy."

Lanu grinned, sitting straight. "That is more fanciful than I would have expected from you. Perhaps under the sensible, problem-solver's skin a mystic waits to be born."

Paul flushed. "It's just," he hesitated. Was he going to share this out loud? Yes, yes he was, because he had to hear if his thoughts were crazy or not. "It seemed ridiculous before, back on Earth. Then we flew through space and met all these big players in the Aoni. Hell, we spent time with a dragon! Now I can't help but think that maybe my family is meant to take charge, when it comes to heralds. There *are* nine of us and our species is so new. Maybe the prophecies, triggers and whatnot, were all waiting on us getting smart enough to handle aliens and sci-fi tech?"

Lanu didn't laugh outright. They took several moments to consider what he'd said. "I can't claim authority when it comes to the Drazoen and all the tales surrounding their return. Nor can I dispute what you're thinking, not with pure logic. But I'd like to think my life has more meaning than assistant to your family legacy." They smiled to blunt the sharp truth of their words. "If you are correct, though, I tremble inside to think every Drazoen herald is on this ship as we speak."

Yuhwa interrupted them, stomping her way to the kiosk. Giving Paul an encouraging look, Lanu excused themself to return to the numig. They wanted to ensure the travel sleds Mandy's bots had been making were correct. If they weren't, Lanu said, people could be hurt.

"There's been enough of that already."

Yuhwa eyed Paul over her mug of coffee. Was she hoping he'd ask for more of what they'd had the night before? Or did she dread him trying to get around her one night rule, like Xanthos and countless others before had attempted? Paul was split in half about it: he didn't want to be a man foresworn. He'd given his word he could handle her limits; did that take precedence over his feelings this morning? What Lanu shared resonated, too. Honesty had power, and deserved a chance. But he'd promised…. Everything ran in circles in his mind.

"It happened," she whispered, eyes shuttered. "The nawa, they're pulling at me. Demanding I return for pâtexi."

"I heard," he replied solemnly. Laying his hand across the table, palm up, he offered wordless comfort. "I'm here if you need me." Friends did that, right? Paul was so mixed up about what signaled what between them now. The last thing he wanted to do was make her uncomfortable, or lose her entirely by overstepping.

She slid her palm over his and her lips curved ever so slightly. "I appreciate it. But," she gusted on a forceful breath, "it means we're heading for Malor instead of Centris. I know Katy wants to get back to the Wheel, but this call," she grimaced. "It aches and burns inside. I never knew it would be so nŭz demanding."

Nŭz *noozh; shared Aoni profanity; so old no literal meaning is known; English equivalent damn.*

Nice. Yuhwa always gave him good toothpaste words. The sadness in her voice reoriented his thoughts.

"Fighting this, I never had a chance. It's like they've wrapped their hands around my organs and keep squeezing."

Paul hated that, knowing it would push all of Yuhwa's buttons. As far as he was concerned, no one should be trying to tell her what to do and when. He could only imagine how badly Humans would react to hearing their path in life was set in motion by magic people who bathed in metal sloughed off of dead ancestors.

"Whatever you need, me and the rest of us, we're here." He debated, then went for it. "You're pretty much family, if we haven't made that clear. I regret to say that means you're stuck with Hurling Days, *way* over the top holiday celebrations, and refereeing Oran and Katy. Heads up, he's a biter. But on the plus side every one of the Phelans will fight to the death for you."

Yuhwa blinked rapidly, her lips trembling. Damn it, he was going to go for it, tell her how he felt. Let her know how completely he wanted to support and comfort her.

"We are under attack!" Mandy's voice blared out from speakers hidden Jesus knew where.

Paul swore. "Why is there never a goddamn break?!"

19

YUHWA SNATCHED HER HAND BACK FROM PAUL, AWARE she'd just dodged what threatened to be a huge emotional moment. His countenance was softer and more eager than a friend's should be. What was worse, Yuhwa might have given in just then. She was scared and needy, her fears about the future weakening her resolve where Paul was concerned. His offer of familial belonging had swamped her for a kaala. She couldn't say she was thankful for an emergency interruption, but she wasn't exactly angry it happened.

"What do you mean attack?" Yuhwa demanded, jumping to her feet. She ran for the numig, Paul at her heels.

"A huge ship, along with an unknown accompanying alien presence appeared in our space without warning!" Mandy's voice was excited and affronted at the same time.

Yuhwa flew into the room, confronted with a Lanu calmer than she expected. Looking at the screens surrounding them she immediately understood.

"Sundancer? That's her, right?" Paul's voice was awe-filled and reverent. "Bug did not exaggerate how fecking impressive she is. She's the size of the biggest planes we have. Bigger, maybe."

The *Eternidad* and Sundancer Orange in full Drazoen glory, side-by-side, here to save the day. Sundancer's nine tails whipped around her body, the only outward sign of her agitation. Yuhwa was so, so relieved to see them. Even if she couldn't go back with them, her family would be safe now.

Heartnote, we are here. We've come for you. Release my herald!

"Oh Christ," Paul hissed. "If she's broadcasting to everyone it's going to be a nightmare up there. We have to find my family before there are riots and fights!"

"The Phelans are in the large biosphere of arm twenty-nine," Mandy said. "Mount Kilimanjaro hemisphere."

"There are whole mountains here?" Paul's voice was incredulous. "Who the shtŭ is the Drafter and how did they make this happen?"

What entity dared to kidnap those under my protection?

Mandy ignored Paul's shout and Sundancer's snarled question. "I have directed a large travel sled to meet you at the portal back into the main ship. Lanu assured me it is built correctly, and I believe avoiding the trains best." She paused. "Confirmed. Stampeding Humans are overloading limits and soon the trains will stop running."

"Let's go," Yuhwa said, impatient to leave Shee and get to the Phelans. Paul was correct and Mandy corroborated: Humans were in a full panic about yet another unknown situation, one more unpleasant surprise. It would only get worse from here on out.

Lanu stayed put. "I will try to broadcast a message of calm to the ship, explaining what's happening. To the best of my ability," they demurred.

Yuhwa and Paul ran for the promised sled. It was big enough to hold all the Phelans and the four M-bots already aboard.

"We are to guide and guard," M42 said proudly. "Mandy anticipates we may need to incapacitate Humans who attack you, or try to steal this conveyance."

"Whoa, whoa, whoa," Paul said. Leaping onto the sled deck, he approached M42. "No attacking Humans. Isn't that supposed to be rule one of robots?" He looked to Yuhwa who'd boarded and was mapping their path. "That's a law or something, right?"

"Typically," she muttered. Damn this huge ship, getting to the Phelans was going to take as long as going from one end of Centris to the other. "But I can't speak for what the stupid Drafter requested." She got them moving as fast as she judged safe.

One of the other bots clarified, "Not attack. Incapacitate." A cylindrical arm slid from a spot that opened on its surface. Electricity arced from the end of the arm. "Stun only."

"Is that a cattle prod?" Paul's voice would hail birds in the sky, it was so high-pitched.

The start of their trip was filled with Paul and the bots arguing about what constituted excessive force. Right up until several large Humans tried to grab the sled. They nearly managed to topple one of the bots off the side, and if Paul hadn't kicked the closest man in the shoulder they might have succeeded.

"Does this go any faster?" he shouted, smacking at grasping hands and one woman who leaped onto the edge rail.

You refuse to answer? We will board and take my Humans back!

Yuhwa grimaced. It was worse out here than she'd expected, and Sundancer wasn't helping. At some point Lanu's voice came over the sound system. Unfortunately, Lanu's assurances were falling on ears incapable of hearing reason. When their face appeared on multiple screens in a connecting corridor, she heard screams.

For many it was the first time their aoiti were kicking in.

And that's if they'd even received them in the underhanded way Mandy had concocted. Lanu looked alien to them, they were hearing voices in and outside of their heads, and the last shreds of their reality had floated out of their grasp.

"We're going to be exterminated!" she heard. From another spot came, "First they dropped us here, took our homes and families, now they come to make us their food." She was most fascinated by a group of women who didn't run at all, hollering, "If they want wives, we're here for them!"

"Paul, sit your ass down, we're going high." Yuhwa knew their only chance was to get above the heads of Humans. Just in time, because Yuhwa heard fights, cries of children, roars and screams from injured and terrified people.

Paul had dropped to the floor while she figured out how to ascend. "Go!" He slapped the hard surface under him repeatedly. "Go, Yuhwa! My family isn't prepared for this!"

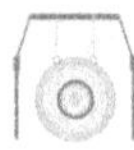

TOO SLOW, this sled was too damn slow! Paul knew Yuhwa was doing her best, and now that they'd climbed, she could open the throttle and let this thing fly. Even from the floor of the sled he heard shrieks of fear and wonder from Humans below watching them speed past.

Sundancer's challenge to the Drafter, heard by all, Lanu's alien looks, it was too much for people. "Thankfully the place my family picked is less populated," he called to Yuhwa.

"There are billions of you on this ship," she replied, keeping her gaze focused forward. They'd already zoomed from command through the dense, urban central ring. Now she slowed, consulted the sled's maps, and made a sharp right into a smaller, greenbelt ring. "Why would that biosphere be less full?"

Paul stood up. He'd never understand why fear transmogrified to violence, but it so often did he believed Humans were just coded that way. Below them were multiple examples of battling people, while others sheltered children or the slower of their groups. Many simply stood in place, crying out to the heavens.

"Paul?" Yuhwa prodded. They were nearing the left side of the belt, where the portal to a connecting corridor yawned open.

"Got distracted for a sec." He moved up to where she stood. "The mountain they went to see is in Tanzania back on Earth. Original flavor Earth, I'm calling it." He'd have laughed at his own joke if he weren't so tense. "That area isn't very dense, not like the cities we just escaped back there."

"M42," Yuhwa barked. "Are the Phelans still in the same biosphere or have they moved?"

The bot produced a few whirs and beeps. "They left the mountain and our bots have not yet located them visually."

Paul got in the bot's space. He couldn't be sure he was facing the damn thing because, well, how did you find the face of a bowling pin? He picked a part he could get close to and demand, "You fucking find them! In case Mandy doesn't understand what's happening, that dragon out there will *destroy* this ship if anything happens to my sister. I will destroy this ship if anything happens to the rest of them!"

"Well said," Yuhwa murmured. "Now come check the specs on these corridors. I think they're narrower than the rings but can't read the words."

Paul stalked back to the console, giving M42 one last stern look over his shoulder. A quick consultation and he said, "They're supposed to be a mile in diameter, two miles long"

Yuhwa paused, waiting for the aoiti to convert. "Three khai. Even dividing the corridor in half leaves more than enough space to stay overhead." She paused once more, then asked, "Why am I also getting something called a kilometer?"

"Humans have a few measurement systems. Metric, imperial, I think China even has their own. And that's before you get into scientific ones." Paul waved a hand.

"Humans," Yuhwa said, "may struggle with assimilation in a few areas."

"The idea of assimilation will be the first place they struggle," Paul replied. "How much longer? Jesus this ship is almost bigger than Centris!"

"Bigger. Centris wasn't intended for so many." She looked at the console. "I estimate three kaalas if I use top speed. Risky given it's a first flight of untested tech, but I'll do it."

Paul's rational side fought the protective need to save his family. "One notch below top, then. No sense tempting the gods."

With that they rocketed through the corridor jammed with panicking Humans, over and through what Paul suspected might be Disneyworld, and into the next corridor. Still filled to the brim with rattled Humans.

"After this sphere we will contact the Phelans," one of the bots announced. "Majio, reverse approach side. Channels in corridor end-caps."

"I don't-" Paul's eyes bugged out and he grabbed the nearby rail. Yuhwa made for a slalom-like track deep in the walls and started a loop-the-loop. "Whaaaaaa!" he gurgled.

Yuhwa smacked his arm. "Infant. Look at the size of this thing. You won't fall out, and the maneuver is required to switch which side of the sphere we exit."

Sure enough, they'd rotated around and past the floor they'd been on. More screams as they appeared, one of which may have come from him. Paul reassured his masculinity that, at their speed, he was perfectly reasonable in freaking out. That right there was hell's own roller coaster.

Yuhwa had slowed a bit on their exit from the track, but resumed burning rubber as they flew past terra cotta tile roofs and sunbaked stone buildings packed closely together. Had to be the Mediterranean or somewhere like that.

"Majio approaches!" M42 belted out.

"Khòchi bot! That isn't correct," she growled.

Khòchi *ho-chi; Jadoube word for an overblown idiot, often one endowed with power and willing to abuse it.*

Paul snorted. "I think it meant we approach where the family is."

"*I* am not a khòchi, Paul Phelan," Yuhwa said. "Or bakyại, the ones you call 'wankers'." The look she gave him would have melted steel.

"Right, right. I'll just start looking for-" He spotted the group immediately, and the fear he'd been masking with jokes fired down his spine. Da was on the ground, surrounded by his family and Raisa. "Shit, shit. Go! They're over there!" He pointed frantically.

Yuhwa saw them and her face turned grim. "Bots, you will play sounds that imitate Human emergency transport. Loudly."

Four different versions of fire, aid, and police sirens went off. The Phelans and Raisa spun around, taking a protective stance around Da's body. All except Ma who was bent over him, crying, begging him to stay with her.

Humans in the vicinity scattered, terrified by the wailing sled descending in their midst.

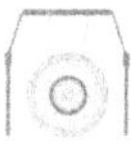

YUHWA KNEW their window was small: the Humans would only stay back so long. She settled the sled close by the family. Right now the frenzy was focused on "run and get somewhere safe", but experience had taught her that flight quickly morphed to a greedy "make sure no one has a better chance to survive than me".

"Go," she yelled at Paul. "Get them over here so we can fly out as fast as possible."

"Sundancer is furious," Katy said, rising from her crouch beside her father. "I'm trying to explain, but she is so pissed the Drafter did this." Katy shook her head. "She wants to rip the walls open, and the only thing stopping her is that she'd kill so many people."

Paul was at his mother's side, hugging her as she cried. "Da? Can you hear me?"

Ian, stiff-lipped, said, "He's coming in and out. I think it's a heart attack. Maybe a stroke."

Yuhwa needed no translation to understand. In any species the heart and brain were critical to survival, worked the hardest, and were the scariest things to have compromised. "Everyone up and over here, we need to go! Carry him slowly, we'll get back to Shee and find healers."

Yuhwa! We are here, trying to get access to a docking bay. The ship is denying us, there's some kind of atmosphere or shield barring entry. Can you assist?

"Shtŭ!" Yuhwa spun, looking at Katy. The *Eternidad* is here, Lia says they're trying to land. M42," she twisted to look at the bot. "Tell Mandy to let the ship and Drazoen land or there will be hell to pay!"

Half the family had lifted Martin, while the others supported his head and held his hands. Deb was clearing a path to the sled, grabbing the satchels they must have dropped when Martin fell ill.

"Mandy will allow docking at the outermost sphere of this arm, but only a few individuals may leave the ship until she and the Drafter have assessed the threat."

"Light their path, so they know where to land. They are no threat, and you are the khòchi I called you. Every one of you!

These are allies, friends. If you try to screw with Sundancer Orange she will wipe you from existence!"

> Lia, look for a light shining on the end of one the Mahoroba's arms. We'll meet you there as soon as we can. Katy's father is sick, we need help.

As she sent the message, she spied Humans encroaching on the team carrying Martin to the sled. Their faces were dirty and flushed, screwed up with determination and, on one or two of them, self-recrimination. No matter their regret for what they were about to attempt, they were going through with it.

"Paul!" she bellowed, pointing to the gang of Humans.

He dragged Katy into his spot holding their father and stepped out in front, arms wide.

"You don't want to do this," he tried in a reasoned tone, pitched to be heard over the still-wailing M-bots.

"Why do you have some fancy space car? Who the hell are you, so important in this crazy place?!" The lead man, shorter than Paul with a ruddy complexion, stopped and crossed his arms. His crew closed in behind him.

"We don't have time for this!" Brianna cried. She stepped to Paul's side and angrily spat out, "Get out of our way! My husband is dying, we have to get him help."

All four M-bots abruptly ceased emitting emergency noises. The bright yellow one, which had to this point never spoken, floated in front of Paul. It adopted a very stern tone to command, "Step aside, Humans. You have no place here."

Oh hål, that wasn't going to sit well with these angry people.

"We needed help too!" screamed the woman standing beside the leader. Tears streaked down her face, trailing through dust and blood. "My son was shoved off a bridge because of all of this, his head cracked like an egg on the rocks! And it's your fault!"

"I am so sorry," Brianna whispered.

Ian said, exasperated, "Why would that be *our* fault?"

We're docking, but someone named 'Mandy'
tells us we cannot leave the ship until you
arrive.

"Time to go," she urged under her breath. "The *Eternidad* can access far superior mediward tech." Her aoiti had made a rudimentary tie with Martin's, and what she was seeing wasn't good. Blockage nearly complete. If they didn't get him to care he would expire no matter what any of them did.

"You're not going anywhere!" the man cried out.

The yellow bot extended its electric prod, current arcing at the end of it. That inflamed the aggressors even more, and Yuhwa noticed previously remorseful faces had hardened. More Humans who hadn't even been in the first group were gathering behind them. She needed to get everyone aboard the sled and fly like a Mikanjo.

"Come on, come on," Oran chanted under his breath. He grunted with the effort of heaving his unconscious father over the edge of the sled.

Deb and Raisa had run around Martin and leaped onto the deck; now they pulled at his legs as everyone else adjusted grip and shuffled his body as carefully as they could until he slid completely onto the sled.

"Go time!" Patrick called to Paul and Brianna, tugging Vasuda aboard.

Yellow bot, spotting someone sneaking behind Paul and Brianna, whirled and zapped them. The man dropped like a stone, and voices around them erupted.

"You're going nowhere!" screamed the woman.

The man beside her shouted, "Everyone go for the car!" He slapped at the white bot hovering in front of him. "We need that car!"

Another man to his left started swinging a baton wildly, going after the bots. Others tried to rush the group but were held back by the bots weaving between them, electric prods arcing. Paul grabbed his mother around the waist, because she'd paled and frozen.

Yuhwa called, "I'm coming!" The bots surround Brianna and Paul, and Patrick jumped off with her to help.

Paul was turning, sheltering Brianna with his bigger body, when one of the attackers slammed into them. They fell, the man punching Paul in the stomach and kicking at Brianna. The Phelan matriarch had finally come out of her fugue state, struggling to stand, and shoving at their assailant. The man jabbed at Paul's face, then stomped down on his leg. A pop sounded.

Yuhwa had never heard any sound like the one Paul made.

20

HE'D BEEN SPRAWLED SIDEWAYS ON THE GROUND
while the man assaulted him. Mofo kept punching at him,
scratching, trying to hurt Ma. Paul got some good swings in;
knew he'd tagged him at least once when he saw blood spurt
from the git's nose. But Paul was sort of turtled, on his side and
trying to help Ma stand up while taking blows.

When the bastard's foot connected with his left kneecap he
felt pain so intense he thought he'd vomit. When someone fell
on top of his attacker, they collapsed on Paul's already injured
leg. Both assholes rolled off, punching each other. Paul knew he
needed to move, take advantage of the distraction and get Ma
away, but couldn't move.

Paul looked down at his lower body and part of his mind
completely dissociated from the agony. Stay in sport of any kind
long enough and you'll see the gamut of injuries. Above his left
knee, his femur looked straight, but below the knee his tibia
hung slightly to the right of where it should connect. The skin
wasn't broken, but human anatomy didn't go that way. *Never do
gymnastics again.*

The part of him not proclaiming his life had lost all meaning was still shouting in anguish. The injury was sharp, burning, and his leg felt so wrong he couldn't process it. Information he'd squirreled away long ago reminded him he could lose the leg if other damage had been done to arteries or nerves.

No time for that now. He pulled himself together as Ma leaned over him, weeping and running her hands over his bruised, scratched face. A new attacker loomed over Ma's back, and Paul braced for the hits to come, unable to do a damn thing about it. But Patrick had reached them, thank all the saints. He shoved the attacker away, reaching for his family to protect them. Then Yuhwa arrived and Paul lost what breath he had left.

Her face was a rictus of fury, like a lavender-haired Valkyrie flying to his side. Before the ass even knew what was coming she landed a wicked belly blow, doubling the prat over and making spittle drip from his mouth. Then she viciously wrenched the guy's head back by his hair, stretching his throat, making him gurgle. With a war cry, she punched his exposed Adam's apple, grinning savagely when he frantically reached for his throat, crying. Paul didn't think she'd fractured his trachea, but the loser would be feeling that for a long time. Yuhwa shove-punched the man, hard, sending him to the ground in a pathetic heap.

Patrick yanked him up, then noticed he wasn't on both feet. "Oh shit," he wheezed. "How bad is it, *dearthàir?*"

"Bad enough, but time for worry later. Get Ma."

Yuhwa inserted herself under his shoulder, taking weight off his injured side. "What is it?"

"Dislocated knee." He gritted his teeth against the pain. Numbness would be a relief, even if it would worry him more. Numbness could mean he was definitely losing the leg. He wiggled his big toe as a reflex to test damage; it responded with a twinge that made him bite his lip, but worked. Thank God.

While he'd been getting his ass kicked, more bots had arrived, forming an electrified cordon around the sled. Oran and

Ian jumped off to help Yuhwa arrange him in a safe place at the center of the sled, not far from Da.

People around them were way past angry. Screaming invectives, swearing and cursing their family line for generations to come, you name it they were doing it. The helpless tears got him the most; babies confused by the fracas, people not fighting at all, but who had lost hope and wept in the middle of the corridor.

Yuhwa moved the sled, ascending rapidly. The bots came with them, floating along as she picked up speed. To distract from the physical torment, Paul tried to remember how far they had to go. Then where the hell they were going at all, because either he'd lost track at some point, or Yuhwa was going the wrong way.

"Aren't we headed back to command?" he asked. "What did you call it, Shee?" He looked at Katy. "*You* had to have named it that."

She blushed and returned to stroking Da's hand. "The *Eternidad* and Sundancer are at the far end of the arm. We're going there."

He must have missed that conversation in the Wild West showdown they'd just escaped. Paul couldn't deny the relief of knowing Sundancer and Lia waited for them at the end of this rainbow.

They reached the final sphere in no time. Their speed caused enough wind noise he barely heard Ma's moans and weeping. She was terrified to lose Da, they all were. But a love like his parents had was special, and it would break her deep down if Da died.

It turned ugly in a second. Ian shouted, he and Oran started CPR and the rest of them stared in horror. Compressions, counted breaths, a chest that wasn't rising. Patrick slotted in to keep the pace as they shouted at Da to stay with them. Ma bit her fist to keep a scream inside. Raisa held a sobbing Katy.

The Phelans couldn't have survived everything they had and have Da slip away from them! He and Ma were the center of their family. Da gave them the laughter and stories, Ma provided practicality and strength. If Paul watched his father die before him on a travel sled, he would hunt down the Drafter and make them pay eternally.

He threw back his head. Giving in to panic and worry served no one, he needed to lock it down and stay in control. White-capped Kilimanjaro rose above them; a sim-sun partially blinded him, adding to the tears already trying to escape.

When the avenging angel in orange swooped down from the sky, he saw her perfectly. Sundancer Orange in her bipedal form, but with the addition of huge wings. They didn't beat even once, and he'd seen her float just fine without them. He was too tired to wonder why they'd made an appearance now.

Katy Phelan jo Faluji, I waited longer than reasonable. Now I come for you. All of you.

Katy broke down sobbing. "She'll fix it, she'll fix Da."

I cannot transport you, your father would not survive it. But I can speed our way.

Sundancer swooped under their sled, centered it on her back, and used the wings to hold it in place. Yuhwa cut the sled power to keep them aligned, and before Paul could blink twice, they'd flown past the summit of the mountain, through a camouflaged panel, into the bay where the *Eternidad* sat. Everyone save Katy and Raisa stayed in place. His brothers had stopped working, Da's chest rose shallowly.

I have him. Fear not.

Da was going to survive, thank the stars! Releasing some of the fear about his father's situation, however, opened him up to feeling more of his own problem. His knee throbbed like it had its own heartbeat.

Lia ran down the ship ramp, puzzlingly alone. Where was Bay? Paul saw Katy's eyes darting all over, waiting for him to appear. When Lia reached her and wrapped strong arms around her, she dissolved into tears again.

"Djilbay is bringing a medisled. Where is your father?"

Katy showed her, and Lia frowned. "The aoiti should be doing something to help already, but I don't like how pale he is. Even with Sundancer's intervention we should get him aboard and checked quickly."

"*Qania!*" Bay shouted from the top of the ramp. He ran to Katy, trailed by a sled that looked like any good EMT gurney; this one just floated instead of rolled. Thuliso, Olak and Pijo followed him. Great, it was a bloody convention. Katy leapt into Bay's arms and they kissed like it was going out of style.

Beeping M-bots, catching up to their group at last, swirled throughout the bay. "Too many aliens!" M42 broadcast. "Mandy demands they return to their ship until proper scans are complete."

Sundancer, wings gone, back to her crowned and terrifying visage, raised her head. Every bot flew to the center of the room and began to shake. Paul thought they were about to vibrate themselves into pieces, and obviously weren't moving of their own volition.

You dare.

Their trembling increased. The yellow one on the edge crumpled like an empty can.

You DARE. I will speak to this Mandy.

M42 spoke in Mandy's voice. "Who are you? What is this you've done to my robots? Release them at once!"

You presume to dictate to a Drazoen? Your Humans are precious to my Herald, but mean little to me. I can destroy all of this with a thought! All that keeps you and your Drafter safe is the need to care for Katy's father.

Another M-bot shuddered its way to self-destruction. Mandy wisely stayed silent.

Katy pulled away from Bay to approach Sundancer. "Don't,

okay? This isn't worth it, and you don't mean any of that." She took a deep breath. "I hope you don't. Let's just go, get Da settled and healing."

Sundancer looked down at her herald, softening.

So it shall be, heartnote.

"Katy, I have to find my family. I left them after an argument earlier; it's killing me to think something might have happened to them." Raisa's eyes were filled with unshed tears, her hands trembling.

"Oh my God, of course. Of course!" His sister spun in a circle, lost for purpose. "We need a sled. Yuhwa, Raisa can take this one back, yeah? Except how do we protect you out there, Riri?" Katy was getting worked up, enough that Bay wrapped a wing around her.

"I can take her back," Yuhwa offered. "I won't be able to go back to Centris, I have to take the *Mahoroba* to Malor."

Katy's face was devastated. "No! The nawa twats called?"

Yuhwa nodded, giving Paul just enough time to make a bad decision. "I'll stay with you. Try to help calm down the Humans out there, then if you need help on Malor," he shrugged. He didn't finish the sentence, worried he'd say something too out of bounds. The ache was making his mind fuzzy, which was often followed by his tongue loosening. That could ruin the careful truce they had going.

"No way," she shot back. "You need to be with your family."

His chest puffed up, ready to fire back several reasons he needed to be with her more.

Lia broke into the mounting argument with words of sensibility. "We are not in a hurry. So long as Irojaku jo Faluji keeps Martin's heart steady, we have time to get aboard, get settled. We'll stabilize him, prepare for any further treatments. Make plans for who goes and stays."

"You have to go, too, get the dislocation fixed," Yuhwa ordered.

"The what!" Ma, who hadn't left Da's side once, now rushed to him. Paul gave Yuhwa a look promising retribution.

She merely smirked in response. "Raisa, hop on. We'll find your family. M42, location please."

"We'll come too, love," Olak said, taking Raisa's hand. Pijo nodded. "I am excited to see the family you've spoken so rarely about." Raisa's countenance was best described as dubious. But she acquiesced and let them join her on the sled with Yuhwa.

"Come back when you're done," Paul demanded. "We can make plans for our trip to Malor."

Yuhwa shook her head and steered the sled out of the docking bay, never looking back.

Hours later, Paul had been unceremoniously carried by Bay onto the *Eternidad*. He lay on a bed beside Da; of the two of them Da was having the better time. Mikanjo mediwards surrounded him, along with a few of the new friends they'd made on the journey to Centris. If Paul were a betting man, he'd lay two paychecks on the odds Martin Phelan would become a Human ambassador. If not to the Calling, certainly to other species. He had a genuine joy in everything around them, and now that his heart attack had been rendered moot, he was gabbing away.

He'd also volunteered to be a learning dummy for the mediwards, who had no frame of reference for Human physiology. That lack was increasingly a problem for Paul, because they were hesitant to perform surgery to repair the damage. Not that he would blame them: his body was alien to them, and losing function because a tendon or nerve was different compared to a seven-foot, winged Mikanjo wasn't on his list of to-dos.

That left him blissfully pain-free and twiddling his thumbs in the med bay. At least the pain relief came without narcotic stupor; whatever these folks had it was better than a full nerve block and didn't make the room spin.

"Majio pet, you look less robust than at our last encounter."

Na had hitched a ride, too? Why? To chase those shadows he'd talked about? Or was there more to it? Paul rolled his head to the side and glared. "I am not Yuhwa's pet."

Na rolled a chair to Paul's beside and settled in. His arms came up in a parody of self-defense. "Come now, everyone in the room saw you two dancing around the obvious attraction."

Jesus, it couldn't have been that blatant, could it? Back then he'd been fighting it as hard as possible, too! Paul grimaced, suddenly reminded that 'back then' was only a day ago. Had it even been twenty-four hours? Time was so screwed up with all this space travel.

"Why are you here, my man? Unlike Bay and Yuhwa, I respect your approach to the namu thing. There are definitely times following laws is the wrong path; obeying unspoken principles takes precedence in cases like that." Paul stared up at the ceiling, suddenly so tired of the cosmic adventure filled with lies, politics, and Big Damn Portents. Secrets and heartbreak. "But you did your thing, right? Fought the good fight all those years. Now Sundancer's outlawed namu'ur, your Nyakisi underground can work directly with the newly freed. Begs the question: what would bring you here, slumming with Humans?"

Glowing eyes had darkened to a navy-grape shade and looked Paul up and down. "Do you know, I think they all underestimate you. Substantially."

"Flattery doesn't answer the question." It made Paul happy, though, no doubt about that. He confessed to himself he might have a teensy fandom worship over Na.

Spreading his arms wide, Na laughed. "Why would I miss the chance to see things that have never happened before? A new species to the Calling arrives, cloaked from exposure by the highest offices in the Aoni. Sundancer Orange, Drazoen of Justice, returns from a prison her herald destroyed with *music*. Now a mysterious ship, capable of teleporting unprecedented quantities of beings, appears in the Mukuru system. Where Sundancer claims the Cho used to exist."

"We're not even in the Milky Way?" Paul whined. "Forget that. Who are the Cho?" Paul knew he'd heard the word, but couldn't tie it to anything useful.

"They were the original species, first to evolve. They disappeared before the Drazoen even left. Many people will claim they're myth now, but I've seen Calling records of Cho ambassadors. From the earliest days."

Thuliso, walking up behind Na, scoffed. "Disappeared? Children's tales. They no more disappeared than my peoples' planet did." He pressed his lips together. "We've always believed they were the first victims of Krylar genocide."

"How would that have gone unnoticed, appointed?" Na asked. He shook his head at Paul. "Exterminating planets draws attention."

Thuliso's voice dropped low. "It was over a kōmilen ago, records and communication were less powerful than now."

"Perhaps," Na's silky voice drawled, "if there had been spies like yourself back then, we would know for sure."

"Jaxolē, you have no tower from which to preach." He kept his eyes on Na who had risen to face him.

"Boys, boys." Katy broke in, peeking around the pair. "You're both pretty." She patted Paul's hand. "More important is you. How are you feeling?"

Paul laughed inside. His sister surely had a way with cutting through crap sometimes. "I'm okay. It's totally numb, which I think is from the drugs. Da is having a ball," he jerked his head to the other bed still surrounded by people conversing with their father, "He's been chatting up a storm with all the mediwards."

"Of course he has." She sighed, plopping down into the seat Na had vacated. "What are we doing about it?" She pointed at his grossly swollen and disjointed knee. "You can't just leave it."

Na interrupted. "Explain what happened, please. Briefly."

Katy and Paul tag-teamed an abridged version of events — their unsanctioned relocation from Centris to the *Mahoroba* and through the fight-n-flight of the last hours. 'Briefly' took longer than it should have, though. There was plenty of frustration with the Drafter and Mandy thrown in for color. Na shook his head, turned on a heel and walked out. Paul looked at his sister, questions in his eyes, but she shook her head.

"He's a weird one. I'm also realizing Humans are once again screwed in the Aoni. Of all the Drazoen meet-cute stories I've heard, we have the worst!"

"The shtŭ are you even talking about, Bug?"

"Mikanjo got wings, Muškikal got accelerated evolution, Jadoube got waja, hell Nyakisi got tips and tricks on being sneaky SOBs. We got running, screaming, panicking." Her tone was flippant but her eyes were sad. "Doesn't seem fair that we didn't get to be discovered by dragons who gave us gifts. We got to be terrified because the Drafter pulled this stupid trick and made Sundancer furious."

Thuliso patted Katy's shoulder. "Take heart, herald. The Sukath people may yet have a worse Drazoen introduction than yours."

21

"Who are *they*? Aoiti aren't giving me anything." Katy smacked her own forehead.

"That's because as yet they're not part of the database. They're the next species being watched for advancement." Thuliso's expression was bland, but his large, cornflower blue eyes twinkled.

Katy twisted to stare at him. "You're watching another species? Of course you are, I bet there are a few out there. Were we being watched?"

"It had been proposed, but not accepted," he chuckled. "The Sukath are beyond Humans, in terms of getting off their planet in a sustainable way."

"We got off our planet, too!"

Paul couldn't figure out why Katy was getting worked up about this. They were well off Earth now, for the love of Pete.

"Your single space station wasn't sufficient for the voting body. They wanted to wait for something more substantial and permanent; a second planet or a satellite of larger stature. Your appearance on Centris has ruffled quite a few feathers." Thuliso's countenance took on a serious mien. "Your Drafter's actions won't sit well, either. Violating the personal sovereignty of so many is grievous."

"Are these the same people who were just fine about namu'ur flourishing for tens of thousands of years?" Paul demanded.

Thuliso nodded just as Na reappeared, carrying M42 who protested loudly the entire way. How the hell had he caught the M-bot? And *why*?

"Cease this at once. I repeat, you must release me, alien. I cannot be on this ship. Mandy has not authorized boarding!"

Na's hand wrapped nearly the whole way around the bowling pin bot's skinny neck. "No one here cares for your objections. We have a critical situation. Tell your Mandy that a Human on this ship requires the precision and technological advancements of 'alien' tech. But these very experts lack the medical knowledge I expect is stored in the *Mahoroba* databanks. Unless you cooperate, you will be directly responsible for whatever permanent damage befalls the Human."

Paul flinched at the words *permanent damage*. He'd prefer Na didn't tempt fate by speaking that aloud.

The ruckus had gotten the attention of Da and the mediwards. "Kweza," called one of them. "Request analysis of this bot-"

"M42," Katy interjected.

The woman looked at Katy a little oddly, but revised her question. "Analyze M42; looking for a way to connect and transfer information."

Paul's arm was just long enough to poke Katy. "Thank God you told them its name. Kweza would have been lost trying otherwise."

She stuck her tongue out at him and he laughed. From the corner of his eye, he saw Na watching them, no expression, but intent. That guy had a steel trap mind; he'd listened to fifteen minutes of their story and figured out how to help instantly.

Paul didn't mind not being the genius here, especially if it meant there was a chance his leg could be repaired.

"Any word from Yuhwa? Or Raisa?"

Katy sagged. "I guess her family was safe, but *furious*. I get the feeling her sexuality is a problem for them, so Olak being there might have made things worse."

"Are they coming back here?" Paul tried not to sound eager.

"Nope, still refuse to associate with me or any of us." Katy's frown trembled a little. "I don't want us to split up! Yuhwa is staying because she has to fly back to Malor. Raisa says she's staying for her family, Olak and Pijo say they're moving into Shee. I assume because of her? You even said you're staying! All the rest us are going back to Centris so Da can get his aoiti tweaked to specially address the blockage. Plus, Sundancer can't leave the Calling for long after what just happened. I hate it. We should stick together." She ended with a whine.

"I know change is hard for you, sis." For once he didn't use the nickname that irritated her, because she was heading into meltdown territory. "We all have to do things that are right for us, even if they aren't what others would want." Paul was divided, despite what he'd said in the landing bay; stay or go? His mind said keep with the family, offer any protection or guidance he could. But his heart pulled to Yuhwa, even if they never left the friend zone again. His spirit wanted the adventure of seeing a new planet, but his habits told him to stick with what he already knew in this dangerous Aoni.

"I too, will stay," Thuliso said. "The *Mahoroba* offers untold opportunities for learning."

Na snorted. "I'm staying to keep an eye on this one," he nodded to the Lunari. "He can't be unsupervised."

M42 had finally quit squawking, beeped several times, then said to Na, "Mandy agrees and will allow me to trade information with the aliens."

"Mikanjo, M42. The ones with wings are Mikanjo." Katy sounded patient, as if she dealt with a child.

Paul was less polite. "Lanu told you all this, robot. I know they did. Stop being prejudiced." He wasn't letting it slide for another minute. "The Drafter says they did all this to be part of the Aoni. Well then. Be part of it! Don't act like a snotty teenager judging everything they don't understand."

Brianna, walking into the med bay at that moment, gave him a little clap. "Well said! It's about time they shaped up." She walked up to M42 and rubbed its top. "You have to be better now, do you hear what we're saying?"

Na arched his eyebrow. "Human relationships to AI are potentially of concern."

When the rest of the Phelans crowded into the room, Na and Thuliso fled the din. M42 hovered by a wall, and when Kweza had created a cable or widget (Paul didn't know and, unlike Da, didn't care) to link their databases the two systems synced. After a few minutes, Kweza flashed textbook imagery of knees onto screens.

The Mikanjo team studied it closely, before one of the men said, "We know what we can do! Do you want to be awake for the procedure?"

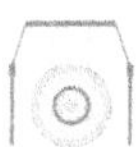

YUHWA WAS weary to her bones. Even the tiniest ones in her hands and feet seemed to ache. Navigating the morass of humanity in order to deliver Raisa to her family had been harder than getting to the Phelans earlier. She'd thought once Sundancer stopped broadcasting in their heads and Lanu was no longer visible on screens, people would calm down. Not so.

It was a self-fueling panic that built and built. Parts of the vessel were on fire, more than one dead body lay trampled along the streets and roads of the spheres. For whatever reason, many of the Humans had run from the simulated Earth sections and gathered in the plain, semi-sterile connecting corridors. There were too many of them to fit; the corridors were never designed to be anything but pathways for trains to join the exponentially larger spheres and rings, but people rammed and pushed into them anyway.

Raisa's family had thankfully stayed put in their area on the central ring, which was a massively populated copy of an Earth city, Bangkok. Getting the sled safely through taxed Yuhwa's abilities, particularly as Humans had taken to throwing objects at them and shouting invectives. Olak and Pijo had retreated to the centermost part of the sled to avoid being hit.

Raisa's posture shriveled the closer they came to her family's location. "They were very angry when I left to meet Katy and her family," she mumbled. "Baba has been unhappy with my 'antics', he calls them." Her head raised and she huffed. "Like I *chose* to be nearly killed and forced to flee the solar system. To protect *them*, for the record!"

"Your father's opinions carry a lot of weight with you." She routed them around a tall, spinning wheel adorned with dangling carriages. Humans had odd cities. "This isn't always true when children become adults."

"In my family, parents dictate for a long time. Especially if you're a girl." Raisa rubbed her face. "Particularly if you're an unmarried girl who's *different*."

"Explain, please. What would make you so different? You seem much like the other Humans."

"I just...." Raisa stopped herself, glancing over to the Lunari voices mid-sled.

Not once did Pijo and Olak look to Raisa. They took in everything else around them with jaded nonchalance, but Yuhwa knew they were impressed. No matter they'd lived aiwaks on Centris, the *Mahoroba* was a wonder never seen before, and being able to fly through Human-designed cities and towns astonished all of them.

Her friend wrapped tense arms around herself. "I haven't always been what Baba and Maman hoped for in a daughter. I'm not as obedient as I should be. My brother is sweet, he tries to help, but I am forever falling short of my parents' expectations."

"Yeòjoda," Yuhwa used the Jadoube term for a dear and close friend, one she'd never felt comfortable saying aloud before. But she wanted Raisa to know her words came from a place of respect and love. "You are more than enough. Katy says without you she would never have had the strength to endure. To discover the part of herself she needed in order wake Sundancer and free the Shadows. If your parents don't respect that, maybe you shouldn't return to them."

Raisa's mouth turned down on one side, head drooping. "That isn't done in our community. Defiance is discouraged as much as difference."

Yuhwa knew she didn't understand the cultural and species dynamics well enough to continue butting in. Her spirit saddened on Raisa's behalf nonetheless. There was an obvious disconnect between what her parents demanded of her, and what she wanted for herself.

Their arrival at Raisa's family's twenty-fifth floor apartment was met with as little joy as Yuhwa expected. Olak, either not reading the tension or being deliberately provocative, had tried to stroke Raisa's arm when introduced. Raisa shrank back; her parents glared even as they nodded politely, then demanded Raisa join them. Her friend climbed over the balcony railing in shamed silence.

They flew away, back to Shee. Olak and Pijo huddled at the far end, talking out of Yuhwa's hearing. Raisa hadn't looked back until the sled was past reach for a change of mind; the longing and heartache on her face tore at Yuhwa.

She was even more uncomfortable with the resemblance to

Paul's countenance when he'd tried to say he would stay on the *Mahoroba*. Or earlier when he'd sworn they were family now. Yuhwa had told Paul she wasn't a khòchi, yet at every turn she avoided the obvious: he wanted more. Both times she felt confident his feelings, not rational thoughts, were behind the ploys. Yuhwa should be stopping him before he could form more attachment. Their night had been wonderful and was at an end. Whether they remained friends was in his hands, hinging on whether he could accept their sexual time was over.

But she didn't confront the problem as she ought. She allowed it to continue because it felt nice. Held in his arms, pressed tight to his side, she'd felt a peace long absent in her life. Any reasons for that didn't bear closer examination, she just wanted to accept it and treasure it for what it was.

Shoving the complication of Paul Phelan to the back of her mind, she showed the voices what Shee had on offer for lodging. They opted for the same unit, despite Yuhwa's impression they weren't a couple. Not her business.

She walked them down to command, highlighted the pool and dining areas, but didn't take them into the numig. Aware she already felt possessive of the *Mahoroba*, she wasn't inclined to fight the territoriality. A side effect for most majio, ship attachment could happen fast.

Yuhwa hadn't even swum the dao on this ship yet, but felt ties forming. The tragic devastation outside of Shee, where Humans had wantonly destroyed areas to vent their fear and anger, grated on her. Inviting Lunari she categorized as self-interested and shallow didn't rate as high priority. Thankfully Lanu had come out of the numig and joined her in welcoming the voices.

They were sampling coffee before Yuhwa returned to the landing bay. It paled overall in comparison to nropita, but the type Deb insisted on had a depth of flavor Yuhwa was coming to appreciate. She knew she had to get back to the *Eternidad*; eventually they had to sort out who was doing what and where, but for now the four of them could take a few kaalas to breathe.

"When this ship travels, it will become a moon wherever it ends up," Pijo marveled. "Or dwarf the satellites it visits."

Olak agreed with Pijo. "There's nothing comparable in Aoni history. Even the largest Dál ships barely approach the size of *one* of the larger spheres."

Pijo leaned over, his hands cupping the coffee mug. "You truly have no idea who the Drafter is?"

Lanu shook their head negatively. "The Drafter hasn't spoken to any of us. Everything comes through Mandy."

"How could they have possibly built something this intricate and colossal?"

"They 'requested'," Yuhwa reminded him. "It was their wishes that someone else brought to life."

Mouth slack, Pijo slowly shook his head. "Incredible."

"The bigger question," Olak said, "is to whom could the Drafter have made such a request?"

"One of the Nine?" Pijo offered.

"We would have heard," Yuhwa said. "Sundancer would mention if one of her siblings came back."

Lanu ran a hand over their hair, making the white strands stick out even more. "Good question for the next person who sees Her." They looked to Yuhwa. "We shouldn't fill in knowledge we don't have. The Drazoen may have ways of cloaking themselves from one another. Or reasons for not telling us another returned."

Yuhwa drained the last of her coffee. Lanu had suggested something called a flavored creamer, but on the whole she liked the beverage better without the sweetened, milky addition. "I'm off to the landing bay Lanu, so I'll ask. Demi-gods aren't sworn to answer us lower beings, though." She quirked a smile. "Are you staying here or going back to Centris? Now is the time to decide."

Lanu leaned back. "I will stay." Their voice filled with sorrow. "I've seen footage of Earth in the wake of the request, and hope to help these Humans cope."

"Bad back on Earth?" Yuhwa asked.

"Apocalyptic," they replied. "Half their population disappeared in front of their eyes, there's been no communication, and they have no idea what's happened. The Drafter's request didn't specify who would be taken; from what I've seen domestic partners were split, families were divided. No children taken from parents that I've uncovered, but extended members have surely been separated."

Yuhwa had heard Katy talk about aunts, cousins, distant relatives. While the core Phelan and Leon family members were here, how many had been left behind? Or ripped from their cherished partner with no clue how they could reunite?

M1616 was waiting for her on the sled when she left Shee, and they rode together in silence. Yuhwa didn't drop her eyes as they zipped along the fastest route back to the *Eternidad*. It was the only way she could avoid the miasma of despair below her; don't look and it isn't real.

By the time they'd reached the bay, her heart was encased in a thin layer of imaginary waja, hardened enough to keep going. The stress of the last few sal-angs had inured her to the nawa's pull, but now it returned with a vengeance. They would not be denied much longer.

Yuhwa sagged under her guilt; she should be trying to take the *Mahoroba* back to Earth so these suffering people could be rejoined with loved ones. But she felt sure that request would be denied by the Drafter as fast as she could ask it. The tug was also getting strong enough it might hurt her if she detoured long enough to fly to Earth. Yuhwa needed to return to Malor and tell them to leave her alone, or she could end up incapacitated, stranding the ship somewhere.

Shtŭ. Na waited at the bottom of the ramp. Who had let him

sneak onto her ship? Her old ship, she revised. Which would need a new majio once Sundancer teleported everyone back to Centris. Paul had a bit of dao deep inside him, could she trust him to help find a new pilot? But he was hurt. She had no good options.

"He's fine," the Nyakisi smirked.

"Drown in hål," she snarled, unwilling to admit it soothed her quite a bit to hear. Unconscious worry for Paul had been pressing on the back of her mind.

Na leaped onto the sled as she flew into the *Eternidad*. "I'm told he asked for you as soon as he awoke."

Yuhwa came to a hard stop, spinning to glare at Na. "I don't know what you think you're doing, or implying. If Paul and I were to have a relationship, *which we do not*, there is no scenario in which it would ever be your business." She jammed a finger into his synth hide encased chest. "Shut the shtŭ up."

"My business, majio, is the delight I take in knocking you off your game." He laughed, a genuine amusement radiating from him. "I am not often in the company of people who are so easily rattled, despite their aiwaks of experience."

"Why are you here?!" Yuhwa was exasperated.

"Chasing answers, just like the rest of you." Backing away, then taking a bow, Na said, "I look forward to our journey together."

"Oh no. No way."

"Oh yes."

Yuhwa swore.

22

By the time they arrived at the med bay, not only had Yuhwa not talked Na out of staying on the *Mahoroba*, he'd taken a few more jabs about Paul. She was ready to smash the sled into a wall. Having M1616 threaten him with an electric prod finally silenced his voice, but not the sly looks.

Blessedly he took his leave as she prepared to enter the room. She had no idea what she'd find in there; every Phelan and half the Mikanjo left on the poor *Eternidad*? The family had been well-liked in their short time on the ship, and a threat to the patriarch's health would be taken very seriously. If the room was overfull she'd say hello and dash out. If that limited Paul time, so be it.

As much as Yuhwa adored them, she struggled at times with the lovable chaos wherever the Phelans went. An only child who'd had to fend for herself more than half her life, who'd had someone ripped from her life, then been abandoned by the person meant to love her the most. Once in a while seeing such a happy family twisted her insides.

Yuhwa reprimanded herself sternly. *Hitch your britches, woman.* She'd gotten that phrase from Katy, and it fit right then. She was healing and overcoming old traumas. She was powerful and gifted, damn it, she could handle whatever came next.

The doors opened silently as three mediwards exited. They nodded politely to her, murmuring hellos but not stopping. She slipped into the room without being noticed. Oran sat beside his father's bed, the pair playing a card game. Brianna was at Paul's side, close to where Yuhwa stood. One step deeper into the room and she could hear their conversation.

"They told you, Paul. You have to rest up. They've fixed the largest part of the damage, but your aoiti won't heal you as quickly as they'd like."

He looked stubborn, arms crossed. "What are you getting at?" His leg hovered slightly above the bed, resting on a floating pillow. It was wrapped tight in bandages from hip to foot, his knee encased in an immobilizing brace that she'd bet drove him mad.

"Sweetie, I know you think you have to watch out for all of us, but you don't." His mother rubbed one of his arms, tangling their fingers. "It's never been your job to care for everyone, even though you always thought it was. You can take time to relax and mend."

"There *is* no time, Ma!" Paul's voice was frustrated. "I don't know how I know, but I *know* this Drazoen crap is going to come fast and furious. Being out of commission isn't something I can allow."

Yuhwa was done eavesdropping and crossed to the other side of Paul's bed. "What, exactly, do you imagine you can do about it?" When the blood climbed to his cheeks, she realized she'd spoken insensitively. Why did she keep doing that around him?

"I can get the hell out of this bed, for one." He pushed clenched fists into the bedding, twisting with real intent, but Brianna stopped him.

"Paul Jacob Phelan!" She grabbed his unbandaged leg and pushed down. "Don't you dare. Oran!"

Paul and Katy's brother left the stool by Martin and took a stand near Yuhwa. "Don't be a shithead," he barked, slapping a hand down on Paul's chest.

"Language," Brianna sighed. "If he tries to move again, sit on him." When Oran bobbed his head, she continued, shaking a finger at Paul. "You're going to respect what those lovely medi-wards spent time learning to do. They saved your leg! You will stay in a bed as long as they tell you to, you'll do whatever PT they tell you to, and *only* when they say you can." Brianna's voice carried as she called, "Martin?"

Yuhwa had the sense this was a call-and-response the couple had perfected over the tuigs.

"Lad, you've upset yer Ma. Best you do as she says now, give in with grace." He winked. "It's the only good answer I've found since the day I met her."

Oran and Paul rolled their eyes.

"In fact," Brianna tapped her lips. "Yes, that will be best. Yuhwa, darling?"

Why was she being dragged into this? Nervous, she stared at Paul's mother. "Yes?"

"Paul's been torn about staying here or coming back with us. I'm afraid he'll overdo it coming back to Centris. You'll watch over him here, won't you?"

Was that a gleam of something manipulative in Brianna's eyes? Yuhwa didn't know how to respond. Was her answer even necessary?

"Ma, you can't do that!" Paul's objection was loud.

Brianna made a dismissive noise. "Just did. You can stay here, you won't be responsible for anything but healing the way they want you to, less stress, all the good things. Katy says the Calling is in an uproar after our disappearing and such, not a good place for you to recuperate."

Yuhwa knew she'd said the wrong thing a time or two with Paul, but what his mother had declared made him grind his teeth. Whether Brianna meant to or not, she'd implied her son would get in the way on the *Eternidad* or Centris. She also assumed he'd have no purpose on the *Mahoroba* and would do nothing but lay about. That wouldn't sit well on a man who wanted to be needed and useful.

"Maybe," he finally said, "it would be good to get away from all of you."

Brianna's face quailed for an atóm, but cleared nearly instantly. "It's for the best, you'll see." She patted his good leg.

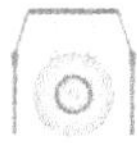

"KWEZA," Yuhwa called. "Please transfer replication patterns and kernel samples for rusim and nropita."

Paul perked up. At least if he was going to be a pathetic shtüing tagalong on Yuhwa's trip home, he could have good eats. "Baijur crackle, too."

She regarded him sadly. "That one can't be replicated. They've tried. They only get it when someone brings baijur from Bankiri."

Damn it. "Fine, can I have jurakeke, then?"

"Kweza, please add it." Yuhwa regarded him solemnly. "If you're staying, you'll need to be happy."

He didn't know how to take that from her. His heart wanted it to mean more than his brain said it did. Responding with playful banter seemed out of reach right now.

Katy saved him from answering when she blew into the room. "Sundancer says we need to leave in the next few kaalas. Storms a-brewing back on the Wheel." Whirling she took in the tense body postures. "What happened?"

"Ma just ordered Paul to stay behind," Oran said with a shit-eating grin. Paul tried to punch him, but couldn't reach when his idiot brother backed away.

"Oh." Katy was nonplussed, then clapped. "Actually, good. I feel better leaving Yuhwa with you here to help. Between Mandy, three Lunari and Na she'll need it."

"You remember I'm a majio of four hundred tuigs who has functioned quite well in difficult scenarios, yes?"

Katy hugged Yuhwa. "Of course I do. He's the cannon fodder so you can get the job done."

"Hey!" Paul was feeling a lot like a punching bag at this point. Between his mother's backhanded swats at his capability and Katy offering him up as a sacrifice, he was going to start doubting his worth.

"Lanu will need you," Yuhwa said seriously. "Humans are going to find out what happened back on Earth and they worry it will trigger more anger and riots. Maybe hearing from a calming Human influence – seeing one of their own species say it's okay – will help."

Mollified, he rubbed his face with his hands. Jesus, none of them had thought through what the other half of humanity was experiencing. "I don't suppose there was a goodbye note? A kind message of 'never fear they're safe'?"

Yuhwa shook her head. Craaaaaap.

"Thuliso and Na are waiting outside for you. What happened with Riri and her parents?"

"She's staying with them," Yuhwa said in a low voice. "They're unhappy. All of them, I think. But she felt she had to stay."

"I can't-" Katy choked. "I don't want to do this without her! Or you!" She hugged Yuhwa again. "Even doofus over there. When the fellowship splits up, I hate it."

Paul tried to give her hope. "This doofus will figure out how to fix things, okay Bug? I'll get Yuhwa safely to Malor, wrap that up tight, then we'll come back to Centris. Things will work out, and in the meantime you can probably come visit as much as you need to." He held out a hand, waited for her to take it, then went on. "You've got Sundancer, who would probably carry you to the ends of the Aoni. Or the *Eternidad*, which Bay and Lia will probably let you use for nropita dates when we get to Malor."

"I can't wait to see how *you* get me to Malor." Yuhwa laughed. "Brushed up on your dao, did you?"

Paul prayed his face wasn't as red as it felt. Before he could get a word in, Bay came through the doors, followed by the rest of the Phelans and Lia.

"Sundancer says it's time," Bay murmured, touching Katy's hair softly.

Wiremu and Zazi, as well as few more Mikanjo, came into the med bay which was pretty freaking crowded now. Da was allowed to stand up and come over to hug Paul and Yuhwa goodbye. Paul's entire bed, meanwhile, was coming with them so he wouldn't jostle his leg and screw up what the mediwards had accomplished.

"Just think," one of them marveled, following as he was floated out to the sled waiting in the hall. "By the time we see you again we'll know the Human body inside out thanks to you and your papu."

"That almost makes it worth the injury," Paul joked as he tickled Zazi.

The boy had taken a spot on Paul's bed, but didn't respond to the Tickle Monster as expected. No wiggling or giggling. A wide-eyed stare, before a whispered, "Kawakona Brother Two, are we now best friends?!"

Paul had to laugh. There went the cosmos teaching him new things. In his *Universe* he knew how to handle kids and was a capable business owner. In the *Aoni* he learned unfledged Mikanjo children weren't ticklish and he was just the second brother of the sacred herald of Sundancer. Perfect.

Zazi was lifted away by Wiremu, who squeezed Yuhwa's shoulder and uttered quietly, "Majio relieved."

Yuhwa, who'd been magnetically locking his bed to the sled

floor, bit her lips and blinked. After a moment she turned to face Wiremu and said, "Thank you, Captain. You honored me with your trust, and I'll carry that with me darû."

Darû *duh-roo; common Aoni word for eternity, forever.*

Paul wanted to reach out, but held back, afraid that kind of comfort wasn't allowed. She'd accepted it this morning, but might reject it now. Thuliso and Na interrupted his thoughts by clapping hands on either shoulder. Na, on his left, had a grip so light he could barely feel it. Thuliso's seven fingers on his right side were gentle, too, but firmer than the Nyakisi. Paul supposed thieves from birth learned to have a phantom touch.

"Human," Thuliso remarked brightly, "we will have many things to discuss. Your rejuvenation sals will spin away quickly."

Paul regarded him skeptically. "Why do I feel like I'm going to be interrogated?"

Na patted him. "You're currently the only Human who doesn't want to kill us on sight. We will take every advantage."

In the end Katy ugly cried, Bay held her, Lia supported Da who was flagging a bit, and Sundancer watched it all with an amused and tolerant countenance. What did a dragon near-god think of all this? She had eight siblings; did they weep when parting? Or were they jejune about it, because they'd lived for eternity? What was that word he'd just learned? Darû. When you had a darû to exist, maybe parting wasn't a sorrow, sweet or otherwise.

All partings, whether desired or not, bring with them small griefs.

Paul met Sundancer's gaze. He really resonated with that thought, and repeated it to himself as Yuhwa flew them back to Shee.

"Mandy requests your presence in the numig, majio." M1616 sounded serious. "There's been an unforeseen complication."

"Damn the Ekletu! What now?"

Ekletu *ecc-leh-too; the Three Ekletu are Jadoube mythological* *shadow forces that exist in opposition to the Five Côttru.* Huh. Katy had told them all that folktales and myths repeated around the Aoni, just like they did across cultures on Earth. The Ekletu sounded like demons or evil ghosts.

M1616 answered calmly. "M42 failed to vacate the alien ship promptly when recalled, and has been removed from the *Mahoroba.* The Drafter is concerned."

"About what?" Paul questioned. "What would they do with a floating bowling pin that would worry the Drafter? Use it for batting practice?"

"Each of the M-bots has detailed information on this craft. Plans, technical specifications, Human data. Aliens might-"

"Stop identifying everything non-Human as alien. That's outdated speech." Yuhwa gripped the console, flexing her fingers. Did she want to throw the bot overboard the way he did?

Thuliso joined in. "No one on the *Eternidad* would abuse the data."

"Mandy and the Drafter say they have greater concern over the chance Krylar or Pu'ulqaari may steal the bot." M616 still sounded calm.

Na tapped his fingers against his upper arm. "They may not be wrong."

"Not helping, dude!" Paul yelped.

"I don't like this word." Na peered at Paul disdainfully. "I don't dress in elaborate costume."

"I don't know what the aoiti just told you, but that isn't right. Not nowadays anyway. Also, irrelevant. Don't help freak out Mandy and the Drafter even more."

Na scoffed. "M42 was compromised before leaving the *Mahoroba.* It hooked into Kweza to share Human anatomy, if you'll recall. A data transfer probably happened on a bigger scale, depending on how they phrased the request."

Paul was getting grouchy. The pain blocking had started to

wear off just before they set off for Shee. He knew there was more in the goody bag one of the mediwards sent along. Plus, the recipe for it had been transferred with the food and drink. But he needed to ride it out a little longer, get on top of it. He hated being dependent on drugs or external things to manage the pain. A man should be able to overcome it on his own.

That didn't mean he had to be happy about it. There was an overall soreness, shooting pains running north-to-south on the back of his knee, and his skin felt tight. Like a cherry ready to burst. That might mean swelling, which he'd need to reduce ASAP. So he didn't have time for Mandy and the Drafter to freak out over nothing.

"You can drop me off at mine, Yuhwa," he called. "I should get ice on this, and call some physios. If any poor bastards got yanked onto this hell-boat, that is."

All three companions looked down on him, pity on two faces and curiosity on one. He went with the guy who seemed to be fascinated by his bad temper. "Na, you can help for a minute, yeah? Just push the bed into my house and make an ice pack in the kiosk?"

Yuhwa snorted. "Asking him to help you without payment is like asking a river to run dry." She huffed. "And your mother said to listen to the mediwards. Calling people for physical manipulation so soon is rash."

"I know my own damn body!"

Thuliso pressed Paul back down to the padding. "Paul, no need for this. We'll help. Give us a chance, and we'll help you heal."

Outnumbered and unable to do a damn thing to help himself until he got out of the bed, Paul gave in. But he'd show them he was capable of rising above this bullshit injury. It wouldn't end his world; he'd walk, run, and someday do a full-twisting double tuck on that damn knee.

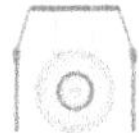

PAUL WAS EXHAUSTING.

After consulting with Mandy, Yuhwa knew what he needed to be doing for his leg, which was the opposite of what he was doing. For more than a day he refused pain blockers as long as he could, calling it "weaning himself". Lanu had tried to reason that feeling so much pain would actually set back his healing, but he'd hear none of it.

Yuhwa tried to intervene with him about calling physical therapists too soon; he threatened to climb out of the bed if she didn't let him. They fought loudly and to a very abrupt end when he spat, "Don't act like you care what happens to me. Yes, we fucked, but that was it, right? You're not someone who gets a say!"

Thankfully the door to his unit was closed when he hurled that at her. She made sure it was shut just as tightly when she exited, fuming. Thuliso, examining the fruiting trees and their green leaves with fascination, watched her emerge and cocked his head.

"Still acting like an injured animal?"

She stomped over and ripped an orange off a branch. She wasn't sure she liked the taste of this fruit, but it made for a satisfying projectile when she chucked it at Paul's door. "He's convinced the aoiti are healing him faster than they are. Won't hear reason."

"Let him hang himself, then," Thuliso said. He crushed a leaf between his fingers and brought it to his nose. "These are remarkable. Someday when I have my own home I'll remember this tree and plant some."

Diverted, Yuhwa teased, "When would a Lunari, especially an appointed, ever settle down? I thought you were the great wanderers."

Wry smile twisting his lips, Thuliso turned to the command center. "Someday, majio; it's the somedays that keeps us going in the nowadays. Right this very now, let's get mediward names from Mandy. Perhaps our Human will listen to one of them." As they walked he added, "I'll go with you to retrieve them. I think it still isn't safe out there for you alone."

Yuhwa thanked him and followed him into the numig. She was distracted, still stinging from Paul's accusations. He was hurting, but why did he have to hurt her? Reducing what they'd shared to mere shtŭing was mean and petty. She would try to let go of the insult, but the chance of them remaining friends seemed far removed from where they were.

23

GODDAMN ASSHOLE. STICK ANOTHER FOOT IN YOUR BLOODY MOUTH. Paul was really angry at himself. He'd been viciously unkind to Yuhwa. She was trying to help him, and he'd verbally slapped her. *Way to ensure she avoids you for the foreseeable future, dinkus.* He was pain free now, having given into a blocker shortly after she left, and clarity of mind brought a buttload of regret.

Her silence as she'd turned and walked out sliced at him most, and told him how deeply he'd offended her. On top of everything else, he remembered she was being called by the nawa. It was a burden she carried alone since he hadn't exactly been supportive. Though she said little about it, it was clear to him the pull was physical in some way. His churlish and infantile behavior might be causing her more pain. That idea dropped the bottom out of his stomach.

Hours passed while he mentally crafted an apology. His ex had told him he was terrible at being sorry, but he had to try. At one point he had the bot in the room record what he said and read it back to him. Nothing sounded good, though! Was there a clever way to say "I'm a douchebag, sorry 'bout it"?

When a chime announced a visitor, he shifted in the bed and

prepared to grovel. Seeing Na walk in, followed by a stranger deflated him. Yuhwa wouldn't even come back, that's how bad he'd screwed up.

"This is one of your Human mediwards," Na said as they approached the bed.

"Doctor," the stout, middle-aged woman said. "Dr. Sofia Vásquez, who wonders where she is and why."

"Hi, I'm Paul Phelan," he began, offering his hand to shake.

She took it, her grip strong. "Why do you both speak perfect Peruvian Spanish, Mr. Phelan? Forgive me for saying neither of you looks like a local." Her mink brown eyes squinted at him. "Do you run this ship we're trapped on?"

By the time Paul had explained what he could, Na had wandered through most of his house and it was nearly time for another blocker. Dr. Vásquez had a million questions about that, too, and demanded to see what had been done. She was an orthopedic surgeon, not the physical therapist he'd wanted, but she could certainly give him advice. When she had the bot project scans and x-rays onto a blank wall to analyze, Na moseyed back to Paul's side.

"She was chosen because she was closest to Shee," he said for Paul's ears only. "Hopefully she's a good mediward."

"I'm sure she'll be great," Paul muttered back. "Bedside manner isn't a dream, but I don't think that's really where surgeons shine. At least she understands Human bodies and what's best for them."

"Speaking of Human bodies. That the bedroom?" Na asked, thumb pointed over his shoulder. "Be back."

"Hey!" Paul objected, rather uselessly. He thought the Nyakisi were supposed to be masters of stealth, but so far Na had been blatant in checking out Paul's space. Did he suspect something about Yuhwa and Paul's encounter, or was he just nosey?

"Do you have any idea how lucky you are?" Dr. Vásquez

marched back to his bedside. "Whoever did this work, you owe them. I can't be one hundred percent sure, but you might have lost the leg. You most certainly would have been permanently disabled without their beautiful work."

Paul nodded. "I know, and I really appreciate their help. But I need to get back on my feet and return to fighting form. How fast can we move to bearing weight, maybe some PT?"

She looked at him like he was rather disappointing. "I can see from your physique you're quite physical, used to exercise or working out."

"Yeah, I-"

"Don't let that go to your head. You are not a superhero." She made a sharp hand gesture to stop his next words. "You are months away from that. Listen to me. Months."

He recoiled. That couldn't be, it just wasn't possible. Not in his version of the future. "The aoiti will help, they'll speed everything up. I'm already tolerating a lot of the pain, and the swelling is going down."

Dr. Vásquez made a dismissive noise, like sucking her teeth and clicking her tongue simultaneously. "You're hallucinating, young man. The records show you are only a day out of intricate surgery on a major joint. If they'd cut out your knee and replaced it I'd have you up and moving. But not for this."

Na, reentering the room, said, "We all tried to tell him."

Horse pucky. Yuhwa, Lanu and Thuliso had. Na and the other two hadn't said a damn thing.

"Listen to your friends," Dr. Vásquez said, reaching for the brace. "Tell that robot to show me the right way to open this device."

About thirty minutes of examination and discussion later, the doctor left with Na. Her instructions were clear and simple: don't move. He'd almost gotten permission to leave the bed for toilet breaks, until Na pointed out the bed handled that. Paul had then been forced to admit it was moving him just enough that bedsores weren't a problem either, so she told him to stay put.

Not long after the doctor left, the bot read him a message from Yuhwa: Dr. Vásquez had been invited to bring her family into Shee as thanks for helping. "The mediward also says she'll be checking on you regularly, so don't 'fug up' your leg."

Paul wasn't going to correct Yuhwa's pronunciation, their relationship was tenuous enough as it was. He wanted to apologize, but needed to say it to her face and couldn't figure out how to get her back in here. The anxieties were building, closing off his mind: he was ensnared in a big ass ship of scared, angry humans; his family was a kajillion light years away; the woman he'd managed to turn into his second pissed off ex was avoiding him.

Instead of asking her to talk like an adult, Paul opted to watch a movie. *Shaun of the Dead* might not have the best relationship advice, but it still made him laugh every time. He needed a little of that right now.

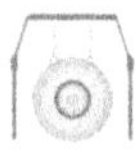

YUHWA HAD SURVIVED QUITE a lot in her four hundred tuigs. Being advanced in dao studies from early on had gotten the attention of many people; some of it good and some not. Her papa's murder, her mother's withdrawal and death from heartbreak. Misspent years at Centris, then gallivanting around the Aoni as a young, hotshot majio desperate to prove her worth. Late nights and lusty affairs to have fun and satiate the hungry beast of loneliness. Lately all the herald mirca with Katy and Bay, plus the associated drama of a Drazoen returning to the Aoni after a kōmilen.

But this latest round of confusion was something not even the Five Côttru could have navigated. Foremost in her mind was regret for crossing the line with Paul. Their night together had been blissful as it happened, but Yuhwa had chosen to ignore her worry he wasn't a one-night man. She cursed herself now. A situation like this could ruin her friendships, not only the one with Paul; first with Katy and the Phelans, then Bay and Lia and possibly even Raisa. When groups were woven as tightly as theirs, one frayed thread could unravel the whole.

It was made much worse by his injury, because Yuhwa knew what it was doing to him mentally. People like him couldn't handle enforced stillness: since the moment he'd gotten on the *Eternidad*, he'd been itching to move and expend energy. Aoiti would do many things to help his recovery, as would the Human mediward they'd recruited. But he felt trapped and useless, not a good mental state for a man who had such a need to manage his environment.

Two sals after the *Eternidad* left, the *Mahoroba* continued to linger in the Mukuru system. Yuhwa argued with the Drafter via Mandy, her demands they make an appearance roundly ignored. The last she'd seen of Paul, he was snapping at the M-bots and arguing with the mediward, a furious, chained Druk raging against his hobbling. She'd departed before he noticed her, certain he saw their relationship as a mistake now, and not wanting to add to his stress. It hurt her more than she liked to admit.

What luck, then, that she could refocus her efforts on sorting out the *Mahoroba*. Just at the moment she was hunting Na for a discussion. After a final, infuriating argument with Mandy, Yuhwa had no recourse but to get the ship moving toward Malor. The nawa call hurt substantially now, and at least flying home would give her some purpose. She felt she'd lacked that for a while, possibly ever since bringing the Phelans to Centris.

M8, a purple bot who had announced earlier in the sal they were her personal bot – "I was redesigned to match your hair!" – copiloted the sled Yuhwa had commandeered to find the Nyakisi. It directed her into an area of Ring Twelve, named Anatolian Steppe, which her aoiti told her was a vast area on Earth in a country named Turkey. She remembered Paul saying "original flavor Earth" and smiled sadly. She missed when he'd joked with her.

She could have commed Na to come to the numig, but she hadn't explored much outside of Shee since the crisis. She wanted to see for herself how the ship citizens were coping. M8 had assured her Humans were calmer now than at 'initial capture' and 'subsequent incident'. Looking at the few people she could see in this bioregion, Yuhwa wasn't sure calm was the right word. They weren't trying to kill one another anymore but they didn't gather as friends, either.

Humans here were overwhelmed. Broken, perhaps. Tired, certainly. There was a hollowness to their eyes, a slackness of mouth, and many shuffled without aim or intent. Moving to move, but going nowhere. She needed to talk Lanu into doing another ship-wide chat. They were afraid their last message had scared more than soothed, but Yuhwa thought these Humans needed a voice promising them an end to the rushing river they'd been thrown into. If Paul had been his old self she would have asked him, but in his current state she was afraid he'd have them all setting things afire again.

She and M8 hopped off the newly produced travel sled; there'd been a variety parked at the Shee train station she could pick from. This was a smaller, four-seat version of the one she'd used before. The trip from Shee to Ring Twelve took longer by this sled, but had given Yuhwa a granular view of how impossibly large *Mahoroba* was. Now she wasn't terrified and flying to save lives, she had to marvel at the construction. It was methodically laid out, from the cylinders connecting the regional spheres and the rings, down to the massive central ring threaded through the arm rings. She thought the Drafter had planned the request well, even if the heart of the dream was faulty. If they'd just *asked* people to go, it might have been idyllic.

Like this spot, nestled inside an entire ring dedicated to natural settings. On Earth the land wasn't highly populated and this replication kept true to that. She wasn't sure if she'd ever like so much green plant life – she was used to more orange and teal – but Yuhwa could appreciate the view.

Na stood a short walk from where she'd stopped; hands on hips, staring into the distance, looking over vast swathes of emerald-covered land. Khais and khais of verdant grasses under a blue sky.

"Greetings alien Na Xan!" M8 blared. "Majio attends!"

Yuhwa pressed two fingers against her forehead. "That's still not how or when the phrase is used. Why do I have to keep repeating that? You will also stop referring to people as aliens, or Humans, or any designation that isn't their name or rank."

M8 wobbled in the air. "But what if I do not know their name?"

"Ask," she grumbled, heading for Na.

Na hadn't turned despite the ruckus, though a few Humans stared at the spectacle Yuhwa and M8 made.

"Exploring?" she asked when she stood at his side.

He nodded. "Based on description, I thought I'd see how close to Godot this place is."

Yuhwa took in the grassy plains, gently rolling hills nearby, larger ones in the distance. Stand-alone dwellings, boxy and squat, infrequently dotted the lands around them. Beautiful, albeit barren. "And?"

Na cocked his head. "Not too bad, but too much light. Godot is always in twilight. This is very bright."

Yuhwa had read once that Nyakisi eyes spotted so many expensive objects because they were trained to see in dimness. She thought that was ridiculous; they found riches because they sought them. And because they were coached from infancy to be little criminals.

"I come to make a bargain with you," Yuhwa said bluntly.

"Weellll," Na dragged out, turning at last to look at her. "How intriguing, majio. What could you possibly need from a sneakthief and liar such as myself. Dating advice?"

Clenching her teeth, she pressed on. "When the Drafter requested this ship, they only specified needing something that makes travel faster than light possible. That's me. They did not, however, ask for a regular pilot. It seems the request details were taken very literally."

Na guffawed. "This is priceless! The most comprehensive species ark ever constructed and it floats in place for want of a captain?!"

Yuhwa scrunched her nose. "This is what happens when immense resources and power are allocated to someone who doesn't understand what they're dealing with." She bit her lip before continuing, "I'm here to offer you the job. Captain of the *Mahoroba*."

"Oh no," he threw out his hands, as if he could push the offer back into her mouth. "I'm here to observe only."

"That isn't an option, Na." She kicked at the ground with her left toe. "Humans can't do it. All the Mikanjo left when the Phelans did. I could maybe do it, but poorly, and only until we get to Malor. You stayed, you have to pitch in."

He pulled back slightly, not responding, then faced the sweeping view. "The sim-sun will set here in a few sal-angs. Perhaps I'll like this place more after it darkens." He waved negligently. "Ask the Lunari voices, they always love to be in the middle of important business. I am not in the mood to take on unpaid work."

"I don't...." Yuhwa debated how honest to be with Na, and decided she had little to lose by sharing. "I don't entirely trust them." When he turned to her, his eyebrow winging up, she twisted her face away this time. "It isn't something I can pinpoint, but part of me has never trusted Olak and Pijo. They latched onto Raisa the second we first arrived at Voice House, and maybe it was Olak's instant attraction to her, but maybe not."

His gaze skewered her. "That leaves the appointed. Thuliso."

"The Lunari appointed. A man who happens to be in all kinds of important places at important times. That's suspicious, too." Yuhwa crossed her arms, disgruntled. Why was Na being difficult?

"There are some who would say I'm the suspicious one. You, yourself, have wondered at my motives in the past." He stepped into her line of sight. "Why do you think you can count on me?"

"You're Nyakisi. If I find the right price, you'll stay loyal for the length of our bargain. The question is, what can I find that would tempt you?"

"I don't open negotiations, I counter or I accept. You have to decide what you think will entice me."

His hair was even shorter than the last time she'd looked him over, but when had he had time to get a haircut? *Why* would he, when the Calling was imploding, the hunt for Budi commenced, and Sundancer transported them all here to rescue her herald? His synth leather suit this time was the finest she'd seen yet, in a softer black than his usual. Was that iridescent brown thread in a wing pattern on the cuffs?

Yuhwa took her time considering each piece of data she had about Na. He'd be entertained enough by their discussion to stay until she at least made an initial offer. It took her longer than it should have, but she gave herself a break since the last buwan had been a hål of a sandstorm.

"I noticed you didn't move into Shee, and I know it's not typical of a Nyakisi to accept living quarters in close proximity to others. But the Lunari have taken residence there, as has the mediward and her family. Paul, me. You would be offered the same. Your pick of the open units; they're very spacious and comfortable." Yuhwa paused. "Raisa visits Olak pretty often, too, and seems happy there. She needs an escape, with how much her family berates her for being a disappointment."

Yuhwa knew she'd hit on the right thing by his utter lack of response. He didn't scoff, laugh, or dispute her words. When he pinned her gaze with his bioluminescent one, the narrow ring of glowing indigo nearly eclipsed by black pupil, she thought she had him. Twice he'd called Raisa *bardu*, which didn't happen outside of committed pairings. The embroidery on his clothing was the same color as Raisa's hair. She spoke to something in Na, the fact she was with Olak notwithstanding.

"We have a contract, majio. Until we reach Malor, then I will either renegotiate or end my service."

"Witnessed!" M8 exclaimed.

24

"ON THE WAY BACK TO THE NUMIG, WE CAN DISCUSS what you think Olak and Pijo may hope to accomplish with the innocent Human. Raisa." Na's voice rolled her name over his tongue, like it was a fine vintage of amstre wine.

Yuhwa worried interactions between Na and Raisa could be as fraught as hers with Paul, but interfering wasn't part of her job. "The Cadre, for all their neutrality, still seeks power. They keep what they have, and always look for more," she said as they boarded the sled.

"What could a member of a new species offer them? One who wasn't the herald."

"Entry-level access to future Human ambassadors, maybe? I could be imagining intrigue that isn't there. But there's a reason their appointed always show up in unexpected places, knowing more than you'd think non-natives would." Yuhwa steered them out of the bioregion. "Like Thuliso. How did he get on-world access to the Imen? I was shocked when we went to recall him at Cadre orders. One of the most protective, insular species of the Aoni, yet he was embedded deeply enough the Imen weren't going to return him until Lia convinced them otherwise."

Na leaned on the sled's rail. "We've heard many things about Thuliso over the tuigs. He actually managed to get into a Pleinarre. I guess that was a milenyo past? Very early sals in his appointed role."

Yuhwa was intrigued. "How did a Lunari get onto Godot and infiltrate the biggest celebration of the tuig? Isn't that where you handle big business, marriage contracts, that kind of thing?"

"Yes, everything. Families rejoin for a brief time, breeding contracts are settled for those less inclined to marriage, starts of feuds and ends to old vendettas. All out in the open, as these things should be. Thuliso Maor out-crept even the Nyakisi. He was discovered in a woman's tent, interrupted in the act." Na's eyebrows arched and he tilted forward. "Some say he planned it all, the scandal of making love to a contracted woman and being caught mid-bedding, to cover up his assassination of a Calling politician."

"What? No!" Yuhwa didn't trust the man, but a murderer?

Na straightened, looking around them as they neared the first locked entry to Shee. "The man was a lobbyist, scheduled to talk with our bloc. Homicide couldn't be proven, Thuliso is too good for that. But it neatly ended talks of Calling motions intended to reduce what Centris pays the Chorus for Cadre maintenance."

Yuhwa blanched. "I don't think I believe that."

"Which part: that the Cadre would send their appointed out to kill, or that the Cadre don't do their jobs out of love and loyalty?" He shook his head. "Any foolishness like that was burned out of them when the Krylar incinerated their planet. Now we watch them closely for any other attempts on political members."

Yuhwa wagged a finger at him. "You're trying to infect me with your pessimism."

"Realism, majio. I've seen much more of the Aoni than you. Take my words to heart: almost no one acts unselfishly."

Yuhwa waited for the first portal to admit them into Shee's antechamber, then zoomed across to the main portal and jumped down from the sled, Na following her. M8, who'd been silent the entire ride back from Ring Twelve, finally spoke.

"This is not the proper location for the travel sled, majio."

"It is now," Yuhwa said, moving through the doors. "We need easy access and having to go through the train station is wasting time."

"But," M8 said, rather judgmentally, "that isn't where it's *meant* to be. A place for everything, and everything in its place."

Both Na and Yuhwa stopped, staring at the purple bot. A couple of lights blipped and flashed, then M8 said, "Mandy programmed that. She acknowledges it doesn't resonate with you, and rescinds the statement." M8 flew past them toward the commend center. "For now."

They'd walked no more than nine steps when Raisa appeared ahead and to the left of them. Three Humans followed her, through a door and into the covered breezeway. Raisa hadn't seen them yet, but they heard her speaking.

"Baba, see? It's beautiful! You could all come stay here, and we'd be safe. This place is secure, no one except those approved are allowed in."

"She's your *almost no one*," Yuhwa murmured. "She's never been selfish in the time I've known her."

Na rumbled, "I believe you are correct."

Yuhwa girded herself for a run-in with the Leon family, who weren't as generous as Raisa. The family interaction was what Yuhwa had expected, especially after the Lunari joined them. Although, Na's response had been surprisingly astute. She'd assumed he was so self-involved he couldn't see the struggles of others, but she'd been wrong. The appreciation for his empathy in Raisa and her brother's eyes was immeasurable.

As they left, Raisa touched Yuhwa, pleading, "Get us back to Centris soon?" before her mother pulled her away.

Yuhwa's heart cracked a little, realizing the amazing woman who'd helped her friend wake Sundancer Orange had been so isolated by her family she didn't know about the nawa call and their upcoming detour to Malor. She'd been integral to what they'd accomplished so far and she was being left behind. Yuhwa couldn't judge what happened inside their house, but it felt wrong that Raisa was missing out on big plans their core group was making.

"You do her an injustice," Na growled. "She is trapped by them and you do nothing to help!"

"Too far, Nyakisi," Yuhwa snarled. "You don't even know her, and you judge me? *I'm* the one who's drunk rusim and talked all hours with her. I know some of what she dreams and fears, and how tightly she holds to her family. A friend doesn't damage another by insisting they know better. Pushing could break her."

Na sucked his teeth in disagreement. "And what of you, great and noble voices? You left her exposed on the tower, gave her no handhold, or guide to a safe landing."

Olak quirked a brow. "I fail to see how it involves you at all, Na. Our relationship is just that. Ours."

Refusing her a response, he shook his head and stormed off. "I'll be in the numig," he shouted. "Time to move this nûzed ship!"

Thuliso enquired, "You made him captain?" Adding loudly, "Him?!"

"He was the best option," Yuhwa replied. Defending her choice without revealing her distrust of the group in front of her would be tricky. "We have history, from our trip to Ishar."

"The trip where he used and lied to you, and that you haven't forgiven him for?" Pijo said. "That history?"

"Regardless of his lies, there's a compatibility in our flight styles. I'll need every advantage when I try to transit. No one has ever travelled the dao with a ship this big, with so many life-forms." She shuddered. "I might not be able do it at all, but if there's any chance I can, I'll take the help a familiar captain provides. My dao will recognize him." Yuhwa was astonished to realize she wasn't lying; perhaps her subconscious had picked Na for more than one reason.

All three Lunari considered her, then one another. Finally, Thuliso clapped and said with false cheer, "Try not to leave us all behind in the veṣu, majio. We're at your mercy and in your hands."

"Shtŭing hỏi hậu appointed." Yuhwa was fed up with all of them. "I'm going to check on Paul." With that she jogged away, determined: she and Paul would work their way to friendship, and get back to the collaborative problem solving they'd excelled at before sleeping together. They had to, because there didn't seem to be anyone else on the ship she could completely trust.

ONCE YUHWA FORGAVE him for being a numpty, they had a great time together. She was leaving Na in charge of easing the *Mahoroba* into motion, saying if he couldn't get them started, she'd never get them through a veṣu. Paul really liked the guy, but questioned how much of their full sal delay was down to honest issues versus milking the attention for all it was worth.

He was pretty proud of himself thinking in Aoni time. Mandy and the Drafter had proclaimed the whole ship would move to Centris time. "Humans need to acclimate, the sooner the better." The AI interface broadcast that message ship-wide in her upbeat, life coach voice.

Yuhwa had snuck out to see how it was received and said most people seemed not to care. "There was nothing new on fire," she said. "I think that means it's okay."

Okay or past caring? Immobile as he was, there was little he could do to get a feel and judge for himself. One thing that *had* caught fire was his mouth: Dr. Vásquez and her family had moved into Shee, thrilled to be out of the biosphere they'd landed in. Her husband made stuffed peppers as a thank you; they called them rocoto relleno. Paul's mistake was thinking the red pepper was like a bell pepper. Incorrect. Very, very, incorrect.

If he'd started crying after the first big bite, they were all kind enough not to point it out. The tears may have been partially due to missing his family, because Vasuda would have gobbled the spicy dish up, laughing all the while. But no one needed to know what a sentimental dork he was, so he left it at pain from the peppers.

There were three Vásquez children, all girls under ten, who ran around the courtyard and splashed in the pool. Upon meeting non-humans, they announced Lunari eyes were cool and wished they had them, but they didn't want extra toes and fingers. And why couldn't the Jadoube and Nyakisi look "more alien"? More like Lanu, who they swore was the coolest person they'd ever met.

Paul got their help, with doc's approval, to float the bed into the courtyard and teach the girls some beginner gymnastics. Yuhwa helped them with some of the moves, smiling and laughing at the children's antics. It was the happiest he'd been since leaving Earth.

Then Mr. Vásquez upped the ante by cooking and sharing ají de gallina, an amazing Peruvian chicken stew that Paul couldn't stop eating. They'd all gathered at the communal tables in command, parked his bed at the head of the table, and given him a tray. The sim-sun was going down, Yuhwa sat beside him, and he felt peaceful, despite Thuliso trying to hog the stew.

Those few moments were precious, transitory though they might be. Watching Na and the others try new foods, laughing at the varying responses, helped him release the frustration that had made him lash out at Yuhwa before. The Vásquez addition to Shee made it feel more like a family gathering, easing some of his heartache at being separated from the Phelan brood.

Raisa walked in, looking tired but relieved. Getting away from her family had to contribute to both states. He introduced the Vásquez family, and Raisa graciously thanked them for their willingness to help.

"I hear we're on Centris Measured time now?" She pulled a chair up next to Olak, who slid a hand onto her thigh.

Na watched their interaction surreptitiously from his side of the table; what was that about? Not my business, Paul thought. I have enough trouble with my own situation. He and Yuhwa were next to each other, but he was careful not to touch or invade her space. She'd have to give him the clarity of where their friendship had landed.

"Not fully CM," Thuliso corrected. "Based on Earth time, that would make a 'forty hour day', which the Drafter vetoed."

Paul scrunched his face up. "We're on sals, but not Centris sals?"

"I suggested a compromise," Lanu answered. "Twenty-seven Earth hours to make up a *Mahoroba* sal."

Raisa laughed. "That won't get confusing at all."

"The growing pains of new-to-the-Aoni species," Thuliso offered in response. "CM is one thing, everyone else has their own version. Your aoiti will keep you aligned."

Yuhwa grimaced and Paul could hear her teeth grinding. He leaned close, or as close as the bed would let him. "You okay?"

"The call gets worse when I forget to focus on pushing it down," she replied softly. "It's like fingers dragging along the inside of my skin."

Paul wasn't having that. "Na, buddy, when are we going to get this rust bucket moving?" He was met with blank stares.

"Buddy?" Na drawled the question.

"You rifled through my underwear drawer, don't think I didn't notice that. That makes us buddies."

"This is a one-of-a-kind work of art, nearly faultless." Yuhwa sounded grouchy, flexing her fingers around the fork in her hand. Was she going to stab him? "Don't call my ship a rust bucket."

"Your ship?" Paul and Na said simultaneously.

She flushed and turned her attention to Raisa. "Your family released you at last?"

"No," Raisa said. "I snuck out. Olak sent a bot and sled for me, and I crawled out the window."

"You are so busted when they catch you," Paul laughed.

"For Nyakisi, children learning to escape their homes and return without being caught is highly prized." Na's voice was soft, a finger tracing around his empty plate. "We would celebrate your small victory of independence on Godot." His eyes came up, a tiny lift of his lips on one side making him rakishly charming.

Not that he'd be trying on someone taken, as Raisa so clearly was; but why couldn't Paul have moves like that? He had to face it, Na was exponentially cooler than he was. "Back to the original question. Why aren't we moving yet?"

"Preening your captain's feathers?" Pijo said snidely.

Thuliso tossed out, "This isn't one of his little smuggling ships. Maybe it's more than he can handle."

Olak laughed, but Raisa and the rest of the table frowned. The catty attitude wasn't a good look from the Lunari trio.

"I thought to give Humans time to heal," Na said, slouching. His hands had curled around the chair arms, but he flexed them a finger at a time. "There are more Humans on this ship than there are Lunari in the Aoni. Or Uilig. Hål, more than

Jadoube, Nyakisi, name your species. You have to combine the entirety of several species in order to get to Human numbers. Just on this ship." He smiled at Paul. "You are a prodigious people.

"They're scared, confused, and hostile out there. What I've learned smuggling namu," Na turned a nasty smile on Thuliso, "is that cornered people react unpredictably. A sal or two spent settling down, teaching them more about where they are, who we are, and where we're going together? I don't see how that can hurt."

Raisa leaned forward, resting her arms on the table. "Thank you," she said quietly and sincerely. "Your insight is true and much appreciated."

Na gave her a single nod, before pushing back and standing. "Tomorrow we can begin flight to the veṣu. That should take half the sal."

Paul leaned into Yuhwa again. "Good enough?"

She sighed. "As long as there's a distraction, I can survive it."

His heart (and southern regions) got excited for a second, thinking she meant sexy times could resume. But a closer glance at her face told a different story; she needed laughter and light to counterbalance the nawa's incessant tugging.

"Raisa, you hungry? How are you with spice? Because we have leftovers of a dish that my doctor and her family tried to kill me with."

The girls erupted with peals of laughter, and Carlos, their father, objected theatrically that he'd merely overestimated a gringo's capacity for "flavor." Everyone at the table was eager to relate how Paul had turned redder than the rocoto, teared up like a baby, and drunk half a quart of milk to recover. Paul pointed out he was an Irish gringo from Seattle, used to seafood, avocado toast, and pizza. Yuhwa laughed too, and the pinched skin around her eyes relaxed. Paul could be the butt of the joke if it made her smile.

"I think," he interjected loudly, throwing his arms into the air, "that it should be movie night!"

Twenty minutes later popcorn was in laps, M13 was projecting an animated movie on the side of the command center, and they'd all gathered in a semi-circle to watch. Mandy had hastened twilight in Shee, and their drive-in/movie-in-the-park mood was heavenly. Paul was deeply content, especially because the new form of entertainment was distracting Yuhwa exactly as he'd hoped.

She poked his arm an hour later. "Give me the rest of your cornpops," she whispered.

"Popcorn," he corrected, "and get your own, woman!" The girls shushed him and he ducked his head in mock shame.

Yuhwa eyed his half-full bowl, looked around, then slid herself into the bed. Quick as you please, she was suddenly squished up against his side. He scooted over to make room. It was barely big enough for both of them, but Paul wasn't about to object to the closeness.

"You still have plenty, and you haven't touched it in at least twenty kaalas." Her whisper was straight to his ear this time, giving him goosebumps. "You should let me have it."

"You can't just steal mine." Paul didn't actually want any more, but felt like he couldn't give in without a little compromise. He settled the bowl half on his thigh, half on hers. "But I'll share.

When the movie ended, everyone else left for their respective units.

"On Earth your animals talk?" Olak and Pijo were on either side of Raisa, questioning her. "If this is true, don't your people object to eating them? Or have the animals consented?"

Paul was leaving that to Raisa to explain. Nor was he questioning the wisdom of her staying the night with Olak; that was her mountain to climb with the Leon family. Dr. Vásquez checked out his knee before going. It was much less swollen than earlier, nearly normal, but she confirmed he wouldn't be "doing anything athletic" overnight, and smiled indulgently when he held up two fingers in the scout's salute.

Na eyed the bed currently shared by Yuhwa and raised an eyebrow, but said nothing as he sauntered to his own room. Soon enough, Paul and Yuhwa were alone. Neither one spoke, neither one moved. They quietly enjoyed the stars appearing overhead, comfortable where they were.

25

"Yippee-ki-yay!"

Paul groaned. "Stop."

"But I love it, why can't I use it?" Yuhwa was having fun driving Paul a little crazy this morning.

"Where are we on the nropita situation?" he grumbled. "And you can't use it a ton because it's a bingo word."

"What the hål," Thuliso interrupted, "is a bingo word?"

"And why do they weigh so much?" added Pijo.

Paul looked to the ceiling, searching for an explanation that would make sense. He'd need to work hard, because the aoiti were throwing strange images of spinning balls with numbers and letters at her.

"Bingo words are ones you only use at the perfect time. Like in the movie; did he use it constantly? No. McClane saved it for the moment it would have the best impact." Fortified with the nropita Yuhwa handed him, he continued. "In this case, 'a ton' doesn't mean weight as much as high frequency. If you overuse the word, then it isn't cool or fun. Say it too often and it loses power. For instance, he never says it again in the later movies."

Yuhwa gasped. "There are more of them?" The movie they'd

watched after the one Paul called a kid's movie had been a brilliant diversion from the pain of the nawa's persistent call. *Die Hard*, and by Nine they had! Explosions and fighting, and that marvelous word. If there were more like it, they'd be watching each one.

"Still good?" Paul asked quietly.

She both appreciated and hated his care. He'd been solicitous without smothering her, after he had apologized sincerely for his rudeness in the wake of his injury. She realized he was comforting her, watching out for her, something that hadn't happened since she was a girl. Did she like that? Did it make her weak to revel the teensiest bit in being eased by his care?

"Still good," she affirmed. "Manageable. Hopefully it eases once we're in my home galaxy." They'd already started to fly, Na estimating veṣu approach in eight sal-angs.

"Mkay. Just let me know if you need more distraction. I'll teach you card games."

"Or," Yuhwa offered, "we see more of the movies. There are more explosions and bad people being outwitted?"

Paul's smile was a wash of cool river over her raw spirit. "Absolutely."

They watched from his unit this time. She didn't climb into his bed again, tempting as that was. The night before he hadn't tried to push for sex. He'd accepted her beside him without comment, giving her the closeness she'd needed in the moment. They could make this work, she thought. Their friendship would be stronger for their night together, give them a comfortable familiarity.

His mediward visited shortly after the first movie ended, marveling at his accelerated healing. "Another few days and I think we could shift to the next phase." When Paul's eyes lit and he sat straighter she firmed her tone. "Gently! Very gentle, low impact exercises. And only after we test weight-bearing, which will not happen today so keep your bottom planted."

Yuhwa's heart twisted at the hope and relief on Paul's face. She'd known he was afraid, hål, that was the source of his earlier anger and lashing out. But now she understood how deeply scared he'd been, especially when he asked the mediward, "Would I truly have lost the leg on Earth?"

"Possibly," she confirmed. "Like I said before, what I saw, that was a real possibility." Shaking it off, she clapped him on the shoulder. "Not the case anymore, though, so put that out of your mind. Focus on being careful. Your healing has to be deliberate and mindful."

A few sal-angs more, playing with the children as Paul taught them his gymnastics. That led to a lot of questions about his work, then to videos of something Humans did called Olympics. It reminded her a bit of the Dál, without the blood and broken bones. Or, at least purposeful bloodletting and breakage, because she watched more than one Human damage muscles or try to staunch bleeding hands, feet and noses.

Paul explained to everyone what was happening as film of gymnasts played. The complexity of movement stirred her, the raw power of forcing a body in motion to freeze, or bend and twist, even to fly in the air. He had been an intensely physical man before leaving Earth, still was, and it went deeper than she'd supposed. The precision of the athletes' movements reminded her of their bed sports two nights past; he'd been flexible and strong, holding her against walls or simply lifting her body over him, maneuvering her where he wanted her to go. Not once did he hurt her or leave a mark, his power a tool he wielded effortlessly.

The blow of his injury would have been acutely felt. Somehow, he'd kept it together enough to help get his father to help, which was yet another overwhelming fear that he'd mastered. Remembering her own frozen, shocked response to her papa's murder begged the question: if she'd been present when the killer attacked, could she have handled the emergency as well as Paul had? She'd undervalued Paul's quiet strength.

Gazing at him over the rim of her rusim glass, something settled inside her. He had snuck up on her, this man who employed Migwa's stealth to climb into her world. Paul was jaejuan to her, just as Katy was. More, perhaps. Chosen family, imperative to her happiness. She knew that she could depend on him and his sturdiness.

Revolutionary thought, that. It was a potent awareness she carried in her heart

Na interrupted their supper, eyes merry. "We approach." Of course he'd view this as a caper, not a life-threatening risk. Damn Nyakisi.

Yuhwa closed her eyes, inhaled until she felt it in every extremity. Standing, she looked to Paul and Raisa. "I may need you, could you join me?"

In this moment, Yuhwa had to face every doubt and concern she'd been ignoring. No Jadoube had ever tried to swim the dao with a vessel the size of the *Mahoroba*. The idea was preposterous, daunting, and nerve-wracking. How could she connect with the life forces of all the Humans, the animals, even the plant life? She was a genetically manipulated pilot capable of things no other being could handle, but this might be too much.

Except.

One other being could do this. Or Nine of them, to be specific. Yuhwa wondered if she could connect with that well of power in some way when she went into the dance. Her ability was a gift from Songmaster, after all.

She remembered a snippet of a nawa text they'd studied in school. The one explaining why they went on pâtexi; she'd used it to seduce Paul. *For all Jadoube must always shift, adjust.*

That's what she would make happen, somehow. Bend, alter, find a new way, as she was born to do. Mind made up, she spun and walked toward the numig. Before she could take more than two steps, three young girls had thrown themselves around her waist, hugging her.

"Papi says what you're doing is very important," the youngest whispered.

The oldest squeezed hard. "Mami says you're our hope, and we know you can do it."

Yuhwa stroked their heads, giving them a moment to power up her resolve. "I will, and then, do you know what you will see? Your first new world! My world, Malor."

That had them running back to their parents, babbling excitedly. Paul, bed pushed along by Raisa, smiled at Yuhwa. "Nice one."

Raisa said, "It only just occurred to me, but someone should probably explain what's about to happen to the rest of the ship."

Sofia, the mediward, offered to do it. "Seeing Humans who aren't afraid of it, perhaps that would help."

Yuhwa nodded, praying this didn't turn into more trouble. But it had to be done; her soul felt scoured like the wadis of Malor at this point. Nawa didn't fool around when they called their people home.

Na, proclaiming the captain was always present for transit, went first. Yuhwa, Paul and Raisa entered the numig right behind him. They all gazed at one another, ignoring wall after wall of screens revealing the fast-approaching veşu. This was a giant one, the sort that might have already consumed others that strayed across its path. Yuhwa was happy about that; it gave her more room to work the dao, more quantum and cosmic river in which to swim.

Na finally broke the silence. "Don't mess this up, majio."

Snorting, Yuhwa climbed onto her dao bed and waved him off. "This? Nothing. You're the one who has to figure out where to park when we arrive." Reclining, sinking in the plush bed and closing her eyes, she chuckled. "Malor has seventy-four moons. Good luck."

She sensed Paul and Yuhwa taking positions on either side of her. Na stayed near the lounge chairs at her feet, but didn't sit. Before reaching for the dao, Yuhwa reached for these three. They would be her anchors as she stretched her senses wider than ever before.

Her linking was gossamer, a touch so light they would never sense it. It gave her the flavor of each of them, just sips that secured them, momentarily, as a unified group.

Raisa, warm spices and gentleness like fur stroking over Yuhwa's abraded senses. Na, the darkness of a forest at midnight, loamy and lush. The combination cradled Yuhwa, centered her between them.

Paul was a balm unto himself. He was the stillness at the center of Lake Bai-Bom, water fed from the heart of Âuke, cool and restful. There was a tang, a bite, earthy metallic traces that spoke of power dredged from fathoms unseen. He invited her deeper, whether consciously or not, to tether to him.

Just this once. Yuhwa would allow herself to depend on these three, praying to the Nine she had the strength to get them home. Just this once.

Weaving their three threads into a rope that she tied around herself, she expanded, reached, connecting as she encountered the living things of *Mahoroba*. Each time, she affixed the new thread to the larger rope; the mediward and her family, the Lunari group, Lanu; moving out of Shee to strangers who had no idea what she did. She had to block individual scents and perceptions, taking them as a whole.

Yuhwa no longer held a rope, it had woven into a net, something she'd never thought to craft when swimming the dao. Her instincts were in charge now, and that's what they demanded. She soon felt the strain of such a heavy net, holding fish too numerous to count anymore. It would drag her under, drown her, if she couldn't find a way through.

Only after an aiwak or two of training were novice majio

allowed to visit their first veşu. It wasn't without risk; the tuig Yuhwa had first gone a young man got overwhelmed and was lost to the dao. Sadly, in cases like that a body could not be returned to his family. He was forever part of the veşu, though the nawa said he wasn't truly gone, only transformed. She couldn't do that to all these Humans.

Sundancer, she called in her mind, feeling the veşu press in on her. *Songmaster. All blesséd Nine. Hear me. Help me guide this ship. Give me the power, the knowledge.* Yuhwa knew she had half of the ship gathered, at best, and transit was mere atómi away. If she couldn't hold all of it, they would be lost in the veşu. They would exist eternally in a state of their last thoughts, like that boy, frozen in time, until they were physically consumed by the veşu's force.

Diving deeper and deeper into the river, begging the dao to reveal a path, Yuhwa pulled on her first connections, bringing more of her friends into herself. There! The waja of Na's resolve and keenness to take mad risks. Raisa's wildness she tried to keep locked away, escaping from around ragged edges. Paul's cavernous well of love, and desire for connection, pushing to the surface and flooding their link.

Down Yuhwa swam, into the darkest, blackest shadows, where instructors told them never to go. It held a warmth she hadn't expected, as though a pocket of dao heated and radiated through her chilled bones.

Child

sweet Child

she returns home

not yet not yet soon not yet

Four voices spoke, though speak wasn't correct. They were in her head and body, her very blood vibrated with their words. Their thoughts coated her in their hope and desire to unite with her. *Help me*, she cried, truly scared. *I don't think I can do this.*

you can

you will
follow the path
love to love be loved

Time ceased. Her mind enlarging, expanding, like ripples from a stone dropped into water. The net of life on *Mahoroba* that she'd built of colorless threads transformed, shining silver in the blackness. New thoughts flashed: rather than connect lines one-by-one, she could allow the relationships to self-attach. They would attract and integrate themselves. Her net grew larger, the weave and weft becoming complex, intertwined, a gleaming, near-solid textile. A sheet that circled Yuhwa as she swam forward, a bubble of life in the dao. One she needed to ferry to safety.

The warm darkness pushed her toward a pinprick of color; one she associated with Malor. Desert tan and brown heated by their orange sun, speckled with multicolor bursts of the plateaus where all Jadoube lived. Green waters inviting her to float free.

come home

to us

we wait for you Child

homehomehome

Their voices, the excitement and urgency, surged inside Yuhwa. She stretched from the inside, swelling, intensifying. The ripples from the dropped pebble expanded her mind, her dao, until it encompassed her and her silver sheet. She dove, moving in a completely new way through the quantum river she'd known her entire life. Instead of aggressively forging through, she harnessed the wave momentum and allowed it to funnel her home.

One final cresting rush and they were through. Yuhwa felt the *Mahoroba* and everything within it squeeze through the pinprick and burst back into open space.

Thank you, she sobbed. *Thank you for showing me the way.* There was no response, only a faint echo of longing.

26

In hindsight, Paul acknowledged that he'd never fully processed his journey from earthbound Human to space wayfarer. How could he? Arriving on Centris had been more like landing at a foreign airport. Sure, there'd been aliens and it was huge, but part of him had always known it was enclosed, manufactured, not a true planet. Kind of the ultimate Duty-Free zone.

Approaching the atmosphere of Malor, aiming for Yuto Port on the Jarog Plateau, watching desert and a massive volcano fill the viewscreen of the shuttle, a few things cleared up for him. Below him sprawled a celestial body formed wholly independently of his own solar system. A bigger planet than Earth according to the M-bots, coalesced and hardened in a completely different galaxy. He was flying in the atmosphere of a planet so far away from his own that he couldn't properly visualize the distance. He, Paul Phelan, was an alien.

Right beside him, flying *Mahoroba*'s first ship-to-planet shuttle, sat Yuhwa. The woman who had managed to carry a spaceship larger than fifteen of Malor's moons through a black hole. Was there nothing she couldn't do?

Something had changed; she was different after the transit. Hell, he was different. He'd felt her on the inside of himself, a link yet to snap. Nor did he want to let it go. He said nothing about it because Na and Raisa didn't mention experiencing anything unusual. But he knew what he'd sensed in that veşu, and that he'd offered her everything in him in that moment. Paul would be Yuhwa's personal dao fuel any time she needed him.

Right this moment, she was debating the best way to explain a semi-mobile member of a new species as her companion. He'd volunteered to stay on the *Mahoroba* if it would make it easier on her, but she insisted. Paul thought she wanted support in case the nawa kidnapped her and force-marched her through her pâtexi.

"Mandy claims the cloaking on the *Mahoroba* is hiding them from Malor sensors." She shook her head. "I don't see how that's possibly true. Our ship can't be mistaken for an asteroid or comet gone astray."

"All things made possible through The Request," Paul intoned. They'd said it enough it had started to feel like a mantra. "Whoever the Drafter was, seems like they thought through everything."

"They also planned with defense capability first and foremost," Lanu added, having joined their small landing party. "Impenetrable concealment is part of the package."

Everyone else had stayed on the ship, uninterested in Malor. Thuliso had muttered, "Still too soon to return."

That guy was a trip. Paul had seen enough movies about secret agencies to understand 'Cadre appointed' was a cover name for black ops. Unlike Na, who was a rakish thief in the vein of Robin Hood (if Robin had stolen from the rich and given to his own coffers), Thuliso was a slippery one. There was darkness in him, and Paul liked to avoid him if possible.

"If it's true and holds out against scans, we'll be in luck,"

Yuhwa drew him back to the matter at hand. "My citizenship and pâtexi will get me in the door with no questions, they'll be intrigued by an Uilig tourist, but what do we say about you?" She looked at Paul, eyes hooded.

"Is being the first Human gonna work in my favor?" he asked. "Or am I a bureaucratic problem?"

Lanu proposed reason. "I suggest we have them look up Sundancer's proclamation. From descriptions of what took place, Paul will be protected by that. He's officially part of Sundancer's close set."

Yuhwa nodded decisively. "Yes, that's the way. Enough time has passed it will be recorded and transmitted officially. Who's going to deny her emissary, someone she awarded her line name?"

Huh. Paul had forgotten Sundancer sort of adopted and renamed him. "Wish I'd heard from the rest of the family," Paul said. Roughly three sals had passed and not a word about Da or how everyone was doing on Centris. "Hopefully they aren't under fire from the PQs or others."

Yuhwa turned wide eyes to him. "I thought your aoiti were transmitting better than that, or I would have shared! They're back, all is well. Your father is a mediward star, fully healed and training their personnel and AI on Human anatomy."

Paul laughed. "I can't wait for them to meet a real medical professional. Da's version of things will be mechanical engineering based, not flesh and bone."

A new voice filled their shuttle, asking a lot of technical things Yuhwa answered. Codes and shuttle numbers, approach vectors and landing berths, that kind of stuff. Paul settled in and let her handle everything because, honestly, what the hell was he going to offer?

At least he'd discovered he could turn the bed into a recliner, quasi-wheelchair deal. He was pretty stir-crazy at this point, but held his feelings of inadequacy at bay. Professor X had a floating chair like his, that had to be worth something.

Yuhwa started talks about Lanu's entry and Paul zoned out to reflect on their getaway from the *Mahoroba*. Having only seen one allegedly temporary landing bay, Yuhwa had pressed the issue of shuttles. Surely the Drafter had thought of that?

Turned out Mandy deliberately withheld knowledge of ports, bays and docks until the Drafter deemed their command crew trustworthy. They'd all burned from the insult, but swallowed it in order to get access to the hundreds of craft the *Mahoroba* apparently sported.

"Included in the 'travel equal to alien capability' sections," M8 had clarified on their way to the secret entry nearest Shee, located on an interior wall of the primary ring. Apparently the walls of the big-ass ring were thick enough to hold dozens of these nooks, tucked between the smaller rings.

Shuttles, scientific probes, and satellites, just sitting in there, untouched. Yuhwa and Lanu had spent an hour or two learning the design of a big shuttle, and debating if they thought it was space-worthy. M8 took it outside the ship, reporting atmospherics and procedural dreck back for a while, which eventually satisfied Yuhwa.

Before them, the inky dark of space and warm-hued Malor were revealed by doors ponderously sliding open. Yuhwa hadn't hesitated and their shuttle barely cleared the edges as they'd sailed free. She'd easily glided them past ship arms too, as they rotated slowly around the central ring; Paul had envisioned shiny, sparkly outsides, but they absorbed light rather than reflected it.

Yuhwa's crisp voice pulled him back to present. "I'll expect you to have accessed the records when we land," she said brusquely, flipping a switch to end communication. "I'm almost entirely sure you'll be allowed on planet."

"Comforting," he muttered.

M8 spoke up. "Mandy wishes to confirm your agreement with the Drafter is not in jeopardy. You will provide a replacement majio as promised?"

First Paul had heard of it, and he knew right off it was chapping Yuhwa's already thinning hide. She got attached to ships. Bringing up this pâtexi-forced handover wouldn't sit well.

"I gave you my word, a vow. Never question me again."

"But-" started the bot.

Paul tuned out the fight: he was closely watching their approach to the insanely busy space hub. Sea-Tac had nothing on this place. Nowhere on earth did, he had to guess. Yuto Port blended beautifully with the natural surroundings. Even from this height Paul saw most of the architecture was made of either Malor's native stone or was simulated to match. No skyscrapers or towers here, mostly two-story rectangles with courtyards in the middle. Some with plants and flowers, some with green pools. No wonder Yuhwa had loved Shee and the pool out front of the command center – it looked like her homeland.

To his sheltered Pacific Northwest eyes, everything outside the plateau and buildings looked hostile to life. Âuke was foreboding and gigantic, an Everest for this planet. Paul caught just a glimpse of green river and a lake that had to be the size of Superior, biggest of the Great Lakes. Everything else was stark. Tan, burnt orange, dirty ivory, brown, dozens more shades of sand and granite. Miles and miles of dunes broken by rocky wadis, sandstone monoliths, and canyons. There had to be wildlife and nature out there. He couldn't see any, but maybe on desert planets those things hid from such bright light.

On that note, Paul was going to need a way to block light. It was bright enough all the vehicles and buildings had a bleached look "Do you have anything like sunglasses?"

Before Yuhwa could respond, Lanu tapped his shoulder and handed over a set of dark glasses "These seal around your eyes. I had Mandy make several pairs just in case."

Thanking Lanu, Paul shook his head. If he wasn't traveling with other, smarter people, he'd be toast in the Aoni. They knew so much more than he did, had experience he might never replicate. How could he ever compete or be part of important conversations if he had only a fraction of their knowledge?

He set those doubts aside. In a few minutes he would step into the air of a new planet; Malor of the Jadoube, the people who had freaky FTL genes and a feel for metal that went way beyond love. He needed to learn more about waja, he reminded himself. Lia said the herald of Songmaster wielded waja...would Yuhwa's pâtexi reveal the right spot for the Drazoen's essence? Bay had found Sundancer's carnelian and shaped it, maybe that's how it would happen for Paul.

The more he considered it, the more right it felt. Mikanjo prophecy only talked about the herald, but it wouldn't have happened without Bay digging up that carnelian in Africa, then waiting around for Katy and giving it to her. He'd been clutch for the win, just not the one to win the game. The herald's helper.

No way was he telling Yuhwa she might be a sidekick. She'd strip off some hide with her cursing, no doubt about it. Even though he'd told Lanu about his theory, Paul didn't fancy explaining to Yuhwa that his family was destined to wake the Drazoen. It would sound egotistical and self-aggrandizing. For the moment he'd keep it bottled up, but he'd also keep his eyes and ears open for more clues.

Malor was as warm as he'd expected. Where they'd landed was open to the outside, and the air had a metallic scent. Felt a lot like landing in southern California, if he were honest. Paul looked everywhere, impressed with the glasses Mandy had made. They dimmed the painfully bright sunlight but didn't distort. He could make out the walls and floor covered with tools and machinery, various servicepeople cautiously approaching the shuttle, and the head woman striding confidently their way. Paul knew she was the head because she carried a tablet encased in waja and a stylus of the same material.

Unless he had this whole quest deal wrong, he was about to meet a lady who went into a mountain and came out with core tools of bureaucracy. Those were the signs of her life's purpose. Having run a small business, Paul was well-acquainted with all the various forms and databases governments torture business owners with. This lady was going to be one of the lifers, who lived for the precision of ticking boxes and filing in triplicate.

The woman, taller than Yuhwa, with magenta hair coiled in a complex twisty thing his sister would love to know how to do, smiled at their group. "I am Onye Ma. Welcome to Malor," she dipped her head to Lanu and Paul. Her grin broadened for Yuhwa. "Welcome home, *sauda*."

Sauda *sough-da; Jadoube greeting specific to other Jadoube; do not use.* Damn it, now he'd been told it was off-limits he'd probably screw up and use it at some point. *Next time,* he thought at the aoiti, *just don't fecking bother to translate!*

"Lanu Ojala, we are honored to have a respected gatekeeper visit us. If you would register your aoiti here, please." She held out the tablet and Lanu hovered his wrist over it for a few seconds. Onye pulled it back, did a swipey move with the stylus, and that was it.

Yuhwa was next. They'd said aoiti were your bank account and passport, on top of the translating and bio-help; this was the real-world proof of it. A step beyond fingerprinting, that was for sure.

"Ambassador Paul Phelan jo Faluji, emissary of Sundancer Orange" Onye turned to him and performed a deep bow. "If we had been given more notice your welcome would be far greater." She took a breath, her brown eyes shining. "On behalf of the Malor governing bodies, I offer our friendship and allegiance.

That Sundancer's ambassador would choose Malor for his first official trip humbles us."

Oh hål. Paul looked to Yuhwa for help, but she raised her eyebrows and hid a grin. "Oh, no, well, yeah." Damn her leaving him to stumble. Really? He knew nothing of diplomacy. Plus, he had to deal with this shit trapped on a floating hospital gurney?! "I mean, of course. The pleasure is mine."

Onye extended the tablet. "If you would be so kind," she said. "Sundancer herself has confirmed your status and requested you receive all due privileges."

"You got Human aoiti upgrades, too?" he asked while registering himself. "You're understanding me?"

Onye beamed. "All of the Aoni has received updates. The primary database intake covered multiple inputs, and the Muškikal are already forming a party to approach Humans for more clarification. So many languages in one species is unknown."

"Humans love to talk," Yuhwa joked.

"These events are portentous, many say. A Drazoen returned, hopes of more to come, a new species joining the Calling. Yes, it all has the ring of destiny." The woman Paul was starting to think might be a big deal on Malor bowed over her tablet. "The Hunzo of Nawa wish to celebrate the occasion, and you, at tomorrow's Feast of the Côttru."

Yuhwa gasped. "I had completely forgotten!"

"You've been away long tuigs," Onye chuckled. "Rest tonight while you can, tomorrow will be like a run through Tizu's rapids!"

Tizu was a river, okay got that, but the jumble of info and pics on this feast were too confusing. He'd ask Yuhwa to clear it up later.

Lanu spoke up. "Would you be so kind as to point me to the safehouse?"

"You're not staying with us?" Paul asked plaintively. As

attractive as alone time with Yuhwa was, Lanu made Paul feel safe to ask potentially dumb questions. They never judged, just spoke patiently and honestly. He was pretty sure tourism as the first Human on Malor would have questions coming out of his ears.

They clasped their hands in front of their chest. "I would very much like to catch up with the host there. I knew them long ago."

Paul gave Lanu a questioning look, to which he got a negative head shake. Not one of the lost loves from the past, then.

A sled was called for Lanu, arrangements made to rejoin in the morning and prep for the feast. That was when Paul learned Yuhwa had a house on Ha-Seng Plateau, her family home that had never been sold or abandoned.

They required a jump-shuttle, unlike Lanu who would stay on Jarog Plateau. Travel between the five plateaus was sounding a lot like short flights between Seattle and Portland, or Spokane. Too much for a sled, too little for a full-sized shuttle. Da used to call them puddle-jumpers; Paul was swamped with fondness and the need to talk with his family.

"We'll swing by to get you well before Feast morning rites commence," Yuhwa told Lanu. "It only takes half a sal-ang to get to Ni-Matak Plateau, but I'd hate to get off on the wrong foot with the nawa by upsetting a festival day's timing."

Onye waved them off, confirming she'd see them at the feast kick-off.

"Can we call Centris from your place?" Paul asked when they'd boarded the jump-shuttle. He was feeling homesick, but for people rather than a place. Home was his family, and he needed to touch base.

"Of course," Yuhwa replied, taking his hand. She wasn't flying the shuttle, they operated like self-driving taxis, so she could give him her full attention. "We'll do a face-to-face, then a quick tour of the neighborhood? Maybe M8 can project the next movie after we eat.”

“Mandy would like status on a replacement majio,” M8 cautiously stated. It was probably still worried Yuhwa might follow through with her threat to throw it into Âuke.

Yuhwa glared. “Mandy will get updates when I have any to give.”

M8 wisely stopped talking.

WHAT WOULD Paul think of Malor? Of her family home, the people she’d grown up with in her earliest years? She wanted him to be awed, to like it and feel comfortable. Her desire to impress him was a new sensation; generally, she didn’t give mirca what others thought of her. She dressed, drank, and lived how she saw fit. If it didn’t have impact on her ability to do her job, someone else’s opinion meant nothing to her.

Paul’s did, though. Especially after their trip through the veṣu. Having seen right to the honorable core of him, enfolded by the fundamental goodness of his spirit, his thoughts and feelings carried more weight in the aftermath. Rather than let herself get tumbled over submerged rocks about it, she chose the deeper water’s path. Accept and adapt. Shift around, like a good Jadoube.

The air inside her house was stale, perfectly logical because the service only opened it every few tuigs. Yuhwa hadn’t been back in several bisous. Last time was when the *Eternidad* had dropped off passengers; she’d ducked down to check on everything and feel the sun on her skin. Stars were literally everywhere in the Aoni, but none caressed her soul the way Malor’s did.

Being here now, seeing it through Paul’s eyes, was revelatory.

Walking through the double front doors and into a large living area wasn't depressing. For once the house wasn't oppressive and dark as it had been when her mother was wasting away. It was quite the opposite. She could see it now, finally moving past the shadows of the past. Her mother had always liked pastel colors, and they filled the space. Pillows and throws, vases, even the frame on the comm screen. Late afternoon sun warmed the floor tiles and endowed the room with a burnished, soft effect.

"I was expecting medieval, because of the inbound view. This feels Tuscan, much better." Paul's voice sounded approving.

Yuhwa hummed. "Most of the architecture is like this, even on other plateaus. What's on Jarog is different because so many people come and go, they build for communal rather than family living."

"I like it," he said, nodding and looking around. "But now, this E.T. would like to phone home." He smiled. "Please."

Connecting with Centris was tricky, because it was pre-dawn on the Wheel. Most of his family was asleep, but Patrick and his father woke and talked with him for a sal-ang. Their conversation centered on three things: hurling and the lamentable lack thereof in the Aoni, Martin Phelan's plans to start selling his ale on Centris, and the delay of Katy and Bay's wedding.

Yuhwa was most interested in the last one, naturally, but the men treated it as expected. Their father explained the rationale: Katy wanted her whole family there, which meant Raisa, Paul and Yuhwa needed to attend. So that was on hold until everyone was reunited.

"Speak true now," Paul said as they prepared to end the call. "Do you want me to leave here and come back?"

She knew his sense of duty was at war with his desire to be with her and explore new places. Her selfishness was equally battling her need to do right by him. Yuhwa wanted him with her, to help get her through this tricky patch with the nawa. The pain of their summoning had ended the moment they'd landed, but Yuhwa wondered what they might have in store for a woman who planned to fight her pâtexi. Instinctively she sensed Paul would find ways to keep her from burning the Binding Bath to the ground; anger at how they forced her hand made her volatile, but he pacified her. Yet, if his family needed him, who was she to keep him here?

"*A mhic,*" Martin laughed. "You're to stay there, heal, and take a thousand pictures for your ma. She's already planning a Grand Tour of the Aoni, and expects you to sort the finest accommodations!"

Yuhwa laughed with them, relief flooding her. Paul would stay, everything would be fine.

27

When they left for a look around Yuhwa's childhood neighborhood, they learned M8 could attach to the head of Paul's medibed and direct it, even in the chair form he liked better. Since she didn't have to steer she was free to walk next to him, pointing out sights and places of note.

As she'd anticipated, their presence got a lot of interest. More from nilnabō than she'd expected, much more. Aware of his soft spot for animals, she'd promised Paul they'd see the creatures as they traveled down side streets and through small parks. Nilnabō were semi-feral, always watching goings on from their perches on rooftops, walls, or in taller trees. Jadoube everywhere cared for them communally.

He'd yelled, "Kitties!" and insisted they take food for an offering. Little did they know the medibed presented a far greater enticement than vittles; nilnabō converged from all over, inspecting then leaping onto the hovering bed. He reclined immediately to take advantage. Paul was covered in at least ten of them at one point. She was going to shoo them away, but he turned shiny eyes to hers and whispered, "They even purr like ours."

Yuhwa introduced Paul to old acquaintances out for evening strolls, who were polite if distant. Her early prowess with the dao, her father's work as a sword on the Wheel, and their infrequent returns to Malor, hadn't helped her make friends and keep relationships afloat. Tangun had tried to ensure she formed ties here, but they'd never fully taken.

Shtŭ. Here came a problem. Given how Paul had reacted to Xanthos, she dreaded how he would handle Isāc. Unlike Xanthos, Isāc never had a problem with Yuhwa's one-off policy. He was one of the rare people Yuhwa had felt safe turning into a two-off, for that reason alone.

Her nerves about Paul's reaction were doubled: would he get jealous if that came out, and would he wonder if he could be with her again? Yuhwa didn't know the answer herself, and therefore was in no position to answer him.

"Yuhwa," Isāc said warmly. He hugged her, then focused on Paul. "What a gift you've brought us! You're the new ambassador? From the new species?" Isāc's enthusiasm was genuine.

Paul flushed. No matter how many times he'd heard the words in their outing tonight, he was adorably awkward over the interest and praise he received. Yuhwa introduced them, noticing Paul's aborted move with his hand. Was he over-tired, or developing a twitch?

The memory of Katy sticking her hand out at everyone in the early days came back in a rush. It was the Human version of a greeting, and she wondered if someday the aoiti would coach other species how to do it, just like his were telling him right then to clasp forearms instead.

"Paul, why are you on a medibed?"

"Hurt myself on our ship," Paul downplayed with a shrug.

Yuhwa clarified. "Another panicking Human damaged his knee. Mikanjo mediwards fixed it surgically, but his aoiti are still new enough the remaining healing is taking longer than he'd like."

Isāc tilted his head. "All right, but why are you in bed? Wouldn't you prefer a hover brace?"

"I, uh, I don't know?" Paul looked to Yuhwa. "Would I?"

"You would," Isāc laughed. "Yuhwa hasn't noticed, but my pâtexi revealed mediward for me. I can fix you up with one. Tonight, even."

"I don't know," Paul hedged. "My doctor back on the ship made me promise not to overdo it." He looked torn between excitement and following Dr. Vásquez's rules.

"We can call her," Yuhwa offered. "Can you come back with us, talk to Paul's mediward?"

Isāc agreed, they returned as quickly as possible, and called the *Mahoroba*. Dr. Vásquez and Isāc talked for nearly a sal-ang, comparing notes, reviewing images, debating the best way forward. Paul followed it all closely, face closed down, afraid to hope.

"What Isāc is describing sounds revolutionary. It essentially bears and redistributes weight, force, all the things that might damage your healing at this stage. You'll be able to walk – slowly! – and get blood flow moving." She shook her head. "I'll be out of a job in this new Universe."

"Not at all," Yuhwa's old friend said. "We are all needed in the Aoni, we merely have better tools at our disposal." He turned to Paul and Yuhwa when they'd signed off. "I'll run back to my house and get what I need for the hover brace."

Paul waited until Isāc left to let out a whoop of joy. "I'm back!"

When Isāc returned, he had supplies in a satchel. "Lavatory still back here?" he asked. He strode down the hallway, calling over his shoulder, "I'll just wash and sterilize, then we'll get started."

Yuhwa looked back at Paul, the fond smile on her lips fading. "What?"

"Nothing," Paul said, evasive.

She knew what she'd seen, despite his pretense now. Surprise and a little hurt. "We knew each other long ago, Paul."

"Not long enough to forget where everything is," Paul muttered.

Yuhwa huffed. "Don't."

Paul scowled. "I didn't! You did. I said nothing."

She tsked and turned away. Her earlier thoughts of relying on Paul came back to haunt her. What kind of touchstone would he be if she couldn't count on his friendship?

By the time Isāc wrapped Paul's knee in the hover brace and helped him to stand, she'd silenced her complaints. The two men were jovial and pleasant with one another, Paul showed no signs of jealously, and Isāc had him laughing several times.

"Yes!" Paul shouted. "The joy of being vertically mobile cannot be overstated!"

Celebratory cups of rusim were enjoyed on the patio; she and Isāc sitting and Paul testing his balance and movements in the new brace. Twice he nearly toppled over, but caught himself with a dexterity that put her in mind of the Olympic videos they'd watched. Despite the hopes he'd told her he had 'overhauled' when he got so tall, he'd kept himself in shape and flexible. Yuhwa shifted, aware that turned her on more than it should now they were done with sex. *No attachments*, she chided herself.

Was it being back on Malor that sent the old dreams her way that night? Maybe it was the looming pâtexi. Or the proximity of Dalchin, the moon that would signal the close of the Feast the next sal. Dalchin only appeared once a tuig in Malor's skies, a pink and yellow wanderer that returned the Five Côttru to their rightful places, watching over the Binding Bath. Who knew what kind of power it held?

Yuhwa was always aware she was dreaming as it happened, but was helpless to stop, wake, or alter the dream. Like every one before, she stood outside herself, watching a stumbling

Dream Yuhwa scrape against narrow cave walls. Dream Yuhwa couldn't see at this stage of her pâtexi, for reasons that were a mystery. Their hands were thrown out for safety and guidance, palms and knuckles scratching on stone. Observer Yuhwa felt her dream flesh abrade as it happened.

Dreamer and observer quested deeper into a cave-turned-funnel into the heart of Âuke. Heat intensified, vision dimmed, until both Yuhwas were equally blind. Their ears filled with a ponderous thump.....thump.....thump. They knew it was the heartbeat of the planet.

Thump.....thump.....thump.

Dream self and observer were of one mind: seek the heartbeat. Within the darkness lay salvation, the reason they'd been created. *Wherewherewhere? Help us.*

our sweet one comes home
not where
who
beloved Child

Had she heard those voices before? Were they the spirits of the Five Côttru, bringing her to her fate? As if thinking of them summoned them, the Yuhwas sensed newly arrived manifestations. The steady plod of Ni-Matak's hooves at her left, ticklish brush of Ji-Cheol Jarog's wings against her cheek, and the softest fur they'd ever felt from Sister Ha-Seng's fur pressing up against her right hand. Though the Yuhwas were still blind, they knew Migwa walked silently before them on long toes, Great Druk protecting them from behind.

Observer Yuhwa tried to flinch from what she knew came next. Dream Yuhwa drifted forward, blissfully ignorant.

Thump.....thump.....thump.

no fear
brave brave
stronger than you know
you are loved

Before the whisper of the last voice faded from their mind, the Yuhwas plunged into a deep lake of waja. They felt the cool metal surround them, cloak them, flow over their head and drown them.

Yuhwa bolted awake, coughing and sputtering. Her heart raced, quadruple the rate of the beats from her dream. Nothing new had happened: same cave, same escort by the Côttru, same submersion in a pool of waja. But that had been the strongest dream she'd ever had; she'd felt trapped and free. Ground-breaking but pre-destined. It was confusing and frustrating.

Shaking off the after-effects, she had a quick shower. She found Paul already in the patio sitting area, drinking nropita, a bowl of food set out for nilnabō opportunists. Just one problem.

"You can't wear that," she said. "We have to wear special clothes for rites like this."

Paul glanced down at his outfit, something her aoiti called *business casual khakis and pinstriped shirt*. "Human clothes won't cut it for the soiree? Too informal?"

"It isn't so much about formal." Yuhwa struggled to explain. "This is a big Feast of the year, and we have traditional ways to celebrate."

"Got it. Can we make something in the replicator?"

She took a deep breath, bypassing the emotional magnitude of what she was about to say. "Actually, I still have my papa's dress clothes. You might fit into some of it."

Paul's eyes warmed, and he reached out to take her hand. "I'd be honored." He turned around, heading for the hall. "This way? And how will we get around the brace?"

"No problem, it's a skirt."

THE DIFFICULTY HADN'T BEEN PUTTING on the fancy, clearly expensive, bespoke outfit. It had been getting his bloody slacks off. He was stunned and privileged she would let him don her father's navy tunic and kilt, both embroidered with silver patterns foreign to his eyes. But both of them were scared to take off the brace, and it was too early for Isāc to make a house call. Not that Paul wanted the guy seeing him be any more pathetic than he already had.

Paul could be reasonable and cool about the whole "ex" thing. Isāc obviously was, Yuhwa was, he *would* be. He was a goddamn adult. He had a past, she had a past, they didn't have a future. Honestly, he should aspire to their level of chill about the scenario, because they'd been relaxed around each other. No awkward desire flaring in anyone's eyes, not a lingering touch that Paul had seen. So yep. Yep. He would be the wine refrigerator of cool: conveniently placed and always in reach, but unobtrusive.

Not so his pants, which they'd had to cut off his free leg and waist. The Mikanjo had already removed the injured leg's fabric when they did the original wrapping. It only now occurred to Paul that he'd been wearing the same outfit for sals. Ionic showers kind of made a guy forget to change, plus who would he let undress him? Yuhwa wouldn't have volunteered and it was a step too far for Na or his doctor.

"Can you give me a low-down on this feast?" he asked once they were underway.

Yuhwa's smile was enigmatic. "I think you should experience your first one as it happens. It's beautiful, and overwhelming. I don't want to spoil you." She took his hand.

"In one sal I'll have seen three of the five plateaus. I'm winning at tourism," he chuckled.

"I can't promise too much," she warned. "President Ma may have other plans for us. Or the nawa."

"Who-" Paul swallowed. "The bureaucrat yesterday? She's

the president? Please tell me not for all of Malor." He felt queasy.

Yuhwa snorted. "It seemed better not to tell you."

"I'm sure the first Human ambassador to Malor meeting the President in a freaking hospital bed looked awesome." Paul told himself to be more like Oran, who wouldn't have given two shits if he'd met Onye Ma in his boxer briefs.

"She seemed to like you," Yuhwa offered.

They touched down briefly to pick up Lanu and were off again. Paul practiced diplomatic silence the rest of the trip, letting Yuhwa and Lanu chat on the way to the feast. He was nervous he'd made a less than impressive emissary the day before, but how could he have done differently? Yuhwa was right, he'd been better off not knowing who she was. But he resolved to ask more questions next time, so he didn't get skunked like that again.

Their jump-shuttle had been directed to a less-busy landing area. It was private, probably VIP or some such. When they climbed out, a travel barge awaited them. Unlike the sleds Paul was used to, this thing had a cover with gauzy curtains falling around the center, and a couple trunks to hold luggage if they'd had any. The sun was blocked enough on the barge he could take off his sunglasses for the ride.

It ferried them to a huge set of bleachers, already filled with thousands of Jadoube in their ceremonial garb. Paul tugged at the hem of his dark blue tunic, nervous about meeting the nawa and seeing the president again. Would he look dumb dressed like a Jadoube?

He heard Da's voice in his head; "No time for doubts, lad, show them yer best!" Back straightening, taking confidence in how much easier it already was to walk in the new brace, he put the glasses back on and followed the usher leading them.

They skirted the edge of the temporary structure, walking down front. It reminded him of a baseball dugout at a stadium;

no one above would see into it, but everyone inside it had ground-level views of the action to come. Dead center was the president, along with a dozen or more people. Five of them wore elaborately beaded robes that must have been heavy as all get out.

This had to be the Hunzo of Nawa, Jadoube-only equivalent of the Cadre. Yuhwa had described them as priest-seer-historians. They'd be there for all the births, deaths, and in-betweens. Currently it was these SOBs that had been causing Yuhwa all that pain. He knew it was their job and a cultural norm here, but he was holding a grudge nonetheless and had told her as much. She'd laughed, smiling radiantly at him.

One of the beaded wonders, shorter than Paul's twelve-year-old cousin Bastien, broke off and moved to intercept them as they approached. His outfit, buttercup yellow covered in navy beads, clacked as he walked. He had olive skin, hair glossy as a ripe blackberry, short cropped and neat, and eyes the green of Malor water. Rounded, bordering on rotund, he beamed at them.

"Ambassadors Ojala and Phelan jo Faluji! Welcome, most welcome." He bowed. "Yuhwa Bon-Gil." Another bow. "Your home rejoices at your return, child."

Calling a four-hundred-year-old woman a child seemed rich, especially considering this dude looked so young. Of course, they all did in the Aoni, didn't they? Humans were going to wither in the time it took these people to move past puberty. Katy better be working that fountain of youth request to her dragon.

Onye, or rather President Ma, had joined them. She was flanked by the other four members of the bead posse. Her hand landed on happy chatty guy's shoulder. "Allow me to introduce Quý Oke-Tu. He's the current head of the Hunzo, and has been most eager to meet you."

Yuhwa wasn't eager. She wasn't openly disgruntled, but Paul

could feel the tension in her arm that pressed his. "Leader, thank you for this honor today."

Quý brushed her formality aside, clasping her shoulders and touching his forehead to hers as she bent down. "When I was blessed with the call of your waja, I thrilled to know I'll share this pâtexi with you. I shared with your mother as well, and I've never eaten bánhti as good as hers once she mastered her skills." He pulled back, still gazing into her eyes. "Something tells me you will be just as gifted as she was. Your father, too."

Paul saw tears in Yuhwa's eyes, but if it was from the kind words, unexpected memories, or the realization she wasn't getting out of her pâtexi since the leader was intent on it, he couldn't say. Leaning into her arm a little harder, he tried to offer silent support. Unfortunately, that move made him the center of attention.

"Paul Phelan jo Faluji, I am never at a loss for words and yet I find myself clumsy with how fast they want to come out!"

"Just Paul is good," he replied, taken aback.

Quý clapped and moved himself in front of Paul, looking him over. "Your ghat is superb. I thank you for respecting our customs, it means much. The first Human on Malor! We have so many things to discuss!" One of the other Hunzo leaned in and spoke in Quý's ear. He shook his head.

"We can take this up later," Onye interjected with a laugh. "Unless you begin the Feast, we will fail to return the Five!"

Quý Oke-Tu pouted momentarily, then brightened. "After the Feast, then. Lanu Ojala, I long to hear your stories, too. A milenyo spent among Humans on Earth! Onye, you'll seat them, yes?" With that he and the other four swept off.

28

Paul, Lanu, and Yuhwa followed the president to seats up front in the dugout. The same seats the Hunzo had been using, which freaked Paul out. How was he, an average guy who taught little kids how to do somersaults, front row to a huge celebration on a foreign planet? If that didn't confirm for him his family was destined for the herald thing, nothing else would.

"I think you should turn off your new word translation feature," Yuhwa murmured, leaning in close. "I can tell you important things, but this is more of a visceral experience. You have just enough dao inside you to appreciate what happens without the aoiti interrupting your flow."

Paul did a double-take. "You can do that? Turn them off?"

Lanu confirmed. "You can instruct them to differing levels of interpretation when you connect actively. You're likely defaulted to highest, normal for beginning."

"All this time I've been on parental control," he griped. "How can I test if I'm active versus passive?"

"Close your eyes," Yuhwa urged. "There should be a sense of something waiting for your input."

Paul, following her instructions, scanned himself inside. Sure enough, something he equated with a blinking cursor prompt, teased his brain. *No auto-translate for the rest of the sal,* he thought. A nearly imperceptible blip and he knew he'd done it.

The Hunzo stepped out from the shaded stands into the still-early sunlight. They moved as one, walking to the pentagonal Binding Bath in front of them. At an unseen signal they split; Quý stopped at the corner to Paul's right, a second nawa to Paul's left. The other three disappeared around either side. Each corner of the building would be covered.

Quý raised his arms, shaking them above his head, stomping his feet. He cried out.

Côttru, Côttru, Côttru Five
Bless us, Bless us, Bless us all
We feed you, we praise you
We sing to you, we praise you
Côttru, Côttru, Côttru Five

The entire stand of bleachers around them shook with feet pounding five measured beats in tandem with the words. Paul nearly jumped out of his seat at the loudness, nearly deafening when you were under the heart of it.

After an hour of ritual, Paul welcomed the break they got between opening ceremonies and story time. He'd jumped in with the stomping and clapping, but hadn't followed all of the details; it involved nawa taking on aspects of the Five and chanting. Then they pulled hidden urns overflowing with dried goods out from the Bath, and swapped them for new ones. During the pause, everyone would wander about as fresh offerings were tossed in to fill the empty containers.

He and Yuhwa walked around the entire Binding Bath, examining carvings and decorations more closely. He wouldn't be allowed inside, but the outside was more than enough.

"Exquisite," he said. He noticed a lot of the Jadoube who dropped off a donation approached the nawa, who would trace their waja tattoos quickly like a blessing.

"What's that for?" he pointed with his elbow.

"The nawa are in touch with all waja. They sense it, commune with it." She turned back to the building. "Inside this Bath they help it join with us. The 'sharing' Quý mentioned? He not only felt my waja surface, but he will coordinate how it bonds to me."

"So tracing the tattoo is like reconnecting?" Paul was fascinated.

Yuhwa nodded. "Something like that."

"Too bad I'll never be able to participate."

"I can't either," she pointed out.

She would someday, though. No matter how hard she fought it, and Paul knew she wasn't ready to give in yet, eventually she'd have those pretty silver tats and a weapon, or whatever a pilot got from their pâtexi. He couldn't imagine her getting anything else, although she'd be a great CEO or a fierce sports coach.

They spent a few hours wandering the plateau, investigating pop-up food stalls for the Feast, and generally having a relaxing time. His knee barely ached, and he'd gotten the hang of walking without a limp in the brace. Trusting that it wouldn't give out and leave him in sudden agony was a big part of his progress.

When they returned to their seats, Paul had been welcomed and even fawned over several times. He was uncomfortable being admired for not having done anything other than be related to Katy. Sundancer loved his sister, so she took care of the whole family. All this Jadoube praise was unearned by Paul. He wanted to tell them to wait until he'd woken up Songmaster.

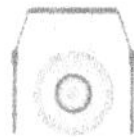

Yᴜʜᴡᴀ ᴏʙsᴇʀᴠᴇᴅ Paul as he watched the Hunzo perform the stories of her people. How the planet formed, how the Côttru came to Malor and became the Five. Smaller stories of the animals all over the earth, all the ones created before the Jadoube.

He was enthralled, leaning forward eagerly, laughing and gasping with the rest of the audience. She knew he didn't understand everything, but she whispered crucial things and left the rest to context. The Feast of the Côttru was about community, and she could tell Paul felt that deeply. Hopefully today gave him the chance to connect with her culture and people. She wanted him to feel at ease here.

Anticipation started to run through her, as it did in all the Jadoube. The sun sank lower in the sky, twilight barely starting to paint the day's end with shadows. "We go out there," she tapped his hand, standing. "Dalchin rises."

Paul followed her enthusiastically. Lanu and Onye joined them, the stands emptying as the crowd left their seats and surrounded them. Everyone turned west, focused on the horizon. There she was, adored wanderer and bringer of blessings. Dalchin came into view, just a pinprick far out of reach at the moment, but she would get closer and closer. Eventually, when she was fat and heavy in the sky, she would bring the Côttru home.

The nawa's voices rose above the hushed crowd.

Côttru, Côttru, Côttru Five
Come home to your people
Return, return, return to us
We yearn to see you again
Côttru, Côttru, Côttru Five

Paul jumped when everyone around him started walking. "We circle the Bath," she said in a low voice. "Just follow."

Moving so many Jadoube in concert took long kaalas, and they would do it five times. Each circuit they paused, looked to Dalchin as the nawa repeated the song, then slowly ambled around again. She sailed so quickly, their adored moon, and by the time the fifth circle was completed, she hung directly overhead.

The night sky above burst with lights from other distant bodies; she was the only one that mattered. *"Home, home, home."* The chant began slowly, never rising to a shout. It was a prayer, a communal hope, repeating until the first reveal.

Every time she saw it happen, Yuhwa was filled with the same innocent wonder she'd felt as a child. Celebrations away from the Binding Bath simply couldn't compare to the miracle happening live. Inside the five empty semi-circles atop the building's sides, the Côttru returned. First a tail, or a feather, maybe a pair of horns or tusks.

Who you saw return depended on where you'd stopped your walk. Each side slowly revealed magnificent sculptures of the spirits who were the sparks of Malor. Their figures faded from the Binding Bath walls before each Feast, and returned only when Dalchin was at her zenith.

Paul gasped. "It's filling in! The Five are returning" He threw his arms around her, joining in the happy cries of the people surrounding them.

Drumming feet and whistles filled the air, followed quickly by an escalating chant. *"Côttru, Côttru, Côttru Five! Côttru, Côttru, Côttru Five!"* People leaped into the air, hands raised to the light of Dalchin. Some wept, overpowered by the raw sensory overload of the Feast culmination.

A boom sounded, a signal commanding all present to focus on the Hunzo; they stood silent, expectant. Quý, filling an entrance of the Binding Bath, bellowed, "We consecrate this Feast of the Côttru. The Five are home!"

Yuhwa spun in Paul's arms, facing Lanu. "And now," she grinned, "the party begins!"

They joined the line of people winding into a nearby village. Every Feast one of the three towns that bordered the Binding Bath hosted closing festivities. Foods cooked from the hearty grains, beans, and seasonings removed earlier were served to all. Yuhwa was surprised by the pride she felt, how she anticipated showcasing everything that would come next to Lanu and Paul.

Never patient unless forced to be, Yuhwa slithered through the crowd, bypassing dozens of slow-mataks. She wanted a drink in her hand, and to move to the beat of music she heard rising from the center of the village. Paul objected to 'jumping the line', but Lanu laughed and followed easily. They were so much taller they could spot breaks in the mass of people and took the lead. For once Yuhwa was happy to follow.

"What smells so good?" Paul asked.

"Mipoy," she replied, pulling him by the hand. "We get in line over there." Yuhwa craved the salty, savory sandwich, could already taste the juicy kamorca meat and how it would drip down her chin.

Lanu, who could see better than Paul, clarified for him. "Resembles a French dip, or more like bánh mì." Their forehead wrinkled. "Though they appear to douse the bread in liquid first."

"The bread is called bánhti; bánh mì and bánhti! Your sister always loves it when words align from your world and others." Yuhwa laughed, blood fizzing even though she'd had nothing to drink yet. "We'll have to tell her."

Paul laughed. "Bug will be sad that I've had a special treat she didn't get first."

"She won't care. You're the one who always wants to be

first," Yuhwa nudged him. "Of all your siblings, you want to be out front most."

"Are you saying I'm an attention hog?" Paul sounded offended, his lips pursed.

Yuhwa snorted. "No. I mean you want to be the one hit first. To protect, or to try and help whenever you can."

"Oh." He bent his head, then scuffed a foot in the sandy ground below. "It's true, I can't argue that."

A few sal-angs later, replete after one-and-a-half mipoys, drink in hand, Yuhwa debated with herself. She wanted to dance badly; people were paired and tripled in front of the musicians, dancing with wild abandon. She longed to lose herself in the beat and the high of Dalchin's remaining hours of visibility. Asking Paul was fraught with risk, though. He might misinterpret; their friendship status was still in its infant stage. But the music seeped into her lungs, her blood, urging her to move.

Lanu returned to the chairs they'd claimed. "I regretfully take my leave," they announced. "There's been another issue on *Mahoroba*. Smaller this time," they hastened to say when Yuhwa sat up in alarm.

"Should we all go?" Paul asked.

Lanu waived them off. "Thuliso and Na believe I'm a less scary alien to talk to the Humans, as they've seen me before. They also know you're needed here. I'll send an update when I have one."

Paul and Yuhwa nodded and watched them walk away, the moonlight-reactive tattooing on their face shining like a beacon. Feeling Paul's gaze back on her, Yuhwa had a choice to make.

Once Lanu's navy and gold caftan disappeared, Yuhwa took a good look at Paul. He'd had one and a half mipoys, too, plus a glass of zaojiŭ, which he said reminded him of Earth rice wine. He was mellow, but not sleepy. Dancing was probably a good idea, to help wake him up and work off the food. She'd be doing him a service.

She stood, jerking her head at the circling dancers. "Think you can keep up?"

"Even with this knee, I know I can." He responded to her taunting exactly as she'd hoped.

They made their way through the crowd, his palm in the center of her back, staying close to one another in the press of bodies and dimmed lighting of the area. Families with children had left already, but hundreds more remained, talking, eating, and dancing. They passed a couple old enough to have white hair sitting and holding hands, tapping their feet to the music.

There was such liberation to be found in the shadows cast by torchlight and candles, she thought. This was good, better than good; Paul was here and it was safe for her to relax, let go. Reaching out with her dao connection, Yuhwa pulled the music into herself. Thrumming rhythms changed the beat of her heart, speeding or slowing it as the popular folk tune demanded. Facing each other, they swayed in and out of the other's space, slowly at first, gathering speed, fingers trailing over shoulders and arms.

A sweet wash of sound from a ceremonial razocông, tickling along her exposed flesh like the lightest rain, stretching her senses wide. Drums underscored the beat of their hearts. Turning her back to Paul and relaxing, she let him cradle her body with his. She opened herself, close to how she had flying the *Mahoroba*, knowing Paul could catch her if she faltered.

Yuhwa's arms wrapped up and around Paul's neck as she watched the razocông player. He coaxed trilling sounds that billowed through the air, mellowing, soon lowering to the deepest vibrations. He did it over and over, a hypnotic wave of sound pulsing from the large metal circle, into the air, over and through the crowd. It entwined with higher piping and midtones of stringed instruments. Yuhwa was floating and blissful, letting the sounds fill her.

She rotated slowly, dragging fingers over Paul's nape until

she faced him. They moved as a synchronized unit, instinctually reading body language. Her hands on his arms, his on her hips, legs slipping between their partner's before retreating. Sliding feet, moving easily over the sand-scrubbed stone below them. Warmth built between their bodies, eyes locked and greedily taking in the other's.

Paul shocked her by gripping her waist and lifting her to his height. One of his hands encouraged her leg to wrap around his thigh.

"You'll hurt your leg," she gasped, fighting the blaze of arousal his strength ignited.

He pressed their cheeks together, whispering in her ear, "I've got you." Was that a kiss to her neck? "Don't feel a thing."

Yuhwa couldn't fight it any longer. The high emotions of the day, knowing how good his body felt against hers, now the intensity of the music and crush of other bodies equally worked up, pushed her over the edge. Tilting her head back to catch a glance of Dalchin, she smiled and threw caution to the wadis far below.

29

Paul knew, rationally, he couldn't die from sexual frustration. Blue balls weren't fatal. But just that second it felt like it could happen. A transformation was imminent, though, right on the verge of erupting. Something about the music, the moon, Yuhwa's undulating body on his. Being her *friend* while dancing the dirtiest tango on any planet in the Aoni strained his willpower.

Then he didn't have to fight it because Yuhwa's throaty laugh preceded laying one on him that would break records. Hell, they could write poems about it. Maybe he would, once he stopped clutching her body like a lifeline, chasing her tongue over and over, feeling her slip a hand between them and down his kilt. Her other hand was buried in his hair as she stroked the edge of his ear with her thumb.

Not completely comfortable having his southern land fondled in public, he pulled her hand back up to his stomach. He'd worked hard for those abs, let her play with them for a bit. He broke the kiss to drag in air, saw her unattended throat and resolved to give it the attention it deserved. Winding his tongue from jaw to clavicle, he reached the hollow at the base of her throat and suckled.

She shivered, bending her head to his ear. "I like that. Do it again."

Paul obliged, reversing his track and kissing her chin when he finished. "Soon I'll trace your tattoos like that. Lick over every single one, learn them all by heart." But when he leaned in to taste her lips, she pulled back.

Realizing her body had gone stiff, he relaxed his hold on her and checked her face. Not good, pinched and withdrawn. What the shtŭ had he said?

"Soon? Because you assume I'll roll over and do whatever they tell me now I'm here?"

He backtracked. "I just thought, I mean," he broke off, frustrated. "What we saw today, the way the nawa traced over the waja marks. It was beautiful. Breathtaking."

"It is," she allowed. "But not so much that it means I should lose what I love. I thought you knew that, were with me."

"I am!" Paul was trapped between his sense of honesty and supporting Yuhwa. "But you heard Quý: there's only so long you'll be able to fight them. All I meant was that when it happens your tattoos will be sexy and cool. Like you."

Yuhwa wasn't mollified, her voice frosty. "Time to head back, I think." She shook her head. "Too much drink, we made a mistake. It happens, no one to blame. But we forget it, yes?"

He assented, even though he wanted to push and question why they couldn't try. Damnit, he knew why. The abandoned little girl inside was never giving anyone a chance to hurt her by fading away again. Short and sweet, that was her way, and Paul was doing a crap job respecting it.

"Yuhwa!" Quý said, having snuck up on them. The head nawa was mere feet away, rosy-cheeked and dressed in less formal robes.

Yuhwa's eyes shuttered before she turned to bow at the nawa. "Leader Quý, we were just leaving I'm afraid."

Paul looked around at the wide gulf between their group and the crowd. Surrounded by powerful people like the grand poobah nawa here, President Onye Ma two feet behind him, and swords protecting the whole kit and caboodle. Back on Centris it had been all dragons and grand folk, movers and shakers every one.

What the hell had happened to his life? This was all Katy's damn fault. She could keep this herald crap to herself, right now Paul didn't want any part of it; he'd be happy if he could help Yuhwa get through her trials. If she was still talking to him come morning.

"Of course," Quý said, reaching out to take her hand and pat it. "But tomorrow we will meet at Hunzo Pavilion, say eleven MM. Your pâtexi awaits!"

As much as he wanted to jump in and fend off the nawa, Paul knew better than to get in Yuhwa's way. She was more than capable of eviscerating her enemies, even if they were harmless-looking, apple-shaped men with Caesar haircuts.

"I regret I can't. I'm due at the dao schools on Druk. My ship, rather the ship we arrived on, needs a new majio, but," she hesitated. "The circumstances are complicated, unique, and I've committed to locating a replacement."

"But your pâtexi must surely come first," the nawa objected. His celadon eyes widened and his hands came together, cradling his chin.

Paul saw the darkening of Yuhwa's face and jumped in. "I'd love to come to the Hunzo, see everything about how you work."

He'd worried he would offend, but Quý's face lit up. "Wonderful! President Ma, you'll come as well?"

Onye moved to stand abreast of Quý. "Not tomorrow, I've

got meetings most of the day," she demurred. "The day after, perhaps."

"Yes, and surely by then, Yuhwa Bon-Gil will have secured a new majio and can join."

Paul eyed Quý, suspicious. Such joy and friendliness; was he genuine? If so, people like the ones he'd seen in the Calling would eat him alive. If not, he was a diminutive mastermind playing all of them.

Yuhwa, face placid, bowed her head. "Naturally, Leader."

They flew back to Ha-Seng Plateau soon after they said their goodbyes. Paul felt like they had a boatload of stuff they should discuss, but Yuhwa didn't look to be in a conversational mood. After confirming MM stood for Malor Measured (which wasn't Centris Measured or Mahoroba Measured), they retreated to their own thoughts. He hated all the unresolved tension and unspoken undercurrents. He'd ignored those with Brittany and look where that got him.

Not that kind of relationship, he reminded himself sternly. Again. Problem was, it wasn't sticking. He kept telling his heart to shtŭ off, that wasn't where this was going, but eventually it circled right back round again. Once more, with feeling.

That's what he'd like to talk to her about first, honestly. Paul got her ground rules, her aesthetic of one-night-only. Except they kept getting closer, hell tonight they'd toppled over the line hard. Didn't that mean they were outside her normal framework? Couldn't they explore that? Together? Naked?

Stop. That isn't what she needs. She's stressed. Be supportive, helpful. Keep the nawa off her back as long you can. Definitely be there if she gets called to be something other than a majio.

Paul could do this, he was built to provide and uplift, guide and enlighten.

YUHWA WAS TIRED, deeply and utterly weary. Sals of talking to majio masters, going over and over how she'd transited the vẹsu, testing ideas and rejecting them. Every time they couldn't replicate what had happened in a controlled environment she felt helplessness creep over her.

No! Yuhwa Bon-Gil didn't do helpless. They would find a solution to this Nine-nŭzed problem and she'd get Mandy off her back.

Part of her frustration was a nagging sense she'd forgotten something about the voyage. Her memory of connecting with Na, Paul and Raisa was clear, but the further she dove into how she'd swum the dao the fuzzier it got. Or, more like it distorted, as though the dao had turned into real water and what she'd done was submerged below the surface. She thought she saw it clearly, but something seemed to shimmer just out of reach when she tried pulling it up.

Annoyed with herself she'd left Druk and flown home. If only she could crawl into her own brain and sift through the memories. What was she missing?

By the time she'd freshened up with a shower and donned her most comfortable clothes she heard Paul come back. Another source of stress. They had moved past the near-miss of Feast night, for the most part. But they hadn't gotten back to the ease of where they'd been before, either. Yuhwa knew she shared blame, both for the kissing and the fight.

But he was supposed to be her support, not her critic. She'd been aroused, emotions high, and his words had felt like dunking in the iciest water. Naturally she'd reacted negatively. Still, she hated their stilted conversations and awkwardness more than what he'd said.

Especially when she appreciated and relied on him running interference for her with Quý and the Hunzo. Their messages had gotten pushier each day she'd begged off. But Mandy, via M8, had made it clear the *Mahoroba* needed to get moving and soon. Raisa had even sent a vid message, asking when they'd get moving again.

"I don't know where we'll go," she said, "but we need to leave. Sitting in one place isn't working for people."

Yuhwa shook her head and sighed. Too many problems without answers. Dinner with Paul might help her reset. "Are you hungry?" she asked softly.

He came into the room with a smile. "I could go for something small." He paused at the end of the table, and she saw his brace was gone. "We had a big-"

"When did that happen?" Cutting him off and stepping into his space, she pointed down. "Mediward Sofia approved?"

His face shuttered in an instant. "I don't need permission from anyone," he said.

She flinched back from his petulant tone. "Ah, of course. Your belief 'what I want is right' can't possibly fail you." Stupid man. He could end up with an enduring problem. If the aoiti began treating the injury as permanent they'd stop trying to heal him.

"You're one to talk, Lady Denial." He pivoted sharply, walking away from her, out the patio doors.

Yuhwa was mainly confused, but irritation was hot on its heels as she followed. "What the shtŭ is that supposed to mean?"

"You know."

"I don't! I haven't ignored anything-"

"How's that pâtexi coming, then?" He bared his teeth. "You can do whatever the hell you want about that; God forbid I have an opinion. But don't lecture me on my choices when you keep running from even making one."

What was happening? He'd come back smiling and now they were fighting. Did Humans suffer mental problems on other planets? Some species had trouble in space long-term, maybe Humans would struggle with new worlds.

Or was this a continuation of the other night? A way for his frustration and disappointment to flay her in punishment for unfulfilled desire.

She stalked out to face him, furious. "Sals ago you claimed to be on my side. You said you understood why I didn't want to go on pâtexi. Now you imply I'm a child running from something?" Yuhwa pointed to the sky. "Go back to the *Mahoroba* if you're so tired of being around me!"

Paul bent his head so close they could have touched noses. As it was, she felt his breath on her lips.

"I never said that! Why do you exaggerate anything I say or do? You are the most aggravating person I've ever known!" He took several steps back and threw his arms wide. "I've spent the last three days with Quý while you've been dragging out finding a replacement majio."

"I am not dragging it out," she spit through clenched teeth. "The top experts of the dao can't find a way for someone to do it!"

"Then get two or three or twenty! Anything is better than how you keep delaying the inevitable." His chest heaved with the force of his words. "Quý has explained a lot; he's feckin' had to because you keep blowing us off. All the Hunzo have taught me things about pâtexi and the Binding Bath. You aren't losing anything, Yuhwa, you're becoming who you're meant to be."

Stung, Yuhwa whispered, "I'm already who I'm meant to be. Waja or the nawa aren't going to *improve* me." She turned away, ready to retreat inside. This hurt her more than she wanted to acknowledge. "I thought…I thought you understood that."

"Jesus Christ, you're so melodramatic," he called from behind her. "Just get it over with, so we can go back to Centris. I told you before: if you believe you'll stay a majio you'll probably stay one." His voice got closer, his hand landing on her shoulder.

She shrugged it off. Leave or let him have it? She whirled on him, truly understanding Human 'pissed' now. "You dare to lecture me about my responsibilities when you couldn't even follow basic medical care rules? For what? Because you're an untried boy desperate to appear important and powerful?"

Paul went nuclear. He felt it happening, couldn't seem to slow or stop it. She'd pushed one of his biggest buttons and they were about to throw down.

"I'm not the one who wasted a couple hundred years living like an irresponsible, care-free party girl. Someone in this room is pathologically afraid of connection and relationships and guess what? IT AIN'T ME!"

Yuhwa stormed back inside. "At least," she shouted, "none of my partners ever had to leave me because I settled into a quagmire of mediocrity."

Paul bit his tongue and tasted blood. He knew he'd reached the point where he might say something he couldn't take back. Trying to rein in his temper, he said, "You know what? Forget it. Forget this. I'll call a shuttle, jump to a hotel on Jarog or something." He brushed by her on his way to his room.

"Of course you'll disappear now. I haven't given in to what you want, so you leave."

When Paul spun back, Yuhwa wiped an angry tear from her cheek. His heart cracked. "I'm not leaving you," he said. "I'm trying to stop us hurting each other for no reason. Tomorrow we won't be so quick to anger."

"Friends stay. Friends support each other, but at the first chance you run." She hunched her shoulders, voice miserable. "You told me we were more than friends, we were family. Was that a lie?"

Paul wanted to placate her, but he was out of patience and Yuhwa didn't like bullshit anyway. "You never said you wanted what I offered. I've tried to give you everything, but you only want a piece here or there. Not the whole. And that is one hundred percent your choice, and valid. I'm sorry I swiped at you about it." He ran a hand through his hair, desperate to make her understand. "I want to respect your boundaries, but you have to do the same. I'm not good at being ignored, which is what you've done ever since the Feast."

Yuhwa walked over, poking a finger into his chest. "Because you angered me! Why would you assume I'd give in to something I've told you I don't want?"

He grabbed her finger. "I was just talking. We'd seen all the waja tattoos, the ceremony seemed to celebrate it, I just thought you'd want that. Everyone who has them seems thrilled to have them."

"I am not them!" She had another tear in her eye, breaking him.

"I know." Paul pressed her hand to his heart. "I know."

She looked deep into his eyes and he opened himself to whatever she needed to see. From one second to the next he had his arms full of Yuhwa, who'd lunged up to kiss him. Should he stop her? They were coming off an argument and were emotionally charged, which – statistically speaking – wasn't Yuhwa's strong suit. What if she had morning regrets?

Then her tongue stroked his and he decided that was a problem for tomorrow-Paul. Tonight he needed to get her to a horizontal surface and reacquaint himself with every sweet curve of her body. He urged her to jump up and wrap her legs around his waist as they kissed. His almost-stumble wasn't because of his knee, it was the indecent way she'd sucked his tongue, pulled back and nuzzled his neck.

His room was the first one down the hall; he swung through the door and lowered them to his bed. Stretched out on top of her felt good, right, like he was back where he was meant to be. She might not feel the same, but he let his soul sing just a bit with the joy of having her close once more. He worshipped her silky skin and her limber body with small, firm breasts and legs he wanted to lick from hip to toe. To say nothing of the gorgeous spot between them: he thought he could set up camp there and happily drive her out of her mind.

Yuhwa directed him beautifully, making it very clear what worked for her and what didn't. As much as he was drawn to her pale nipples they didn't do much for her. She was far happier with his attentions focused on the backs of her knees and where her neck met her jaw. Hot air breathed over the tops of her ears made her whimper. Anything she wanted, he was going to give her.

Paul was going to find a way to convince her to take a chance on him. He promised himself when he got lost in her pleasure and found his own. Yuhwa would see they could work, because he needed her.

30

Yᴜʜᴡᴀ ʜᴀᴅ ᴡᴏᴋᴇɴ ᴡɪᴛʜ ᴛᴡᴏ ᴛʜᴏᴜɢʜᴛs, ᴀɴᴅ ᴛᴏ her shock regret was neither of them.

Before she acted on either idea, she gave herself another kaala or two to enjoy the sight of Paul in the early light. He was adorable when he slept. Black hair falling over his forehead, chest bared to the hips, mumbling incoherently every now and then. She even liked it when he made little smacking noises with his lips.

Last night's fight had started the day they'd met, she saw that now. She and Paul were two people who tried to govern and direct situations. They'd been trying to control each other from the start. He was especially pushy about her pâtexi because he thought he understood the outcome, and had decided what was best for her.

Sweet man, she thought. *I'm the only one who does that.*

Up and dressed, she addressed her two duties. First, she'd sent a suggestion to the dao teachers based on something Paul had said. He'd been mad and sarcastic, but the potential of multiple majio being able to transit with the *Mahoroba* was worth investigating.

They wouldn't need her to test that, which was good because, thought number two; she admitted it was time to go on pâtexi. Not because of anything specific Paul had said, more that he'd highlighted how juvenile she was being. Refusing any longer served no purpose, and a multi-sal journey away from Paul and the nawa had profound appeal. She could use some time to examine her future.

She messaged the Hunzo she was leaving immediately, which wouldn't give them time to interfere or pontificate. Nor did she share that even if she found her waja, she wasn't committing to entering the Binding Bath. That choice was hers, no matter what they tried to say, and part of her journey would be an internal quest.

Did she accept Jadoube norms, or did she reject them? Both options were valid as Paul had said last night. But if her rejection sprang from the unwarranted fears of a child scared to change, that shifted the landscape. There was something to be said for the shared experiences of her people, the beauty in their legacy and stories. But not if they locked her into a future she didn't want.

Dressed, a pack filled with protein and water sachets over her shoulder, Yuhwa looked in on Paul one last time. She was tempted to kiss him goodbye, but didn't want to wake him. There was a voice message M8 was set to play when he woke, that would suffice for now. When she returned, they would talk about what they were doing, and how they might move forward together. If that was an outcome they both wanted.

Right now, she needed to focus on a part of her dao that didn't tie to veşu. Maybe. No one coached them on how this worked, just that you'd *feel* what to do. You'd go wander in the wadis and stumble around Âuke until you found the magical right spot. She thought back on her dreams, wondering if she'd recognize the cavern based on what Observer Yuhwa had seen, or if she'd be sightless by then, as Dream Yuhwa usually was.

Yippee-ki-yay she whispered to herself.

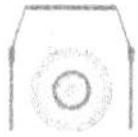

PAUL WAS PRETTY sure he loved Yuhwa like he'd never loved before, but damn her to perdition. Yet again, after a stunning night of pleasure, she'd left him to wake up alone. He buried his face in the pillow she'd used, getting a dopamine rush from the faint hit of her minty melon scent.

Two cups of nropita and one message relayed by bot later, he waffled between irritated and pleased with himself. Something he'd said or done had gotten through to her, she was off on pâtexi, and he wanted to take the win. But she'd snuck off without waking him. Did that mean she resented his input? Or that she wanted to maintain it was all her idea?

Either way, he thought, he was a free agent as long as it took her to go out and back. He'd had hours upon hours of chats with the nawa, and they'd all said it could take hours to days. In a few rare cases weeks had been needed.

Yuhwa had plenty of supplies to get her through. Supplicants were encouraged to take as little as possible as it allegedly made the quest more potent if they were deprived of everyday comforts. But she'd be fine. Were there dangerous animals out there? Yes. Did he want to be out there with her, beating them back? Yes. But he'd been assured that unlike the Outback or East African wildlife, not all of it was trying to kill people at any given moment. And her pâtexi was for her alone.

Paul wasn't great with downtime. He needed to be out, about, doing something useful. What was there for him to do, though? The *Mahoroba* seemed to be in fine hands without him. Yuhwa couldn't use his talents out in the desert. He was too far away from Centris to help his family and the political bloodbath probably still churning on the Wheel. As much as he wanted to go to the dao schools on Druk Plateau and see the kids learning there, he wasn't sure he'd be welcome.

That left hitting up Quý and team. Paul enjoyed being around Quý, who was a pretty cool dude for the head of a domineering religious crew. Paul tried to come up with a good reason to go back to Migwa Plateau. He loved the Hunzo Pavilion, but that didn't feel like a good enough justification to just show up. Should he tell them he thought he was probably a herald? It would definitely raise eyebrows. Would they shoot him down before he could lay out his theories?

What had Katy done when presented with roadblocks like this? Paul ran through her stories. That was it! Research! It wasn't glorious, but it needed to be done, and last time she said had helped knock loose some ideas. Obviously, his case was different from his sister's: the trigger was already in her hands by the research point, whereas he'd have to wait for Yuhwa to return with his. No reason not to lay an early foundation and get some facts, though, and where better than the Pavilion housing their sacred scroll room?

An hour later, his jump shuttle landed and he was escorted directly to Quý.

"You bring such a fascinating project to us!" the leader said, clapping his hands. "Let me gather a few other nawa, and we'll meet in the scroll room to discuss!"

The new people, most of whom Paul hadn't yet met, had a thousand questions. His voice was getting hoarse from telling the tale of Sundancer, Katy and Bay. It wasn't lost on him that he was truly acting as Sundancer's emissary at that moment, rehashing the events from a few weeks back.

"A nefeslo cage? I'm having a hard time even picturing it," a bald woman with skin the color of skim milk said. "Somehow the Pu'ulqaari have turned their precious mud into a shadow prison capable of holding Drazoen?"

"That's what I was told," Paul confirmed. "A collapsed dark

star is part of the mix. Katy's assassin, Yfaun, told her the cost to open them is death."

Quý paced rapidly, his robes swishing as he strode back and forth. "None of the Mikanjo Seekers have found the next 'Kawakona'? The herald remains hidden, as does the next Drazoen slated to return?"

Paul waffled a hand. "The Mikanjo are split on the matter. Some think they're done seeking, that just finding the first one was their purpose. Others believe they have to find all Nine."

Another member of the Hunzo popped up, his eyes merry, curly hair bouncing. "I have an idea! Be right back," he called over his shoulder as he trotted into the shelves on the other side of the room.

Paul gazed at the inner courtyard while they waited, visible from the open wall of the scroll chambers. This whole place was capital-Z Zen. Single story, square, almost like Shee in layout, but more Southeast Asian in sensibility. He wasn't a designer, he just knew he liked how serene and fresh it looked. Polished white granite floors and white walls accented here and there with plants or desert rocks. There were fabric-covered walkways shading most of the interior from Malor's hot sun, and magenta bougainvillea crawled over all the entrances.

He was happy he'd thought to come here; surely they'd find something to help in this oasis of calm. If Quý would stop pacing, that is.

"How did your sister know who her assassin was?"

Paul sat up straight before he answered Quý. "The guy came after her, before they'd left Earth. Then he showed up at the safehouse and told her. Called it his 'life's purpose'."

"And no one else has been attacked?"

"That we know of," Paul said.

A lot of rumbling and *hmming* commenced from the nawa. Finally bald lady said, "How incredible that the Pu'ulqaari have bred people just for this. That they were given the power to create shadow prisons. They've spent a kōmilen preparing for this day, while the rest of us have ignored the whole problem. We've been too passive."

Paul didn't like how admiring she sounded. "The Mikanjo prepared just as much. Sounds like the octopeople-" he stopped, letting his aoiti feed him the right word. "Muškikal, they've been waiting for the right time, too."

"Found it!" Curly jogged back to their group, scroll in hand. "This is the oldest copy of our *Origins*. Of course, we have cloud versions, but this was written by hand. Likely three kōmilen ago."

Three kōmilen *equivalent two hundred seventy thousand years.*

Paul almost fell out of his chair. How could they have something preserved so perfectly that was older than all of Human civilization? *Nûz*, he thought, *were we even out of the trees by then?* "Should you be touching that?" All the nawa looked at him like he'd burped the words. "I just mean it's so old."

"The atmosphere on Malor was quite friendly to keeping things unspoiled," Quý chuckled. "Very little moisture to damage documents before we perfected conservation and moved to digital."

"Great," Paul said, relieved. "Then let's get to it!" He looked around the circle. "Who wants to read first?"

More odd looks before it dawned on them he couldn't read the scroll. "I'll read it the first time." Curly was eager, rolling on to the balls of his feet. "It isn't long, but you may have many questions."

Paul listened all the way through once without interrupting. It was handed to another to read for the second go-round. Apparently the text was old enough to present a challenge for these scholars, who were translating as they went. He thought it equated to someone who'd never read Beowulf giving it a go, converting Old English to modern on the spot.

"Can you read that again, please?"

"We are neither young nor old. Neither new nor aged. We are not originals like Lunari and Cho. We are not ingenue like Oti and Rixat." This woman's voice was mellow and lovely, her cadence measured.

"Right, what is this saying? The Cho were the first species the Drazoen found, yeah? I heard a rumor the Krylar destroyed them before they went after the Lunari." Were these terrifying Krylar going through species in order of evolution?

He got puzzled frowns. "I've never heard that before," the bald woman said. "It seems unlikely. The Cho did, however, disappear suddenly."

The current reader kept going when there were no more questions from Paul. By the time she finished, he had one burning question. "Twice in there, the writer said jabbing the Aoni. Not swimming it, which is what I've always heard Yuhwa say. I don't want to make a big deal out of nothing, but are they the same thing, or different?"

The nawa gathered around the scroll, reading it through repeatedly. His aoiti couldn't really keep up with the rather spirited debate that ensued over how to translate the word he'd picked up on. Finally, Quý turned to him, hands on hips, blackberry hair askew, and grinned.

"Outstanding interpretation, Ambassador!" He took a few steps forward, making space for rigorous arm gestures that punctuated his words. "We've come to an agreement; the word translates as 'needle', and the text would therefore say Song-master *remade our souls to needle the Aoni*, as opposed to jab."

Paul got excited. "And that part about how majio needle the Aoni with the dao, you think that's different from the swimming concept?"

Curly nodded, his rambunctious hair bobbing in concert. "As long as can be remembered, the dao instructors have used the metaphor of traversing a river. Lose yourself in the flow, be like the little fish who out-swim the currents." The nawa all looked nostalgic at his words. "Needling is a far sharper implication."

The woman with the nice voice said, "I'd argue it's the opposite of swimming, in fact. Even if you swim against the flow, you're in the water. When you sew, you take opposing things and join them. We don't think of it as a violent act, but that's because we aren't fabric or thread."

Paul wanted more. "Are there any other texts this old? This was a great start."

Quý smiled, kind and patient as ever. "We will set a team to look. For now, most of us have to return to duties." He chuckled. "Bindings shouldn't wait, even for ideas on how to wake Drazoen."

Mortified, Paul tried to apologize to the group but they were having none of it.

"When was the last time we were challenged like this?" the bald lady said. "This has been a delight, and I look forward to tomorrow."

Quý escorted him to a shuttle, where Paul gave apologizing another try. "I am truly sorry for abusing your time like that. I had an idea and barged in with it, assuming no one else had anything better to do," he said in chagrin.

"Do you know, I've been a nawa for a milenyo. Only three or four are chosen every generation like the *Origins* said, so there aren't that many of us. I've been leader for less than an aiwak." Quý laughed. "Today was the first time I've seen such animation in those nawa. You have been good for us."

Paul blushed. "I never want to infringe."

"Normally we would have had a little more time, but several members have binding ceremonies today, and the rest of us attend Spirit Bath tonight." At Paul's blank look he said, "When Jadoube pass, no matter where in the Aoni, their body returns here." He swept his arm out to indicate the beautiful building adjacent to the Hunzo Pavilion. It resembled the Binding Bath with carvings and semi-circular pediments, but it was a pale, sand dollar stone rather than black.

"Right! Yuhwa mentioned this once. That's the Spirit Bath? I thought it was part of the Pavilion."

"It is off limits to most," Quý said. "Only nawa and the dead enter the Spirit Bath." His tone saddened. "Tonight we must lay to rest an unjust deceased. Rarely are those easy."

Paul reached out and shook Quý's hand. At the nawa's puzzled look Paul grinned. "That's Human for hello, goodbye and, in this case, good luck."

Back on the shuttle, Paul decided to stop on Jarog plateau. He wanted to explore a little and grab a bite that wasn't from a replicator. Or just came from a different replicator, he wasn't picky. Five minutes of research in the shuttle's recommendations interface and he was dropped off, not far from Yuto Port where they'd first landed. The neighborhood was reputed to be a hive of cultural activity and food options.

As he exited the shuttle, he caught sight of the president, walking with a group of Pu'ulqaari. Paul froze. What were they doing here? Trying to get a good look through the crowd between them, he recognized the PQs from the Calling. Koala clan; the people who replaced the family Katy's suicide assassin had come from.

He was so busy trying to spy on them he failed to notice the guards Onye Ma had sent his way. In a minute he'd been escorted to the group, rather unwillingly. But he wasn't going to make a scene. Unless one of these people tried to kill him.

"Ambassador Phelan jo Faluji!" The President beamed, and rested a hand on his shoulder. "May I introduce Ambassador Getnet of the Ko'olak clan, and his aide, Leah."

Leah, not of the Koala but the much harder to say Ko'olak clan, was a woman who deserved attention. The whole time

Paul nodded at the other guy, he evaluated Leah. Her bearing and posture were imbued with casual strength, nurtured and controlled. Her face markings – her ruh – mesmerized. Close up he could verify it was deliberate scarification; each raised bump was painted white, blue, or green. It made an offset petal pattern where the flower would have centered around her ear. Stunning.

She made him nervous. Leah never looked at him after the initial greeting, but his skin crawled with the sensation of being watched. He was very glad his hover brace was gone and his eyes had adjusted so he didn't need sunglasses anymore, because showing weakness in front of Leah felt dangerous. She was well-muscled, taller than he was, and prowled around without moving an inch.

PQ assassin concerns fresh in his mind after their session at the Pavilion today, Paul tried to get out of a meal with the dignitaries. But the president insisted, so excited to have multiple Calling emissaries on Malor. By the end of the night he didn't know what he'd eaten or where (it had been fancy, he thought, and he hadn't paid despite all the money Sundancer had loaded on his aoiti), and he'd managed a private conversation with Onye Ma to explain the predicament.

Her doubt was clear, but he urged her to message Centris and verify what he told her. When she got confirmation, she clenched her jaw, ordered round-the-clock security for him, and still managed to act perfectly normal in front of the PQ. Paul demurred when invited for drinks, and fled as casually as his mounting anxiety let him.

The herald had summoned his assassin.

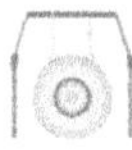

IF PRIVATION WAS the route to pâtexi, Yuhwa's protein sachets were shoving her right down the road. She was damn sick of the things already, and hadn't regretted losing the one she threw at a papimogu who'd attacked her. Why did her quest have to happen during insect mating season?

She'd tried to meditate, even laid down in the dried wash of Wadi Tak, eyes to the moons and stars. Not the area of wadi by Nay or Aru Rivers; that would be stupid because they could flash flood and drown her. This had been a slightly inclined flat area against a medium-sized spire. Gave her nothing but a few sal-angs of rest.

Her dao wasn't saying mirca to her. Civilization had receded almost immediately when she descended Ha-Seng Plateau to the desert floor. All those aiwaks of dreams had primed her to think her pâtexi would feel rehearsed, or too easy. Laughable now, as she wandered, lost, along the high ridge above the Aru. The river was straight at the moment, but would bend east as it got closer to Âuke.

The sacred gulrã, Cholgŭ, was supposed to be around here somewhere. How she would recognize a fabled cosmic desert winding around and linking up the regions of Malor, she had no clue. A full day of walking through the sands of a regular gulrã around Wadi Tak made her short-tempered enough to kick at rocks in her path. Stupid pâtexi. Stupid nawa. Stupid Nine-nûzed quest she never wanted anyway. But had anyone asked her what *she* wanted? No!

Yuhwa readied her foot to let another rock have it. This time when she kicked, the rock didn't move. No bone broke, but it violently rebounded her foot, threw off her balance and sent her tumbling. She fell off the ledge, flailing as she dropped. Nails tore as she tried digging into to the rocky, sandy earth to stop her slide into to the river, which ran swiftly despite the dry season. She was moving too fast, her body pummeled by the shale and large stones at the water's edge.

Her head cracked into one of stones, wet from splashes of

river racing by. She cried out, pain shattering her focus, and couldn't see for the blood running in her eyes. Yuhwa's final thought before everything went dark was a wish she'd woken Paul to say goodbye.

31

"I'm not hiding," Paul said to Na. Again.

"You are," Na replied. "It's been three sals, she'd have killed you by now if she planned to."

Pacing in front of the vid screen, Paul chewed his thumb. "You don't know that. The guards-"

"Can't stop a killer who was bred to do nothing else in life." Na smiled, not unkindly. "You should be safe to go back out. Visit your nawa brain trust in person."

"There's not much left for us to talk over. They haven't found any scrolls older than the first one, and after sals of discussion they're all set that 'needling' is right, but can't agree what that means." Paul stopped, hands on hips, facing the screen and Na. "I don't know if it helps our Drazoen wakeup theories anyway. We needed something that said, 'look here, go there, find a person named Bob who holds the keys to the kingdom'. Not obscure references to sewing space together."

The Nyakisi pilot regarded him silently. Finally, he said, "You don't have to figure this whole problem out yourself. You do know that, yes?"

Paul dropped onto an ottoman. "I do know," he sighed, voice

low. "But if I don't focus on that, I dwell on how Yuhwa needed me to support her and I didn't. I pushed when I should have just listened. From the beginning she's talked about wanting to stay a majio, that she's happy and fulfilled." To his horror, he felt himself choke up, but a quick glance said Na either hadn't noticed or didn't judge him for the emotions.

"The nawa aren't what I expected," he kept on, swallowing a few times to cling to his composure. "Her fears made me expect them to be cruel, like religious dictators who forced their down-trodden people to do whatever they say. When I met them, and I saw how happy most people here are to have gone on pâtexi and have their binding marks, I guess I…yeah. I bought the hype and stopped seeing her side of it."

Na shook his head. "Her message didn't say she was mad, or blamed you. Only that she realized it was time to undergo the quest."

"But *I* blame me." Paul struggled to forgive himself, as he had every hour since he'd woken alone. "What kind of partner, friend, or man am I, that I could so easily trample her wishes and dreams with my assumptions of what she should want?"

"One who is fallible and learning," Na responded. "None of us is perfect, we are adventures always in progress. Whether you've gotten it right or wrong is measurable moment to moment, and the opportunity to be better is eternally available."

Paul let the hope in Na's words flood his tired brain, then laughed, heart lighter. "Back on my world, you could write for greeting cards." He counted the seconds until the aoiti shared the concept with Na, who glowered once it hit.

"Do you know what term I learned today," Na said, voice silky. "Boy toy. Mandy taught us that you are Yuhwa's boy toy, because she's so much older."

Sputtering, Paul yelled, "Tell Mandy to update her terminology, that's offensive!" Truthfully, he wished he could claim the name. He would grovel to be her boy toy if he thought it would work.

"Go out, Human, do something. Anything. In fact, check on the progress of a new pilot for us. Mandy pesters every few salangs." With that Na signed off.

Paul hadn't yet gone to the dao schools on Druk Plateau. A quick check-in with his guards later and he had a shuttle plus armed escort. Crossing over Wadi Tak he gazed down, knowing Yuhwa was down there somewhere, seeking her divine Aoni-orchestrated chunk of waja.

This part of Malor desert really did look different from the other areas he'd seen. Wadi Abisah, around the Migwa Plateau-Spirit Bath area, was filled with buttes and flattop mesas. Wadi Gwansee, which surrounded Ni-Matak Plateau and the Binding Bath, was a far more open land, fewer foothills than he was seeing now.

"I never would have thought I could tell them apart," he said to his companion.

Laci, a sword who normally guarded the president, gazed below them. "We're taught as children that each of us is as unique as the grains of sands in the wadis."

"That's really nice. I could use that with the kids I teach. Taught, I mean." His heart clenched, wondering if he'd ever get it back.

She rolled her shoulders; ones bulked with enough muscle Paul thought Laci could easily do free ring gymnastics. Pommel horse, too. "Eh. I always thought it all looked the same out there. Brown." She laughed, flashing a few crooked teeth, nutmeg eyes merry. "But kids need to hear they're special, don't they?"

Chuckling, Paul agreed. They flew the rest of the way in silence. Paul missed Yuhwa, how they could talk so easily. She never minded his endless questions, dumb or not. He couldn't fight the ache in his heart as they headed for the part of Malor where she felt most at home.

Druk Plateau was where they taught Jadoube children how to access their dao. It was home to multiple large schools. As they flew overhead, he thought it looked like a college campus; the University of Washington minus cherry trees and green grass. But they did have a fountain, he spotted, five in fact. That tracked; most things on Malor came in fives.

Paul reviewed what the nawa had told him about majio studies. Down there they spent decades, bisous, honing their skills: first were years in physical rivers, forging links in their young minds between flowing water and the dao. Next came more years of meditation and physical discipline, training the body to handle the connections and remain relaxed. Tensing up to the point of pain or, worst case, causing a heart or brain problem, wasn't out of the realm of possibility.

It didn't matter they were genetically touched by a dragon, bodies were flesh and blood, prone to break if poorly prepared. Once all of that came together, there were yet more years of tests with veşu and the fabric of spacetime itself. Yuhwa had shared a few stories, the nawa shared even more. Young Jadoube got lost in the dao semi-regularly because the pull was so strong and, he'd been told, it felt like being wrapped in the arms of angels.

Okay, they didn't say angels. They said something about Ji-Cheol Jarog's wings enfolding you, but Paul didn't want to hug a giant raven-Jadoube hybrid. So he'd subbed baby cherubim; same concept but more suited to his Human nature.

Their arrival today was met by several very excited majio teachers. "Ambassador, we think we have it!"

He trotted after them into the closest school. They were inter-connected and their ultimate destination was a massive pool two buildings south and three floors up. Dao schools were the rare Jadoube buildings more than two stories high.

On Earth most of the "kids" he saw would be considered adults. But aging really differed, and a Jadoube under one hundred was still a child in their eyes. These ones raced through halls, bowing respectfully to the instructors and eyeing Paul and Laci with open curiosity. Of the two of them, she was way more interesting. Her daggers looked dangerous and sexy, their waja hilts peeking above embossed leather arm-sheaths. The edges of her binding marks peeked out the bottoms, snaking down her wrists, palms, and onto her fingers.

"Seeing you is a story they will brag about for tuigs." Laci pitched her words for his ears only.

Paul was sure she was confused until one boy approached, tentative but determined. "You are the *Hooman?*" When Paul nodded the boy surged forward, only to be held back by Laci, who shook her head.

"Did you need something from me?" Paul said over Laci's shoulder.

Frozen, mouth agape, the boy just stared. Then he suddenly came to himself and said, "I graduate soon, if you need a majio I would be your personal pilot. Free, completely free!"

The instructors tutted loudly, apologizing. Laci pushed the kid to move on, telling him he'd overstepped. Paul wasn't sure about that; had to give him points for trying. But Paul's pilot would only ever be Yuhwa, he was pretty sure about that. Even if the pâtexi turned her into a freaking knitter, she'd still be his majio.

If she ever came back, that is. He wanted her with him, and three days had felt interminable without her.

By the time they reached the pool, his knee burned. He'd call Isāc or Dr. Vásquez when this was done. Contrary to Yuhwa's assumptions, he had consulted both of them before removing the hover brace. They'd agreed he could give it a shot, so long as he went nice and easy. No prolonged exercise or strain, no twist-ing, that kind of thing. But he'd carried Yuhwa to bed and, perhaps, hadn't been as careful as he should have in the hours that followed. Not like he'd been feeling any pain that night.

It was more likely days of pacing in circles around her house, then climbing all these stairs for the first time in a while was just stretching the healing his aoiti had done. The burn didn't feel like tearing, it was more like a good leg day would feel.

Seven more Jadoube awaited them, four arrayed in a diamond pattern, three others waiting nearby. The excited man who'd greeted them coming off the shuttle took up the conversation again. "Yuhwa told us of your brilliant idea, Ambassador."

"I bet," he said wryly, "she didn't use those words."

Everyone laughed. "She was ruder about herself," head guy went on. "But we are able to see it was truly inspired. Just this morning, we think we've connected sufficiently to fly the *Mahoroba* through the veşu."

"Could we impose on you?" asked a woman with turquoise hair the same length and style as Yuhwa's. She was one of the corners of the diamond. "We hoped you would allow us to connect with you, as she did?"

"You can tell us if the experience resembles when Majio Bon-Gil brought you here," said another corner of the diamond. His voice was soft and optimistic.

Paul very much doubted they could connect the way he and Yuhwa had, therefore the experiences couldn't compare. Hell, he didn't even know any of their names. Jesus, he was *the worst* ambassador. So effing bad.

But he would try for them, otherwise the *Mahoroba* and all her occupants were stuck here. No telling what kind of shape Yuhwa would be in when she returned, and the Drafter (via Mandy) was insistent they move on soon. Malor wasn't the right location for billions of Humans to cut their alien world teeth on. Nor could the planet support such an invasion; Onye Ma had hinted that more than a time or two.

"Tell me where you want me," was all he said.

They left him where he was, waiting for their move. It was weird. Gentle, but weird. They were polite, mentally knocking before trying to connect with him. Yuhwa had slipped in like she was meant to be there, had every right. These folks were being too nice.

"Just go for it, okay? I'll squawk if you start to hurt me, otherwise have at it."

After a startled pause, they listened. Since Paul was a complete novice at linking consciousness, he was pleasantly surprised to learn he could discern differences in who was where. More importantly, he could tell them it wasn't working. "I don't know what's missing, but it doesn't have the same... snap. When she connected to all of us it was like air filling up a balloon, right? And then we synced and boom! The balloon was fully stretched and we floated away."

Laci walked over while the others conferred. "One more try, then we need to go. An armored shuttle is coming to pick us up."

Paul raised his eyebrows. "What happened?"

"When the Pu'ulqaari contingency left Malor last night, Leah's aoiti didn't register for departure." Her face closed down. "They've lost sight of her, and the president is taking no chances. She'd like you relocated to her secure residence."

"But when Yuhwa comes back-"

"We have cameras watching Âuke; she'll be picked up as soon as she comes out."

That put paid to his chance at grilling experts on how they saw needling vs. swimming veşu. Hopefully he could comm with them after he'd been secured wherever they were going. He also took a moment to regret mocking his sister's frustration when she'd been in lockdown at the Voice House. Was this the lot of heralds: house arrest in the nicest jails of the Aoni?

SHE WOKE TO DARKNESS; this wasn't nighttime, it was opaque and blank. Dream Yuhwa's fate had befallen her and she couldn't see a thing. She could only pray her aoiti would repair it fast enough for her to escape the dream prophecy of drowning.

Her backpack of water and protein sachets had survived, and Yuhwa took her time ingesting one of each. Relax, she told herself. Stay calm and rational. You've seen this play out hundreds of times. *Of course, I always die in the dreams.*

not die never die

you must come home

sweet Child

see differently

She was hearing voices now? How hard had she hit her head? Wait, why were these voices familiar? She knew she'd heard them before, when was it? Damn! The answer teased at the edges of her mind. Was it part of her recurring dream? Were these the Côttru? The sacred Five of Malor coming to her aid, leading her to her waja. Yuhwa had heard stories, of course, but never fully believed it could happen. Especially to her, only a semi-faithful Jadoube at best.

attention

embrace darkness

homehome come home

focus and see

The dull blackness behind her eyes changed, brightening with dozens of colors in swirling lines. They slowly resolved and, in shock, Yuhwa rose to her feet. She was in a cave, just like her dreams, but in real life she could see contours of everything around her. Like a 3D model she'd see projected on the *Eternidad*: irregular, jutting rock walls, a high arching ceiling above, loose gravel strewn along the path forward, all of it clearly outlined in multichromatic lines.

When she was unconscious, she must have floated down-river. Yuhwa knew the Aru went underground as it neared Âuke. Had she truly been dragged so far? Howsoever she'd gotten where she currently stood, she'd been spit out of the water and enough time had passed for her to mostly dry off. These mountain caves blocked most sunlight, which meant sals could have passed as she lay unconscious. Yuhwa was lucky to be alive. Hopefully Paul wasn't worried. The nawa should be filling him up with tales of glorious pâtexi that lasted multiple sals and signified glorious things for the Jadoube it happened to.

Nothing glorious would happen to *her* unless she made a decision to move. Choosing her path was going to be a challenge; threads of every color she'd ever seen spun through the cave walls and seemed to offer multiple options. Taking several slow, deep breaths to steady and center herself, Yuhwa opened her spirit, actively asking for guidance from the Five. If they'd been speaking to her before, perhaps they'd help her again.

She didn't get an answer in words, but her inner sight sharpened, plucking at ghostly, silvery-white threads leading her downward and to the left. The part of her brain suddenly processing invisible light waves in an Aoni-level blackness saw those lines were vibrating, humming, teasing her into following them.

yesyes
birthright
sweet Child
come home

Yuhwa, as she'd attested many a time, was no bakyai. Not a khòchi, either. There were as many anecdotes about the Five helping on pâtexi as there were dunes shifting between the wadis above. How they led, provisioned, even nagged Jadoube who started to flag on their quest. They were benevolent helpers, guides and good omens. Sacred to Malor, beloved by all. Their Feast was so recent she could practically still taste the mipoy.

Only one person she knew had heard different voices: Katy. Herald of Sundancer Orange, who said she and her Wataño only heard each other in the shadow prisons. At first. Once they'd been released by Katy's music, she heard them all the time, she said.

A rush of memory overtook Yuhwa as soon as the thought crossed her mind: transiting the veşu, these were the spirits who'd guided her through! These voices had given her the know-how to carry the entirely of the *Mahoroba,* a feat the top majio teachers couldn't replicate.

Only a bakyại would ignore the signs Yuhwa was putting together, and she was no useless fool. Ethereal commentary giving her advice and aid. Dreams about waja for aiwaks. The threads she felt compelled to follow in darkness were the very color of Songmaster Silver, the Drazoen Lia had made sure to tell her needed waja to wake up.

A khòchi would find a way to turn it to their advantage, but Yuhwa wasn't a power-hungry idiot, either. She didn't want to believe she was a herald, despite mounting evidence, and struggled to grasp the enormity of it. What she was – a woman who wanted to survive a pâtexi gone sideways – needed to take precedence now. Losing herself in fantasy and fears of failing to rouse dragons wouldn't help. The danger of being inside Âuke remained very real, despite her ability to see the aura of stone that surrounded her.

> *not wrong*
> *all as planned*
> *downdowndown*
> *trust*

Côttru, Shadow Drazoen, even possibly just annoying nawa who'd found a way to keep messing with her dao, whoever they were they wanted her following the glowing waja path. Arms out, just in case, she walked forward and down. It would be her luck to watch those lustrous strands closely as she descended, and miss a head-height rock that knocked her out again.

She couldn't help but recall this was about the time in her dreams that she'd be flooded and drowned. And, her newly expanded memory also recalled, these same voices were the ones who'd pushed dream-her to walk right into the subterranean waja lake.

Well shtû.

32

Yuhwa's eyes hadn't adjusted, her mind had. Appreciating the subtle difference had taken her several sal-angs of slow trudging along her route. Cavern walls had narrowed to body-width (if she held her breath) at one point, but right now she heard her footsteps echoing in a way that signaled a large open space. Combined with the topographical images in her head, outlined in intensifying silvery white, she could "see" almost perfectly.

The lines called for her to cross a bridge over a long drop and Yuhwa didn't care that she could make out the edges. Relying on this new second sight was scary, dangerous, and she took each step slower than she might have with regular vision and a glow-light. She'd spent the time trying to recapture the voices she'd heard before, both earlier this sal and previous times. Were they Shadows or Côttru? Did it matter?

Quite a lot. Yuhwa had no plans to be a herald; she couldn't commit to dating more than a night or two, she certainly wasn't cut out for a lifelong bond to a Drazoen. If Great Druk or Sister Ha-Seng wanted to give her tips, show her the right path to her soul-mated waja, that was all fine and good. Shadow Drazoen wanting her to break them out of their prison, now that might be a problem.

Even worse, what if she was the herald of Songmaster and couldn't do it? Yuhwa wasn't musical like Katy. The way her friend had explained that transcendent moment, playing her flute was one of the biggest parts of it. Yuhwa didn't sing or play an instrument. She danced, but her artistic side stopped there.

Depending on me isn't going to get you what you want, she thought at the voices. *You need someone like Paul. He can't play either, far as I know, but he'd teach himself in three kaalas to be what you needed.* She halted, halfway along the span, foot scraping against the ground. He would, wouldn't he?

Paul Phelan was a man someone could lean on; honorable, generous. All these years, she must have met others with the same traits, but none of them had resonated with her the way he had. She looked back on their time, aware her initial distrust had sprung from dueling instincts telling her to trust, while bitter experience wanted to escape such intimacy. He was kind, a person driven to lead and mentor, who could encourage or challenge others to be better. Unlike her, he would acknowledge and apologize for mistakes. There was merit to the man.

Of course, on the other end, if you pushed him too hard he wouldn't give. Stubborn as Ni-Matak, he was.

A loud snort echoed from her left side.

Slowly, slowly, she turned her head. She knew what she'd see, but had trouble accepting it even so.

Glorious, curly-furred, steady Ni-Matak. Their head towered above hers, reaching more than halfway to the ceiling, though their feet were situated below the path Yuhwa trod. Ni-Matak, right there, floating beside her.

Their light in her mind's eye was the warm reds and oranges of a low-burning fire. They radiated hearth and home, and the pleasure in following a life that celebrated Malor's earthen splendor.

Paul had said he liked them best because they had great presence, but would lay waste if they needed to. Another snort from above. Yuhwa sensed Ni-Matak's amusement, and thought they agreed with Paul. When they lowered their head and liquid brown eyes peered into hers, she *knew* they did. Ni-Matak was a bulwark; they were how Malor stood firm, cradled its creations, kept enemies at bay.

Being nuzzled by one of the Côttru was nothing Yuhwa could have ever imagined, and she broke wide open. She stopped trying to think and rationalize. She released her worry, stress, fear, every bit of burden she'd been carrying since childhood. They were here; they'd spoken to her and come to show her the way. She didn't need to know more than that, she only needed to let it happen. She'd been shattered, and with new awareness she was remade.

As if that epiphany opened a portal, she felt all of them, just like her dream. But in this version, there was weight to the visitations. Ji-Cheol Jarog was heavy, talons digging into her shoulders for purchase; his threads were shimmery blue and black, a dull silver flecked along the outermost lines.

Migwa's feet, spread wide to carry a large furry body made to break rock, barely fit on the bridge. Yuhwa was delighted to see they tip-toed along, just as in legend. But unlike the desert colors they were said to be outside Âuke, in here Migwa was made of blues like Human lakes and oceans.

Great Druk behind them she couldn't really see, but the strength and heft of stone they were said to embody pressed against her. Yuhwa could see the ends of their wings, nearly as black as a veṣu, scraping the cavern sides.

Finally, soft fur rubbing against her hand, hip and outer thigh, then pressing against her body: Sister Ha-Seng. Her incredible feline shape pulsed with obsidian and cloud-white threads, patterned as she was said to be out in the wadis. She prowled on Yuhwa's right side, predatory power incarnate.

Together they would seek, together they would succeed. With their spirits to guide her, Yuhwa knew she would not be made less by her calling. It would surpass everything she'd known, and when she let it fill her with purpose, she would become more. A Jadoube that honored Malor for the gifts and sacrifices it had made.

Their traveling party crossed the bridge quickly, nearly running, Yuhwa no longer afraid of falling now she had the Five around her. Chamber after chamber, down they went, following the silver threads that pulled at her. She couldn't say how far they'd gone, but the heat was sufficient to drench her in sweat, which reactivated previously dried blood. Damp strands of hair plastered to her neck and face before she pulled the whole mess back and knotted it.

Sal-angs passed. There were no words from the Côttru, no sounds they made were heard over the noise of Âuke. Stalactites crashed in distant caverns, rodents scurried and winged animals flitted, always out of sight. Yuhwa was losing her enthusiasm and holistic unity feelings.

This was boring, hot, and her feet hurt.

They rounded a sharp corner too fast and Yuhwa slipped, the path sloping so radically that she'd have tumbled but for Ji-Cheol Jarog beating his wings to keep them upright. She lowered her head, annoyed at herself. Inattention like that was inexcusable, potentially fatal. And how could she so easily let go of the hallowed feelings she'd experienced, like it was that new normal Paul talked about? She had no idea how many people before her had been blessed with help from all Five, but she refused to lose sight of how precious it was.

Her view of the threads was compromised with her head down; they'd disappeared from the path. She raised her eyes, only to realize her vision was completely gone. Physical and mental, neither showed her anything. Absolute darkness surrounded her. This had always led to the scariest part of her prophetic dreams: drowning in waja. Panic crept through her body, insidious, cold, spiking into her lungs, stopping her breath.

Talons in her shoulders tightened and drew blood. Fur to her front and side warmed flesh gone clammy in fear. A large wet snout huffed hot breath directly into her face. Leathery wings wrapped her close.

callcallcall

call your waja

call

call it

How?! She couldn't see anything, sound was gone now, too. How was she meant to call her waja? Whistle like a kamorca herder? Yuhwa scoured her mind for ideas of how Katy would have handled it. Dead end, because Katy swore by "gut instinct" but Yuhwa's was telling her to turn and try to escape.

The Five pressed her more tightly, almost too much to bear. All right, different approach. What would Paul do? Yuhwa thought back to Shee and the time spent with the mediward's children. Physical to ground the mental, he'd said. She didn't know his gymnastics, but she remembered early training in the dao schools. Forms they were taught to help align body-mind-spirit.

She knelt on the ground, palms to earth, willing her dao to open her to the body of the mountain pressing down on her. Each of her five fingers on both hands were conduits, and she jolted when the Côttru spirits dissolved from around her and funneled through her fingers. They wanted to return home, to the heart of Âuke where the Cholgǔ rose up to begin its journey girdling all of Malor. Their power dragged her with them, sinking to a place no Jadoube could physically go.

Yuhwa couldn't see, but didn't need to. She smelled molten waja, a lot of it. One part, hidden somewhere in there, was hers, meant to bind to her and carry her life and memories. More than anything she wanted to be joined to it, hold it and let it surround her.

Come to me, she cried, her spirit flaring like a beacon in the fount of waja. *Come to me!*

She felt the Côttru release her, stamping themselves inside of her, then floating away. Unencumbered and unafraid of what always came next in her dreams, she shouted *Come to me!*

Observer and Dream Yuhwas hadn't understood; not their body, but their soul was drowning in waja, exactly as it needed to. Only together could they rise to the surface, consummate the pâtexi, be whole.

A soft, pleading call. *Come to me.*

And it did.

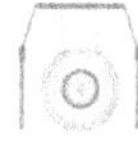

"Ambassador!"

Paul was jolted out of a doze by the shout across the president's courtyard. He'd barely slept the night before, scared for Yuhwa, scared for himself, and frustrated by the limitations of this place. Secure it might be, relaxing it was not.

"Ambassador Phelan jo Faluji!!"

"Yeah, yes," he grumbled, wondering when the hell he'd just accepted having a new name in the Aoni. He'd bet Da loved it, though. "I'm up. What's going on?"

Laci waved him over. "They're getting ready to test majio linking and need your feedback."

"I'm allowed to go back to the schools?" he asked eagerly.

"Ah, no." Laci shook her head. "They've come here."

Great. Ugh. "Okay, lead the way."

Forty minutes later, Paul bid adieu to the new *Mahoroba* majio crew. Turned out seven was the right mix. He also said goodbye to M8. Mandy wanted her bot back, and she and the Drafter couldn't wait to head out.

"Thuliso has convinced them to go to Pała·č," Na said drolly. "Man like him probably has orders to get as deeply lost in that carnival as possible.

Pała·č *paw-law-tch; Tschuele festival held every three hundred tuigs. Lasts for 1 tuig and all serious traders consider it a pilgrimage. Rotates between the Tschuele planets, current stop on original home world Quiltac.*

"Isn't this the thing Katy was going to play her symphony at? And you're sticking with them?" Losing contact with his sorta-friend made him tense, plus Paul thought Na would get bored. But if Raisa went, Na was likely to follow. "Maybe you'll get lost in this potluck."

"Pała·č, and I've been to them before. Fun, good place to introduce Humans to nearly every species in the Aoni. I doubt it's got anything to do with Shadow Drazoen and prophecies, which is just what your people need. No more cataclysmic events for a while."

It felt ridiculous to say, but Paul had to anyway. "Call when you get there. Or text. Just to let me know everything went well." Na frowned, so Paul added. "If you don't I'm going to worry half of my species disappeared into a veșu along with you and the Lunari."

Understanding dawned and Na signed off with a promise to send word when they arrived at Quiltac. "At least it has less damn moons than this place."

Paul couldn't stand it, the juxtaposition of mind-numbing fear and utter boredom. Resolute, he tracked down Laci again, hoping she could show him a gym. A light Pilates workout would go a long way to soothing his frayed nerves and stretching sore muscles. She understood immediately what he wanted and showed him to a training center for the president's guards. Their quarters were aimed more at weapons practice, but he found some equipment he could use to meet his needs.

Paul left the room after an hour, endorphins and the pleasant ache of used muscles making him happy. President Ma had left a message inviting him to dinner. She didn't have obligations to the state, he guessed, and he RSVPd yes, thankful for something to look forward to.

He'd just stepped out of the shower when his comm screen blared a siren noise and flashed neon yellow. What fresh hell was this?! Paul touched the frame to accept the call from whoever needed to shout at him so loudly.

"Yuhwa!" Leader Quý gasped. The normally happy and relaxed nawa was pale and agitated. "I felt her return, her waja signaled it surfaced! But it was upset, something may be wrong."

Jesus, their metal had *feelings*? Paul was never going to get used to the weirdness of the Aoni. "What do you mean wrong?" Dread stole his strength and he had to grab the back of a chair to stay upright. "Like Leah found her, that kind of bad?"

Quý looked horrified. "No, I don't think so. But it could be, I hadn't thought..." He shook his head, firming his expression. "I'm coming in a shuttle, nearly there, be ready. I've told all monitors to scour the perimeter of Âuke in the meantime. If they spot her, we will go there immediately. Otherwise we patrol until we find her."

A fight commenced, with Laci and the swords refusing to let him leave, but you can't argue too much with the leader of the Hunzo. In the end, two swords would fly with them, and Paul accepted a vest from Laci that would repel most shots and blades. But she reminded him nothing was perfect, telling him to stay in the shuttle at all times.

"It's the best protection you can have out there."

Quý didn't have to wear a bullet-proof vest, Paul noted with irritation. Crap on a cracker, being hunted seriously sucked.

Settling up front, next to the control panel and his nawa friend, Paul exhaled shakily. "No sightings, I take it?"

"No," Quý replied, tone soft. "But my instincts tell me she will emerge soon."

Paul looked more closely at him. "Do you connect with all the folks on pâtexi like this?" At the negative head shake, Paul pushed, "She's special, right? Something different from the rest?"

"Oh, yes."

"Is she," he started. Stopped. Went again. "Do you think she's herald-level special?" This was the secret thought he'd been chewing on for several sals now. Yuhwa would be a better savior of Songmaster than he would. She had an aura that couldn't be denied: it had taken seven freaking people to try flying the *Mahoroba*, something she'd done alone and barely broken a sweat. Always calm...well, almost always. Unless Paul had pissed her off.

Quý brought him back. "I do. In aiwaks past we would have suspected Yuhwa was destined for the nawa, likely the Hunzo."

"Not now?"

"She doesn't want that, would hate it." At Paul's surprised look, Quý laughed. "Come now, I am not a bakyại. Yuhwa had no desire to go on pâtexi, much less join our ranks. In all my years, I've never seen the waja choose a path for a quester that they would despise."

They'd been flying low, cruising over low buttes and dunes that curved like crescent moons, smooth on one side and rippled by wind on the other. Paul got glimpses of emerald green Lake Bai-Bom in the distance, cradled between higher mountain ridges.

"I still don't get how you're connected to her waja. I thought it was personal, a one-way conversation. Like these guys," he pointed behind them at the two swords. "Their pâtexi gave them different weapons, took them different places. But you, the nawa, can feel all the waja?"

Quý pursed his lips, tilting his head. "Remember the *Origins*? Songmaster placed all the waja here, it comes from the same source. When nawa are called our waja retains a connection with the original source. That's strengthened by the Spirit Bath."

"Where Jadoube bodies are laid to rest?"

"The Spirit Bath is made up of all the waja of every Jadoube. At death, when we put them to rest, we are submerged for a time in the memories and lives of each one of them."

Paul's jaw dropped. "That's got to be billions of people!"

"More," Quý countered. "We don't remember specifics when we leave the Bath, just that the waja has been reunited and the general sense of a life completed." His voice roughened. "Some happy and fulfilled, others well-lived but with bad ends, like Yuhwa's parents."

"Theirs were like the one you had to handle the other day. An unjust deceased." Paul felt sadness for the child-Yuhwa who'd had to deal with that.

Quý flashed him a glance. "You are perceptive."

He hoped so. "My heart is telling me we should aim for the lake." He focused on what his instincts wanted. "Her dao will want water, the river. How do I know that?"

Quý punched some buttons, redirecting the shuttle. "Perhaps you are touched by the dao. We once had a Lunari go on pâtexi; she was able to commune with waja. Perhaps you are a Human who can do the same."

"Isae Zam! I met her. Yuhwa had a major case of hero-worship for her." Scanning everywhere, Paul pointed. "Maybe over there?"

In defiance of his instincts, Yuhwa did not magically appear. They made endless loops, tracking back and forth in a grid pattern, hoping to see something. No luck. The swords let him off the shuttle when they reached the far side of the lake because he needed a bathroom break. That was as exciting as it got.

Finally, at hour six, sun setting, Quý sat up straighter. "I feel-"

"Over there!" Paul said at the same moment. "There's something shining like crazy on the shore, right there where the river comes out of the volcano."

They were on the ground in minutes, running to what Paul had spotted. The swords tried to keep him between them, but he shoved right past them. She was there! Yuhwa, alive, curled in a fetal position on a huge waja shield. Thank God!

Quý reached her first; for a portly man he moved like a freaking cheetah. He drew up short, devastation on his face. Paul dropped to her side. Yuhwa was a mess, bad enough his entire being seized, horrified he might have lost her.

No, there, a breath. But she was battered; her lavender hair half knotted on top of her head, some strands wrapped around her throat and streaked with blood. There was a gash in her scalp toward the back, probably the source of her bloody hair. Her bodysuit was shredded in places, her arms and hands scratched to hell and back. Something had attacked her shoulders: he could see pierced fabric, and blood stained it front and back. Claws, maybe? Her feet were gag-worthy, gory and damaged enough he wouldn't be letting her walk any time soon.

"Shtŭ, shtŭ," he whispered. "Baby, are you there? Can you wake up?" He knelt down, gently stroking the top of her hand. "Yuhwa, come on, come back to me."

Please, please, please! He begged internally to whichever deity wanted to answer. *She's got to be okay. I'll do anything, give anything, just bring her back to me.* Paul saw nothing but Yuhwa's face, her battered body, the blood that scared him silly. She had to be all right, he needed her and damn it, she needed him. *Please.*

Eyes as black as midnight fluttered open, confused and hurting. "You," she rasped, licking her lips, "aren't Songmaster Silver."

33

If Paul didn't stop hovering she was going to unleash her full temper. It was a rare occurrence, primarily because being mad enough to lose it on someone meant she cared. That's how Yuhwa knew she loved Paul. She wanted his arms around her constantly, but if he was any more solicitous she was kicking him out of their room. Forcefully.

That was another clue she loved him: they were sharing a room and she didn't object. She was, frankly, very content to be there with him.

He'd been carrying her from the moment they'd found her, which was great before her aoiti had done any healing. Yuhwa had never experienced pain like that, coming awake above ground where the waja and her spirit had erupted from deep below Malor's crust. She had no memory of how her soul rejoined her body, but the state of her body would support *dragged straight through the rock of Âuke* as a possibility.

"You awake?" Paul whispered, pressed against her back, cradling her close.

"I don't know how I'm alive," she whispered back. "I don't

know how much of what I experienced was real. It's," she paused. "I'm confused."

He traced her arm, down to her hand, linked their fingers. "And that?" he aimed their joined hands at the wall by the door.

Yuhwa stared at the massive shield her waja had made. She was a sword like Tangun had expected, but without an offensive weapon. Meant to stand between those who would hurt others and their intended victims? Some of that idea resonated, but part of her denied it. Her story wasn't that kind of tale.

"You'll think it's foolish," she kept whispering, trailing circles on the back of his hand. "I remember being surrounded by waja, hearing the voices, and I thought, 'I'm a herald like Katy and when I open my eyes Songmaster Silver will be there'." Her sore throat made her chuckle almost inaudible. "Silly! I never wanted to be a herald, but when I woke and he wasn't there, I was sad."

Paul was silent longer than she liked. Rolling in his arms to face him, she released his hand and used newly freed fingers to trace his brows. Then his mouth and jaw. He smiled, dipped his head and gave her a gentle kiss.

They weren't speaking of what was happening between them. But when he'd refused a medibed for her, scooped her into his arms and carried her to this room, she hadn't protested. He'd said something about a PQ maybe-killer on the loose, but she hadn't cared in the moment. Him holding her close was all that mattered.

First a shared shower, using real water he'd begged to get to wash her. Dried off with a fluffy towel, hair combed gently to detangle it. He deftly avoided the healing spot where she'd smacked into a rock before plunging in the river. He wrapped her feet, shaking his head at the damage, inhaling raggedly. Then straight to the bed, where they'd stayed together as she napped fitfully.

It was all wonderful until it was time to go out for a meal and he wouldn't stop asking her how she felt, if she needed anything, was she okay. Once he tried to get a pillow for her, and she gave him a glare that got him to shut up for ten whole kaalas. She refused to admit the pillow was nice, or that eating and talking had worn her out so much she was grateful he carried her back to bed.

"Hate to break it to you," he rumbled, "but you're the herald."

Yuhwa jerked away. "What?!"

Paul's strong arm gently scooped her back into his body. "I've thought about it, quite a lot. For a while I was sure I was the herald." He snorted. "Figured it ran in the family."

"I don't want to be the herald," she protested. "You do it!"

"This doesn't seem like a job offer they let you turn down, *a stór*."

His treasure. She melted when he used the endearment she'd heard his parents use with one another. Imagine being a couple as strong as they were. "I can't be."

"Katy," he murmured, "says you should trust yourself in these situations. Let your instincts lead you. Think it through, walk me with you the last few sals. You heard voices?"

Safe in his arms, Yuhwa talked and talked. She held nothing back, recounting her arrogance, fear, confusion. Every moment. When she told him of the Côttru, and Ni-Matak's thoughts on Paul, he laughed. He tightened his embrace reflexively when she spoke of stumbling in total blindness.

"And then I heard your voice. I was out of the mountain with a giant shield, opened my eyes and you were there." She yawned, tired despite having slept only a sal-ang ago.

Paul's eyes moved back to her waja gift, narrowing. "I don't get it. You're too active for something as passive as a shield. If it shot darts at people, I could see it."

"What the hål do you think of me?" she said, pretending outrage.

"Only good things, promise," he smiled, giving her another slow kiss.

She returned it, feeling effervescent and depressed simultaneously. Being with Paul, accepting his affection and letting herself return it was new and precious. But the loss of closeness to the Côttru, severing her connection with the voices, not to mention physical separation from her waja.... Yuhwa mourned it, felt discouraged and heartsick that outside Âuke she had to sacrifice the joining that had felt so natural and essential. She hoped the binding ceremony would alleviate the sorrow.

Their room's com dinged with several messages. Groaning, Paul withdrew from her arms and activated it. First was a message from Na, reassuring them the *Mahoroba* had safely arrived in near-Quiltac orbit. Paul was relieved and sent back an effusive thank you.

"You have a crush on him," she teased.

Paul quirked his lips. "About the same as you with Isae. We're even."

Rolling onto her back as she giggled, Yuhwa waited for him to open the second message.

"Congratulations, Yuhwa! Your pâtexi is concluded, and the Hunzo requests your presence at the Pavilion to hear more about it." Quý's voice was eager and happy. "We can also schedule your Binding. Tonight, if you're able. Tomorrow if you need more time to recover."

Paul sat next to her hip, caressing her arms. "Your call. I'll support you either way."

"Even if I say I want to go alone?"

She watched him go from determined to crestfallen to resigned.

"Whatever you need. I can be there for you to lean on in person, or I can wait here while you sort out the nawa." He swallowed. "I bulldozed over your feelings before, and I'm sorry about that. If you want a separate room, I'll get it sorted, too. When we got back I was so freaked out I didn't even think-"

She stopped him with a finger to his lips. "I'm very happy where I am, and who I'm with. I don't need space, and I do need you next to me." She poked his cheeks, gone red with the beaming grin he aimed her way. "There's something not right about this." She pushed into a sitting position, staring at her waja.

"Us being together?" he asked, dread in his tone.

"No! I mean that," pointing at her shield.

"You think it formed the wrong thing?"

"Not exactly," she said slowly. "But what I've heard about waja joining, I don't have that. It feels incomplete. Like I missed a step."

Paul turned to sit next to her, gazing at the shield, too. "Not everyone has Five Côttru helping them, right? Or those voices that I truly think were Shadow Drazoen."

"Katy didn't hear them until she was in the shadow prison," she pointed out.

Paul jerked around to face her. "That's why you didn't see Songmaster. You didn't go into a shadow prison!"

"I think I did. The darkness, the loss of sight and feeling, it all matches."

"BUT," he insisted, "no one died."

"Of course not, although I might have come close," she mused.

Paul's jaw clenched. "Don't even joke." He shook it off. "Katy says Yfaun had to sacrifice himself to open the prison. These things were built to require death's release of energy to open. The PQ bred willing offerings, but we've lost sight of the one I think was sent after us."

"Leah Ko'olak," Yuhwa breathed. "She can't kill either of us, that would risk another herald rising someday in the future. But she'll want us in the shadow prison."

"Us?" Paul cocked his head. "Why us? You're the herald."

Leah rose to her knees and straddled his stretched-out legs. She'd seen how well he was moving on his previously damaged limb, and knew he could handle her weight since he'd been hefting her everywhere. "She doesn't know that. No one does, not even us. You think it's me, I think it could be you. Either I found the essence of Songmaster myself, or I did it to give to you like Bay did for Katy."

"If we go together, that's eternity. You don't do eternity," he joked tentatively.

"If I had to do it with anyone," she bent her head to bump his nose with hers, "I'd accept you."

They came up for air after twenty good kaalas of kissing. His hands cupped her butt, eyes heavy-lidded, his breathing heavy. She liked making him lose his cool demeanor.

"We're getting back to that when you're fully healed," he growled. Shaking himself, he said, "But for now, what should we tell Quý?" He picked her up and moved her off his legs, away from his obvious arousal. Standing, he stared at her with his heart in his eyes.

Yuhwa bit her lip, almost unbearably aroused by his strength. "Tell him we'll go tomorrow. Tonight, I want you to show me gymnastics. Your best-loved one."

Paul shuddered. "Why does that turn me on so much?" After sending the message to Quý, he turned back to her. "I haven't done the rings in a while now, plus I doubt they have what I need onsite. But I can do floor ex for you."

"No, we'll find something or have it made. I want your favorite." Yuhwa was determined. This was a way to bring him a little joy, and it was going to happen. "We're in the president's house, surely they can help."

She made to stand, but he tutted, giving her his back. "Hop on, little rufucebus. I've got you."

Happier than she could ever remember being, Yuhwa obliged.

OF COURSE, Onye had a majordomo, or head butler or whatever this person was called. They were wicked intimidating even as they were soft-spoken and sweet. Paul thought it was the sheer efficiency of someone about five-three, dressed in a pink fringed jumpsuit, who solved their problem in two seconds flat. They already had people scrambling to set it up to their vision.

"Oh yes," they said when Paul shared a crappy drawing and described what they did. "I know just the thing."

He and Yuhwa stayed out of the way, marveling at how quickly a spare room was transformed into a small gym. Floor lined with soft padding and all furniture removed. He stared at the rings, not particularly surprised at the longing washing through him. Working on them had always brought him peace; the focus and strength required to nail his moves, discipline that honed his concentration and took it to a higher plane. Free rings were Paul's way to meditate, and now he'd be using them to seduce the woman of his dreams.

Scratch that. He couldn't have dreamt of a gift like Yuhwa. She was more than he deserved, but he'd soak up every minute she gave him. When she'd said he was the only person she wanted to be locked in a shadow prison with, whoo daddy. That was a *moment*.

He had no hope of playing it cool, wouldn't even try. No scaring her with words like love yet, but he wasn't pretending he could go back to hit-it-and-quit-it status. Yuhwa was it for him.

Paul claimed her from the lounge chair she'd occupied while

he supervised the apparatus installation. She laughed at being on his back again, resting her chin on his shoulder. Her breath, warm and scented with her natural mint and fruit mix, teased his throat. Part of him wanted to skip the gymnastics foreplay and toss her on the bed in their room.

Not until she was fully healed, though. Once she was? They were spending days making love. Hopefully the presidential residence had good soundproofing.

"Oh!" She'd gotten her first look at the rings. "Wait, those, I know those."

"I guess they normally use these to hold up some kind of instrument, but with wrapping they work for me."

She started out tapping his shoulder, quickly escalating to smacks. "I need my shield!"

Astonished, Paul jogged to their room, snagged it, and jammed back to the newly set up ring-nasium.

"Put me down," she commanded. "Chair, floor, anywhere."

Paul wasn't dropping her, but letting her slide down his back at her own speed was awkward. Especially when he didn't want her landing on her feet, so he had to squat for her to dismount to a kneeling position.

"Now," she croaked, nervous for some reason. "Take it and hold it by the rings. No, right in front. Like that."

Paul saw what she was getting at just as her eyes welled with happy tears. She choked, the emotion overwhelming her. "It's not a shield. It's a razocông, that's why it's so round, so big."

Jadoube called them razocông, his sister would call it a gong. A helluva big one, too. Had to be five foot in diameter, smooth front with a rolled edge.

She looked at him, hands clasped in front of her heart. "There was nothing wrong with it, only with how I interpreted it. I feel it in inside me now, like an empty place is filled." Yuhwa broke into silent sobs.

He set her cymbal down and went to her. Paul held her for

long minutes, while she came to terms with the true fulfillment of her pâtexi. He tried to deal with the fear it brought him: Yuhwa had to be the herald, she'd been given a musical instrument just as Katy had. This for sure put her in the crosshairs of a sociopathic PQ assassin. Paul resolved to do whatever it took to put himself between Leah and Yuhwa, to keep his love safe.

He also wasn't dumb enough to tell her he'd be doing that, because she'd get mad. For the first time he properly appreciated what Bay had gone through when Katy went missing. To love someone and have them stolen from you, pronounced dead because you'd failed at protecting the one person who mattered more than the rest of the Universe. It would destroy a person.

After a while she settled, curled into his chest. He loved the way she took little sniffs of him, much like he did with her. What was it about your lover's unique scent that grounded and calmed you?

"When we go tomorrow," she hedged, "I don't want to tell them about this."

"Okaaaay," he hedged right back. Why didn't she trust the nawa like he did? "Can I ask why?"

When she shook her head, he noticed her scalp injury had healed already. Damn, mature aoiti kicked serious ass.

Tilting her eyes up to his, she said, "Seeing the Côttru, Ni-Matak and the others, they made a new place in me. It was like being on a ledge. I could stay on it, deny what was happening, tell myself I was imagining all of it and feel safer that way. Or I could open to my instincts and what they told me: I was deep inside the heart of my planet, protected and guided by the chosen sparks of Malor, all for a greater purpose. I chose the second path in there, and I'm choosing it out here." She closed her eyes. "My instincts tell me to stay quiet."

Paul rubbed her back, trying to offer comfort. "If that's what you want, then my trap is shut. I am a vault for your secrets, promise. But if you change your mind, I think the nawa could be useful."

Yuhwa frowned. "Maybe." She brightened, mischievous. "That's for tomorrow. For tonight, I want to see your gymnastics."

"I can't guarantee a good show," he said. "I haven't gotten a decent warmup or practice in a long time."

She leaned up, licked his throat and Adam's apple. "I have confidence whatever you do is going to work for me. More than you know." She licked again. "Then you're going to carry me back to bed, unwrap my feet to see they're fine, and fulfill my needs."

Paul hoped his look was smoldering and not stupefied; her words left him a combination of both. If she wanted him flexing for her, he'd do it night and day. "You just sit there and look pretty," he ordered, stripping off his shirt as he stood.

NAKED WITH PAUL was the right way to wake up, especially after a night of scorching lovemaking and achingly tender cuddling. Yuhwa hadn't ever done that before, cuddling, and decided it was nice. Probably only with Paul, and only if he wasn't pushing her buttons to get a rise out of her.

"On a scale of one to ten, where am I when it comes to getting the job of your personal hairdresser?"

They'd taken another shower together, sadly ionic instead of water this time. He was combing her hair, a task he really seemed to enjoy, and making something he called a French braid.

"Since I don't know what you're doing or how your scale works, I can't answer."

He tugged a lock gently, pulling her head back until their

eyes met. Upside down he was still the most handsome man in the Aoni. "I did this for Bug when she was younger. Your hair is a damn sight easier to work than hers, TBH." His voice got dreamy. "Ma taught me. Funny how you remember things you learned so long ago."

"Talk to me when you're a couple aiwaks old, you'll see. A lot fades over time." Yuhwa sighed. When Paul stopped working on her hair, she glanced up. Why was he sad?

"Unless there's a miraculous intervention, I won't live to see that long. We Humans top out around eighty, and that's if we're lucky." He shrugged nonchalantly, eyes telegraphing his sorrow, and resumed platting.

"Katy already plans to get Sundancer to change whatever the aoiti don't fix." Yuhwa hummed, reaching up to caress his arm. "If that doesn't work we'll demand it from Songmaster."

They said no more on the topic, but Yuhwa believed that conversation was the most intimate one she'd ever had. At the core of it was the implication they would be spending aiwaks together. Instead of panic, she warmed at the idea. Paul all to herself for a milenyo or two would be fine by her.

Sooner than she'd like, they left their secure residence for the Hunzo Pavilion. The president sent along three swords as guards, but Yuhwa knew it was futile. If Leah Ko'olak was the PQ chosen one, sent to open the shadow prison, nothing was going to stop her.

To her dismay, the Hunzo and larger nawa collective was in full attendance. They'd set up a large banquet to celebrate her pâtexi, rather than the simple meal she'd expected. Yuhwa didn't get why they made such a big deal about her quest; millions of other Jadoube had survived theirs and didn't get state dinners for their trouble.

"We welcome Yuhwa Bon-Gil and her partner, the Ambassador!" Quý was loud of voice and dress, wearing fuchsia robes that matched the flowers at the entrance he occupied. Other nawa had gathered behind him to greet her.

"I, erm, thank you?" She'd never been nervous in social gatherings like this, but the connection to her instincts that she'd left wide open whispered things were wrong. Misaligned, broken. She felt Sister Ha-Seng's fur brushing inside her skin, a warrior's strength infusing her.

What battle loomed that she needed this from one of the Côttru?

The five Hunzo approached, touching her razocông, patting her arms, murmuring what an incredible pâtexi reward she'd gotten, how blessed they were to witness this. Yuhwa didn't like other hands on her personal waja, she found. Was it because it wasn't fully bound to her yet? Until she'd endured the Binding Bath and its painful process that joined her with her waja, the razocông felt fragile to her senses.

Paul, detecting her unease, took her hand, bending his head to hers. "I'm here," he said quietly.

"I love you," Yuhwa blurted. She was horrified at her slip of tongue, the sheer inappropriate timing of it, and came the closest to apologizing since her youngest tuigs.

Paul's eyes widened, then his lips bloomed into a giddy grin. "How could you resist all this? You never stood a chance." Raising their joined hands to his lips, he kissed her knuckles and said, "I love you, too."

Relaxing into the glow of being loved back, Yuhwa fortified herself for the dinner to come.

34

Paul could have crossed the entire gulrã of Malor, every single wadi and river, plateaus and all, just to hear her say it again. Any tall buildings that needed leaping? He was your man. Yuhwa loved him, and he would take on marauding hordes to keep her safe. This bizarrely fancy dinner wasn't the most opportune time to revel and wallow in the feelings, but he let himself have just a minute. Holding her hand, both of their backs protected by that huge gong slung over her shoulders, he was invincible.

"Please," said one of the Hunzo, gesturing for them to follow. He was a short, trim man with hair like a salmon berry and deeply tanned skin.

What was up with Jadoube and fruit colored hair? Maybe it was a nawa thing? Paul remembered Malor wasn't likely to have either blackberry like Quý's hair, or salmon berry like this dude. Was Paul just hungry?

"Why the lavish spread?" he asked, quietly he thought. When every nawa in the vicinity stopped talking, he knew he'd failed at subtle. "I thought we were just getting together to casually talk about Yuhwa's pâtexi."

They'd reached the head table, and Quý settled them in the center chairs. Four other tables, seating a good fifteen to twenty nawa each, spread before them. Paul thought every nawa on Malor had to be in the room tonight.

"This is a momentous occasion! We celebrate the Yahdo Ascension, now that she has arrived!"

Yuhwa froze, Paul's jaw dropped.

"I, what, I don't understand," Yuhwa stammered.

Paul thought he did, and apparently his herald got the moniker Yuhwa the Yahdo. Or would it be Yahdo Yuhwa? Back on Earth she'd be a superhero with a rhyming name like that.

Every nawa in the room spun and bowed to her, hems swishing along the stone floor. Paul saw most robes were shiny silver. Except Hunzo members; they wore bright pink like Quý. In the chamber's warm, soft light the silver robes flashed and gleamed, embroidered with geometric patterns. The magenta of the Hunzo were like a blooming five-petalled flower in the center.

"We've held this secret for a kōmilen, since the day Song-master Silver gave us the task to wait for his Yahdo to rise." Quý's voice intoned words like a sermon.

My Yahdo may not be Jadoube, but their waja will cry out for them regardless. Do not hinder them, encourage and aid them. Their abilities will be unparalleled, yet guidance from you will still be necessary. Raise them up, show them their path, give them tools to accomplish what seems impossible. They alone can do it.

Paul squeezed her hand in support as Yuhwa objected. "How do you know this is me? In your own words they may not be Jadoube, why me?"

"Not our words, Yahdo." This from a Black Hunzo with deep set amber eyes and russet hair framing her face. "Songmaster's final words to the Jadoube before leaving the Aoni."

Salmon berry hair jumped in. "We thought for a time Isae Zam might be the Yahdo, but her waja never burned bright in our minds, the way it was promised to happen."

Quý approached them, reaching out a hand. Yuhwa reluctantly clasped it. "I hoped it was you," he smiled, eyes twinkling and voice so damn cheerful. "From your childhood, I thought there was a chance. You didn't merely burn, you scorched my senses. Your early facility with the dao and piloting. The strength of surviving your parents' deaths. How hard you fought returning!" He laughed.

"She's not a fan of being ordered around," Paul volunteered. "You shouldn't have pulled so hard." Yuhwa's nails dug into the back of his hand and he made a note not to interfere again.

"It took all five of us to do it," Quý muttered. "You are a very strong woman."

"I still don't understand. You've been waiting for a Yahdo, heard about another one turning up at Centris, and decided I'm a good candidate?" Yuhwa pulled away from Quý and Paul, crossing her arms over her chest. "Seems convenient."

"Not 'a Yahdo', *the Yahdo*. There is only one, Songmaster's Yahdo, his spark embodied." Amber eyes lady spoke with reverence.

"A kōmilen since Songmaster and the rest left the Aoni, I take it you've known about heralds and the Yahdo since then? Why would you keep this hidden?"

Paul thought Yuhwa's question hit the nail on the head. What was it about prophecies that made people go *ooh, I'll have that to myself and never speak of it until nearly too late?* Then he thought about people spending centuries debating Nostradamus and realized being out and proud with it wasn't a sure thing, either. Still, it made the nawa seem less noble spiritual order and more like the Illuminati. Between Muškikal hidden libraries, Mikanjo concealing names of triggers, and this lot hoarding info on the Yahdo, he was miffed.

Quý stepped back, a serious mien taking over. "Leader Pema Achi-Yao, from all those tuigs ago, knew the job fell to us. We are the ones who sense the connections between Jadoube and waja; our shoulders carry the weight of potential and futures realized. If knowledge of Songmaster's foresight was common, we would have had dozens of self-appointed candidates every generation." He rocked on his heels. "This way we could control how the task was approached and fulfilled."

"Sounds to me that you all like having the power," Paul said, saddened. "When I came to you, desperate to find information that could help, you kept this back. You had the chance to be forthcoming and you deliberately blocked me."

"What would have been gained if we recited his words to you?" Quý raised his hands waist high, palms up, a Jadoube gesture Paul had learned meant peace and conciliation. "We have no information on the greater problem, how to bring back the rest of the Drazoen. Only Songmaster's hints of how to recognize *his* spark."

"Our help was genuine," the bald nawa from their scroll sessions called out. "Without the research we did together, the needling question wouldn't have been uncovered."

"What 'needling question'?" Yuhwa rounded on him, exasperated.

"Just a thing we found in an old scroll," he said. "Not super relevant right now, but interesting. We can talk about it after this Yahdo thing ends." Slouching, he murmured for her ears only, "Told you it was you." Her kick to his ankle nailed him right on the bone and hurt, but he laughed to himself despite the pain.

"I am not what you think," Yuhwa tried again.

Every nawa in the room started chanting. Nothing his aoiti could translate, but it came together in a beautiful harmony. After a minute the random sounds resolved into a two-part sound: half the nawa said *yah* and the other replied *do*. Yahdo, Yahdo, Yahdo.

"You are exactly what we know you to be, Yuhwa Bon-Gil," Quý said. "Talented beyond any other, your light in our dao is that of a star, incandescent and fiery. Blessed by all Five Côttru, Malor itself put you to the test and you emerged victorious. Once we have bound your waja to your soul, the path for Songmaster's return opens!"

His triumphant shout at the end was echoed by the rest. Paul felt Yuhwa's panic, saw her hands clenching on the chair arms and how her thighs tensed for flight.

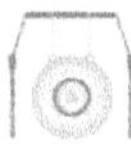

YUHWA NEEDED OUT. She needed to run, to get away from this madness seeking to trap her into something she wasn't. Because Yuhwa wasn't their Yahdo, not a nawa savior born to bring Songmaster back. She couldn't be like Katy, survive something like this and come out smiling. She didn't have the tools, the know-how, nothing useful.

Paul's steadying hand on her arm helped her take a breath and push away the anxiety. Remembering the freedom she'd felt in letting go on her pâtexi, in accepting what was happening as a necessary part of the journey, she tried to apply it here.

What the nawa wanted was irrelevant; this was her journey, her quest. Once she decided what *she* wanted, they could move forward. Where they aligned was on the binding, so she could start there. Until that happened she wasn't as grounded as she knew she needed to be. Whether she was a herald or not, odds were good Leah Ko'olak was coming for her and she needed to be ready. Having her razocông embedded with her dao might give her the strength to outwit, or just outlast, a PQ killer. She looked at Paul and saw nothing but acceptance and encouragement on his face. Together they'd get through this. Nodding at him, she rose from her seat.

"I don't like playing games with lives, and that's what you've done. Since the Drazoen left, you've hoarded information that could have helped others. Maybe you thought there was a good reason, maybe it made you feel powerful and in control. But know this: you don't control me."

Every nawa in the room gaped at her. Stunned she took a shot at them, were they?

"You need-" Quý started, then stopped. He hung his head.

Paul pushed his chair back, rose and stepped behind her. His height gave him a clear sightline over her head to the Hunzo, and the man Yuhwa thought he might have considered a friend. "I'm disappointed. You've really let me down." His hands clasped her shoulders, thumbs rubbing gentle circles. "So much for teamwork making the dream work."

Quý looked near tears at that. "Our time was a delight, Ambassador. Paul. All of us were genuinely excited to meet with you, talk about our culture and ancient texts. Just not this one."

"You should have," Yuhwa insisted.

"We couldn't," he replied, despondency making his voice a thin, wavering thing.

Shaking her head, she gave up. They weren't going to see it from her side, nor she theirs.

"Devil's advocate time," Paul whispered from behind her. "As much as it sucks, all these secret squirrel prophecies came to light right around the time they needed to. Would it have helped or hindered if they'd said something a hundred thousand years ago?"

Yuhwa grudgingly admitted his point was valid. Leave it to the Human to find a way to make her see their point of view. "Let's move past this. My waja binding – the faster the better. We can all agree on that. I think it's best done on an empty stomach, so how about we skip these festivities and leave for the Bath."

One step to the side, one step back, and her razocông was back in her hands. The makeshift strap she'd attached earlier still held, so she swung it on her back and walked to the Hunzo Leader. His face was miserable, until she took his hand.

"Shall we?" That was as close to forgiveness as she was getting, at least until this whole thing was resolved one way or the other.

Quý's eyes welled, but his face creased in a little smile. "The honor is mine."

Paul had stayed at her side, so they turned as a unit and exited the Pavilion, back toward the president's shuttle. The swords Yuhwa had all but forgotten ranged in front of their group, scanning for danger. Their relaxed body language said all was well.

A sudden pang speared her chest as they cleared the Pavilion and stood under open sky. Not a projectile or blade from the outside, but an inner twinge. She was transported back to her pâtexi, and the feeling of summoning her waja. Separating it from the whole had been hard. Her memories were sparse about most of it, but she did recall her waja's heartbreak to leave the collective, even as it was ecstatic to join with her. That's what she felt now: her waja longing to join with the Spirit Bath.

"Why do you not return ancestral waja to Âuke?" The question was important even though she wasn't sure she should ask. So many things the nawa did were never probed; what Jadoube society accepted as normal was treated as beyond examination, above reproach.

"The Spirit Bath is what tightens our association to the unclaimed waja, and allows us to connect with Jadoube who will need a bond. As you know, I think." Quý's voice in the darkness seemed perfectly rational.

"I do," she said. Except… "My waja wants there. Not the Binding Bath. It says we need to go to the Spirit Bath."

"Whoa," Paul muttered as Quý gasped.

"That's forbidden, as you also know." Taking her elbow gently, Quý tried to steer her to the shuttle. "Waja doesn't want things, my dear."

She yanked free, spinning to regard him skeptically. "It wants each of us, in our time. It reaches out and calls us. Or is that mirca you've been telling Jadoube for føns?" She huffed and speared a finger toward the Spirit Bath. "My waja wants. It desired me, none other. Now it desires to go in there, and I'm in the mood to give it what it wants."

Quý wrung his hands. "You can't, it isn't proper protocol."

"If I'm this Yahdo of yours, I can do whatever I bloody well like."

"Too much time with Katy," was muttered behind her, but Paul followed her to the Spirit Bath entrance.

35

Fire bowls burned day and night here, to respect the deceased and pay homage to the history held in the Spirit Bath. One hundred generations or more had been laid to rest in this spot; existences and experiences of those who'd gone before were held here. A final resting place the Jadoube had created.

From all to one.

Those were the words they chanted when the dead were released. For only in death was the link to the communal dao relinquished. None save the nawa breached these consecrated waters of waja. They alone touched the sacred substance no longer merged with its chosen Jadoube; they alone collected and revered it in person. She shouldn't be here. Yet her own waja told her she must be.

Yuhwa's most deeply held beliefs were being challenged even as she walked beyond the portal, through a waiting area, and finally into the Spirit Bath chamber itself. It was huge, bigger than Shee had been. But it had to be, to hold the waja of all Jadoube who'd lived and died since Songmaster gave them his Gift.

Light from several of Malor's moons shone through stained glass windows and glinted off the Bath. The brilliant silver of liquid waja was mostly quiescent, but rippled here and there. Walking to the edge of the fluid, Yuhwa knelt down. Somewhere in this lake of memory floated her mama and papa's lives, as recorded by their bonded waja. Her razocông heated against her back.

What if they'd been wrong all these milenyo? Should the nawa have been returning the waja to Âuke all along? That's what hers seemed to be telling her right now. It had been created as a whole, then carved up bit by bit over the milenyos, never to be rejoined. Fractured, splintered, longing for the union it had once known. Driven to seek out the Jadoube it was meant to enhance, it still yearned for an elastic reabsorption when its service was complete. But Jadoube, nawa especially, had enforced separation, unknowingly cruel, thinking it right.

So strange for a people who prized community the way theirs did. But often, Yuhwa knew, even the best-meaning ideas could twist into something pestilent and harmful if left unexamined. She heard what her waja was telling her, and she intended to listen and act.

"Feels like spirits are watching us," Paul uttered softly.

Quý, still uneasy with how she'd barged in, said, "There aren't any spirits here. We ensure they are released from the body when we return their waja to the Bath."

"This is what's broken," Yuhwa said, standing and facing him. "I'm sure it started from a good place, but we're keeping something here that should be returned to its home." Her razocông heated more, stopping just shy of pain, and the edges curled slightly around her. A hug, acknowledging her words?

"I hate gainsaying you, Yahdo, but we've always-"

Before he could finish speaking, Yuhwa's razocông pulled her backward into the Spirit Bath. One atóm she was standing, the next it had connected with the giant pool of waja and yanked her back. Both men shouted, running for the edge as she toppled over. She landed on her back, arms and legs flailing, sinking faster than she could fight it.

"Yuhwa! Baby, can you reach out? Swear to fucking God I will dive in there if you don't!"

What the shtŭ, she yelled mentally at her waja. *I was giving you what you wanted!*

ChildChildChild

so close

come closer

nearly home

The voices were back! Shadow Drazoen or Côttru, it didn't matter, because if she drowned in waja she wasn't anyone's herald. Her thought must have gotten through; Yuhwa felt her body shifted upright and her head raised above the surface. She had almost no control of her limbs; the waja that surrounded her did all the moving.

She blinked her eyes and Paul was the first thing she saw. Quý beside him, utterly gobsmacked (another excellent Human word). Liquid metal rolled down her face, coated her hair, and even slipped in her mouth when she opened her lips. "I'm okay, I'm okay. Don't come in, I don't know what it will do if anyone tries to interfere."

"DO YOU KNOW, I EXPECTED MORE." A tight, high voice preceded Leah's appearance. She seemed to detach from darkness like a silhouette come to life, her gait leisurely and relaxed.

Paul's chest pounded with adrenaline from Yuhwa's dive and now this. He hadn't felt spirits earlier, he'd felt the PQ assassin. Damn it all, he needed to listen to his heebee-jeebies more closely. He and Quý both spun to block her view of Yuhwa. Paul had a fleeting moment to consider what he'd be willing to do to protect her, and believed he'd kill if he had to. She wasn't just important to him, she was needed by the entire Aoni. His Yuhwa, their Yahdo.

"Do I disappoint?" Yuhwa sounded nonchalant, slowly blinking waja out of her eyelashes, but she had to be terrified. Assuming you wouldn't be killed and coming face-to-face with the person who might do it anyway had to be scarier for her than him, and he was shaking.

Leah stopped a few feet away, ignoring the men completely, meeting Yuhwa's gaze in the gap between their bodies. "A little, perhaps? The way your waja tried to protect you from me, that seemed monumental at first. You splashing into the Bath, your lover desperate to save you, the clergyman torn between his care for you and the dogma of his calling." Leah's black eyes had swirling yellow centers. Creepy reverse black-eyed-Susans to go with the floral motif on her face. "But you weren't magically whisked away to safety, were you? I thought for sure you would be. Nor did you realize I was here. You were so surprised, did you not feel it recoil from me when I entered?"

This woman's casual questions and unsettling proximity were setting off klaxons in Paul's brain. GET OUT. GET OUT. But he had to stay, to protect Yuhwa and help her raise Songmaster. His anxiety had narrowed his vision until all he saw was the PQ's unnaturally emotionless face.

He squared off, posture straight and eyes focused on the danger in front of him. She wore loose, palazzo pants with a camisole. The outfit gave her flexibility, and hid no weapons.

What need? The way Katy had talked of these inbred hit-people, Leah Ko'olak *was* the weapon.

YUHWA KEPT up the chat from behind Paul, determined to keep Leah's focus away from him. "My trigger has other things to say to me, I suppose. Is this the part where we fight to the death?"

Leah tittered, a doll's sound in her high voice. "You need me, you know." She took a step forward, but Paul and Quý pressed arm-to-arm in a counter move. "You can't get to the cage without my help."

Yuhwa appraised the PQ, unafraid. Wasn't that a surprise? But it was true. Yuhwa didn't feel fear, worry, anything. In this place, this time, she was free from all the negative things that had held her back. She acknowledged what Paul had been saying, what she'd subconsciously known but fled from, and what the nawa had tried to honor and celebrate. She was Song-master's Yahdo, and one way or another she would be reunited with the ancient benefactor of her people.

"You can't kill me, or else you risk calling up another herald," she reminded the killer.

"True." Leah said.

Quý sagged against Paul's side, pulling on him hard enough to twist Paul away from Leah.

"Let's see if his sacrifice is enough to open the prison up. Then I'll throw you in."

PAUL LOOKED DOWN, horrified to see a gory line yawn open on Quý's throat. He gurgled as Paul caught his falling body. The Hunzo Leader's hands raised to his neck, eyes rolling, blood pouring over his twitching fingers.

"No, stop, ohmygod no!" Paul cried, laying Quý flat, cradling his face, looking into his eyes. "The aoiti will fix it, just hang on. This can't-"

Leah squatted next to Paul, Quý's blood dripping from the knife she held in her hand. "Your species is truly new, isn't it? The aoiti cannot save anyone from a wound such as that." She tilted her head, like a curious bird. "I am sorry for the pain it caused you. Watching you the last few sals I've seen your relationship building. You gave him joy."

"Why?!" Paul howled.

The older man's eyes dulled, pupils fixing, all breath and movement ceasing.

"NO!" He heard splashing from the Spirit Bath as Yuhwa scrambled to get to him, and he bent over his friend's body as he tried to pull himself together.

Paul was devastated, aware he didn't stand a chance against Leah, and feeling angry and disempowered. What possible use was he to anyone if he was just a dumb, weak Human?

"It was either him or you, before me. I chose him because she loves you, and I don't want to hurt her." Leah was trying to peer into his eyes, on hands and knees now. "But I've hurt you, and for that I'm sorry."

PAUL REARED BACK, abject devastation warring with horror on his face. Yuhwa felt trapped in waja, unable to get to him and give comfort. Worse, if Leah had gone for him instead of Quý, there would have been nothing she could have done. It was infuriating, and she surged to the edge of the pool, thinking to climb out and protect her love. "What are you talking about?" she shouted. "I thought your life plan was to destroy *me*? Not innocents who have no part to play in this farce!"

Leah crawled to the edge and squatted in front of Yuhwa this time. "For a very long time it was. Not that I knew it was you, but I always knew Songmaster was my most likely candidate. We have dreams, too, you know."

Yuhwa gazed into Leah's eyes. She was reminded of a comment Katy had made, late one night: Yfaun and Bay had both dreamed, sought, and found a herald. Seemed in Yuhwa's case, the PQ assassin and the herald had been the dreamers. What a strange Aoni this was, to link beings from opposing sides in such primal ways.

Leah rested her butt on her heels as she continued. "Everything changed when we traveled to the Calling this last time. I changed. Hearing Sundancer speak of a future that was light and just, and seeing what pain my people caused others… I decided I wouldn't accept what my people decided I had to be. I could make my own choices. I visited Budiasa, listened to his story, and set him free."

Yuhwa gasped, a grudging admiration growing despite the dreadful act Leah had committed.

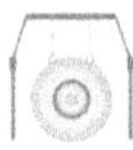

"HE DIDN'T BELIEVE I was releasing him. Why would he, after all? I'm the Pu'ulqaari all fear. But eventually he took the currency and escape I offered."

Paul almost warmed to Leah, until his palm connected with Quý's body. "It doesn't make up for this. Nothing will ever make up for it," he growled.

Her face was sad when she twisted to look at him. "I know. He was harmless, but my recent enlightenment didn't void the entirety of my innate selfishness. We're all trying to live, aren't we?" When she got glares in response, she sighed. "Before I forfeited my life to open the prison, I sought another path. Using Paul would damage you, not something I wanted."

"Are you looking for pity? Or thanks?" Paul asked, incredulous.

Leah's eyes rose to the stained-glass windows, gazing into the night for long minutes. "Not that. Perhaps I hoped for understanding, but that seems impossible. My only hope now is to greet Sula of Shadows with dignity." Leah rose up, standing over Yuhwa, and smiled. "Tell Them I said hello when you get there."

Before anyone could react or say another word, her skin split open, light beaming from inside, shooting like rays out of her raised scars. It covered Paul and Quý's body, crept over the walls and floor of the Bath, and its inevitable march found Yuhwa, floating in the waja pool.

His *stór* met his eyes, resignation in hers. Then she was dragged under the surface. Darkness replaced the beams of light, crawling out to cover every surface. Before he lost his vision, Paul saw Yuhwa's body shoot out of the Spirit Bath to hover above the pool. She was coated in waja, it dripped and streamed from her arching body, and she screamed.

36

It happened faster than she could track. Leah killed Quý, then herself. Not a vicious Pu'ulqaari assassin, but a woman hoping not to die and trying to be more than everyone had told her she could be. Yuhwa related to that more than she probably should, given Leah was still willing to kill without hesitation.

dreamer
sad child
she goes
to her home

Inside this dark place Leah's suicide had opened, the voices were all-encompassing. Yuhwa felt them at a cellular level, integrating with the rush of her blood. Warm, gentle, loving. *Why does it happen? Why must someone die to let us come together?* Yuhwa could cry with the pain of it.

not our rules
we would have loved
bigbig makes rule
beautiful Child
You're the Shadow Drazoen, right? Katy told me all about you, how

you've been left out of the story for darû. Yuhwa firmed her mental voice. *Not any more, not with me, not with anyone. You're just as loved as the other Nine.*

Rab's Child!
knows us!
loves us!
we are yours!

They were an invisible, vocal clutch of baby nilnabō, playful and happy, swarming her with softness. She felt protected and adored, sure that she was the center of their Aoni right now.

What she wasn't sure about was step two. She was Songmaster's Yahdo, Rab's Child (had to be his truename), and she was locked up tight in a shadow prison but didn't know if she still had her razocông. She'd been wholly submerged in the Bath as Leah's sacrifice took effect, what if it had slipped loose? Several gulps of waja had gone down her throat before she could stop them. She was coated in and out, but what good was that if she didn't have the trigger?

Even if she held it, she wouldn't know what to do with her razocông. Bash it repeatedly until Songmaster was annoyed enough to come out and yell at her to stop making a racket?

feel home
Wataño home
come home
come home

What does that mean? Am I not home now, here with you? She was baffled. When Katy spoke of her Shadow Drazoen they had clear voices, distinct personalities, even presumed genders. Yuhwa had gotten the impression they spoke in complete sentences to Katy. This group, *her* group, was more opaque, almost indistinguishable from one another and borderline childlike. That made understanding harder.

we have displeased
sweet Child regrets

unhappy

we are wrong

No! Yuhwa beseeched, horrified they'd read her thoughts and come to that conclusion. She felt their withdrawal and shame. *The issue is me. Not you,* never *you. I will learn your communication, the ways you are unique, and we will be the happiest Wataño. The Orange Wataño will be jealous of us, I promise.*

yesyes

do we

love them

too

Her clutch returned to her, slithering around her psyche, showering her with adoration.

knew them

longlonglong ago

have missed

love them

She answered the question at the end. *We do, but we probably love ourselves best.* Yuhwa reconsidered. *And Paul, we love Paul.* She let herself miss him for a few atómi (or sal-angs, or bisous; time was awfully fluid in shadow prison). *Any tips on how I'm supposed to wake up Songmaster?*

no sleep

Rab trapped

come home

open door

She wracked her brain for what going home would mean. Home to the Wataño? Home to Malor? Home to a Jadoube, which would be the dao, she guessed? Her nilnabō Shadows pounced.

trust

swim

trust

soar

All right. She let herself settle, then sank into her dao, seeking the river Songmaster had woven into the fabric of Jadoube biology. Back to the beginning, to that very first day the instructors laid her in the Uyu River. She didn't remember everything, barely older than a babe and overwhelmed with instincts and fear. But as she concentrated, she remembered a sound that rang loud when their hands withdrew, leaving her floating in the cool, still water. Her spirit had sent out ripples of sound, connected with her dao, and the low humming vibration of their union kept her afloat.

Without conscious thought she'd known how to ride the current her teachers would subject her to in the coming sals, before they'd even told her what they would do. That sound had carried her for tuigs as a majio, it was how she attuned herself to ships and people when threading them to herself in transit.

Her memories connected part of her with the majios of the past, their sensate experiences whispering to her of the dao and how it connected every Jadoube. Songmaster hadn't merely bestowed one Jadoube with an ability, he had found a way to bind each of them together through the warp and weft of navigating veṣu. They were a People who could never truly be torn from one another.

As that realization settled in, Yuhwa found herself looking back in time again. The Uyu River of training years was so different from the last river she'd been in, the Aru. The Uyu was broad and ponderous with a few racier spots. The Aru ran narrower but deeper, swift and treacherous as she'd learned. But it had ferried her where she needed to be, so she held no grudge.

More Jadoube reached along the bonds, showing her their journeys, their quests, endowing her with a powerful *knowing*. Each story was unique, but together they made a tapestry, large as the one she'd made transiting with the *Mahoroba*. Just like that one, it floated around her, cradled and cloaked her.

If she hadn't fallen into the river, she wouldn't have ended up deep in Âuke. She wouldn't have met the Five Côttru, and she wouldn't have her razocông. Her pâtexi would have failed.

Perhaps in this nefeslo prison she could accept the truth of her own journey. *I am blessed beyond measure. Even if I never break us free, I have been given gifts I can hardly understand.* She lacked physical sensation to confirm, but her mind told her she wept. *Plenty in the Aoni go their whole lives without the friendships and love I've known. I made my own way, asking no permission and making no apology. Who I am got me through difficult times, and gave me strength to live a life that prepared me to come back to Malor and meet my destiny.*

us we yours

Wataño

precious one

beloved

This time, behind the playfully happy voices, Yuhwa felt another presence. She reached for it, only to find it was Five. The Côttru were here in the shadow prison with them!

in you

never left

Rab's Child

Malor's daughter

Yuhwa's heart swelled nearly to bursting. They were here, and just as much a part of her as the Shadows. Cherished Ni-Matak, Great Druk the guardian, fearsome Sister Ha-Seng, curious Ji-Cheol Jarog, Migwa the mystical. Their power and presence bled into the tapestry, reaffirming their bonds with the Jadoube of Malor's past. In Yuhwa's mind they caressed the strands, just as the nawa would trace binding tattoos during a Feast. They blessed, and were blessed in return.

One at a time, the Côttru turned to her, embraced her, the truth of their spirits spellbinding. Malor's sparks were the embodiment of love. They expected nothing in return, offered all they were freely, wanted nothing more than for Malor's greatest creations to thrive and daringly stretch themselves. Jadoube were meant to pierce the Aoni with their souls, bring species together, and above all be true to their natures.

As they pulled back from the joining, Yuhwa found she held something from each of them in her hands. Sister Ha-Seng's claw, sharp and light, slotted itself to the end of Ji-Cheol Jarog's feather shaft that he'd left behind. Great Druk bequeathed a shoulder scale; it fastened to the end of Ni-Matak's freshly-shed horn. The open end of the horn connected with the feather-claw combination. Finally, Migwa's soft, dense fur wrapped around the scale, leaving her with a club of Côttru parts, held tight in her fist. Yuhwa didn't understand; what was she meant to do with this?

The greatest Jadoube musicians' knowledge surged into her like rapids, flashes of concerts zinging through her mind like arnat zingo. They revealed the immeasurably priceless gift she'd been given. The Five had left her with the greatest ajan ever crafted; the tool used with a razocông to coax soft sounds, ringing tones, resounding and reverberating crashes. Whatever was needed.

Whether spirits of Jadoube remained in the waja contrary to beliefs, or the metal itself reshaped her could be debated later. But she knew they gave her something precious, and patience was required. Yuhwa felt where they gently buried a seedling of music inside her soul. That hadn't been her path originally, but in this place, all roads were open to her if she was brave enough to follow. To listen. She watered the tiny speck with some of her dao and watched it germinate. A sprout, then a sapling, roots spreading throughout her essence. It demanded nothing of her, save the space to expand and unfurl. Once it did, she and her tree rested in a silence so elemental Yuhwa thought it must be the kind from before the Aoni was born. Peaceful, with inherent promise.

Soon, she felt something new and undeniable rising within

her. A need as inescapable as the search for her waja had been. It was a demand to make a sound, one that expressed more than how she felt. It had to encompass her life, her hopes, her joy at being joined with the Five Côttru and her Wataño. How her life had come full circle, and the brilliant future she envisioned as part of a society working to better the Aoni and restore balance. At Songmaster's side, no less. So much to try and say with a sound.

youyou always you
make one from all
unity strong
Child sees

Yuhwa wasn't sure she could do it, but she would try. The deep-rooted tree pushed at her, showed her how to funnel the dao between its leaves and branches. How her music would flow and be hers alone, but built upon the experience of all who had come before. Harmony in individual threads joining as one.

open door
trust
swim
freefreefree

Her razocông hung before her; had it been there the whole time? Or had it separated from the Spirit Bath and come to her because it was another gift she'd been given in this place that was nothing and all things at once? What did it matter now that it was here. It was hers and together they would try.

The heft of the ajan in her hand felt good and right. Yuhwa knew this would be difficult, she wasn't a musician despite all the endowed memories. But she burned to make music nonetheless. She contemplated the hardest thing she'd ever done; transiting a veşu holding the entire *Mahoroba*. The only way she'd managed that was by committing and diving in.

She rubbed her hand along the face of the instrument, feeling tiny dimples where before there'd been none. Pressing her fingertips to the indentations triggered flickers of more ancestral Jadoube emotions, thoughts, and ideas. Her instrument carried the spirits now. Their trip into the Spirit Bath had reshaped her razocông, and though the impact was necessary, she longed to soothe her waja that had endured so much. Using the soft Migwa-fur end of the ajan, she ran it slowly in circles around the rim, spiraling closer and closer to the center as she went.

A tone so deep it must surely echo the cosmos itself poured forth. Yuhwa let it wash over and through her, accepting how it reached into her and pulled her emotions, thoughts, and ideas back to her razocông. Her Shadow Drazoen hummed in concert, a tone so deep she felt it in her very bones. The sounds wound around one another, floating around the rim of her instrument, slipping down the face. There was a raised center to it now, a representation of how her hopes burgeoned.

She ran the ajan around again. Again. The cavernous tones blended into one another, building to something greater. Five times she did this, once for each of the Côttru, in thanks and veneration. As that sound began to die down, she turned the ajan and used the claw side to draw a wave between the rim and center. This sound was melodic and higher, sweet and light. Both sounds combined to create something exponentially grander.

Four wavy circuits for her beloved Shadows, who had been instantly precious to her, and whose love for her was unconditional and eternal. Their humming rose to join the new top notes, strengthening and enhancing. Instinct told her to repeat the patterns, so she did. Five sonorous cycles for the Côttru, four chime-like rounds for her Wataño.

Except, that wasn't quite right. A proper Wataño had six members. She was missing Songmaster, who slept on. No, he was trapped. That's what they'd told her. Yuhwa made another circuit of the patterns, letting the sound calibrate her heartbeat and the speed at which her blood flowed.

I am a conduit, a way through.

The sounds were bouncing off one another now, but instead of cancelling each other out they built to a crescendo.

Reach for me, I will find you.

Just as it seemed destined to twist from symphony to disharmony, Yuhwa grabbed the ajan with both hands and swung at the center of her razocông as hard as she could. A boom with the power of colliding veşu tore through her, the shadow prison, her Shadow Drazoen, even back into the Aoni she'd been ripped from.

Yuhwa's inner eye observed waja from Âuke tunnel down and south, speeding through rock and earth, meeting up with waja that had blown through the floor of the Spirit Bath and traveled north. Reunited, the two parts were jubilant to be whole, and added as one an alto-frequency tone to the still ringing note Yuhwa had created. She thought Malor itself heaved from the power of their Song.

Come through Rab and meet your Child! I. Am. The. Open. Door.

PAUL'S SIGHT had returned sometime after the three swords dragged him from the Spirit Bath.

"No, damn it, no!" Paul fought their hold, desperate to get back inside. "She needs me!"

"Where is the Pu'ulqaari? Are you still in danger?"

He shoved them away, catching them by surprise and sprinting for the doorway. "Dead, the evil cow is dead!" He made it back inside to see empty space. No Yuhwa suspended above the Bath. Empty air, and a waja pool smooth enough that plenty of time had passed between Leah's death and the swords pulling him out.

Sunlight blazing through walls filled with stained glass windows told the story of just how long he'd been knocked out. The brightly colored patterns were a direct contrast to his bleak despair. What the hell was he supposed to do? He'd thought he would pull her down, keep her from falling into the Bath and drowning when whatever had her trapped let her go.

His mind went in circles, reliving those last minutes. Murder, suicide, bam! She'd been an inconceivable sight, coated in silver like that, and he couldn't accept that that was his last vision of her.

An earthquake brought him to his knees, stone tumbling from the roof to crash beside him. "Give her back!" he bellowed at the empty air before him.

37

It was warm where she was. Not burning like the sun-heated wadis and dunes, but rather the delicious, snuggly warmth of blankets and hugs. She was overcome by a feeling she associated with her parents and their love and protection; the happiness they'd shared as a family.

Yahdo, Child. You found me.

Songmaster Silver's voice was like the smoothest cup of toasty forsikla. Just like that beverage – a rich, spiced indulgence drunk during biannual festivals for the shifting seasons – Songmaster's dulcet words filled her with relaxation, ease, and more warmth. Yuhwa was near tears, or maybe she'd never stopped crying.

I missed you. How can that be? I've never known you, yet I missed you terribly.

You are my spark, the one being in the Aoni tied to me as closely as my siblings. Your soul knows mine, your heart beats with the one in my body. I longed for you from the moment we were separated. That time is done, and we return to one another.

Yuhwa gave herself permission to bask in the wonder and hugeness of his affection. She could tell they weren't back in the regular part of the Aoni because she still couldn't see. But for this brief interlude, eyes were superfluous. She had her dragons, they had her, and their Wataño was complete. Pure satisfaction and a sensation of being enfolded in wings filled her mind.

One point of interest, spark of mine. There is a very angry person demanding things of me. Things I am not inclined to give just yet.

Yuhwa's heart and soul sang. He was here! They needed to fly or run, even swim to the Aoni where Paul waited for her. Were they not there?

Not quite yet. One more small door to open, but this…Human? Hm. New species.

Please, let's go back. Yuhwa needed Paul as much as she needed her Wataño.

Yes. Songmaster's voice was coated with satisfaction. *Our Wataño, together at last. But this new being, you're sure about it? I do not think I like it.*

In her mind's eye, Songmaster was a sleek Drazoen, as unlike Sundancer as Yuhwa was unlike Katy. Every shade of silver, pewter, waja, titanium and metals she might not know coated his scales. They didn't overlap the way some of Great Druk's did, they were slotted together and appeared flexible. Instead of Sundancer's crown, Songmaster's head was covered in feathers and small, smooth horns that swept back along the top. Facial patterning kind of like Tschuele, but less symmetrical and raised up like Leah's ruh had been.

He was perfect. Breathtaking, wonderful. And, apparently, hated her boyfriend. *He's going to love you, though. Not as much as I do, but he'll try.* Yuhwa felt like she'd drunk three bottles of rusim. Somehow, she'd pulled it off; given all of herself to bring them home, and that had been sufficient. She was drunk on the accomplishment and at feeling the gamboling Shadow Dragons.

HAPPY

family

please free
we fly free

Yuhwa sensed Songmaster's mortification as fast as he felt it. *I've blocked your freedom, sweet ones, and I'll never do it again. We will never be contained.*

With that they burst back into the Aoni, knocking Paul flat on his ass.

THE WOMAN PAUL loved stood over him, naked but for epic waja tattoos covering eighty percent of her skin in spiraling circle patterns. Something wild had gone down in the shadow prison. Her lavender hair floated behind her because the wings of a ginormous fucking dragon were making a lot of wind. Her razocông floated back there too, with a funky new mallet hanging off the edge of it.

She was there! He'd known she'd come back, of course. Of course. She would win and be Songmaster's Yahdo. But seeing the proof, her returned, unharmed and happy, was a balm for his soul.

She was everything to him, and he'd have been a complete disaster if anything had happened to her. He scrambled to his feet, refusing to let the big damn lizard distract him from what mattered: holding Yuhwa immediately. Yuhwa looked at him, fathomless black eyes changed from whatever had happened to her in there. Now they were flecked with silver, like stars in the night sky. But her smile remained the same as she stepped into his arms.

"Songmaster is returned! We're back!"

"I always believed you'd do it," he whispered, hugging her tightly.

She squeezed him back. "Once you stopped assuming you were the herald, you mean."

"Don't embarrass me in front of the dragon, please."

Together they turned to take in Songmaster. He was almost beyond description: bigger than Earth's jumbo-est jet. Silver as the name implied, but there were more metals in there. Probably adamantium or promethium, for all Paul knew. Instead of shadowed highlights where fore and hind legs met body, the bright sun of Malor glinted off his hide and highlighted the sleek musculature under scaled skin. He didn't have nine tails like Sundancer, or her crown. Songmaster had horns curving back from his head, like a gazelle or antelope. His single tail was incredible, serpentine and long, whiplike. The eyes were a little creepy, though. Lanu's were white and odd enough, but this was weirder. Pale, nearly colorless, honestly, and shining as though lit from within.

Do I offend you, pup?

Yuhwa, nestled under his arm, huffed good-naturedly.

"No, no, never. Of course not. It was just a stray thought."

Songmaster lowered his huge eye and focused on Yuhwa. *You are sure this is the one you want? Inexperienced and from an infant species?*

Shite. Getting used to dragons talking in his head would never be normal. He was also realizing that, unlike Bay, he hadn't gotten instant Drazoen approval. Sweat trickled down his spine; what if Yuhwa had to dump him to move on as a herald? If he was dead weight he didn't want to ruin things for her, but it would kill part of him to walk away. She was Songmaster's only Yahdo, though, so that had to mean she had plenty of sway. He hoped.

"Stop scaring him, please. I'm keeping him. For the record, without him you'd still be back there."

The *Hmph* ringing in his mind didn't make Paul think he'd won Songmaster over. Before he could think of a response

Yuhwa took his hand, pulling him closer to the Drazoen. He didn't remember when it happened, but her nudity had been covered in a graceful silver gown.

"We've destroyed the Spirit Bath and most of the surrounding building; very upset nawa will be here any atóm. Was there an earthquake? Or was that my imagination?" she asked Paul.

"It got a little wobbly, yeah." Paul coughed. "I left three swords outside; they'll probably be here any minute."

"Unless they're in too much shock from seeing you." She peered around Songmaster. "You're hard to miss and rather dazzling. If we stay there will be endless questions, and probably several new Feasts. Should we escape to Centris before the chaos starts up here? You and Sundancer can catch up, then everyone will keep trying to figure out where we go next."

Very well. I'll carry you in my palm. Bring the pup since you're so insistent.

My, what big claws you have, Paul thought. A little more sweat slipped south of his nape.

I'll do my best not to cut you with them.

Songmaster's mention of sharpness reminded him of the open research question. Paul suddenly had questions, not concerns. "When we go back to Centris, are you swimming the Aoni or needling it?"

Needling. I haven't heard that term in a very long time. Where did you learn it?

He'd surprised Songmaster, go him! "It's in one of the scrolls from ancient times. We found it studying how to bring you guys back. They'd forgotten all about it, actually. What does it mean to needle? The nawa are debating it pretty hard."

Yuhwa turned in his arms. "I love your mind. You have so many interesting questions." She rested against Songmaster's foot. "Needling sounds more intense than swimming. What have majio been doing in veṣu all these kōmilen?"

Piercing dimensions, Child. That's what allows us to move so quickly, and what I endowed the Jadoube with. Not to the same extent as the Nine, but enough to ensure the People of the Aoni could reach one another and grow together.

"By Nine," Yuhwa breathed. Then her face twisted, eyes losing focus, and she said, "Yes, you too. All of us. More than Nine, I know."

Paul stared into eyes of sheerest white and grimaced. "Other dimensions! I can't process that. At all."

Your inability doesn't surprise me. My sweet Child, you deserve more. Let us leave him.

Fed up with being bullied, even it was by a demi-god, Paul pushed back. "I know you love her. She's your spark. Songmaster's Yahdo. And *she* loves me, so your threats are a little hollow."

She is the Child of Rab, He Who Captured Song, Lord of Music, Father of Arts; her partner should be the best the Aoni has to offer.

"He is," Yuhwa said. "You know it, too, or else you wouldn't have just given him your truename."

Paul tried not to gloat, but Bay didn't have Sundancer's truename. He was totally winning.

As you say, Child. The whelp may yet grow on me. Songmaster's voice was indulgent, and Paul marveled to see a dragon smile.

They stepped inside the circle of his claws, Yuhwa shaking her head. Before she could take him to task again, Songmaster scooped them up and they toppled into his velvety, soft hand.

Breathe in.

Paul pulled Yuhwa closer, dragging her arm over his body in case of turbulence. Of the two of them, she had way more experience with this kind of travel. The last time Sundancer whammied them from jail to Voice House he had wanted to puke. He needed to make a better showing this time, with Songmaster watching and judging.

Gut wrenching took on a new meaning, and he barely kept breakfast down. How absolutely incredible, though, to see the Wheel from this view. He'd been lectured enough that he knew he wasn't supposed to think up, down, blah blah, but to him it looked like they viewed Centris from above. It felt like coming home.

Breathe out.

Songmaster flew them around the big port and right into the smaller one. Katy said that's how Sundancer had done it as well.

This port was created for our convenience, but I see it's been repurposed in our absence.

He set them on their feet, and by the time Paul had his stomach under control and looked up, Songmaster was a two-legged man.

YUHWA THOUGHT Songmaster was even more striking than Sundancer.

Child of Rab
laughing
biased
sillysilly

Maybe, but I'm not wrong either, am I? she thought back to her Shadows.

Matching Sundancer's bipedal form in height, Songmaster's skin was so pale it was virtually translucent and managed to give his eyes some color by comparison. He eschewed a dragon head and went with a more expected one. Silvery white hair and horns, his forehead and cheeks covered in raised, flowing rivulets of waja. The Drazoen skin below his face had transformed into a grandiose version of the robe the Voices wore: it seemed to flutter in a wind of its own, made of liquid waja rippling and shifting around his body.

He was, on the whole, magnificent. *Our Wataño is better than Katy's.* Yuhwa froze. *Shtŭ, don't tell Sundancer I said that, okay?*

Five Drazoen laughed into her mind. She tapped Paul's arm, wanting to share what she'd just thought, when two things happened.

I sense more siblings than Dikaios.

"What?" Yuhwa asked, sure she'd misheard.

Paul replied before Songmaster. "I just got a message from Katy. Two more Drazoen showed up right before we did."

"Who?!"

He shook his head. "She didn't say, just said get back to Voice House ASAP."

Songmaster bolted, running toward the exit and the Wheel, leaving them no choice but to sprint after him. The adventure, Yuhwa thought, was only beginning.

TURN THE PAGE
FOR A PREVEW OF
BOOK 3 IN THE
DRAZOEN HERALDS SERIES

RESONANCE

RESONANCE
EXCERPT

Thirty-seven divers clung loosely to ropes hanging from thirty-seven small boats. Eyes closed, separated by no more than one or two swim strokes, breathing in sync. Yemoja wouldn't need to watch her companions to time her dive. By this, her fourth performance, it was second nature. That didn't make it less special, and a shivering rush of anticipation flooded her. She led, and younger women may look to her for their first time.

Raising the Tøtimzahler each Paɫa·č was a privilege, and she didn't take the honor for granted. Every three hundred tuigs, Tschuele women hosted the greatest open market of the Aoni. Music, crafts, tech, poetry and storytellers; every artist in the Aoni came to participate, haggle, observe and enjoy. The Tøtimzahler served as the center of the carnival here on Quiltac: it marked where vendors would start raising their tents and booths. Favored traders and lauded artists blessed their spots closest to it. Over the tuig the market stayed open, participants came and went, but closest to center was the goal of all of them.

Yemoja slowly inhaled, filling her lungs as little as possible, held the breath, then exhaled. A longer pause, before starting again, feeling her heart rate slowing as the cycle repeated.

Tschuele learned young to prepare physically and mentally for diving. The ceremony she was about to commence lasted for thirty kaalas, most of which happened underwater. She'd need to be focused, relaxed, and well-oxygenated.

Sunrise had teased the horizon for half a sal-ang, but at last the first slivers of true light broke over the oceans of Quiltac. That was their signal. A horn sounded, low and piercing, cutting through morning mist. Thousands of observers managed to keep their excitement hushed enough not to distract. Only when the single note died out did Yemoja dive.

Yemoja and the rest of her yptà – ocean sisters of Quiltac diving this sal – told the creation story of the Tschuele. Their interpretive water dance shared with all present how their world had once been a great desert, barely sustaining life. Against all odds, their people survived, eking out sparse lives. Then one day Giftgiver Red and Waterbringer Blue arrived. With their advice and gifts, Quiltac became a planet of oceans, vibrant life, and plentiful resources.

As they wrapped up the ancient story, the yptà dove in synchronicity to the ocean floor. They circled a sacred spot: this was where the Drazoen had first set foot on Quiltac, and it was from here the Tøtimzahler would ascend. Yemoja felt her heart start to quicken, but forced it back to a more sedate rhythm. She would be under water a while longer and a faster pulse led to a greater need for breath she couldn't access.

This Pała·č's chosen divers joined hands, dancing, feet kicking sand and silt into the water. From the ancient desert floor that was now a clouded sea, the Tøtimzahler emerged and rose toward the sunlit surface. Carvings of Quiltac's greatest animals swirled around the cylinder; orcuvig chased schools of inktvis round and round, while a playful zeerhej flared its wings to land on the einlinwal's horn. All Nine Drazoen were presented in their fullest glory; the colors on the Tøtimzahler remained bright as the day they'd been applied, the chiseled wood unworn despite the kōmilens gone by. No one knew what was inside it or how exactly old it was, just that it took more than thirty Tschuele to circle it, and it was tall enough to stretch one third of a khai beyond the surface of the ocean.

Milenyos of history and ritual dictated how the yptà moved. Their group kept pace, floating higher and higher, exhaling as they went, until they broke into open air, gulping huge breaths. Yemoja let the ceremony's euphoria flood her, grinning and shouting with joy. Their cries were echoed a hundredfold by the crowds, thrilled, knowing the Pała·č would begin in earnest.

Many sal-angs later, dried off and walking the temporary platforms to check they floated as expected, Yemoja smiled to herself. This Pała·č would be the greatest of all time, better than any that had come before. Something told her there was extra luck to be found in this gathering, provided she was canny and willing to take a risk.

A Lunari man bumped into her, and she glanced down. He was handsome: dark hair secured in a queue at his nape, eyes the blue of a javetchi's dorsal scales, and nice teeth he revealed in a wide smile.

"Please accept my apologies! I wasn't paying attention, so overwhelmed with the wonders here." His eyes, Lunari large and beautiful in the sunlight, gazed up earnestly.

Yemoja liked the look of him, especially when she noticed he was barefoot. Tschuele almost never wore shoes, and always appreciated when others did the same. To them it was a sign of strong character. Would this man be a candidate for genetic contribution?

"The ocean rolls," she responded with a laugh, the Tschuele phrase indicating no offense taken. "Are you setting up a stall for the Pała·č?"

"I'm no vendor," he replied, a self-deprecating grin turning his plump lips inward. "I am an importunate collector and enthusiastic shopper only. I saw you this morning, calling the

Tøtimzahler to the surface. Very impressive. May I ask your name?"

"Yemoja Tahir," she answered, amused by the suave, casually dressed man. He might be a very good candidate indeed. "And yours?"

"Thuliso," he said, voice low and husky. "Thuliso Maor."

ACKNOWLEDGMENTS

Heartfelt gratitude to every scientist who helped me define where I wanted to take my Drazoen Heralds and how I could get them there. To name only a few: Michelle Thaller, Neil Degrasse Tyson, Brian Greene, Laura Danly, Chris McKay, Matt O'Dowd, Aowama Shields, Amber Straughn, Alex Filippenko, Hakeem Oluseyi, Michio Kaku, Lawrence Krauss, Nina Lanza, Jani Radebaugh, Brian Cox, Stephen Hawking.

My Dogwood Playpark Crew who have been a deep well of support: all my thanks and love to the Small Dog Mafia, Tiny Tuesday friends, Active-Side Switch Hitters, BILs (Big Identifying as Little), the incredible staff, and the amazing owners who made a small spot of heaven for Seattle dog owners.

To my Twitch friends and Found Fam who have supported, encouraged and cared for me, you mean more to me than I can say. I *will* keep trying, though. There's got to be an emote for that somewhere…

For Amber McCulloch, the Voice of the Aoni: voyaging with you is both a privilege and a joy.

Last but never least. Love to my family who are farther away than I would like, but always close in my heart.